AT THE POTTER'S WHEEL

Day by Day

Devotional Readings Through the Year

AT THE POTTER'S WHEEL

Day by Day

Devotional Readings Through the Year

Preethi Alice Jacob

2019

At the Potter's Wheel–Day by Day: Devotional Readings Through the Year – published by the Rev. Dr. Ashish Amos of the Indian Society for Promoting Christian Knowledge (ISPCK), Post Box 1585, Kashmere Gate, Delhi-110006.

© Author, 2019

Online order: http://ispck.org.in/book.php

Also available on amazon.in

All Scriptures quotations are taken from THE HOLY BIBLE, NEW INTERNATIONAL VERSION®. NIV®.

ISBN: 978-81-938241-7-7

Laser typeset by

ISPCK, Post Box 1585, 1654, Madarsa Road, Kashmere Gate, Delhi-110006 • *Tel:* 23866323

e-mail: ashish@ispck.org.in • ella@ispck.org.in
website: www.ispck.org.in

Contents

Foreword

It is indeed an honour for me to have been asked by the author, Preethi Jacob to write the Foreword for her book on daily devotional with biblical reflections. As a woman and for a woman, I am encouraged to write the Foreword for her maiden publication. The Lord commissioned Preethi to write these daily readings and to share with the world.

> Consider it pure joy, my brothers and sisters,[a] whenever you face trials of many kinds, 3 because you know that the testing of your faith produces perseverance. 4 Let perseverance finish its work so that you may be mature and complete, not lacking anything. James 1:2-4

We may face many trials and temptations, but we have one assurance, the word of God which I strongly believe will speak to us through these readings. God tells us that our lives will be filled with challenges, but it is how we face them that makes all the difference not only in our lives but the lives of others too.

I present before you a daily devotional reading written by Mrs. Preethi Jacob. The readings are led by the Holy Spirit and will speak personally with the reader with easy and lucid language for all ages and backgrounds. The NIV has been used almost throughout the Readings.

Hope the Readings will touch you and make you spiritually strong in faith and action for the Lord. May the Lord use each of you mightily and may these devotions be a blessing to you.

Ella Sonawane
Assistant General Secretary, Publishing
ISPCK
Delhi, 2019

Introduction

Be the change you want to see.

This has been the unwelcome answer to my prayers over the years for a relevant devotional book for young people.

As a teacher of the young adult class of our Sunday School for many years, it was a regular practice to instill in the young people the importance of the habit of a daily time with the Lord and His Word. And when they left I always longed to have a relevant devotional book to hand to these young people. Such a book was hard to find.

Through my interaction with young people over the years, I have come across two responses to the Bible that caused concern. One that the Bible is an ancient book written centuries ago for a people who lived ages ago. Hence, the Bible is not relevant to us today in our fast and current world. The other that the Bible is too difficult to understand or be applied. **At The Potter's Wheel, Day by Day**, is a humble attempt to address these two positions.

The reading plan for this book takes you through the Bible in a year, but with a twist. The readings are found in chronological order, which means that the readings are in the order that the events in the Bible took place and not in the order we have them in the printed Bible today.

The devotions are based on key verses taken from every book of the Bible. The two sets of reading portions enable you to choose either to read a small portion of scripture, found at the top of the page each day, giving the context for the devotion. Alternatively, you could challenge yourself to read through the Bible in a year, using the 'Extended Readings' found at end of each devotion.

It is my prayer that as your journey through the Bible this year, you would find that all Scripture is God-breathed and is useful for teaching, rebuking, correcting and training in righteousness, thoroughly equipping you for every good work (2 Timothy 3:16-17).

Preethi Alice Jacob

A New Day

As this new day, you start
May you go with him in your heart
As he leads, directs and guides you today
And with his love fills you through the day
His channel of blessing to be
To the needy world that you see
And so your candle in your corner
To shine stronger and brighter!

KNOW GOD
Divine Legacy

So God created human beings in his own image. In the image of God, he created them; male and female he created them.

Genesis 1:27

God created.

Genesis in Greek means 'origin' or 'creation.' The first book in the Bible sets the stage for the entire plan of redemption which unfolds in the rest of the books. Genesis begins with the beginnings. The first few chapters give an account of creation. The Bible simply and clearly declares the world did not create itself or come about by chance. The world was created by God. And God, by definition, is eternal and has always been.

In the first five days, God created the heavens and the earth. He spoke all of creation into being. And it was good in his eyes. But when on the sixth day, God created man and woman he created them in his image. God formed them with his own hands and breathed life into their nostrils.

Humans are the crown of all God's creation. We are created to love God, worship him and enjoy fellowship with him. Zephaniah 3:17 says he will rejoice over you with gladness, he will quiet you with his love, he will rejoice over you with singing. What a privilege and legacy.

You and I are created in God's image. To be in God's image is to be like him. It is to have his nature and reflect his character. It is to live in unity with one another.

Human parents love to hear that their children are like them. How much more then is God who created us? How are you reminding others of your heavenly Father?

Lord may I grow to be more and more like you in this new year.

Extended Reading – Genesis 1-3

SIN / TEMPTATION
Before It's Too Late

If you do what is right, will you not be accepted? But if you do
not do what is right, sin is crouching at your door; it desires to
have you, but you must rule over it.   *Genesis 4:7*

Cain was working late.

Another day was drawing to a close. But today was different. As he continued to work in the field, Cain's mind was racing. What would he tell his parents? How could he explain what happened? How could he tell them that he had killed his only brother Abel? They would not even understand. And yet, it was all Abel's fault, really. He had always made him so mad. Pretending to be good Abel managed to do all the right things and make him look bad.

And today was just the final straw. God had required both to offer sacrifices. And when they had brought their offerings God accepted Abel's sacrifice and not his! How come Abel is the one who is always right and accepted and not he? This just had to end.

Even as Cain was re-living the events of the day, there came the unmistakable voice of God cutting through the silence, 'Where is your brother Abel?' Cain though taken aback, retorts 'I don't know' and quickly adds the now infamous counter query – 'Am I my brother's keeper?'

Sin has a way of creeping in on us. Sin steals our peace of mind. Sin makes us touchy and defensive. The decision to kill his brother Abel was a buildup of resentment and jealousy. Temptations are a given in this fallen world. God's word says we are to resist the devil and he will flee from us (James 4:7).

What sin is lurking near your heart's door today?

Lord help me recognize and resist sin every day I pray.

Extended Reading – Genesis 4-7

PRIDE
What is the Purpose?

Then they said, "Come, let us build ourselves a city, with a tower that reaches to the heavens, so that we may make a name for ourselves; otherwise we will be scattered over the face of the whole earth."
                                                          Genesis 11:4

The earth was full again.

The floods were over. The Lord had saved Noah and his family. And the number of people on the earth had increased substantially. Though the people were many the language was just one. And that was a great advantage.

And now, the people had arrived at a plain in a place called Shinar. It was a good land and they hit upon a great plan. They decided to build a city for themselves. They would bake bricks and use tar to build themselves a city for all of them to live. Great plan. Great unity. So far so good.

But their plans didn't stop there. They were not content with just building a city to live in, they wanted to build a tower too. The purpose of the tower was to reach the heavens so that they could make a name for themselves. Pride and selfish ambition overtook their good intent. Their confidence in their unity led them to believe they could achieve anything, even reach the heavens. Now that sure spells trouble.

Unity is wonderful and much needed to achieve great things. But when driven by the wrong motive the extent of harm and destruction caused can be extensive. Pride and selfishness can never lead to any good.

Does pride have a role in why you are doing what you are doing?

Lord keep my motives ever pure as I serve you I pray.

Extended Reading – Genesis 8-11

PERSPECTIVE
Worship Through Tears

At this, Job got up and tore his robe and shaved his head. Then he fell to the ground in worship [21] *and said: "Naked I came from my mother's womb, and naked I will depart. The LORD gave, and the LORD has taken away; may the name of the LORD be praised."* *Job 1:20-21*

Job was crushed!

Job had just received devastating news! In a matter of less than twenty-four hours, Job lost not just all his cattle, all his crops, all his wealth, but all his ten children as well! The magnitude of his loss is almost unimaginable. If these losses were distributed among even a dozen people, still the loss would be extremely painful to each. And here, one-man Job loses all he has which matters to him in a single day!

Job's pain was unbearable. But the way this godly man handles his painful reality is a powerful lesson for all of us. The Bible says, in his unspeakable sorrow, Job's response was to worship God. He expressed his pain honestly, he mourned. But he did not shake his fist in God's face. He was not angry or bitter. Instead, he fell face down in surrendered worship.

Job recognized and acknowledged God's ownership and his own stewardship. He recognized that God has the unquestionable right to take back that which is his, whenever he chooses, no questions asked. Many of us wrongly assume that all that we have is the result of our own hard work, talent, and abilities. But the truth is that all that we have is his, we are only stewards or caretakers.

Are you able to trust the loving sovereignty of God through tough times?

Lord help me never forget that all that I have is yours, I pray.

Extended Reading – Job 1-5

SUFFERING
It is Okay

"What strength do I have, that I should still hope? What prospects, that I should be patient?   *Job 6:11*

Job is exhausted.

Job was one of the most God-fearing men that ever lived. God, himself was so confident in Job's faithfulness that he allowed Satan to test him. And as part of that test, Job loses all that he owns, including his family except for a wife he could have done without.

Literally, everything that he owned was gone. And all in a matter of a single day. And if all this were not enough, there came the next set of trouble. Job was afflicted with sores from head to toe. Sores that were extremely painful and left him so badly scarred that his friends couldn't even recognize him. That he was devastated is an understatement.

Job was truly exhausted. This was way more than he could bear. He was exhausted from grieving. He was exhausted from the pain he was going through. Job broke down, he grieved deeply. Human emotion got the better of Job. And there is nothing wrong with that.

Few of us may be able to identify with Job's level of pain and suffering. But in our times of suffering and pain, we too express our pain and our emotions do get the better of us. Sometimes we are too tired to even listen to any counsel. And that's okay.

It is okay to grieve, to express our sorrow, to cry. We can come to him with our honest fears, our pain, and questions even. God understands and loves us still. He remembers that we are mere dust.

What tough situations in your life has made you weary and overwhelmed?

Lord, I choose to rest in your loving arms through my pain.

Extended Reading – Job 6-9

SUFFERING
Seeking Answers

I say to God; Do not declare me guilty but tell me what charges
you have against me.   *Job 10:2*

Job has questions for God.

In the previous chapters, we find that Job's friends have come visiting. As genuine good friends, they come to spend time with their suffering friend. They sit with him in silence for seven whole days. They then take turns speaking to Job, suggesting their own reasons for the suffering that he is going through. Job replies to each of them.

Now he has turned to God. He is asking some basic questions. Why Lord, is all this happening to me? What have I done? He is simply not able to understand what he has done to go through so much suffering.

In Job's case, we know that God used the sufferings as a test and as part of his sovereign plan in Job's life. God blessed Job twice as much as he had before (42:10). But this is a very pertinent question that many of us ask when we go through suffering of different kinds.

Trials often discover sins.

Charles Spurgeon says it is true that God does often contend with both saints and sinners to deal with their sin. He also suggests several reasons why we sometimes go through trials. One reason could be to awaken us to our lost condition. Trials could also be to test our earnestness. Or a way to bring to the fore sin which we are unwilling to turn over to the Lord. Trials could be because we have not yet fully understood the plan of salvation. Could any of these be the reason for the suffering you are going through in your life?

Lord help me learn whatever you are teaching me through the suffering in my life, I pray.

Extended Reading – Job 10-13

GRIEF
It is Not Our Place

I have heard many things like these; you are miserable comforters, all of you!   Job 16:2

Today, let's look at Job's friends.

Job's friends, Eliphaz, Bildad, Zophar, and Elihu were good friends who came to be with their dear friend Job during his time of grief. They took time to be with Job. When they saw him from a distance, they could hardly recognize him; they began to weep aloud, and they tore their robes and sprinkled dust on their heads (2:12). They empathized with him.

They spent the first seven days with him in silence. They just sat on the ground because they saw how great his suffering was. Sometimes that is one of the best things we can do when we visit those who are suffering. Just our physical presence can be a great comfort.

But they soon each took turns to give Job lengthy lectures. They told him that he was going through troubles because of the judgment of God. But they were not right. Even God was angry with them (42:7) for not speaking the truth about him.

We are not to pass judgments on those suffering. It is not our place. We are called to mourn with those who mourn. We can encourage them to endure faithfully. In and through their pain help them keep their trust and focus on the truths about God. Though we don't always understand why we can always rely on who God is. He never changes. He remains faithful and true, our loving heavenly Father. And that offers great encouragement and hope. How will you be a blessing to a friend who is suffering?

Lord help me point those who are suffering to who You are, I pray.

Extended Reading – Job 14-16

GOD
Proclamation of Faith

I know that my Redeemer lives and that in the end, He will stand on the earth.   *Job 19:25*

Amid his sorrow and his pain Job has a flash of profound prophetic faith.

Job, though going through immense suffering and complaining, has this time of proclaiming his faith. He affirms his faith in the fact that his Redeemer is alive, not someone dead and distant. He also states that he will stand in the end on the earth, clearly pointing to the divine. Job was also declaring the truth that in God, man has a Redeemer in all the fullest senses of that great word.

A redeemer in the Old Testament language was a vindicator of one who was unjustly wronged. He was a defender of the oppressed and a champion of the one who was suffering. A redeemer was the advocate of the unjustly accused.

When Christ chose to be the Redeemer of his people he came down to earth redeem his people from their sins. Christ redeemed us by paying the price for us upon the cross of Calvary. He also redeemed us by the power of his divine Spirit coming into our heart and renewing our soul.

During his suffering, Job's faith was intact. He did not become bitter. He did not curse God in all his pain. Rather Job proclaims his faith in his time of suffering. Times of suffering are times for us to turn our focus on God. To choose to affirm God and his faithfulness in our lives.

What is your response when you go through suffering?

Lord help me focus on you and your faithfulness when I go through times of trial, I pray.

Extended Reading – Job 17-20

GOD
What is your Greatest Desire?

Then Job replied: ² "Even today my complaint is bitter; his hand is heavy despite my groaning.³ If only I knew where to find him; if only I could go to his dwelling!   Job 23:1-3*

Job was not comforted.

Eliphaz, Job's friend had just finished a long speech in his effort to comfort Job. But Job continued to feel desperate. All the wisdom and counsel of Eliphaz and his other friends did not really help. It made his mental and spiritual agony only worse. Do your friends feel comforted or more miserable after you try to comfort them? We need to be careful with our words and the way we comfort others.

Job's greater need or desire was not to be healed of his disease or see his children brought back from the grave or even to get his properties back. His longing was for God. Job longed for and sought God. His first and greatest desire was to find God and get back in communion with him.

Job felt separated from God. He was not able to feel the presence of God. A man who previously had been in fellowship with God now felt utterly forsaken. And that was the greatest source of torment for Job. Job not only felt separated from God, but he was longing to get the fellowship back. He was not content without the presence of God that he had always enjoyed. Job's greatest desire was for God, even above his family, his money or even his own health.

Times of crisis reveal our inmost and deepest desires. What is your greatest desire?

Lord, you know my heart, increase in me my desire for you I pray.

Extended Reading – Job 21-23

HONESTY
Gracious Words

- as long as I have life within me, the breath of God in my nostrils, ⁴ my lips will not say anything wicked, and my tongue will not utter lies. Job is on the search for wisdom.

Job 27:3-4 (NIV)

Job was honest and spoke from his heart.

There were many negative features in Job's response, but there were positive aspects too. Job loved truth and righteousness and desired to walk in them. At the beginning of the book of Job, God described Job as one who loved righteousness, feared God and turned away from evil. And Job in the above passage reiterates that he would continue to hold on to his integrity and would not speak lies or what was wicked.

Honesty is good. But being honest does not mean expressing whatever comes to our mind, whenever we want, without restraint. People try to justify such behavior as 'just being honest.' But they are not. They are speaking out a negative and critical spirit and have also failed to exercise restraint. Such behavior fails on both counts of self-control and honesty.

On the other hand, some think that being spiritual and positive is to say nice-sounding things which they don't mean or believe in. But if the words do not come from the heart, we should not say them. God sees through our outward conduct. He knows our heart. And God hates hypocrisy. He desires truthfulness in us. When there are issues that disturb us, we need not pretend they do not exist. We can honestly acknowledge our thoughts, graciously to the Lord and to those around us.

Is there someone whom you need to seek forgiveness from for hurting them with your 'just honest' words?

Lord help me come to you humbly and honestly with issues that disturb me, I pray.

Extended Reading – Job 24-28

SUFFERING
The Value of Pain

"I cry out to you, God, but you do not answer; I stand up, but you merely look at me.   *Job 30:20*

Job was perplexed.

Job was frustrated and discouraged too. He just could not understand his situation. He wanted to know why God was afflicting him this way. He was quite certain that it could not be that God was judging him for his sins. Rather the trials came on Job because of his righteousness. They came because God appreciated and had so much confidence in him that he allowed Satan to test Job.

Job was also rather lonely. He didn't seem to have anyone to turn to. His friends did not understand. They believed that Job's suffering came from God. They did not understand the existence and work of Satan. His wife was no help at all either. And so, Job wanted to reason out, to discuss what was happening with God (Job 23:3-4). But the Bible says he felt like he just could not find God (Job 23:8).

Job's situation was difficult. And if we look only at the pain and suffering, it sure seems like a real terrible situation. But we see in the later chapters that Job came through these difficulties a wiser and more mature person. God values these qualities in us and they are very important in his kingdom.

The difficulties and pain we go through need not have a negative effect on us. When we continue to trust and hope in God even through situations we do not understand, you and I too can emerge as better, stronger and wiser, by his grace. Would you trust and hope in God today, even through your tough situations?

Lord help me trust you especially through the trials of my life, I pray.

Extended Reading – Job 29-31

COMMUNICATION
Honest to God

*My words come from an upright heart; my lips sincerely speak
what I know.*   *Job 33:3*

Elihu finally speaks.

The youngest of the friends that came to visit Job, Elihu, had been
quietly listening to the taunting words of the other older friends of
Job. He had also been listening to the somewhat exasperated replies of Job
himself. But finally, he breaks his silence and addresses himself to Job.

He begins his address with a powerful statement that is relevant to each
of us. He states that he is speaking from the uprightness of his heart
and that his words are sincere. Basically, Elihu is saying that he will only
say what he knows and shall try to say it simply and clearly so that no
one would mistake his meaning.

That is a great example for us of how our conversations need to be. We
are to speak from upright hearts. We are to be sincere before God in
what we say. We need to honor God with our words. Harsh words do
not come from an upright heart.

There are times when we need to speak up, but we hesitate because we
fear what people would think or say. But we are to speak with courage
and not with the fear of being judged.

Sincere and clear communication is great for keeping relationships healthy.
When our thoughts are not clear, our words will not be clear either. It
is necessary that we speak plainly so that we are easily understood to
avoid misunderstanding. Is there a relationship that needs your honest
to God communication to bring healing?

*Lord help me always be upright and clear when I speak to others I
pray.*
Extended Reading – Job 32-34

FAITH
Spirit Led

I would like to reply to you and to your friends with you.

Job 35:4

Elihu though young was a man with a wise spirit.

Elihu's message was different from the other friends. His message was not another misguided effort to comfort Job with bad theology. His message had distinct marks of being guided by the Spirit of God. When Elihu is finished at the end of chapter 37 Job is silent. He does not dispute with Elihu. And interestingly when God finally turns to Job's comforters to express his anger at them, he only mentions Eliphaz, Bildad, and Zophar (42:7) not Elihu.

Elihu's message shows that he was stirred by the Spirit of God. Young Elihu was slow to speak. He took his time, he listened to all the others. Often when we feel we have a message from the Lord, we can become presumptuous and lose the meekness and gentleness of a learner. But those whose burden is from the Spirit will be slow to speak, quick to listen and learn and grow.

But after a point, he could not keep quiet any longer. He was burdened with a message from God (32:18). A person stirred by the Spirit of God is passionate for the truth of God (Psalm 39:3).

Elihu was also very angry. He was angry with Job for justifying himself rather than God. He was also angry with the three friends because they did not refute Job (32:2-3). The mark of righteous anger is that it is triggered by the belittling of God and not the belittling of ourselves. Elihu though young was led by the Spirit of God.

Does your life reflect marks of one being led by the Lord?

Lord help me be slow to speak and quick to hold your name up high, I pray.

Extended Reading – Job 35-37

QUESTIONS
The Right Recognition

Brace yourself like a man; I will question you, and you shall answer me. ⁴ Where were you when I laid the earth's foundation? Tell me, if you understand.   Job 38:3-4

God rebukes Job.

As we go through the book of Job, there could be many possible questions that come up in our minds. Questions about why God allowed righteous and innocent Job to suffer so much. Even questions about Job being the helpless object of contest between God and Satan. It is fine to ask questions and try to understand them. But we need to guard against drawing improper conclusions that contradict the perfect character and ways of God that are clearly taught in the Bible.

In the above passage, God seems to be asking Job a series of tough questions. There Is no indication of God sympathizing with Job's suffering and pain. It could seem like God is simply exerting his power to subdue Job and force him to submit to him. That could lead to feeling that God was unfair to Job. And yet we know that God's response to the situation must have been wise because God is perfect in wisdom.

It is crucial not to harbor or entertain negative thoughts about God. The evil one is waiting to evoke and provoke such negative thoughts within us. God is open to reason and not One who will simply overwhelm and try to overcome us by the sheer weight of his power. If we submit simply because someone is powerful, then we could end up submitting to Satan because he is also a powerful being.

Job had enough recognition of God's goodness and greatness. Do you?

Lord guard my heart against Satan's attacks to provoke wrong thinking about you, I pray.

Extended Reading – Job 38-39

FAITH
Attention Please

Then Job replied to the LORD: I know that You can do all things; no purpose of Yours can be thwarted. Job 42:1-2

Satan is out of the picture.

The book of Job began with the focus on three beings, God, Satan, and Job. Now by the end of the book, Satan is nowhere in the picture. Just God and Job. And as Job begins to see how God is working out in his vast cosmic plans and what he is making possible through Job's suffering, he has no more questions.

The book of Job closes with an amazing view of God, the One of incredible wisdom. The One who puts things together way beyond our greatest dreams and imagination. A God who is working out incredible plans and purposes that will bring us immense delight and joy if we are willing to wait for his purposes in his time.

In time, the Bible says, the LORD restored Job's fortunes and gave him twice as much as he had before (v10). And Job lived a hundred and forty years; he saw his children and their children to the fourth generation. Job died an old man full of years (v16-17).

Pain is often God's megaphone to draw our attention to our loving and gracious Lord.

Job went through a lot of pain and suffering. But he trusted God and remained faithful to him through it all. And so, he came through the whole experience richer and stronger.

Is God trying to draw your attention to him through a painful situation in your life? Would you, like Job chose to trust him, even when you don't always understand?

Lord help me trust you especially through the painful situations of my life I pray.

Extended Reading – Job 40-42

DISAPPOINTMENT
ABC of Disappointment

So Lot chose for himself the whole plain of the Jordon and set out toward the east. The two men parted company.   Genesis 13:11

God called Abraham out of Ur.

And Abraham brought along Sarah his wife and Lot, his nephew. When God promised Abraham that he would bless him and make him a mighty nation, Lot was with him. As Abraham increased in his wealth and possessions, Lot was with him. Lot benefited from being with Abraham. Lot shared in the blessings that Abraham enjoyed. Abraham taught him the tricks of the trade. Lot grew under the mentorship of Abraham. Lot gained all his possessions when he was with Abraham.

Over time, however, both Abraham and Lot grew. They grew so much that their herds were too many and the pastures were not enough for their combined flock. And strife arose between their servants. Obviously enough for Abraham to decide that the time had come to part ways.

Abraham took the initiative to make peace. He gave Lot the option to choose the land he wanted. And Lot chose the seemingly, better part of the land with no thought or concern for his uncle. Seriously? After all that Abraham had done for him? Abraham had every reason to be disappointed and hurt.

Yet the Bible records no such thing. Abraham was not upset or hurt by Lot's behavior. Instead, he showed maturity that is worth a mention. He trusted God. From the way Abraham handled this situation, we can arrive at the ABC of handling disappointments.

Accept, know, that people will disappoint. Don't be taken by surprise.
Be gracious. Remember others are dust, just as you.
Continue to trust God. The best is yet to come.

Lord help me to continue to trust you when I face disappointment, I pray.

Extended Reading – Genesis 12-15

SUBMISSION
Called to Return?

Then the angel of the LORD told her, "Go back to your mistress and submit to her."
                                                    Genesis 16:9

All that Hagar did was obey her mistress Sarah.

When Abram was seventy-five years old, God called him out of Ur to follow him into the Promised Land and told him that he would bless Abraham with descendants as many as the stars in the sky. A humanly ridiculous and impossible promise.

And yet, now ten years into the promise, no child. Hadn't they waited long enough? Maybe the Lord had forgotten? Did they actually hear God right, Sarah wondered. God could do with a little help, maybe?

And so, Sarah in all her human wisdom, and with Abraham's willing compliance, gave Hagar her slave to Abraham, that they might have a child through her. And sure enough, Hagar conceived. But then began trouble. Hagar despised her mistress. Sarah mistreated Hagar. And when Hagar could take it no longer, she ran away.

An angel of the Lord met Hagar in the desert and asked her what happened. Having heard the entire story, the angel asked Hagar to go back to her mistress and submit to her. Hagar would have expected some sympathy and concern, right? At least a promise of harm to those who have been troubling her? But Hagar trusted God. Her willingness to humbly obey led to God's blessing her.

God's ways are truly higher and much wiser. Going back to the place of suffering or injustice takes faith and humility. And yet, God's blessing is often linked to our humble obedience to him.

What place of suffering are you running from? Would you humbly trust God even if it means returning, submitting to the very same difficult situation?

Father help me humbly trust and obey you in my tough situations, I pray.

Extended Reading – Genesis 16-18

CHOICES
Where are You Headed Today?

The two angels arrived at Sodom in the evening, and Lot was sitting in the gateway of the city.   Genesis 19:1

Each choice is a progression.

When Abraham followed God to Canaan, the Promised Land, he had brought Lot with him. And over time they both prospered so much that they had to part ways. When given a choice by Abraham, Lot had chosen the land that seemed all fertile and lush, the whole plain of the Jordan toward Zoar. And the Bible says Lot lived among the cities of the plain and pitched his tents near Sodom (Genesis 13:10-12).

However, over time, Lot moved and began to live in the city of Sodom (Genesis 14:12). And now if you notice, just a few chapters later, Lot is sitting at the gateway to the city of Sodom, among the elders of the city. He has moved away from Abraham, to the plains near Sodom to finally being inside the city and now is an integral part of the evil city of Sodom.

The Bible records how God destroyed the cities of Sodom and Gomorrah, because of the extreme evil in it. Would Lot have known that these cities were bad? Of course, he would have. Did it happen overnight? Absolutely not!

We make choices, big and small, every day of our lives. Some choices we make may seem small and insignificant. But the truth is every choice has a consequence. And every choice leads to the next, in progression. From the time you chose to wake up this morning, to the sequence of dressing up and getting to the tasks for the day, all are choices which have consequences. How much more the bigger choices of life.

Where have your choices brought you today?

Lord for courage and wisdom to make right choices, I pray.

Extended Reading – Genesis 19-21

TEMPTATION
Not to Return

"Make sure that you do not take my son back there," Abraham said.   *Genesis 24:6*

Abraham was very clear.

Abraham now lived in Canaan, the land that the Lord had promised to give him and his descendants forever. Abraham had grown to know, love and trust Yahweh and had experienced his awesome leading and faithfulness. Though Abraham had grown immensely in wealth, he did not involve himself with the people of the land, for they served foreign gods.

And now lay before Abraham the all-important task of finding a bride for Isaac, his son. He never forgot how God had called him out of his father's house, to bless him. He knew that he was not to return to the place from where God had called him out. But he also needed to find a bride for his son from among his people and not from the people of Canaan.

So, Abraham calls his oldest servant, Eliezer and gives him clear instruction. Eliezer was to find a bride for his son Isaac from among his father's house. But Isaac was not to be taken there. Isaac was not to return or move out of the promise that God had given.

We are called to stay out of the places of temptation and sin that God has called us from. We are not to return. God calls us to stay in the place of his promises to us.

Is there some such place that God is telling you not to return to? A place where you could be tempted to sin or go back to your old ways? Maybe an old habit or addiction? Or to stay away from some friends who could lead you back to your old ways?

Lord keep me in your place of promise, I pray.

Extended Reading – Genesis 22-24

CHOICES
Your Bowl of Soup

"Look, I am about to die," Esau said. "What good is the birthright to me?"   *Genesis 25:32*

All for the love of a bowl of soup.

Jacob and Esau though twins, were very different in nature. Esau the outdoorsman, loved a good game any day, while Jacob more at home, enjoyed cooking.

When Esau came in weary from the field that day, all he could think of was food. Jacob never one to lose an opportunity, lost no time. Pat came the offer. Yummy piping hot soup in exchange for Esau's birthright?

Esau responds rather dramatically. Was Esau going to die for the lack of one meal? Absolutely not! He was just so overtaken by his own passions and desires that his birthright didn't seem worth even a meal.

Birthright in the Bible refers to the rights and privileges of the family's firstborn son. In the absence or after the father died, the firstborn son assumed the father's authority and responsibilities. He also inherited twice that was received by the other sons.

We all agree that Esau was foolish in trading something precious and long lasting for something small and temporal. But before we judge him too much, just pause and think, don't we all have our 'bowls of soup?'

Do you compromise time with God and his word, to pursue careers and wealth? Do you overindulge your favorite foods, or are addicted to harmful substances, at the cost of your health? Are you addicted to the various screens of your phone, television, computer etc. to the exclusion of your family time? Are there unhealthy relationships in your life that are ruining your home? What is your 'bowl of soup' today?

Lord I give my misplaced priorities to you today, help me choose right I pray.

Extended Reading – Genesis 25-26

FAITH WALK
Are You Running?

I am with you and will watch over you wherever you go, and I will bring you back to this land. I will not leave you until I have done what I have promised you."   *Genesis 28:15*

Jacob was on the run.

Jacob had messed up, messed up so bad that he literally had to run for his life. Not only had he manipulated Esau, his older brother, out of his birthright in exchange for a bowl of soup. Now he had deceived his father, Isaac, by pretending to be Esau and had stolen his blessing.

Esau was so furious with him, that he was waiting for an opportunity to kill him. And Jacob ran. On Isaac's instruction, Jacob is now fleeing to Haran. Isaac told him to go to Laban, his mother Rebekah's brother, to take for himself a wife from among Laban's daughters. And so, he goes on this journey through the desert.

And as he rests for the night, all he has is a stone for his pillow. But in that place, God meets him. The Lord appears to Jacob in a dream and comforts him. He promises to watch over him and not to leave him. For all that Jacob had done, he may have expected to be punished even. But instead, God comes and meets him at his point of need. What an awesome God.

And this God has not changed. He is the same yesterday, today and forever. He remains the same loving God, who promises to be with us, provide for us, and never leave us nor forsake us. He calls you to run to him with all your needs and problems.

Is this God your God?

Lord thank you for the loving and amazing God you are. Help me always run to you, I pray.

Extended Reading – Genesis 27-29

WORK ETHICS
How will you be Missed?

But Laban said to him, "If I have found favor in your eyes, please stay. I have learned by divination that the Lord has blessed me because of you." He added, "Name your wages, and I will pay them."   *Genesis 30:27-28*

Jacob had served Laban long years.

Jacob had served Laban seven years for Leah, his older daughter. Then another seven years for Rachel the younger daughter. He had all his sons and daughter, except Benjamin, while working for Laban. And now, Jacob asks to leave. But Laban entreats him to stay.

Laban recognizes that he was blessed because Jacob was with him. He recognizes his stocks have increased, he has grown in wealth because of Jacob. And so, Laban is willing to pay him anything, to keep Jacob back. Jacob asks for his wages in the form of every speckled or spotted sheep, every dark-colored lamb and every spotted or speckled goat. Laban agrees. Jacob ends up staying another six years.

In just the next chapter, we find Jacob's description of how he worked for Laban and why Laban valued his service so much. Jacob reminds Laban, how during the twenty long years he worked for Laban, the ewes had not miscarried (31:38). Jacob bore the losses of sheep killed by wild animals (31:39). He worked hard, day in and day out (31:39).

Laban was no easy boss. He demanded payment from Jacob for the flock that was stolen (vs.39). He changed his wages ten times in twenty years (vs.41). Despite all that, Jacob remained faithful and took good care of the flock. He took his job seriously. He was hardworking and diligent.

How would your boss or those you serve respond if you were to leave today?

Lord that I may be a blessing where I serve, I pray.

Extended Reading – Genesis 30-31

KNOW YOUR GOD
For He has Said

But you have said, 'I will surely make you prosper and will make your descendants like the sand of the sea, which cannot be counted.'"   *Genesis 32:12*

Jacob is scared.

When his men tell Jacob that Esau was on his way to meet him, Jacob is petrified. And rightly so. And if that is not enough, Esau is not alone, he was coming with four hundred men. At the thought of meeting Esau, all the events of the past flash past his eyes in a matter of minutes. The many ways Jacob had deceived and wronged Esau, just came back in waves.

The description of the huge number of men with Esau, scares Jacob. The circumstances are not favorable. Jacob is confused and has no clue how to handle the situation. But one thing he knows and does. He turns to God.

He turns to God and reminds him of what he has said. Jacob knew his God well enough to know that he could turn to him in times of need. He knew that his God was a God who kept his promises. He knew his God was faithful and true. So, he calls on the Lord in his time of trouble. He has not forgotten the promise that the Lord had given him. He claims the promise. He remembers and reminds the Lord of what he had promised.

God remains the same and is ever faithful to his word and his promises even today. Do you know him and his word to go to him in confidence when in trouble?

Lord help me turn to you first and claim what you have said in your word, I pray.

Extended Reading – Genesis 32-34

TRUST GOD
When Life is Not Fair

Meanwhile, the Midianites sold Joseph in Egypt to Potiphar, one of Pharaoh's officials, the captain of the guard.

Genesis 37:36

Joseph's life changed radically and oh so quickly.

His father Isaac had sent him to Shechem to see how his brothers were doing. And Joseph obedient and willing, set off immediately, only to find that they had moved to Dothan. Now Dothan was a good twelve miles further.

Joseph could have returned from Shechem, he would still be obeying his father. But the fact that he goes the extra mile shows his genuine concern for his brothers. And what did he get in return? His brothers sold him as a slave to Potiphar.

Joseph's life changes, drastically. From being the favorite son of his father Isaac, he became a slave in a strange land. From the happy comfort of his home to the hard reality of slavery. From being the one who is served in his father's house, to be a servant. What a sea of change.

And all because Joseph obeyed his father and went the extra mile for his brothers? Now how is that fair? Joseph's situation was not fair. And to be treated like this by his very own brothers made it even more painful. He sure did not deserve to be treated like this.

Now Joseph could be angry and bitter, or he could choose to trust God. Joseph chose to trust God and the rest, as they say, is history.

God's thoughts are not our thoughts nor are his ways our ways (Isaiah 55:8). God has a plan for your life too. Would you choose like Joseph to trust God, even when you don't understand?

Lord help me trust you even when life is unfair, I pray.

Extended Reading – Genesis 35-37

CHOICES
The Fragrance of Choice

From the time he put him in charge of his household and of all that he owned, the Lord blessed the household of the Egyptian because of Joseph. The blessing of the Lord was on everything Potiphar had, both in the house and in the field.   Genesis 39:5

Young Joseph was a slave.

Sold as a slave by his own brothers, Joseph finds himself in the house of Potiphar the Egyptian. In no time, Joseph moved from being the favorite son of his father to the hated brother, hated enough to be sold as a slave. Why Lord why, could easily have been his response.

Joseph had a choice to make. He chose to trust God enough not to question, whine or complain. He chose to trust God enough to accept his circumstances and to serve happily with honesty and integrity.

And the result? Potiphar's household was blessed.

Potiphar the pagan, was blessed because Joseph trusted and honored God. Potiphar the master was blessed because the slave chose to serve with integrity. Potiphar the rich man got richer because the slave Joseph was faithful to his God. Now how is that for fairness? Potiphar was blessed and Joseph's reward nowhere in sight.

God's children are to serve him faithfully, wherever we are. We are called to trust him for who he is and not depending on how our circumstances are going. And God does surely use his children to bless others.

Who is being blessed because you are serving joyfully, trusting God, despite your circumstances?

Heavenly Father, for the times I have whined and questioned you, forgive me. Give me Lord the grace to serve you joyfully with integrity, I pray.

Extended Reading – Genesis 38-40

HUMILITY
Not About Me

Pharaoh said to Joseph, "I had a dream, and no one can interpret it. But I have heard it said of you that when you hear a dream you can interpret it. " I cannot do it," Joseph replied to Pharaoh, "but God will give Pharaoh the answer he desires."

Genesis 41:15-16

Young Joseph had been through a lot in his short life.

Sold into slavery by his own brothers, Joseph ends up in the household of Potiphar. His misery did not end there. Though he was hardworking and sincere in all his work, he soon enough finds himself in Pharaoh's prison, falsely accused of seducing Potiphar's wife. And there Joseph remained for more than two years.

When in prison God gives Joseph the ability to interpret dreams. He interprets the dreams of the baker and the cupbearer. Soon enough, Pharaoh has dreams that disturb him. None of his wise men could explain the dream to him. Then the cupbearer remembers and tells Pharaoh how Joseph had interpreted his dream correctly.

Joseph is brought in from the prison. And when Pharaoh tells Joseph that he had heard that Joseph could interpret dreams, Joseph is clear and quick to bring perspective. No, it is not Joseph, but the God he served, who could interpret dreams.

Joseph was very clear. He knew he was but an instrument, whom God uses for his own purposes. Joseph explains the meaning of the dreams, it makes sense to Pharaoh. Joseph is elevated to the position second only to the Pharaoh himself.

All that we have is from the Lord and so none of us have reason to boast. (1 Corinthians 4:7)

Do you tend to take pride in your talents or gifts?

Lord may I always be humble about what you have given me, I pray.

Extended Reading – Genesis 41-42

KNOW YOUR GOD
Choose to Trust

"So then, it was not you who sent me here, but God. He made me a father to Pharaoh, lord of his entire household and ruler of all Egypt.   Genesis 45:8

Joseph had every reason to be angry and bitter against his brothers.

Joseph's brothers had come to Egypt looking for food as there was famine in all the land. And now Joseph has just revealed himself to them. His brothers are petrified.

Joseph is no longer the young lad whom they had bullied and sold. He was in a position of great power over them. Joseph had risen to be the second in command of Egypt.

Now if he did not forgive those who sold him as a slave he couldn't be faulted right? After all, it was injustice done to him. And that too his very own brothers. Joseph could claim it was by his own hard work and diligence that he had risen to the heights of power in the land he had been sold as a slave. But Joseph doesn't.

Joseph's reliance and perspective of God gave him a humble heart. His great attitude gave him the ability to work hard and with integrity. His faith and willingness to trust God and his timing gave him the strength to persevere.

The Bible says all things do work together for good for those who love him and are called according to his purpose (Romans 8:28). And they that wait upon the Lord shall renew their strength says Isaiah 40:13.

Would you choose to trust him today and let it show in the way you respond to life?

Lord give the grace I need to trust you through the challenges of life, I pray.

Extended Reading – Genesis 43-45

FORGIVENESS
Above and Beyond

So Joseph settled his father and his brothers in Egypt and gave them property in the best part of the land, the district of Rameses, as Pharaoh directed. Joseph also provided his father and his brothers and all his father's household with food, according to the number of their children.   Genesis 47:11-12

Joseph's brothers were literally at his mercy.

The famine in the land was very severe. There was no grain, no pasture for the herds and flocks. The situation was grim.

Now as the second in command of Egypt, Pharaoh had put Joseph in charge of the entire land and especially the distribution of grain during this long time of famine. And his brothers had come all the way from Canaan in search of food. Joseph was now the lord of Egypt and in control of all food. Joseph could easily have used the opportunity to get back at them.

But Joseph instead goes above and beyond what he needed to do. He forgives them. He is gracious to them. He provides the best he can for them. And in his position and the favor he enjoyed with the Pharaoh, his best was quite something. He was able to provide all of them property in the best portion of Egypt. He took care of their everyday needs of food and provision. Joseph gave food to those who harmed him and provided for them. (Proverbs 25:21-22)

Who needs your above and beyond today? Whom can you return good for evil? Like Joseph, you too can do it, by God's grace.

Lord help me to go above and beyond what is expected of me, even it means those who have hurt me, I pray.

Extended Reading – Genesis 46-47

RECONCILIATION
Not My Place

But Joseph said to them, "Don't be afraid. Am I in the place of God?
Genesis 50:19

Jacob the patriarch is dead.

Jacob had lived a full life. Twelve sons and a daughter. He had the privilege of seeing his favorite son Joseph again, who he thought had died. Not just see Joseph, but the joy of seeing him doing very well in life despite all the troubles he went through.

And now Jacob died, after blessing each of his sons, including giving a double portion of blessing to Joseph's sons. And that is exactly the reason why the brothers are scared now. With Jacob their father gone, there is nothing to stop Joseph from taking revenge for all that they had done to him. But Joseph was able to forgive his brothers and not hold any bitterness in his heart. And that came from a place of love, God-given love.

Bitterness is like an acid, someone said, that only damages the container. Those who hold on to bitterness and un-forgiveness, only make themselves sick at heart, sometimes even sick in the body. The only effective anecdote for bitterness is love.

As the Bible says in 1 Peter 4:8, above all, love each other deeply, because love covers over a multitude of sins. We love and forgive not because the other person deserves it. We love and forgive because we are loved and have been forgiven much. When we can look at others in this light, it is difficult to hold on to bitterness.

Is there someone against whom you have been harboring bitterness? Would you ask God for his grace to love and forgive that person today?

Lord would you give me the grace to forgive, I pray.

Extended Reading – Genesis 48-50

CALLING
No One but You Will Do

*When the LORD saw that he had gone over to look, God called
to him from within the bush, "Moses, Moses!" And Moses said,
"Here I am."*   *Exodus 3:4*

God *did* call and *continues* to call people out of their comfort zone, to
serve him even today!

God called Noah to build an ark when the earth did not yet know
rain. God called Abram out of the land of Ur when he was still
an idol maker. God called Moses from a burning bush, while he was
a shepherd in the back of beyond. God called Joshua to bring down
the fortified city of Jericho, by walking around it and a loud cry. God
called Esther to stand in the gap for her people using her position as
queen. Jesus called his disciples each by name, to follow him. The Lord
called Paul on the road to Damascus, to serve the God whose followers
he had been persecuting.

God throughout the Bible did call his people to serve him and that
same God continues to call us to serve him. God has called his children
to do things that may seem decidedly different, even ridiculous to us!
But the fact remains, each one is unique and only you can do what
you are called to do!

God does not just call, but also equips, with his presence and his
guidance. We just need to obey. If God is calling you, would you say,
yes Lord, today, in humble trust and obedience?

*Lord give me a heart that is sensitive to recognize your call and to
say yes to you, in humble trust, I pray.*

Extended Reading – Exodus 1-3

PRAYER
When Confused

Moses returned to the Lord and said, "Why, Lord, why have you brought trouble on this people? Is this why you sent me?

Exodus 5:22

Moses is confused.

It was surely God who had called him. God had called to him out of the burning bush to lead the Israelites out of their slavery in Egypt. The Lord had even shown him signs to assure him that it was the Lord himself, the great I AM who had called him.

God had specifically asked him to go to Pharaoh and ask him to let his people go. Moses just obeyed. Then what went wrong? Why had the Pharaoh made it even more difficult for the Israelites, rather than let them go? Why had the Israelites themselves turned against him? Moses just could not figure out.

The Bible says Moses returned to the Lord and he asked some real honest questions.

Now, is there anything wrong in asking questions to the Lord? Absolutely not! It is interesting that it was the Lord to whom Moses returned to when he was confused. He didn't go around asking Aaron or talking to anyone else. He went straight to the Lord. In his asking though, Moses isn't shaking his fist at God, but asking from a place of humility, genuinely trying to understand. The fact that he goes back to the Lord also reflects that he is still willing to listen to him. His confusion does not mean he has lost faith in the God.

There may be times when we are confused and have questions too. Let us come to him, as Moses did, from a place of humility and with a heart willing to listen and obey.

Lord help me humbly trust you even when I don't understand, I pray.

Extended Reading – Exodus 4-6

FAITH
A Pharaoh in You

When Pharaoh saw that the rain and hail and thunder had stopped, he sinned again: He and his officials hardened their hearts.   *Exodus 9:34*

Yet again!

The exodus of the children of Israel out of Egypt must have been a spectacular sight. God had called Moses to lead his people out. He gave Moses careful instructions for each step of the way. Moses was to go and tell Pharaoh to let his people go. And if he refused God would send plagues on the Egyptians. But time and again, when Moses went and spoke to him, Pharaoh refused to listen.

The plague of the rain and hail and thunder was the seventh in a line of ten plagues. For all the six earlier plagues, Pharaoh had gone back on his word. Pharaoh remained stubborn. He and his officials hardened their hearts again, says the Bible. As we read this account, we tend to think, what a stubborn man this Pharaoh was. And rightly so. Would he never learn? How many more times did he need to see the amazing hand of God, before he believed that the Lord is truly God?

We live and breathe miracles every single day of our lives. The fact that we are alive to see this day, is a miracle. If we have eyesight to read this devotional today, we are among the privileged few who have both vision and the freedom of religion in your country. The health, the resources, the talents and the abilities that we have are all gifts and miracles from the Lord. And yet, when faced with challenges in life we don't believe. We worry, complain and whine. Isn't there a pharaoh in you and me?

Lord forgive me for my stubbornness and increase my trust in you, I pray.

Extended Reading — Exodus 7-9

SALVATION
The Last Plague

*The blood will be a sign for you on the houses where you are,
and when I see the blood, I will pass over you. No destructive
plague will touch you when I strike Egypt.   Exodus 12:13*

The final plague was the most painful.

From the Pharaoh to the servant, every Egyptian lost their first born
that night, including the first born of their cattle. The sorrow and
loss of the Egyptians was immeasurable. Pharaoh finally relented. He
agreed to let Moses lead the Israelites out of Egypt.

In the Israelites camp, however, it was a time of hope, deliverance, and
new beginnings. The Israelites were finally leaving to go and worship
God in freedom. Their centuries-old life of slavery was ending.

God had very specific instructions for his people as they prepared to
leave. Every Israelite home was to select a perfect lamb with no blemish,
kill it and put its blood on the doorframes of their houses. That blood
was the sign for the Lord as he passed through and struck down the
Egyptians. The Israelites were to be dressed for departure and the lamb
was to be roasted and eaten with haste. They were to remember this
night, observe and teach it through the generations.

Passover is a reminder that salvation requires the shedding of blood. For
New Testament believers, the shed blood of Jesus earned our salvation.
We no more need to make any blood sacrifices for our sins. We only
need to believe in the Lord Jesus to be saved. As John 1:12 says, yet to
all who did receive him, to those who believed in his name, he gave the
right to become children of God. Have you believed in the Lord Jesus?

Lord Jesus, thank you for shedding your blood for my sin.

Extended Reading — Exodus 10-12

WAIT ON GOD
Be Still

The Lord will fight for you; you need only to be still.

Exodus 14:14

Hemmed in!!

The Israelites had just seen the amazing hand of God as he freed them from four hundred years of Pharaoh's cruel slavery. They witnessed the ten deadly plagues which tormented the Egyptian people but did not even touch the Israelites. What wondrous miracles and a dramatic exit! And then began the exodus.

An exodus of people, cattle and livestock, into the desert. They journeyed with the Lord personally leading them each day with a pillar of cloud and a pillar of fire at night. What a sight they must have been.

But their joy was short-lived. They were soon faced with the swirling Red Sea in front of them and six hundred of the best Egyptian chariots, pounding on their heels, behind. Hemmed in on all sides, with literally no place to go, they were terrified. Their fear caused them to blame Moses. They blamed Moses for the situation they were in and for bringing them out of slavery?

But Moses did not react to their accusations. He reminds them that the Lord will fight for them. There was just one catch though, they were to be still!! Be still! That small little phrase may easily be *the* most difficult command for a believer to obey.

And yet, that is exactly what God asks of us. When crisis overwhelms and fear grips, we are not to run or take things into our own hands. We are to trust him and be still. He will work it out for us. What crisis are you facing today, that you are yet to trust God with?

Lord help me trust you enough to be still and let you fight my battles for me, I pray.

Extended Reading — Exodus 13-15

GRATITUDE
Do You Remember?

The Israelites said to them, "If only we had died by the Lord's hand in Egypt! There we sat around pots of meat and ate all the food we wanted, but you have brought us out into this desert to starve thisentire assembly to death."   Exodus 16:3

Memory is short lived.

The Israelites had been slaves in Egypt for more than four hundred years. In their misery, they cried to the Lord. God heard their cry. He called Moses to lead the Israelites out. With a great display of his power through ten plagues, God led his people out of Egypt. When the armies of Pharaoh pursued them, the Lord parted the waters. He took the entire two million people of Israel across in just one night. The armies of Pharaoh that had pursued them perished in the waters of the Red Sea. The miracles that the Lord performed to deliver his people were amazing and mighty.

And yet, here they are, complaining already. Complaining about the lack of food. After all the amazing wonders the Lord had done they were still doubting God's goodness toward them. They had already forgotten God's marvelous provision and protection. Peoples memory is too short.

Complaining reflects that we have forgotten God and his goodness towards us. Complaining is always against God and not the person we are angry at. It displays a lack of trust in God's goodness or confidence in God's sovereignty. When we complain, we blame people around us, even those who have helped and done us well. A heart that trusts God is a grateful heart. Take time to recall at least five ways God has blessed you in the past week.

Increase in me an attitude of gratitude Lord I pray.

Extended Reading — Exodus 16-18

OBEDIENCE
Treasured Possession

Now if you obey me fully and keep my covenant, then out of all nations you will be my treasured possession. Although the whole earth is mine.   *Exodus 19:5*

God's promise with a condition.

Even though the people of Israel grumbled and complained, the Lord remains forgiving, patient and faithful. He does not change. He is the same, yesterday today and forever. God told Israel that they would be his treasured possession among all the nations. But there was a condition. They were to obey him *fully*.

God's people today, however, are not restricted to the nation of Israel but includes anyone who believes in the Lord Jesus Christ as Savior. God's people are from every tribe, every nation, and every tongue. Apostle Peter in 1 Peter 2:9 reminds us as believers that we are a chosen generation, a royal priesthood, a holy nation. And so, as Christians we are called to obey God fully as his treasured possession.

Obedience is an essential part of Christian faith. Jesus said in John 14:15, if you love me, keep my commandments. We cannot call him Lord, Lord and not do what he says to do (Luke 6:46). Obedience is submission to a higher power or authority. When we obey God through what he says in his word, we show our love for him. Partial obedience is disobedience. Delayed obedience is disobedience too.

God's word is his love letter to us, his children. It is our guide to obeying him. Our obedience to him through his word reflects our love for him. What is one area where you have only done the part that is convenient to you and avoided obeying Him *fully*?

Lord, please help me love you by obeying you fully, I pray.

Extended Reading — Exodus 19-21

GRACE
High Calling

Six days do your work, but on the seventh day do not work, so that your ox and your donkey may rest, and so that the slave born in your household and the foreigner living among you may be refreshed.   *Exodus 23:12*

On the seventh day, God rested.

This chapter begins with specific instructions God gives on how his people were to handle legal situations. They were to be fair. They were to be true. They were to stand firm in doing what is right, even for those who hate them.

Next, the Lord moves to Sabbath laws. After six years of plowing the field, the seventh year was to be a year of rest, so that the poor could get food from their fields. And after six days of work, the seventh day was to be a day of rest to allow the slave and foreigner to be refreshed.

What an amazing God. A God who so graciously provides for the slaves who had no rights and the foreigner feeling lost away from his home. God calls his people to be like him. To care for the poor, those who have no rights, for those who are lonely and needy.

Someone said, if you are a Christian, even the dog in your home will know it. You and I have not done anything to deserve the homes, resources or talents we have. God in his infinite wisdom and plan has allowed it. There is no way that we can take credit for it or be arrogant about it. Instead, we are called to care for and bless those less fortunate than us.

What can you do differently this week to be a greater blessing to those who serve you?

Lord help me reflect your love to those who serve me, I pray.

Extended Reading — Exodus 22-24

GIVING
Privileged to Give

The Lord said to Moses, "Tell the Israelites to bring me an offering. You are to receive the offering for me from everyone whose heart prompts them to give.   *Exodus 25:1-2*

It was time to build the sanctuary.

The Israelites had come out of Egypt. God had protected and provided for their every need. The Lord had also given them detailed laws concerning every area of living. And now the time had come for the Lord to dwell among his people. It was time to build the sanctuary.

And so, God called Moses and gave him instructions. The Israelites were to bring offerings to build the sanctuary. Moses was to receive offerings on behalf of the Lord. But he was to receive an offering from everyone whose heart is prompted to give. And therein an undergirding principle regarding giving.

Could the Lord have built the sanctuary without the offerings from the people? Of course, he could! Then why did the Lord require the people to contribute? The Lord who owns cattle on a thousand hills is more than able to accomplish all that he needs. But God in his graciousness allows us to partner with him in the work he does. What a privilege!

And so, when we give, it is to be from that place of being privileged to give and not as if we are doing the Lord a favor (is that even possible?). Giving is to be voluntary. Giving is never to be forced. 2 Corinthians 9:7 says, each of you should give what you have decided in your heart to give, not reluctantly or under compulsion, for God loves a cheerful giver.

Do you give and serve with a cheerful heart?

Lord help me always give from a grateful heart, I pray.

Extended Reading — Exodus 25-27

PRAYER
Priestly Duties

Whenever Aaron enters the Holy Place, he will bear the names of the sons of Israel over his heart on the breast piece of decision as a continuing memorial before the Lord.   Exodus 28:29

Aaron was the first high priest of Israel.

Aaron was being prepared to begin his service. There are very specific priestly garments that he would wear in God's presence, within the tabernacle. And one of those garments was the breast piece mentioned in today's text. The Lord said that Aaron was to wear the names of the sons of Israel over his heart on the breast piece, as a continuing memorial before the Lord. He had the responsibility to intercede on behalf of the people. The people could not even approach God in their sinful state.

Today, New Testament believers are like living stones and are being built into a spiritual house to be a holy priesthood, offering spiritual sacrifices acceptable to God through Jesus Christ. (1 Peter 2:5). Every believer is called to intercede on behalf of others and offer spiritual sacrifices. We are called to offer our bodies as a living sacrifice (Romans 12:1). Spiritual sacrifices are deeds you do, words you speak, songs you sing, in reliance on the power of the Holy Spirit.

To be the royal priesthood of God is an awesome responsibility and privilege. How you worship God matters. We are to rely on the Holy Spirit to help us worship God in truth and in spirit. We are to be diligent to intercede on behalf of others and our words and actions are to be motivated by his love. How can you pray more diligently for those around you?

Lord help me worship you through my actions, words, and prayer for others, I pray.

Extended Reading — Exodus 28-29

COMMITMENT
A Price to Pay

The Levites did as Moses commanded, and that day about three thousand of the people died.   Exodus 32:28

Moses went up the mountain to meet the Lord.

Aaron oversaw the Israelites while Moses was away. As time went, the people grew restless and began to grumble. Grumbling is often a precursor to sin. And sin they did, very gravely. The Almighty God who had led and provided so miraculously was easily forgotten and Moses taken for dead. The people convinced Aaron into creating a golden image for them to worship.

Moses came down to the sound of revelry gone wrong and was furious. In his anger, Moses threw the tablets to the ground. He grinds the broken pieces to powder and makes the people drink it.

Moses next calls the people from the entrance of the camp. He asks them to choose. Whoever was for the Lord was to come to him. Only the Levites come. Moses then called the Levites to do something tough. He told them to go through the camp from one end to the other and each killing his brother and friend and neighbor. And the Bible says, three thousand men fell that day. What a heavy price to pay.

Commitment to Jesus Christ comes with a price too. Jesus said if anyone comes to me and does not hate his own, even his own life cannot be his disciple (Luke 14:26). You and I are called to choose Christ in the small and big happenings of life, among family, friends and in the marketplace. And that could sometimes come with a heavy price. Are you willing to choose to follow Christ daily, anyway?

Lord may I choose you every day, even when it hurts, I pray.

Extended Reading — Exodus 30-32

MENTORING
What are you Reflecting?

The Lord would speak to Moses face to face, as one speaks to a friend Then Moses would return to the camp, but his aide Joshua son of Nun did not leave the tent.   *Exodus 33:11*

God prepared Joshua to lead Israel after Moses.

Joshua had a huge task ahead of him and the Lord knew it. And one of the ways Joshua was trained was as he watched Moses, day to day.

The richness of Moses' life and relationship with the Lord came from the time he spent in the Lord's presence. The Lord would speak to him face to face, as one would speak to a friend. Each time Moses met with the Lord and came out, his face was so radiant that he had to wear a veil on his face. (Exodus 34:35). What a privilege for Joshua to watch this at close hand.

Moses invested time in Joshua. Joshua got to watch Moses, closely. He saw how Moses interacted with the Lord. Joshua watched Moses, on a regular basis. And that is mentoring.

Mentoring is more than the words you speak. A mentor is a counsel, a guide, a life coach. A mentor not only counsels, but also walks alongside. Mentoring is a biblical mandate. All of us as believers need mentors, someone to look to for counsel, for guidance. But each of us are also called to be mentors, to lead, to point others to Christ. Older believers are called to mentor those younger in faith.

If you don't already have one, would you prayerfully seek out a godly older man or woman to mentor you? Whom are you investing in?

Dear Lord, help me have the humility to be mentored and to mentor someone you lead me to, I pray.

Extended Reading — Exodus 33-35

CALLING
Step into the Water

So Bezalel, Oholiab and every skilled person to whom the Lord has given skill and ability to know how to carry out all the work of constructing the sanctuary are to do the work just as the Lord has commanded. The Lord calls.   Exodus 36:1

There was a task at hand. The tabernacle was to be built. And so, the Lord called and equipped Bezalel and Oholiab to lead the work of constructing the sanctuary. The Bible says, God not only called Bezalel and Oholiab by name for the task, but he also filled them with his Spirit and gave them the wisdom and skill for the task (Exodus 31:1). God gave them the ability to know how to do the work and to teach others too.

God continues to call people to do various tasks for his Kingdom purposes. And those he calls, he equips with all they need. But many of us are scared to take up the tasks that God calls us to do. We feel inadequate and ill-equipped.

That's a great place to be. When it is God who equips us, our reliance on him is greater. Our confidence is replaced with his confidence. When we trust him completely instead of on our own resources and abilities, it leads to humility. It is finally all about him and him alone. And so, the responsibility to make it happen is also is not ours but his. All we must do is stay close to him and obey him completely. There is immense freedom in that.

Would you take courage and step out into the waters, to do what he has called you to do? You will walk the waters with him.

Lord help me obey your call and step out in faith, I pray.

Extended Reading — Exodus 36-38

KNOW YOUR GOD
Practice the Presence

So the cloud of the Lord was over the tabernacle by day, and the fire by night, in the sight of all the Israelites during all their travels.   *Exodus 40:38*

The Lord was with Israel.

God did not just deliver his people from the hands of their Egyptian masters, he continued to be with them. He led them through the desert and provided them with manna and quail all their years in the wilderness. Their clothes did not wear out nor did their feet swell (Deuteronomy 8:4). He took care of their every need. Most of all, he was with them. The Israelites enjoyed his presence through the cloud and the fire, which went with them, led them, direct them when to pitch the tent and when to move.

In Hebrews 13:5, the Lord says he will never leave you nor forsake you. God continues to be with his people. That promise remains true for each of us even today. When the sun shines brightly, when someone gives you a warm hug when you are feeling low, when things simply fall into place it is the presence of God. When you wake up to a new day and your needs are met, it is the presence of God. We often tend to take for granted the many ways God makes his presence felt.

Even through the times when you feel all alone, and you doubt if he really is with you because of your sin, he remains true to his word. He is with you, he will never forsake you.

Look out for ways he reveals himself to you each day.

Lord help me to be increasingly aware of your presence in my life, each day, I pray.

Extended Reading — Exodus 39-40

SALVATION
In Your Stead

The Lord called to Moses and spoke to him from the tent of meeting. He said, "Speak to the Israelites and say to them…"

Leviticus 1:1-2

Leviticus begins at Mount Sinai.

The glory of the Lord has just filled the tabernacle. The priests and people are instructed about sacrifices, worship, and holiness.

The central theme of the book of Leviticus is that God is holy, and his people are to be holy. Leviticus talks about the corrupting nature of sin and how sin separates us from God. It also provides laws and requirements for the holy and separated people of God. Leviticus shows God's requirement of blood for the penalty of sin and his provision of a substitute.

Now the Bible is clear, that all have sinned and have fallen short of the glory of God (Romans 3:23). And yet the Bible also says, God calls us to be holy just as he is holy (1 Peter 1:16). And so, God sent his only Son to die on behalf of us or to die in our place. Christ stood in our place as a sinner and bore the full force of the wrath of God for our transgressions. As a result, you and I can stand before God, "like Christ" and be his righteousness.

Holiness cannot be achieved by human nature or effort. Christ's substitutionary death on the cross provided a way for you and me to be reconciled with God. If we accept him as our Savior we don't have to pay the rightful penalty for our sin, which is death. Have you chosen to accept this amazing offer of life and salvation?

Lord thank you for dying on that cruel cross for me. Help me love and obey you each day, I pray.

Extended Reading — Leviticus 1-4

WORSHIP
Nothing But the Best

These, then, are the regulations for the burnt offering, the grain offering, the sin offering, the guilt offering, the ordination offering and the fellowship offering, which the Lord gave Moses at Mount Sinai in the Desert of Sinai on the day he commanded the Israelites to bring their offerings to the Lord.

Leviticus 7:37-38

The Israelites were commanded to bring offerings.

The book of Leviticus lists five kinds of offerings that the Israelites were required to bring to the Lord. The profound sinfulness of humans and the need for atonement is the premise for these offerings. It made a way for everyone to repent and come back to fellowship with God.

There are three undergirding principles about offerings that are relevant even today. Firstly, the offerings were open to all. Anyone could bring an offering. And that is the wideness of God's grace and true human equality. Though salvation is through none other than Christ, anyone may come to him.

Secondly, there is a cost involved for the worshipper. Salvation is a gift for us because Christ paid the full price to redeem us. And only he could pay that price. But disciples, are to deny themselves and take up their cross daily and follow him (Luke 9:23).

The third principle is that only the best could be offered. Jesus' sacrifice was the ultimate. He gave his very life and the last drop of his blood for you and me. We are to offer ourselves as living sacrifices (Romans 12:1). We are to offer our praise, our gifts, and service to others in Christ's name. We have received the best and the ultimate sacrifice, how can we offer anything but our best?

Lord give me a heart that offers you my best each day, I pray.

Extended Reading — Leviticus 5-7

CONSECRATED
Washed, Dressed, Anointed

Moses then said to Aaron and his sons, "Cook the meat at the entrance to the tent of meeting and eat it there with the bread from the basket of ordination offerings, as I was commanded: 'Aaron and his sons are to eat it.' Leviticus 8:31*

Moses did as the Lord commanded.

This is one phrase you will find repeated over and over in these chapters of Leviticus. What an amazing relationship between God and Moses. Moses knew and understood God. The Lord found Moses reliable and obedient. Would the Lord be able to trust you as he did with Moses?

The next task Moses had was to consecrate Aaron and his sons as priests. He was to wash, dress and anoint Aaron and his sons. Then there were sacrifices to offer. And finally, Aaron and his sons had to cook the meat and eat it.

To consecrate is to set apart as holy. As the preparation for this awesome responsibility, Aaron and his sons had to be washed, as a symbol of being cleansed. They then had to be dressed in clothes specifically made for them to make them presentable before the Lord. They were then to be anointed with oil as a symbol of being set apart. All these were done by Moses for them. But finally, Aaron and his sons had to cook and eat the meat in full view of the people, as their symbol of acceptance.

Jesus Christ's perfect sinless sacrifice paid the price once and for all. Everyone who believes in him is saved and made righteous before God. But like Aaron and his sons, each one needs to accept this salvation that is ours for the asking. Have you chosen him?

Lord, I choose to accept your gift of salvation today.

Extended Reading — Leviticus 8-10

HOLINESS
Enslaved to What?

I am the Lord your God; consecrate yourselves and be holy,
because I am holy. Do not make yourselves unclean by any
creature that moves along the ground. I am the Lord, who
brought you up out of Egypt to be your God; therefore, be holy,
because I am holy.   *Leviticus 11:44-45*

Do Old Testament food regulations apply today?

As early as the time of Noah, God made the distinction between 'clean' and 'unclean' animals. However, it is only in Deuteronomy that God specifies the kinds of clean and unclean animals. Some of the food laws may have protected Israel from the disease. But health cannot be the primary reason for these laws, because God has rescinded the food laws. Jesus in Mark 7:15 says "Nothing outside a person can defile them by going into them. Rather, it is what comes out of a person that defiles them."

And yet, at the end of the food laws, the running theme of Leviticus is reiterated. The Lord calls his people to be holy because he is holy. And that is the crux of the matter.

The prohibition of certain foods as unclean was a temporary part of God's way of making Israel distant or distinct from the nations of the world. With the coming of Christ, God's people are no longer a political-ethnic people like the Jews, but a global people from every tribe and language and ethnicity and race.

To be holy is to be set apart, to be consecrated for the Lord's use. We are alive for his purposes, to worship him the way he wishes to be worshipped. We are called to be slaves to righteousness which leads to holiness (Romans 6:19). What are you enslaved to?

Father help me live my life as a worship to you, I pray.

Extended Reading — Leviticus 11-13

HOLINESS
Do You Not Know?

'You must keep the Israelites separate from things that make
them unclean, so they will not die in their uncleanness for
defiling my dwelling place, which is among them.'"

Leviticus 15:31

The Israelites were to separate themselves.

These two chapters deal with uncleanliness that comes from skin diseases and body discharges. But again, the crux of the matter is what is summarized in this verse. The Israelites were to separate themselves from things that make them unclean so that they would not defile the Lord's dwelling place, which was among them. The tabernacle with the presence of the Lord was with the people of Israel wherever they moved.

New Testament believers, however, don't have a physical tabernacle that moves with us. But the Bible in 1 Corinthians 6:19 reminds us, that our bodies are temples of the Holy Spirit. Today the temple of God has moved from being outside to the inside of each of us.

Jesus Christ the perfect Lamb of God, died on the cross and paid the price for our sins. He died in our place. He paid the price of our sin with his blood. We have been bought with the blood of Christ. When you accept Christ as Lord and Savior, the Holy Spirit comes to live within us. Our body becomes the place where the Holy Spirit dwells.

We owe our life and all that we are to Christ. We are not our own but called to live a life for him, on his terms. A life that is separated lives to please him and obeys him.

Does your life reflect that you are set apart for the Lord?

Cleanse me, Lord, today and make my heart a clean place for you to
dwell, I pray.

Extended Reading — Leviticus 14-15

SIN
Serious Business

> *In this way, he will make atonement for the Most Holy Place because of the uncleanness and rebellion of the Israelites, whatever their sins have been. He is to do the same for the tent of meeting, which is among them during their uncleanness.*
>
> *Leviticus 16:16*

Two of Aaron's sons died because they offered unauthorized fire before the Lord.

After their death, God gives specific instruction about how Aaron was to enter the Most Holy Place. Aaron was to deal with his own sin first, through specific sacrifices and symbolic clothing and with incense. Then he was to offer sacrifices and incense for the atonement of the sins of the people. God takes sin very seriously. Sin so offends God that sinful people would die in his presence if their sin were not concealed.

Sin is any lack of conformity to the will of God. Sin is an outrage against God and the source of untold harm to us and others. Sin is subject to the eternal wrath of God and has eternal consequences (Romans 6:23). The Bible teaches that all are sinners and that there is no one righteous, not even one (Romans 3:10).

Sin has affected our moral, intellectual and thinking capabilities. As a result, we fail to understand the gospel even when explained. We flee from God rather than seek him. Sin deceives us and blinds us to the truth of the Scriptures. When truth makes us uncomfortable we often try to redefine the truth to justify our behavior. Trust in the word of God increases our discomfort with sin and propels us towards God. Is the sin in your life making you uncomfortable or are you prone to justify your behavior?

Lord help me see sin as you see it, I pray.

Extended Reading — Leviticus 16-18

RELATIONSHIPS
Reverence for God

*Stand up in the presence of the aged, show respect for the elderly
and revere your God. I am the Lord.*   *Leviticus 19:32*

Standing up, is it that important?

The Lord is instructing his people regarding daily living and how to interact within a community. And one of the things he says is stand up in the presence of the aged, show respect for the elderly.

Interestingly the sentence does not end there. When we respect the elderly and stand up in their presence, we are respecting them, but more importantly, we are revering God. A worshipper of God, someone who loves and honors God, is to respect the elderly. Also, at no place does the Bible say, respect the elderly who are good people or those who have been good to you. We are called to respect the elderly, period. No clauses or options.

Isaac showed respect to Abraham, Jacob to his parents, Joseph to his aged father, Ruth to her mother-in-law, and the list goes on. Christ is the ultimate example of tender care toward his mother even during his dying moments.

We respect the elderly for the rich and sometimes tough experiences they have come through. We respect them for the long years they have invested in serving us. We respect them for their maturity and wisdom. We respect them because they remind us of the nearness of eternity and the imminent brevity of life. We respect our elders as we set an example and legacy for our children. Whom have you been disrespectful to? Would you ask God to forgive you and help you find creative ways to respect them always?

Lord help me respect the elderly in my life by my words and actions, I pray.

Extended Reading — Leviticus 19-21

SIN
No Two Ways About It

*The Lord's Passover begins at twilight on the fourteenth day of
the first month.*   *Leviticus 23:5*

In ancient Israel, Passover was the first and most joyful festival.

Passover memorialized how God delivered his people from slavery
in Egypt. The celebration of Passover began on the evening of the
fourteenth day of the month of Nissan, the first month of the Hebrew
calendar (late March to mid-April). Passover is one of the three festivals
for which all Israelite males were to appear before God in Jerusalem.

The Feast of Unleavened Bread began the day after and lasted six days.
This feast was a reminder of the departure of the Israelites from Egypt,
where people left so suddenly that there was no time for bread made
with yeast to rise.

The Passover meal and the Passover lamb are the highlight of this
festival. All the lambs of the Passover point to Jesus Christ, who went
intentionally to Jerusalem to die on the Passover as the perfect Lamb
of God, sacrificed for his people.

Without the shedding of blood, there is no forgiveness of sin (Hebrews
9:22). The thought of blood and sacrifice is repugnant to many. That
may be the reason too, that many see Jesus as a fine example, but reject
him as the crucified Savior. The Bible clearly teaches that the wages of sin
is death (Romans 6:23) and there are no exceptions. Either the person
who sins must bear the penalty of death or accept the gift of salvation
through the death and resurrection of Christ Jesus.
Have you grasped and accepted this deep truth? Whom will you share
this truth with this week?

*Lord, please help fully grasp this amazing truth and share it with
those around me, I pray.*

Extended Reading — Leviticus 22-23

LAW
Rest and Freedom

Consecrate the fiftieth year and proclaim liberty throughout the land to all its inhabitants. It shall be a jubilee for you; each of you is to return to your family property and to your own clan.

Leviticus 25:10

The Jubilee was probably the first ever land reform program in history.

This chapter begins by describing the sabbatical year which occurred every seven years. The fields were not to be plowed or planted. In the seventh year, the land was to have a year of rest.

Jubilee was about freedom from captivity. Every fifty years the Israelites were to remember how they had once been oppressed as slaves in Egypt and how the Lord had liberated them. The laws for the Jubilee looked forward to the day the Israelites would live as free citizens in the land that the Lord gave them. It was to remind them that man does not live by bread alone.

The Sabbath and Jubilee years called the people to trust God to provide. Jubilee prevented massive accumulation of wealth, especially at the expense of poorer people. The Jubilee year began with the sounding of the trumpet. And the Bible says, one day the trumpet of the Lord will sound for us. The dead in Christ will rise first and those alive will be caught up in the clouds to meet him, to be with him forever more. (1 Thessalonians 4:15-17). Is this hope yours? Then you will set little value on possessions and more value for God and his Word.

On what is your heart set?

Lord help me set my mind on you more than on my worldly possessions, I pray.

Extended Reading — Leviticus 24-25

OBEDIENCE
Rewards Follow

If you follow my decrees and are careful to obey my co mands,
.... I will walk among you and be your God, and you will be
my people.   *Leviticus 26:3,12*

The first thirteen verses of this chapter point to the consequences of obedience.

Many of the law codes of the ancient east ended with a section on rewards and punishments. Rewards for those who obey and punishments for those who don't. In the Bible, this twenty-sixth chapter of Leviticus is one such section.

Here, the Lord is making promises to his people. If the people are careful to obey the commands of the Lord, he would bless them with good rain in season and rich harvests. He promises to protect them and keep them safe from wild animals. He promised peace through victory over their enemies. But the greatest blessing was the promise of God's Presence. He promised to walk among them, to be their God.

The Bible is full of promises of God's presence. In God's presence is fullness of joy; At his right hand are pleasures forever (Psalm 16:11). Draw near to God and he will draw near to you (James 4:7). The Lord is near to all who call upon him, to all who call upon him in truth (Psalm 145:18).

God promises his presence to those who obey him even today. Obedience to God proves our love for him (1 John 5:2-3), demonstrates our faithfulness to him (1 John 2:3-6), glorifies him in the world (1 Peter 2:12), and opens avenues of blessing for us (John 13:17). Would you choose to obey God and enjoy his presence in your life, daily?

Lord give me an obedient heart that I may enjoy your presence every day of my life, I pray.

Extended Reading — Leviticus 26-27

CHRISTIAN WALK
Prepare For Battle

Take a census of the whole Israelite community by their clans and families, listing every man by name, one by one.

Numbers 1:2

'Numbers' is not a trick title!

This book, at least the initial chapters is about numbers. It's about numbering the people of Israel. These chapters are also about how the Lord reordered his people's camp and their lives around himself and prepared them for the Promised Land.

This census is of all the men of Israel who were of fighting age, a total of 603,550. With women and children, the nation's total population would have been between two and three million. That's quite a number indeed.

This census matters to us today for two reasons. One, all the fighting men were counted. Every single one was important just as every single member of God's family is important. God knows us and has recorded the name of each of his children in the Lamb's book of life (Revelation 21:27). Two, the census prepared the Israelites for battle.

Christian life is a spiritual battle. We fight stronger forces than those that opposed Israel. We are important to God and are made in God's image, fearfully and wonderfully. But the devil is constantly trying to fight this truth. And so, the battle for our soul is a daily reality.

In Ephesians 6:12-13 Paul reminds us that, our struggle is not against flesh and blood, but against the powers and spiritual forces of evil in the heavenly realms. And so, he calls us to put on the full armor of God so that when the day- of evil comes, we may be able to stand our ground. Are you equipping yourself for battle by reading the Bible and praying every day?

Lord help me diligently put on my armor each day, I pray.

Extended Reading — Numbers 1-2

CHRISTIAN WALK
The Business of Your Life

> *The Lord said to Moses, "Count all the firstborn Israelite males who are a month old or more and make a list of their names. Take the Levites for me in place of all the firstborn of the Israelites, and the livestock of the Levites in place of all the firstborn of the livestock of the Israelites. I am the Lord."*
>
> *Numbers 3:40-41*

All Israel's priests were Levites but not all Levites were priests.

Only the male members of one family, Aaron's family, offered sacrifices. The rest of the Levites assisted the priests in their work and carried parts of the tabernacle when Israel traveled.

The census of the Levites is described in chapters three and four. This census was different from that of the other tribes. In the Levitical census, every male from age of one month and more was counted and not just those twenty and upwards as in the other tribes. The reason for this goes back to the time of the Exodus when God claimed all the firstborn of the Israelites, including their cattle, as his own. Firstborn of the cattle were sacrificed. But since human firstborn could not be sacrificed, God claimed all male Levites as his own. And this showed that the whole nation belonged to the Lord.

In the church today, however, not just firstborn male but all believers are God's purchased possession. And Apostle Peter reminds us in 1 Peter 1:18-19, that we are not redeemed with perishable things, but with the precious blood of Christ, a lamb without blemish. If you belong to Christ, you will make it the business of your life to serve him, as the Levites did. Do you?

Lord help me serve you with all my heart I pray.

Extended Reading — Numbers 3-4

HOLINESS
The Priority of Preparation

The Lord said to Moses   *Numbers 5:1*

The next phase begins.

Now that the people were all numbered and organized, God moves to prepare his people. Preparation to move into the Promised Land involved being pure. The Lord gives Moses instructions about different ways people were to make themselves pure. They were to remove from among the people who were ritually unclean (v1-4) they were to pay restitution to those they had offended (v5-10) and they were given a way to resolve marital distrust and jealousy (v11-31). In all of this, God's purpose was that his people would be pure and set apart from the idolatrous cultures around them. God gave great importance to preparing his people. He brought the Israelites from a disorganized mass of former slaves to a disciplined nation ready for battle now.

Preparation to do God's work properly takes time. God gives different tasks to different people, but every one of us is to take the Gospel to others. We are also called to prepare to worship and to serve him. But we need to prepare our hearts so that we can serve him.

We are called to be holy as he is holy. If God's people are to be in fellowship with him and useful in his service, they must be pure in heart. Disharmony with God or with people makes spiritual victories impossible. We are to be humble and quick to repent when the Holy Spirit convicts us of our sin. Our lives are to be pure, in thoughts, words, and deeds.

Are you preparing your heart daily to be useful to the Lord?

Lord, cleanse me and make me pure, I pray.

Extended Reading — Numbers 5-6

GIVING
From a Place of Love

Then the leaders of Israel, the heads of families who were the tribal leaders in charge of those who were counted, made offerings.   *Numbers 7:2*

This chapter is about the offerings by the heads of the twelve tribes.

The tabernacle was set. Moses had anointed the altar, the furniture and all the vessels in the tabernacle. And now the Lord tells Moses to accept the offerings that the leaders of the tribes bring which were to be used in the work of the Tent of Meeting.

The dedication of the altar extended over a twelve-day period. Each tribal leader presented his gifts on a day set aside for his tribe. God is interested in what each one does. And the careful repetition of the nearly identical words in each case makes the point that each one was important to God.

Jesus noticed the offering of two small coins by a widow. Others had much bigger gifts to give. The gift of the widow amounted to much more than all the others' gifts because she gave her all. God measures our gifts by what we have left rather than by what we give. Nothing misses God's eye. The Lord never overlooks the very least we do for him.

The Bible says in Matthew 5:23-24, if we are offering a gift at the altar but are not reconciled with a brother or sister, we are to leave the gift at the altar, first go and be reconciled to them and then offer the gift. Ask God for his grace to make peace before you bring your offerings to the Lord.

Does your offering of money, talent and time come out of genuine love and gratitude for the Lord?

Lord help me present offerings that please you, I pray.

Extended Reading — Numbers 7

WITNESS
Encourage in Love

But Moses said, "Please do not leave us. You know where we should camp in the wilderness, and you can be our eyes. If you come with us, we will share with you whatever good things the LORD GIVES US."   *Numbers 10:31-32*

The Israelites set out, finally.

The tribes of Israel had been waiting for this time when they leave Sinai for Canaan. After their three-month journey from Egypt, they had camped near the sacred mountain for eleven months. And now they set out, in the same way God had commanded at the time of the census. What an amazing sight it must have been. And yet their joy was short lived. Though the people possessed ample evidence of God's power and goodness, they would soon reject God and doubt his ability to give them the Promised Land. And their tragic unbelief led them to wander in the desert for the next forty years.

As they prepare to leave, Moses urges his brother-in-law Hobab to come with them. Though he refuses initially he agrees eventually. When we share the gospel with people, they may not agree immediately. Don't give up. Continue to encourage them to come with you and that you will share your blessings with them. Continue to witness to them.

A witness is one who testifies to what he has seen or heard and verifies what is true. As believers who have tasted and seen that the Lord is God, we are to share out life's experience with those who don't know him. We are to testify to God's goodness and faithfulness in our lives, to share it with others.

When is the last time you shared the gospel with someone?

Lord help me encourage and point at least one person to you this week, I pray.

Extended Reading — Numbers 8-10

COMPLAINING
Tough Silence

Now Moses was a very humble man, more humble than anyone else on the face of the earth. Opposition within and without.

Numbers 12:3

Today's text is found in parentheses in some translations as many scholars believe it was added later by a later scribe.

In the previous chapter, the people complain against Moses. Their latest complaint is about the lack of meat. Moses is exhausted and overwhelmed. The pressure had been high for so many months now. He has had enough. He turns to the Lord in frustration and angry prayer. But the Lord is so gracious, he does not condemn him instead he provides for him. God sent quails. And now his own family turned against him.

Miriam and Aaron are angry with Moses and start questioning his authority. The trouble was probably instigated by Miriam, which explains why the judgment later came to Miriam and not Aaron. They began by complaining about the Cushite wife that Moses took. They now moved to question his authority. "Has the Lord spoken only through Moses?" they asked. Pride was at root the root of their problem. However, Moses remained silent when accused.

When God's honor was at stake, Moses tried to do something about it, but when the accusations were against him personally, Moses is silent. That is a mark of true greatness. Truly great or strong people do not constantly defend themselves.

Unfortunately, most of us feel a strong need to speak in our defense when people accuse us. We are quick to defend ourselves but slow to speak up for the Lord. How do you respond when those you love, and trust turn against you?

Lord help me like Moses, be humble enough to be silent when I am attacked personally, I pray.

Extended Reading — Numbers 11-13

TIME
Important vs Urgent

Teach us to number our days that we may gain a heart of wisdom.   *Psalm 90:12*

Life is short.

The brevity of life stands out sharpest at the untimely death of a loved one. Death does have a unique way of bringing into focus and perspective, things that truly matter. And that perspective brings with it a whole set of different priorities to life. A perspective that moves from the temporal to the eternal, from petty to profound. If you knew that today is the last day of your life, would your day be any different from the other days?

If today were to be my last

Would my day change? Would it be different?

Oh yes, it would Oh yes It would!!

If today were to be my last

Things would change and real fast

Much less my concern with unwashed dishes

Much more with unsaid wishes

Much less with untidy beds and bathrooms

Much more ensuring loved ones' eternal rooms

If today were to be my last

Things would change and real fast

Much less my concern with airs and graces

Much more that from me overflows His praises

Much less with petty and insignificant points to prove

Much more that loved ones know His love is absolutely true

Yes, if today were to be my last

My one and only desire would surely be

To those around, one last time, quick and fast

To plead with all my heart, that they eternally His would be!!!

And so, my friend to live each day as if it were my last

Would be the wisest choice to make wouldn't you agree?

Lord help me each day choose the important over the urgent for your
glory, I pray.
Extended Reading — Numbers 14-15; Psalm 90

PRIDE
Grim Consequences

They came as a group to oppose Moses and Aaron and said to them, "You have gone too far! The whole community is holy, every one of them, and the LORD is with them. Why then do you set yourselves above the LORD's assembly?" Numbers 16:3

Pride goes before a fall.

Korah, a Levite, along with two hundred fifty leaders of Israel, rebelled against Moses and Aaron. He accused them of exalting themselves above the congregation. Korah obviously thought he could do a better job of leading the people than Moses was doing. But he rebelled against God's divinely appointed leaders, it was against God that Korah was revolting (Numbers 16:11).

Moses proposes a test to prove the source of his authority. Both Aaron and Korah with his men would present incense to the Lord. And the man whom the Lord chooses will be the one who is holy. Korah fails the test. God opens the earth. Korah, his men with their families and possessions are swallowed up. The rest of Israel were terrified.

But by the next day, the Israelites complain that Moses and Aaron had 'killed the Lord's people.' God is angry and sends a plague. Moses and Aaron interceded on behalf of the people. A complete catastrophe was averted. The plague killed fourteen thousand seven hundred people that day (Numbers 16:41-50).

God calls and appoints people that *he* chooses. God called Moses not Korah. Korah was arrogant and self-promoting. God's true leaders are humble and they submit to him. True leaders are called by God to their offices. They are not self-appointed. How are you respecting the leaders that God has appointed?

Lord help me accept and submit to the leaders you have appointed, I pray.

Extended Reading — Numbers 16-17

SALVATION
On His Terms

The Lord said to Aaron, "You, your sons and your family are to bear the responsibility for offenses connected with the sanctuary, and you and your sons alone are to bear the responsibility for offenses connected with the priesthood.

Numbers 18:1

God appointed Aaron and his sons to be priests.

As God's chosen priests, Aaron, and his sons were responsible for the purity of the sanctuary and the priesthood. The priests continually offered sacrifices on behalf of the people. Day after day every priest stood and performed his religious duties. Again, and again, he offers the same sacrifices, which can never take away sins (Hebrews 10:11). Their work was never done. They never got to sit down.

Aaron's role as priest, though extremely important, anticipated the greater and final priesthood of the Lord Jesus Christ, which was yet to come. The offerings of the Hebrew priests pointed to the way of salvation. But when Jesus Christ the High Priest had offered for all time one sacrifice for sins, he sat down at the right hand of God and since that time he waits for his enemies to be made his footstool (Hebrews 10:11-14). Jesus the High Priest sat down.

God created us. But our sin separated us from him. Now, God did not need to make a way for sin to be atoned for. He could have simply condemned us all. Instead, he loved us so much, that he opened a way for all to come to him. He gave us his Son as the one-time atonement for our sin. (John 3:16-18). We need to come to him, on his terms

Have you believed in Jesus as your Savior?

Lord Jesus, I accept you and your finished work on the cross for my sin.

Extended Reading — Numbers 18-20

SALVATION
Look and Live

The Lord said to Moses, "Make a snake and put it up on a pole; anyone who is bitten can look at it and live." Numbers 21:8

The people complain.

The people of Israel must have been hugely disappointed. They had been on the verge of conquering Canaan and they now had to make this detour. They needed to travel from Mount Hor along the route of the Red Sea, to go around Edom. And so, they complained.

This time they complained about the lack of bread and water. They 'detested the miserable food'. The Lord had been providing manna and quail in the desert. They never knew hunger or thirst even for a day. And yet here they were, complaining again.

And so, the Lord sent venomous snakes among the people. The snakes bit the people, and many died. The people came rushing to Moses in repentance, asking him to intercede to the Lord on their behalf which Moses did.

The Lord told him to make a bronze snake and put it up on a pole. Anyone who was bitten could look at it and live. Now there was no therapeutic value in the bronze snake. The healing was not in the piece of brass. The healing is in the Lord. The people bitten had to look at it, not pray to it. So also, salvation.

We receive salvation by faith alone. It is not earned. The Bible says in Romans 10:9, if you declare with your mouth, "Jesus is Lord," and believe in your heart that God raised him from the dead, you will be saved. You have nothing to do but look and believe. What is stopping you from looking to Jesus?

Lord Jesus, I look to you today and believe in your death and resurrection for my sins.

Extended Reading — Numbers 21-22

WORD
Whose Word?

God is not human, that he should lie, not a human being, that he should change his mind. Does he speak and then not act? Does he promise and not fulfill? Numbers 23:19

God's word is full of promises.

A promise is a declaration or assurance that one will do something. The one who promises is bound to keep it and the one who receives the promise needs to believe it.

In the Bible, it is God who makes every single promise. He is the God who is the King of kings and Lord of lords, the Creator of the entire universe. Yes, the same amazing God who also created every cell in our body when he fearfully and wonderfully knit us together in our mother's womb.

And this Almighty God who is making these promises has never once ever gone back on his word or broken his promise. From the almost ridiculous and impossible promise God made to childless Abraham of innumerable descendants, to Simon, whom he named Cephas, the rock on which he would build his church. God came through on every single promise. Not one of his promises in the Bible failed. And there is absolutely no reason why they should begin to fail now!

However, a promise is only of worth, when the promise is believed and received. Unless you are ready to receive the promises given in God's word, believe it and claim it for its worth, they simply remain nice sounding words, printed in the Bible. What promise from God's word would you choose to believe today?

Dear Lord, help me believe and receive every promise in your word, I pray.

Extended Reading — Numbers 23-25

DEPENDANCE ON GOD
Heavy Price

For when the community rebelled at the waters in the Desert of Zin, both of you disobeyed my command to honor me as holy before their eyes." (These were the waters of Meribah Kadesh, in the Desert of Zin.)   *Numbers 27:14*

Moses led Israel for forty long years.

The Israelites had been in slavery in Egypt for four hundred years. They cried for help and the Lord sent them Moses. After forty years of preparation in the palace and yet another forty in the wilderness, God called Moses to lead his people out of bondage.

And Moses did faithfully lead the Israelites. Despite their grumbling, murmuring,and rebelling, he led them, patiently. Even when they angered the Lord many times, Moses faithfully interceded on their behalf. And yet, in one moment of weakness, Moses faltered. And for that, he paid a heavy price.

The Israelites came to the desert of Zin and were thirsty. They grumbled against Moses and he cried out to the Lord. The Lord told him to speak to the rock and that water would come out. But Moses in his frustration struck the rock instead. Though water did gush out, Moses had made a grave mistake. Moses had taken his eyes off the Lord and somewhere taken the situation and glory for himself. Moses lost the privilege of going into the Promised Land.

When you and I take our eyes off the Lord and try to solve situations on our own, not relying on him, we are being proud. The Lord opposes the proud but shows favor to the humble (1 Pet 5:5). What do you need to depend on the Lord in humility?

Lord forgive me for being proud, and may I never take the glory due to you, I pray.

Extended Reading — Numbers 26-27

SALVATION
It is Finished

The Lord said to Moses, 2 "Give this command to the Israelites and say to them: 'Make sure that you present to me at the appointed time my food offerings, as an aroma pleasing to me.'

Numbers 28:1-2

The second census was taken.

This second census replaced the first census. Only three names remained from the first census, Caleb, Joshua, and Moses. The Lord had said that all who disbelieved the report of Caleb and Joshua would die in the desert. And they did. Unbelief and disobedience have very serious consequences.

Generations had changed, their wanderings were over. But the way to approach God had not changed. The offerings, feast, and vows were at the very heart of the Israelites' religious practices. These offerings would continually remind the people of who they were and who God is. Their continual reminder to respond in enormous gratitude to the Lord for all that he had done for them.

Reading the endless repetitions of the sacrifices should cause us to rejoice in Jesus Christ and his triumphant cry from the cross, "it is finished." The blood of Christ has put an end to the endless sacrifices. We no more need to offer sacrifices. Jesus Christ provided the one perfect sacrifice, once and for all. And today all we need to do is to believe in Jesus Christ, his finished work on the cross and we will be saved.

Our circumstances may change but the nature of our sins does not change. Our need for a savior and redeemer does not change nor does the way to salvation. Jesus Christ is the only way to salvation. Have you chosen to believe him? Who is the one person you will share this truth of the finished work of the cross today?

Lord fill me with gratitude that compels me to share you with others I pray.

Extended Reading — Numbers 28-30

JUSTIFICATION
Why Not Me?

The Lord said to Moses, [2] *"Take vengeance on the Midianites for the Israelites. After that, you will be gathered to your people."*
Numbers 31:1-2

The Lord tells Moses to exterminate the Midianites.

This is the first time in Israel's history that God is mandating a war of extermination. And this is a story that troubles a lot of people. God told Moses to have the army take vengeance on the people of Midian, except very young girls. And it was done.

The question that arises in many minds is how could God give a command to kill the people? The Midianites were guilty of seducing Israel into sexual immorality and idolatry (Numbers 25). This was God's decision not the Israelites'. God alone gives life and he alone has the right to decide death.

The Bible says for all have sinned and have fallen short of the glory of God. We often tend to forget our own sinful nature. Thus we should be reminded of our weaknesses and not justify ourselves. Jesus said unless we repent, we will perish too (Luke 13:5).

Would you ask God to give you a contrite and repentant heart?

Lord help me to be ever conscious of my sin and your grace, I pray.

Extended Reading — Numbers 31-32

LOVE GOD
Partial Obedience?

*'But if you do not drive out the inhabitants of the land,
those you allow to remain will become barbs in your eyes and
thorns in your sides. They will give you trouble in the land
where you will live.*   Numbers 33:55

This chapter is a record of Israel's journey from Egypt.

Moses in his record recounts the warning and the instruction that
the Lord had given his people. The Israelites were to drive out the
Canaanites from the land and destroy their idols. And if they did not
drive out every single Canaanite, the Lord had warned them that ones
that remain would become thorns and barbs to the Israelites.

The Israelites did drive out the Canaanites, but not completely. They
failed to destroy the Canaanites. And in the years to come, that led to
the Israelites repeatedly turning away from the Lord to worship idols.
They forgot the Lord their God who graciously led them out from Egypt.

Partial obedience is disobedience. When God asks us to do something
we are to obey Him, completely. Often, we obey just parts that are
convenient to us. The tough parts we tend to ignore or pretend we
don't understand.

We are called to love all, even those who are tough and seem unlovable.
We are not to steal, even in 'small' or intangible areas like our time and
quality of work. We are to be holy and set apart, not just when others
can see us, but even when we are alone, and no one is watching. Jesus
said if you love me keep my commandments (John 14:15).

In what area of your life are you not obeying the Lord, completely?

**Lord help me obey you fully in the things you are showing me each
day, I pray.**

Extended Reading — Numbers 33-34

SALVATION
Tower of Refuge

Six of the towns you give the Levites will be cities of refuge, to which a person who has killed someone may flee. In addition, give them forty-two other towns.   Numbers 35:6

Cities of refuge were among the Levites cities.

These cities were the place a person, whether Israelite or foreigner, who killed someone unintentionally, could flee to. If a person killed another, the victim's family could appoint a family member to avenge the death of their relative. The avenger was to find and kill the murderer. This led to justice for the intentional killing but injustice for the accidental ones. The provision of cities of refuge was not to condone the killing or to protect the murderer. Rather provide the offender an opportunity to prove innocence.

Once inside a city of refuge, the person had to appear before the elders of the city to explain why the killing was accidental. If the person was found guilty he could not stay in the city of refuge. But if the elders were convinced that the killing was not intentional the person could live in the city of refuge. And when the high priest in office died, the person could return home without fear of harm. The high priest's death seemed to serve as a symbolic atonement for accidental deaths.

God is our refuge, fortress, and deliverer who provides safety for all who come to him for refuge from sin and its punishment (Psalm 18:2). Christ's death and resurrection have provided us with freedom from the condemnation of the law and from an eternity in hell. But we need to choose him.

Have you found your refuge in Christ?

Thank You, Lord, for the refuge I have in you.

Extended Reading — Numbers 35-36

KNOW GOD
Not to Forget

In the fortieth year, on the first day of the eleventh month, Moses
proclaimed to the Israelites all that the LORD had commanded
him concerning them.   *Deuteronomy 1:3*

Deuteronomy is Moses' final and personal challenge to the people he loved.

A t the end of Numbers, the people of Israel stood on the banks of the Jordan, ready at last to enter the Promised Land. Moses knew he would soon die. God appointed Joshua to lead the people in the conquest of the land of Canaan. In the first thirty-three chapters of this book, Moses is passionately instructing, challenging and warning the sin-prone people that he had led for forty years.

In Deuteronomy, Moses restated God's law. Although this book contains much law, it is not just a law code, it is a passionate teaching and application of the law. Moses longed for the people to do what was right and good in the Lord's sight.

The recurring theme of this book is – remember. Moses entreats his people to remember God has led them, to remember that they were a chosen people, a people for whom God had a purpose. And most importantly to remember to love and obey God and not follow other gods.

A Christian too is called to remember. Remember Christ's sacrificial death on the cross that gives life eternal. To remember, how the Lord has led, provided and answered many a prayer. To remember that all that you have is a gift from the Lord. Remembering keeps us humble and provides much-needed perspective to life. Would you pause right now to prayerfully remember and thank God for his goodness to you and your loved ones in the past one week?

Lord help me be ever mindful of you in my life I pray.

Extended Reading — Deuteronomy 1-2

BIBLE
Alive and Active

*Do not add to what I command you and do not subtract from
it but keep the commands of the Lord your God that I give you.*

Deuteronomy 4:2

Faith and obedience are always the right response of God's people.

Deuteronomy is sometimes viewed as a series of sermons by Moses.
They are words that Moses spoke to all Israel in the wilderness,
as the very first verse of this book records.

Moses begins with the all-sufficiency of God's word. He reminds the
people, not to add or subtract from it. God's word is all they needed,
and they needed all of it. Moses knew the importance of God's word.
He pleads with the people to keep the decrees and commands, that he
gave them, so that it may go well with them and their children after
them and that they may live long in the land the Lord gave them.
(Deuteronomy 4:39-40). Moses knew that a heart response of obedience
was the undergirding need for the people to be safe.

The Bible is God's great gift to us. It provides us all that we need to
discern his will, to live in love and harmony together as a society, to
grow in grace and to share his word with the lost.

What is your response to the Bible? Some boring book of ancient
history? Or do you recognize as the true living word of God, alive and
active, sharper than any double-edged sword, which penetrates to even
dividing soul and spirit, judging the thoughts and attitudes of your
heart (Hebrews 4:12)?

Would you ask the Lord to reveal himself to you through his word and
give you a heart that is willing to listen and obey?

Lord help me love your word more each day, I pray.

Extended Reading — Deuteronomy 3-4

CHOICES
Choose to Love

Love the LORD your God with all your heart and with all your soul and with all your strength.   *Deuteronomy 6:5*

God loved human enough to allow them to have free will to choose.

Moses had summoned all of Israel and was giving them the commands that God had given for his people to follow. The first and foremost law was that God's people would love him. Their love for God was to be all-encompassing, passionate, consuming love, involving all their beings.

You and I are created by God and for God. We are created to live out his glorious purposes in and through us. If we live for him, we obey him. And the foremost command is that we love him, wholeheartedly, with all our being. We are to love God with our heart which involves our emotions and feelings. Our thoughts and choices are to be guided and driven by our love for God. The use of our God-given resources needs to be directed by our love for God.

Love is an act of the will, it is a choice. We don't love because we *feel* like loving the person. We love someone because we choose to love. A good way to gauge your true love is to start noticing the first thought on your mind when you wake up each morning, also the last thought before you fall asleep. The one thing that occupies your mind would be the thing or person you love the most. Is it God?

How much of your love for God did those around you see in you last week?

Lord give me increasing love for you and may it be evident to those around me, I pray.

Extended Reading — Deuteronomy 5-7

DISBELIEF
No I Don't Think So

*And when the Lord sent you out from Kadesh-Barnea, he said,
'Go up and take possession of the land I have given you.' But
you rebelled against the command of the Lord your God. You
did not trust him or obey him.*   *Deuteronomy 9:23*

Moses is stating some plain facts.

Standing on banks of Jordan, before crossing over into the Promised
Land, Moses pauses to give the Israelites perspective. Israel has been
a stiff-necked, rebellious people themselves. They have no righteousness
to call their own. Moses reminds them that the Lord is routing out the
peoples in Canaan for the Israelites not because of Israel's righteousness
but because of the wickedness of those nations.

The Israelites rebelled repeatedly. When Moses went up to the mountain
to receive the tablets from the Lord, the people were impatient and
doubted Moses' return. So, on Aaron's watch, they made for themselves
an idol to worship. Another time was when the Lord asked the people to
go up and take the possession Kadesh-Barnea. They did not go because
they did not trust him.

How often we are like the Israelites. We have a wonderful God who
waits to bless us. He has already done all that it takes to forgive our
sins, give us abundant life here on earth and then amazing life in his
presence forever. All we need to do is accept what he has already done
for us. Trust him and live by the promises in his word. And yet we don't,
why? Unwillingness to believe and obey him is rebellion.

Are you rebellious?

Lord forgive me and help my unbelief, I pray.

Extended Reading — Deuteronomy 8-10

LOVE GOD
Experienced, So Obey

*But it was your own eyes that saw all these great things
the LORD has done.*   *Deuteronomy 11:7*

Moses continues to exhort the people to remember.

The people of Israel have seen and experienced firsthand, God's
provision, God's protection and God's discipline too. Moses is
reminding them, it was not their children but *they* who had seen God
do the wonderful signs and wonders.

God had led them out of Egypt with a mighty hand. He had routed
the pursuing Egyptian armies. He had parted the Red Sea for the entire
Israelite nation to walk across in just one night. The Lord had provided
them with all their needs through the years in the desert. They had also
witnessed the discipline of the Lord. They had seen the earth split open
and swallowed up Korah and his men who had rebelled against God.

Moses is telling them because you have seen, you have experienced God's
goodness, therefore, love and obey God. You know that the Lord has
been faithful and true. So, the least you can do is to obey him. God
continues to be the same God. All of history reflects that he continues
to the one who provides, protects and disciplines his children.

Every one of us has experienced God's goodness and faithfulness in
our lives. From the air that we breathe, the fact that we are alive to
see another day, to the innumerable blessings of food, clothes, health,
talents, resources, opportunities, loved ones. For the gift of his word,
the gift of salvation and life eternal in him. And the least we can do is
to obey this gracious and faithful God.

How is your life reflecting your gratitude to God?

Lord help me increase in me the desire to love and obey you, I pray.

Extended Reading — Deuteronomy 11-13

CHOSEN
What Guts!

for you are a people holy to the Lord your God. Out of all the peoples on the face of the earth, the Lord has chosen you to be his treasured possession.   *Deuteronomy 14:2*

Have you ever thought about it?

God of all creation, the Lord who is sovereign over all the earth, has chosen you and me to be his prized possession? To be his ambassadors to a world gone bad. To be the salt and light of the world, to be the ones to point this watching world to Christ. Truly, what guts right? What's your response today?

Who but he would dare
To choose, use and prepare
The least, the weakest of them all
To be ones to live daily, to show all
His amazing salvation and eternal plan
For his precious and chosen clan
> *Now if that ain't awesome, my friend, what is?*
> *That the King and Lord of the entire universe*
> *Would stoop to mortals such as you and me*
> *To partner with him and create history?*
> *To be the light and salt in a world gone bad*
> *Because of the impact that sin has had*
So what say, dear friend are you up to this task?
Or would you rather in praises of men, bask?
Choose him dear one, who is ever your friend
Let him use you to reach and bless your world
As he remains to you true and faithful, eternally

Father for choosing me for this enormous task, thank You. Help me be your light to this watching world, I pray.

Extended Reading — Deuteronomy 14-16

BIBLE
Write to Know

When he takes the throne of his kingdom, he is to write for
himself on a scroll a copy of this law, taken from that of the
Levitical priests. [19] It is to be with him, and he is to read it
all the days of his life so that he may learn to revere the Lord
his God and follow carefully all the words of this law
and these decrees.   *Deuteronomy 17:18-19*

There was no king in Israel yet.

And yet, God inspired Moses to anticipate a Hebrew king. Through
Moses God provided clear guidelines and strong warnings for the
kings that would rule Israel. Moses warned about three excesses that
could draw the heart of the king away from God and lead to his fall.
Excess of weapons or horses, wives and wealth.

Each time a king came to the throne, he was to write for himself a
copy of the law. Writing the law would lead to him to dwell on every
word. It was not enough that he has the law, the king was to meditate
on the law every day of his life. The king needed to know God and his
Word personally so that he would revere and obey him and lead the
people to obey him.

In our digital world, though we have multiple options for the Bible on
our phones and other devices, a personal hard copy of the Bible remains
a treasured possession. Writing down or marking your Bible each day
as you read and learn, is a very edifying practice. A well-read and well-
marked Bible is a great testimony and reminder of God's faithfulness
as you journey through life.

Do you have your own copy of the Bible? If not, get one today.

Lord teach me to love and obey your Word, I pray.

Extended Reading — Deuteronomy 17-20

LOVE GOD
Worse than Death

If someone guilty of a capital offense is put to death and their body is exposed on a pole, [23] *you must not leave the body hanging on the pole overnight. Be sure to bury it that same day, because anyone who is hung on a pole is under God's curse.*

Deuteronomy 21:22-23

To be exposed on a pole was worse than death itself.

In ancient Israel to hang on the tree did not mean to be executed by strangulation. Rather it was to have the corpse mounted on a tree or other prominent place, with the purpose of exposing the executed one to disgrace and the elements. To be put to death for an offense was bad enough, but to then have your corpse left exposed to scavenging animals and birds was the ultimate humiliation.

But even in the most severe judgment, there was a tempering. To ensure that the humiliation of the person and family is not excessive, the body was to be brought down and buried the same day. This kind of punishment was thought to be so severe that it was reserved for those who were under God's curse.

And yet, Christ voluntarily, took on this kind of punishment when he died on the cross to save you and me from our sins. Jesus Christ died on a cross, outside the city. He died a death of utter shame and humiliation and his body was exposed on a cross for all to see. God loved us so much that he sent his only Son, Christ the sinless one so that we could be reconciled with God.

What kind of love is this! How is your life reflecting your gratitude for this amazing love?

Lord may I never take your love and sacrifice for granted, I pray.

Extended Reading — Deuteronomy 21-23

MARRIAGE
Priority of Marriage

If a man has recently married, he must not be sent to war or have any other duty laid on him. For one year he is to be free to stay at home and bring happiness to the wife he has married.

Deuteronomy 24:5

Newly married men were exempt from military or state service for a year.

The purpose of this law was not to encourage men to become lazy. Rather they were to prioritize and invest time and effort into their marriage. The man was to bring happiness to his wife with the purpose of building strong foundations for their marriage. God takes marriage seriously and so gave detailed laws about marriage.

Matthew 10:39 says we find our lives by losing our lives in Christ. So also, man finds most happiness when he makes his wife happy. The husband cannot make his wife happy without being happy himself. Neither can he make his wife unhappy without being miserable himself. A happy wife is the foundation of a happy home. A bitter and quarrelsome wife makes a miserable home (Proverbs 27:15).

A man who does not provide for his family has denied the faith and is worse than an unbeliever, says 1 Timothy 5:8. The husband is to prioritize his marriage above his career, job, and responsibilities, even above himself. Wives are not to take this out of context but they should be responsible to make their husbands happy. God expects the husband to lead the relationship and has commanded them to love their wives as Christ loved the church. Wives, on the other hand, are to respond in kind. A long-lasting happy marriage can only be the result of a deep God-centered foundation. In what new ways can you make your spouse happy?

Lord bless and direct our marriage I pray.

Extended Reading — Deuteronomy 24-27

ASTROLOGY
Pry Not

The secret things belong to the Lord our God, but the things revealed belong to us and to our children forever, that we may follow all the words of this law.   Deuteronomy 29:29

Moses has come to the end of his life.

H is greatest desire was that the people he had loved and served all these years would continue to faithfully obey God even when he was gone. And so, in this chapter Moses leads the people in renewing their covenant with God. Moses calls the people to obey God so that it may go well with them. He also cautions them of the consequences of abandoning the covenant.

The final verse in this chapter, however, is an unusually important verse. It simply and plainly states that the actual future of the people is known only to God. And that God's people are to live by faith not sight. They were to keep God's law and leave the future to him who alone holds the future.

As God's people, there are things about God and the future we do not know and need not know. All we need to know is found in the scripture. Astrology, zodiac signs, tarot cards or other similar methods of trying to figure out the future is not for a child of God. We are to focus on learning, understanding and applying God's word to our lives. We are not to go prying into figuring out the future. God alone holds the future. Our job is to trust him and walk day by day with him, in the light of his word.

Are there practices for finding out your future that you need to confess and abandon today?

Lord help me trust you and your word alone, I pray.

Extended Reading — Deuteronomy 28-29

RESTORATION
Hope Through Hopelessness

Even if you have been banished to the most distant land under the heavens, from there the LORD your God will gather you and bring you back.   *Deuteronomy 30:4*

There is hope in the most hopeless situation.

Honestly, the terrible warnings in the Bible can be scary. But thankfully, punishments are not the final word on the matter. Moses warned of terrible judgments that would befall the Israelites if they turned away from God and worshipped other gods. And yet, he quickly also reminds them that God would always remain faithful to his covenant. And so, even though they may sin terribly, if they return, if they genuinely repent, God would willingly and lovingly accept them back.

Sin they say is a slow leak. Very few of us are sinners because we have committed some "grievous" sins. Sin often begins with our compromise on small things. One small sin leads to another. And before you know it, doubt and unbelief creep in and God is slowly relegated to some small corner of life. Material possessions, selfish passions, and ungodly desires become the gods.

Soon enough you find yourself far away from God. And the evil one is waiting to tell you, you have gone too far *this* time, God will never forgive this sin. And you begin to believe it. But the truth is, however far away from God you may have gone, the Bible says if you repent and come back to God, he is waiting to welcome you back. What is stopping you from coming back to the Lord in repentance, right now?

Lord, I have been far away from you for a long time. But I come back to you now, please forgive me Lord and accept me I pray.

Extended Reading — Deuteronomy 30-31

LIFE PURPOSE
Divine Testimonial

Since then, no prophet has risen in Israel like Moses, whom the Lord knew face to face, ¹¹ who did all those signs and wonders the Lord sent him to do in Egypt—to Pharaoh and to all his officials and to his whole land. ¹² For no one has ever shown the mighty power or performed the awesome deeds that Moses did in the sight of all Israel.

Deuteronomy 34:10-12

Moses died.

And the scripture records this amazing testimonial the Lord gave about him. Moses is uniquely known as a man who knew God "face to face." The scriptures called him "the man of God." Although Moses was outstanding in many ways just as others were also in their generation, his focus on God set him apart. God was Moses' first and true love. God was Moses' constant companion, his life's goal.

Moses was a great man of prayer. Though one of the greatest leaders, Moses was also known as the humblest man that ever lived. He never drew attention to himself. Moses' faith was unshakeable. Immense intellectual capacity marked his life. Moses was also the greatest spokesman for God and the greatest worker of miracles by the power of God in the Old Testament.

Moses was a man of great courage. Nowhere did he show greater courage than in his final hours. Moses was prepared to die, as only those who deep-rooted trust in God can be. After he delivered his final exhortation to his people, Moses walked confidently up Mount Nebo to be taken home to God.

Lord, I want to know you more and more. Help me I pray.

Extended Reading — Deuteronomy 32-34; Psalm 91

BIBLE
To Obey, Meditate

Keep this Book of the Law always on your lips; meditate on it day and night, so that you may be careful to do everything written in it. Then you will be prosperous and successful.

Joshua 1:8

Joshua with the people of Israel is standing at the threshold of the Promised Land.

Joshua is one of the two people (Caleb, was the other) that survived the desert journey. All the others of his generation are dead because they rebelled against the Lord by not believing, that the Lord could take them into the Promised land. Joshua is also one of the few that has seen at close hand the challenges that Moses faced while leading these people. And now Moses is dead, and he is to take over this staggering task. The Lord speaks to Joshua, commissions him to the task at hand. "Do not be afraid, do not be discouraged" is the repeated message and encouragement that the Lord gives him in this first chapter. The Lord also tells him to meditate on his word, day in and day out. night and day. Does that mean you only read the Bible all day? No! But it does mean that you reflect on the word all day and be governed by the word in all you do and say. Obey and live by the word.

Every one of us has fears. We are worried about situations in our life, fearful about what the future holds. And the Lord is saying to you, be strong and courageous for he is with you, he will never leave you nor forsake you. Meditate on his word, draw strength from him.

Lord help me know and live by your word, all day, every day, I pray.

Extended Reading — Joshua 1-4

SIN
Your Sin Effects More than You

The Lord said to Joshua, "Stand up! What are you doing down
on your face? [11] *Israel has sinned...*   *Joshua 7:10-11a* [10]

Joshua is heartbroken and totally confused.

Israel has just been routed by a relatively small army of Ai. Three thousand men went to fight and were routed. The army of Ai even killed thirty-six of the men of Israel. Joshua turns to the Lord questioning the Lord. The Lord replies, very simply and clearly that Israel has sinned.

The Lord had clearly commanded that the Israelites were to destroy everything and not take anything for themselves from Jericho. And yet, Achan had coveted and stolen some of the things. Achan had done wrong and deserved to be punished. But why then does the Lord say to Joshua, Israel has sinned? Why did the Lord punish *Israel* for Achan's sin?

The Bible says in Exodus 34:7 that the Lord maintains love to thousands, forgiving wickedness, rebellion, and sin. Yet he does not leave the guilty unpunished, he punishes the children and their children for the sin of parents to the third and fourth generation. Yes, the message is clear. Your sin impacts not just you but those around too. It impacts your family, your loved ones, even your community, and nation.

Our God is a loving and gracious God, but he is also a holy and just God. And we his children are called to live holy lives in complete obedience to him. 2 Chronicles 16:9 says for the eyes of the Lord range throughout the earth to strengthen those whose hearts are fully committed to him.

Is your disobedience punishing your loved ones?

Help me Lord to obey you in all I do, I pray.

Extended Reading — Joshua 5-8

BIBLE
Just Another Proof

> On the day the Lord gave the Amorites over to Israel, Joshua
> said to the Lord in the presence of Israel: "Sun, stand still over
> Gibeon, and you, moon, over the Valley of Aijalon." [13] So the
> sun stood still, and the moon stopped, till the nation avenged
> itself on its enemies.   Joshua 10:12-13

Gibeon is in trouble.

Adoni-Zedek, king of Jerusalem leads a band of five Amorite kings to
attack Gibeon. Gibeon rushes to Joshua for help and he comes to
their aid. He leads the Israelite army against the Amorites. They march
all night and arrive at Gilgal and take the Amorite armies by surprise.
The Lord throws the Amorites into confusion and hurls hailstone at
them. Thus the Amorites fled.

On that day, Joshua commanded the sun to stand still and it did. The
sun stood still till the nation avenged itself over its enemies. The Bible
says, that there has never been a day like it before or since, a day when
the Lord listened to a human being.

Have you had times when you've had doubts if all that is mentioned
in the Bible did happen? This extraordinary event recorded in the
Bible is just one of the many that have been proven to be historically
and scientifically true. Researchers claim that this epic Biblical story is
the earliest account of annular eclipse that occurred more than three
thousand two hundred years ago.

The Bible is the infallible word of God (2 Peter 1:20-21) and is God-
breathed (2 Timothy 3:15-17). The Bible is alive and active and is
sharper than any double-edged sword (Hebrew 4:12) The Bible is
without error (Numbers 23:19). Whom will you prayerfully share this
awesome truth with today?

Lord increase my faith and help me obey your word I pray.

Extended Reading — Joshua 9-11

PERSEVERANCE
A Long Wait

Now give me this hill country that the Lord promised me that
day.   *Joshua 14:12*

Caleb had a long wait.

Caleb and Joshua were among the twelve that Moses sent to explore the land of Canaan. Only the two of them came back with positive reports, believing that the land could be conquered by God's grace. The ten others gave a conflicting report of giants and fear. The people chose to believe the ten and not Caleb and Joshua.

When an entire nation headed in one direction, Caleb was one of the four rowing the other way. The people's lack of faith made the Lord angry. And so, the Lord said, not one of that generation would live to see the Promised Land, except for Joshua and Caleb.

The Lord promised to bring Caleb to the Promised Land because in him was a different spirit and he followed God wholeheartedly (Numbers 14:24). Caleb had not forgotten the promise of God. He waited patiently, in faith, trusting God to keep his word. And now after forty-five long years, he comes to Joshua to claim the land that the Lord had promised him. And Joshua gives him the land of Hebron.

Caleb waited long but in faith and hope. He was not bitter, nor did he give up. He remembered the promise of God and he claimed it. God's children do have periods of waiting. We are called not just to wait, but to wait with a good attitude, with faith and hope.

How can you be more like Caleb as you wait for God to fulfill the promise that he has given you?

Lord give me hope and patience as I wait for you, I pray.

Extended Reading — Joshua 12-15

FAITH
You Need to Move

*So Joshua said to the Israelites: "How long will you wait before
you begin to take possession of the land that the Lord, the God
of your ancestors, has given you?*   *Joshua 18:3*

The Israelites were taking it easy.

The land of Canaan had been brought under the control of the
Israelites. Allotments had been made to five out of the twelve
tribes. The remaining seven tribes were yet to take possession of their
inheritance. And they did not seem to be in any hurry. Joshua asks
them, how long are you going to sit around on your hands, putting
off taking possession of the land that GOD, the God of your ancestors,
has given you? (MSG). The land had been fought for and won. Now
all that was remaining was to go and take possession of it. And yet the
people are slack.

Joshua stirs them to action. He tells them to appoint three men from
each tribe to make a survey of the land and write a description. Then
he would cast lots before the Lord and assign the lands to the remaining
lands. Joshua is ready to do his part if the people will do their part.

As Christians, you are given the title deed to the promises in the Bible
that comforts, strengthens and directs our life on earth. But you need
to believe in God and his promises. You need to move out of your own
prison of unbelief, fear, doubt, worry etc. God is willing to do his part
if you will do your part.

What will you do to take possession of one promise from God's word
this week?

*Lord forgive my slackness. Help me believe and live by your promises,
I pray.*

Extended Reading — Joshua 16-18

KNOW GOD
To Trust, Remember

*Not one of all the LORD's good promises to Israel failed; everyone
was fulfilled.*   *Joshua 21:45 (NIV)*

God remains faithful and true.

When God called Abraham out of Ur, he was seventy-five years
old and had no children. And yet God promised that he would
make him a mighty nation with offspring as many as the stars in the
sky and the sand on the seashore. And throughAbraham and Sarah, God
blessed Isaac and the twelve tribes of Israel.The Lord called the Israelites
out of their bondage in Egypt. He promised to give them a land for
themselves, a land flowing with milk and honey. And he did. The book
of Joshua records in detail how the Lord enabled the Israelites,under
Joshua's leadership to acquire the land of Canaan,the many battles that
were fought and won,how the land then was distributed and allotted
to the twelve tribes.

Through the Bible, we see how time after time God has proven himself
to be faithful and true. And yet one command that the Lord gave his
people was, "remember" (Deuteronomy 8:2). Remembering all that God
had done for them helped them continue to trust for their future too.
Christians too are called to remember. Remember the many ways God
has provided for and delivered us in the past. Remembering equips us
to continue to ask and expect answers from God. When we forget,
we give ourselves reasons to be fearful or even arrogant. When we
remember and come to him in prayer, we are confident that he always
hears us (Philippians 4:19) and makes everything work together for
good (Romans 8:28). How will you regularly remind yourself of God's
faithfulness in your life?

Lord may I never forget your faithfulness in my life, I pray.

Extended Reading — Joshua 19-21

WORSHIP
Other Gods?

But do not rebel against the Lord or against us by building an altar for yourselves, other than the altar of the Lord our God.
Joshua 22:19

The lands had been acquired, the battles won.

The Reubenites, Gadites and the half tribe of Manasseh, who had crossed over the Jordon to help their fellow Israelites to settle into their inheritance, had now been sent home with Joshua's blessing. Joshua acknowledged their faithfulness in doing all that the Lord had commanded them to do.

These men, having got back to their own land, the first thing they did was to build a huge imposing altar, at Gelioth, along the Jordon. This perturbs and infuriates the ten tribes of Israel, who rush out up in arms to wage a war against these two and a half tribes, assuming the altar to be a sign of their rebellion against God. But all is at peace when the men of Reuben etc. can honestly clarify their intention and prove their innocence, that their hearts were loyal to the Lord God alone.

So, what does true worship look like? Joshua in verse 5 of this chapter, gives a beautiful picture of what it means to worship God. He says they were to love, obey, and serve God wholeheartedly. These three go together and are dependent on one another. You will only obey and serve the one you love.

Make a quick look at how you spent your time and resources in the past few days. Whom or what are you serving and using your talents and resources for? The Bible clearly states you cannot serve both God and money. You will hate one and love the other. (Matt 6:24) Is God truly the recipient of your love and worship?

Lord help me to love, obey and serve only you, I pray, Amen.

Extended Reading — Joshua 22-24

PRAYER
Give me a Blessing

She replied, "Do me a special favor. Since you have given me land in the Negev, give me also springs of water." So, Caleb gave her the upper and lower springs.   Judges 1:15

Aksah seeks a favor.

Joshua is dead. The Israelites still have some battles to fight against the Canaanites. They seek the Lord and he gives them victory. As part of the land acquisition, Caleb promises to give his daughter Aksah in marriage to the man who captures Kiriath Sepher. Othniel his nephew does and marries Aksah. Aksah comes to Caleb and asks for a blessing (ESV).

Aksah's request is a great example in prayer. When she came to meet her father Caleb, he asks her what she wants. Her answer is very simple and clear. She asks Caleb to give her the upper and the lower springs.

Aksah had thought through her request. She was humble and eager in her request. She did not hesitate because she knew she was talking to her father. Aksah was grateful for what she had received and used the past blessing as a reason to ask for more. Interestingly, Caleb does not criticize her request in any way but gave her what she asked for.

We have a Heavenly Father who knows and understands us way more than any human father. We are called to come to him with our specific prayers. God loves to hear us ask him for what we want. He does not criticize or mock our prayers. We can approach him humbly and yet with grateful and humble hearts.

Like Caleb asked Aksah, God is asking you today, what can I do for you?

Lord help me to confidently come to you with my needs, I pray.

Extended Reading — Judges 1-2

OBEDIENCE
No Ifs

Barak said to her, "If you go with me, I will go; but if you don't go with me, I won't go."   *Judges 4:8*

Conditional obedience is disobedience.

After the death of Ehud, the prophet, the Bible says, Israelites again did evil in the eyes of the Lord. And so, the Lord sold them into the hands of the Jabin, the king of Canaan. His commander Sisera cruelly oppressed the Israelites for twenty years. The people cried to the Lord. The Lord raised up Deborah.

Deborah was the unique combination of a judge and prophetess. The only other one who was both a judge and prophet was Samuel. Deborah was also a good singer and songwriter. Deborah called on Barak and said to him, that the Lord God of Israel was commanding him to take his army and go up to Mount Tabor. And that she would bring Sisera and his armies there for battle. Barak responds by saying he will go only *if* Deborah would go with him. His conditional obedience causes him to lose the blessing of the victory. Deborah prophesies that the victory would go to a woman. God does deliver his people from Sisera, but not through Barak. Sisera ends up in the tent of Jael the wife of Heber the Kenite. She drives a tent peg through Sisera's forehead when he was asleep.

When you put conditions on your obedience God doesn't lose, you do. What conditions are you laying before you obey what the Lord has asked you to do?

Lord help me obey you fully and unconditionally, I pray.

Extended Reading — Judges 3-5

FAITH
Unreasonable Requirements?

The LORD said to Gideon, "You have too many men. I cannot deliver Midian into their hands or Israel would boast against me, 'My own strength has saved me.   Judges 7:2

The Midianites had been oppressing Israel.

They ravaged their fields leaving Israel nothing to live on, forcing the people to live in mountain clefts and caves. And in their suffering, Israel cried out to the Lord (Judges 6:6). God answered. He raised Gideon to deliver Israel from the Midianites.

Gideon had questions. (6:13). Questions about God and his own weakness. The Lord graciously answers each of these questions, including Gideon's fleeces. Finally, Gideon is convinced.

The Midianite army was one lakh thirty-five thousand strong, and Gideon had a mere thirty-two thousand men. The odds were heavily against Gideon. But the Lord tells Gideon there are way too many people in his army for God to work? And so, he asks Gideon to do something almost ridiculous to human understanding. God asks Gideon to send the men back. And the Bible says, in two rounds, the Lord brings Israel's thirty-two thousand strong army down to a mere three hundred men! (7:3-8).

And yet, with those three hundred men Israel won a convincing victory against Midian with trumpets and torches. They totally routed them (7:15-25). What a victory! Though God asked Gideon to do some real strange even ridiculous things, Gideon trusted and obeyed God.

We often choose our own defeat when we rationalize what God asks us to do. The Lord sometimes takes us through seemingly insignificant tests that determine how he will use us in life. Does what God is asking you to do today seem ridiculous and even impossible to you?

Even when it doesn't always make sense, help me obey you, Lord, I pray.

Extended Reading — Judges 6-7

RELATIONSHIPS
Choose a Gentle Answer

Now the Ephraimites asked Gideon, "Why have you treated us like this? Why didn't you call us when you went to fight Midian?" And they challenged him vigorously.   Judges 8:1

The Ephraimites were offended.

When Gideon called out to them, the Ephraimites joined in the fight against Midian. Yet, they were upset that Gideon did not call them *before* the battle started. They seemed more concerned with recognition rather than the overall good of Israel. Instead of being jealous about the recognition that others received, the Ephraimites should have been happy that God's people were rescued and that had some part in the victory. Jealousy often hinders the work of God.

Now Gideon could have taken offense too. But Gideon chose to take the high road. He deals graciously with them. He recounts their accomplishments and took very little credit for his own valiant effort. That response caused the resentment of the Ephraimites to subside. (v2-3)

We have friends like this too. Gideon's response is a great example to follow. Take a humble view of yourself and focus on the other. Give a gentle answer.

The Bible says in Proverbs 15:1, a gentle answer turns away wrath, but a harsh word stirs up anger. When someone chides or quarrels with you, it is easy to answer back in anger. It takes greater and God-given strength and grace to give a soft answer.

Is there someone who has been vehemently quarreling with you, who needs a gentle answer from you?

Lord give me your grace to give a gentle answer when someone offends me, I pray.

Extended Reading — Judges 8-9

CALLING
God Is Not Limited

Jephtath the Gileadite was a mighty warrior. His father was
Gilead; his mother was a prostitute.   Judges 11:1

Jephthah had a difficult past.

This brave and notable man was born to Gilead and a prostitute.
Now Gilead had other sons through his wife. And they did not take
kindly to this son of a prostitute. They drove him away. But soon
trouble arose from the Ammonites. And these very people come
to Jephthah for help. Jephthah was willing to help, but only if he
would remain leader after the crisis too. He didn't want to be rejected
again. They promise to make Jephthah their leader.

Jephthah tries to avoid war by negotiating, but the King of Ammon
refuses. War becomes inevitable. Jephthah makes a vow to the Lord
promising to sacrifice whatever came of out his house when he
returns in victory (v31). Jephthah must have expected an animal to
come out of his house.

Jephthah, enabled by the Lord, defeats the Ammonites. God used
Jephthah despite being born of a prostitute. But sadly, when he
returns home, his only daughter is the one who comes out of his
house to greet him. Jephthah bound by his vow ends up sacrificing
his only child.

You and I cannot change where we come from or our backgrounds.
But thankfully God is not limited by any of it. God continues to
use people despite their past. However, we are to be careful with
the promises we make to the Lord. Jephthah lost his only child
over such action.

In the task that God has called you for, are you feeling limited by
your background?

Thank You, Lord, for using me despite my limitations.

Extended Reading — Judges 10-12

HOLINESS
Full Potential

The woman gave birth to a boy and named him Samson. He grew, and the LORD blessed him.   Judges 13:24

Samson was set apart.

The cycle of sin, repentance, deliverance, and sin again continued in the history of Israel. And into such times was born the next judge of Israel, Samson. Born a Nazirite, Samson was set apart. God had given him the great supernatural strength to do his work in Israel. But Samson soon fell. He became great in his own eyes. He was vengeful. He began to pursue women. And that was not God's plan for his life.

During his wedding ceremony to a Philistine woman, Samson was humiliated. He took revenge by killing thousand Philistine men. Then Samson fell in love with Delilah, another Philistine woman. But she, bribed by the Philistines, coaxes Samson to reveal that the secret of his strength.Delilah cuts his hair in his sleep and Samson loses his strength. The Philistines overpower him and gouge out his eyes.

A repentant Samson cries to the Lord. The Lord strengthens him one last time. Samson pushes against the pillars and brings down the temple where he was held captive. Samson dies with thousands of people that were in that temple that day.

Samson, though mentioned in the Bible's hall of faith (Hebrews 11:32), also serves as a great warning. A man of great physical strength, he also displayed great moral failure. Samson did not live out his full potential of what he could have been if he had lived as the set apart one, he was, in obedience to God. Are you living out your life, set apart unto the Lord and to your full potential?

Lord help me live for you, to the fullest of my potential I pray.

Extended Reading — Judges 13-15

IDOL WORSHIP
As You Please

Now this man Micah had a shrine, and he made an ephod and some household gods and installed one of his sons as his priest. ⁶ In those days Israel had no king; everyone did as they saw fit.

Judges 17:5-6

Everyone in Israel did as they saw fit.

There was great spiritual confusion and sin in Israel. And the story of Micah (not prophet Micah) recorded in chapters 17 and 18 of Judges, is one such example. Micah stole 1,100 shekels of silver from his mother and then returned it to her. His mother blessed her son for returning the money, though he had originally taken it. Now ten shekels was a year's adequate wage (17:10). Therefore, 1,100 shekels was a great fortune.

Micah's mother directs that a part of the money be used to make an image for worship. And so, Micah makes a shrine and makes an ephod. He even appoints his own personal priest for the worship. He thought he was pleasing God by all this (17:13).

But Micah did wrong. Whether this image was of a false god, like Baal or was meant to represent Yahweh, God strictly forbids idols. Idol worship stands against the very first of the Ten Commandments (Exodus 20:3). Micah also chose to worship God the way he thought right rather than how God wants to be worshipped.

Idols need not only be gravened images. Idols can be religious activities or even just good deeds. God calls us to worship him the way he commands. And the Bible says, God is Spirit and those who worship him must worship him in truth and in spirit (John 4:24). What in your life is keeping you from worshipping God in truth and in spirit?

Lord teach me to worship you the way you command, I pray.

Extended Reading — Judges 16-18

SIN

Apart from the Grace of God

But she was unfaithful to him. She left him and went back to her parents' home in Bethlehem, Judah. After she had been there four months, ³ her husband went to her to persuade her to return.   *Judges 19:2-3*

Evil follows where God's authority and leadership are not acknowledged.

There was no king in Israel. That sets the stage for this terrible story in the following chapters. No king meant more than the absence of a political monarch. It meant that they refused to recognize God's leadership over them.

This story of the Levite and his concubine is one of the most grotesque and distasteful events. It reveals the depths of depravity to which humans can sink apart from the grace of God.

This is the account of a Levite and his concubine who had run away. There are two distinct problems with this situation. The Levite of the priestly tribe of Levi was not to have a concubine. And then there is the problem of the woman being sexually involved with someone else. The Levite travels to bring his concubine back.

The Levite is an example of how an offended spouse should behave in the event of adultery. The woman had broken the bond between them. But he worked hard to bring the relationship back together. Jesus says that divorce is never commanded even when there is adultery (Matthew 19:8). If a partner in marriage is sinned against by adultery, they should still work to make the marriage survive and succeed, to the best of their ability. And yet, apart from the grace of God, it is not an easy task.

How would you help someone you know rely on the grace of God to bring healing and forgiveness?

Lord help me be your agent of healing and restoration, I pray.

Extended Reading — Judges 19-21

CHOICES
A Choice to Make

But Ruth replied, "Don't urge me to leave you or to turn back from you. Where you go, I will go, and where you stay, I will stay. Your people will be my people and your God my God.

Ruth 1:16

Ruth had a choice to make.

When the famine worsened , Elimelech moved to Moab, with his wife Naomi and sons Mahlon and Kilion. The sons married Moabite women Ruth and Orpah. But over time, Elimelech and his two sons died, leaving Naomi, Ruth, and Orpah as widows.

Naomi heard that the famine was over in Bethlehem and decided to return. However, she encouraged her daughters-in-law to return to their homes in Moab. After much coaxing, Orpah agreed. But Ruth did not.

Ruth was a Moabite. She grew up worshipping pagan gods. She did not know the God of her Israelite husband Mahalon. Over the years of her marriage, however, Ruth must have heard about the spectacular hand of Yahweh in delivering the Israelites from Egypt. Also, how the God of the Israelites had parted the waters of the Red Sea to deliver them from the hands of Pharaoh and his pursuing army. How he had led, kept and provided for his people through the forty years in the desert and much more.

And for Ruth, these did not remain just stories. Hearing about this amazing God of the Israelites led her to believe in him. When the time to make a life-changing choice came, she was clear and ready. She chose to follow this God. This same God is alive today and continues to faithfully deliver and provide for his people. The question is, have you chosen to follow this God?

Lord help me chose you today and every day of my life, I pray.

Extended Reading — Ruth 1-4

CALLING
A Listening Heart

So Eli told Samuel, "Go and lie down, and if he calls you, say, 'Speak, Lord, for your servant is listening.'" So, Samuel went and lay down in his place.   *1 Samuel 3:9*

Hannah's tearful prayer was answered.

Samuel was born, and she dedicated him to the Lord for all his life. And when he was weaned, she left Samuel in the temple. Samuel ministered to the Lord under Eli, the priest.

One night, God called Samuel. Samuel did not recognize it as God's voice because the Bible says, Samuel did not yet know the Lord (v7). So, he ran to Eli, thinking it was Eli who called him. After a couple of times, Eli figured out that it must be the Lord calling and gave Samuel some wise counsel.

Eli told Samuel, to go back and lie down. Be quiet and available to hear when he would call again. He said if he calls again say, 'Speak Lord for your servant is listening.' Samuel was to wait for the Lord to call again. If God did call, Samuel was to respond, humbly.

Samuel was a good and obedient boy living in the temple and serving God faithfully. Yet he still didn't know the Lord. So also, being born in good Christian homes and 'doing good' is not enough. Every person needs to know God personally.

God almost always confirms his calling more than once. It is generally wise not to act on just 'one inner voice of God'. Our response to God's word is to humble ourselves and take time to personally listen. We may also hear God's word spoken through many teachers, preachers, and pastors. The important thing is to keep our heart tuned to listen as God speaks.

Are we listening?

Lord give me a humble and listening heart I pray.

Extended Reading — 1 Samuel 1-3

COMMITMENT
An Undivided Heart

So Samuel said to all the Israelites, "If you are returning to the Lord with all your hearts, then rid yourselves of the foreign gods and the Ashtoreths and commit yourselves to the Lord and serve him only, and he will deliver you out of the hand of the Philistines."   1 Samuel 7:3

Samuel strikes when the iron is hot.

Samuel is in the prime of his life. He is active in the reformation of the Israelites from idolatry. He is instrumental in praying for them against the invading Philistines over whom God gives them victory.

The ark of the Lord had been recovered from the Philistines and kept in the house of Abinadab for the next twenty years. The threat of the Philistines attacking Israel looms large. The people lament and show the inclination to turn to the Lord. Samuel is quick to act on this change of heart among the people.

Samuel calls them to do two things. First, the Israelites were to rid themselves of the idols and foreign gods in their midst. Two, they must commit to wholly serving the Lord and him only.

We are called to remove idols from our lives. An idol is anything or anyone who takes precedence in our life, above God. We are to worship God and him only. Some of the idols in our lives could be work, money, talent, power, career, friends or even people and relationships.

To serve God with a whole heart begins with taking time to know him. Make it a priority to spend time with him and his word. What idols are dividing your heart today?

Lord help remove things that take more importance in my life over you, I pray.

Extended Reading — 1 Samuel 4-8

REBELLION
Freedom in Yielding

But if you do not obey the Lord, and if you rebel against his commands, his hand will be against you, as it was against your ancestors.   *1 Samuel 12:15*

Israel gets the king they demanded.

Israel was the only nation which did not have a king over them. They were a theocracy, where God was their Ruler and King. But the people wanted to be like the nations around them.God instructs Samuel and he anoints Saul as king over Israel.

Samuel gathered the people of Israel and gave   his farewell speech. He reminded them how he had faithfully served the Lord and led the Israelites from his youth. He called them to testify against him if in all these years he had been unfaithful in any way. The people were quick to affirm that Samuel had served faithfully and not been dishonest.

Samuel recounted how the Lord had faithfully appointed leaders who had led the Israelites over the years. And how now finally gave them a king over them because of their insistence.

God always answered their prayers and provided for them. Asking for a king was wrong and evil in the sight of the Lord. Samuel proved it by praying and calling down thunder and rain on the harvest. The people realize they have sinned.

As God's chosen people we are called to trust and obey God, our King. To accept and yield to the Lord and his authority requires a trusting and submissive heart. Insisting on your own way is rebellion.

In what area of your life are you insisting on your own way today?

Forgive my rebellion, Lord and help me submit to you, I pray.

Extended Reading — 1 Samuel 9-12

OBEDIENCE
Obedience Sometimes Means Waiting

You have done a foolish thing," Samuel said. "You have not kept the command the Lord your God gave you; if you had, he would have established your kingdom over Israel for all time.

1 Samuel 13:13

Saul is anointed king at Gilgal.

Samuel obeyed God's command and anointed Saul. Samuel told Saul to wait for him for seven days at Gilgal. Samuel would come and offer the sacrifice and then the people of Israel would be spiritually ready for battle.

In the meantime, Saul's son, Jonathan initiated a war against the Philistines. The Israelites, however, were scared to attack the Philistines. They scatter themselves and hid in the caves.

Saul waited six days and most of the seventh day. But by the evening of the seventh day. The pressure was building. Saul knew that the Philistines were gathering a big army. And time was running out. And the people had begun to scatter. So, Saul in his anxiety took matters into his own hands. He decided to go ahead and offer the sacrifice himself. Just as he finished Samuel arrived. Samuel rebuked Saul.

God had not permitted kings to be priests and priests to be kings. When King Uzziah tried to do the work of the priest, God struck him with leprosy (2 Chronicles 26). Fear or anxiety caused Saul to disobey. He made excuses for failing to trust God. Saul was ruled by his feelings rather than his faith in God. And that turned out to be a great mistake. Saul lost his kingdom. Anxiety and worry often get the better of us and cause us to act in ways that we end up regretting. Obedience sometimes means waiting.

Lord give me the grace to wait for your perfect time, I pray.

Extended Reading — 1 Samuel 13-14

OBEDIENCE
Beautiful You

But the Lord said to Samuel, "Do not consider his appearance or his height, for I have rejected him. The Lord does not look at the things that people look at. People look at the outward appearance, but the Lord looks at the heart."   *1 Samuel 16:7*

Samuel is at the house of Jesse.

The Lord rejected Saul as king over Israel (1 Sam 15:23). God told Samuel the next king would be from the house of Jesse. Samuel went to Jesse and asked him to bring his sons. Seven tall and strapping young men passed before Samuel. And each time Samuel thought this might be the one, it turned out that none of them were the chosen one.

When Samuel asked, Jesse said he had his youngest son David, who was out in the fields with the sheep. Samuel insisted on having David. It turned out that he was the one that the Lord had chosen. And the Bible says Samuel anointed David as the next king of Israel in the presence of his brothers and the Spirit of the Lord came powerfully upon David (v13).

People are impressed by our outward appearance. But that is not what impresses God. The Lord very clearly states that he looks at the heart. And the Lord alone knows the heart of each one.

A heart that is pleasing to the Lord is obedient to him (1 Samuel 15:22). To obey him we need to know what he says. The Bible says, meditate on the word continually (Joshua 1:8). The Lord found David's heart good and right before him.

How would the Lord find your heart?

May You ever find my heart good and right in your sight, I pray.

Extended Reading — 1 Samuel 15-17

PERSECUTION
Fear in Action

*Saul was afraid of David because the Lord was with David but
had departed from Saul.*   *1 Samuel 18:12*

David was the new blue-eyed boy, and everyone loved him.

David's trust in God enabled him to defeat Goliath, the huge,
intimidating foe of Israel, in an epic combat. All of Israel was
pleased with David. They sang his praises. Saul retained him in his army.
And whatever mission Saul sent him on, David was so successful that
Saul gave him a high rank in the army.

But sadly, that didn't last very long. Soon enough, Saul, who was so
relieved and grateful for the amazing victory, was bitten by the green-
eyed monster. Jealousy raised its ugly head in Saul's heart and he began
to compare and resent the praise David received.

Over time Saul also realized that the Lord was with David and that the
Lord was no more with him. This caused Saul to fear David. And that
fear kept David in the wilderness and caves until Saul died. And though
David had the opportunity to kill Saul more than once, the Bible says
in 1 Samuel 24 and 26, that David chose the high road. He chose to
honor the anointed of the Lord and let the Lord deal with him.

When you do right before the Lord, expect to get noticed,one of the
responses you get from people could be fear. And fear often causes people
to be irrational and extreme in their thoughts and actions.

There could be people in your life whose behavior baffles you. Would
you choose to take the high road, as David did, while you stay faithful
in honoring the Lord and his word?

**Lord help me honor you and trust you to deal with those who trouble
me, I pray.**

Extended Reading — 1 Samuel 18-20; Psalm 11, 59

SUBMISSION
Not in my Hands, but Yours

The men said, "This is the day the Lord spoke of when he said to you, 'I will give your enemy into your hands for you to deal with as you wish.'" Then David crept up unnoticed and cut off a corner of Saul's robe.   1 Samuel 24:4

What wrong have I done?

That could very well be the question that tormented David, as he for years, ran for his life, from King Saul. Yes, this very David who had saved him and the entire Israelite nation, from the giant Philistine tormentor, Goliath. This very David who was his son Jonathan's best friend. This very David who had bravely brought the bride price of two hundred Philistine foreskins, to marry his daughter, Michal. And yes, this very David who had never once done him any wrong. And yet Saul was bent on killing David.

As they hid in a cave, from Saul, Saul came to the very same cave, to relieve himself. And the men with David saw this as a 'God-sent' opportunity to put an end to the years of torment. But David refused. His men could not understand why David would give up such a golden opportunity.

But David knew that it was not his place to harm Saul, whatever the reason. Saul was the king anointed by the Lord, placed in authority over him. And so, he dared not raise his hand against him. Romans 13:3 says if we rebel against authority we rebel against God. Hebrews 13:17 calls us to submit to our leaders.

Would you like David, choose to respect those in authority over you and trust God to do the rest?

Lord help us trust you enough to submit to those you have placed over me, even when they are difficult, I pray.

Extended Reading — 1 Samuel 21-24

WAITING ON GOD
Hold On

Wait for the Lord; be strong and take heart and wait for
the Lord.   *Psalm 27:14*

When the heart is sad and heavy
With many a care and worry
When you have for days on end
Prayed, as on your knees you bent
For that thing which causes so much pain
That you bring it to the Lord, over again
You've cried, and you have pleaded
As long on your knees, you've waited

It feels like ages, yet you see nothing
Problems only seem to be worsening
Though you've asked daily, time set apart
For this need so close to your heart
Yet no answer seems to be coming
Rather the problem is only increasing
Now exhausted you are truly wondering
If it will ever end, this pain excruciating

Though dear one, you have no idea why
The reason for this seeming delay
Keep your eyes fixed on him, your Lord
And be firm in believing in his word
He does for his children, who him seek

Ensures no foe, nor evil one can ever keep
That which he has purposed in his perfect will
For them, that remain humble, trusting him still

He promises to restore with every passing day
The years that the locusts have eaten away
And the times that have been lost in strife
He is sure to heal and restore with added life
To bring to pass his perfect will, he will not delay
As on him, his word, his children rest each day
So, do not give up, instead sing him a hymn
He is an on-time God, so simply hold on to him.

Extended Reading — Psalm 7, 27, 31, 34, 52

WAITING ON GOD
Choice to Rest

When I am afraid, I put my trust in you.   *Psalm 56:3*

Why Lord why is life so confusing
What Lord what is it that you are teaching
How Lord how should I respond
To life and all that goes on around

When what each day takes me through
Makes my mind cook and stew
How Lord how should I respond
To life and all that goes on around

Teach me Lord to, on you to wait
As you keep me on the path narrow and straight
To even when confused and distressed
Know, that it is only a test

A test to mature and to grow me
Into that which you are shaping me
To be more and more like you each day
Until You, I see face to face one day

So, Lord when life is confusing
And I know not how to respond
Help me choose to in you be resting
And you follow with all my heart, trusting

Extended Reading — Psalm 56, 120, 140-142

WISDOM
A Quick Wise Response

His name was Nabal and his wife's name was Abigail. She was an intelligent and beautiful woman, but her husband was surly and mean in his dealings—he was a Calebite. 1 Samuel 25:3

Abigail's wise response saves the day.

As Nabal's wife, Abigail, had a choice to make that day and quick. The servant had just come and given a very disturbing report about her husband, Nabal's response to David.

Sheep shearing was a time of festivity and celebration. And Nabal was in great spirits. When David heard that Nabal was shearing his sheep, he sent his men to him, asking for compensation for the protection that he and his men had given his shepherds. David politely reminded Nabal of the traditions of generosity that surrounded sheep shearing and counted on Nabal's generosity. But Nabal gave a foolish and arrogant reply. He refused to give David anything and went to the extent of asking who David was. David was furious and set out to kill Nabal and his household.

Abigail acted quickly. She loaded her donkeys with food for the men and rushed to meet David. She met him on the way, fell at David's feet and pleaded for favor. She accepted that Nabal was foolish in his response and asked for forgiveness. She was quick to remind David that he would be sinning greatly by choosing to avenge himself. David impressed by her good judgment, stopped.

When Abigail returned to Nabal the next day she reported to him all that happened, and his heart failed. He died ten days later. David later proposed Abigail and took her as his wife. What difficult situation needs your wise humble response today?

Lord give me a wise and a humble heart I pray.

Extended Reading — 1 Samuel 25-27

PRAYER
A Confident Plea

Contend, Lord, with those who contend with me; fight against
those who fight against me.   *Psalm 35:1*

David is in trouble.

D avid had enemies that pursued him, enemies that were too strong
for him (35:10). People who falsely accused him and repaid him
evil for good (35:11-12). What was David's response? David called
on the Lord and asked the Lord to contend with his enemies on his
behalf. That is his first and confident response.

David's confidence came from a vibrant relationship that he had with
God. From knowing his God who was more than able to save him.
David came to him in humility acknowledging his own helplessness
and his need for the Lord.

Psalm 63 gives a vivid picture of David's relationship with God. He began
the psalm saying, you, God are *my* God. David had a very personal
relationship with the Lord. His relationship with the Lord involved his
whole being. He said he had seen the Lord in the sanctuary (v3) and
his eyes have beheld the glory of the Lord. Then he said he will praise
the Lord as long as he lives (v4) and that involved his mouth and lips.
Further, he says that he remembers the Lord on his bed through the
watches of the night.

The Lord was part of David's entire day and night and all through his
life. And it is based on this relationship that David confidently turned
to the Lord when in trouble.

Every one of us has times of trouble. If we like David are to turn to God
for help, we need to have an on-going vibrant relationship with him.

Lord I want to know you so well that I can turn to you for my every
need, I pray.

Extended Reading — Psalm 17, 35, 54, 63

GRIEF
Bitter or Strengthened?

But David found strength in the LORD his God. 1 Samuel 30:6

David was distressed.

A chish the Philistine King was preparing to fight Israel. David who had sought shelter with Achish had also found favor with him. And so Achish asked David to accompany him into war. However, the Philistine army commanders were not pleased. They insisted that Achish send David and his men back, for they feared that David could turn against them in the war. And so, David and his men returned to their homes in Ziglag.

On arriving at Ziklag, David and his men are in for a shock. The Amalekites had attacked, raided and burnt down the town and taken everyone, all their women, children and the old, captive. David and his men were distressed, and they wept until they could weep no more. Does that kind of pain sound familiar?

And if this was not enough, David's men became bitter and turned against him. They were so overwhelmed by their sorrow that they even began to talk about stoning him. David was distressed and his loss heavy.

David in all his pain and distress, the Bible says, strengthened himself in the Lord. David's pain was real. It was more than he could bear. He cried, and he cried. But then David didn't stop there. In his pain and his sorrow and when he was overwhelmed, David turned to the Lord for comfort, direction, and guidance.

Life is tough and can sometimes be very painful. We can either like David's men, become bitter in our sorrow or like David, seek the Lord for comfort, strength, and counsel. How does life's situation leave you, bitter or strengthened in the Lord?

Father that I would choose to strengthen myself in you, I pray.

Extended Reading — 1 Samuel 28-31; Psalm 18

DEPRESSION
Remember to Remember

Out of the depths I cry to you, LORD;² Lord, hear my voice. Let
your ears be attentive to my cry for mercy. I wait for the Lord,
my whole being waits, and in his word, I put my hope.
Psalm 130:1-2, 5

When your heart is sad and heavy,

And you have no idea why

Gloom seems to have stopped by

And you just want to cry

You feel no excitement, no joy,

Life seems to barely crawl by

What do you do, how do you control?

This absolute listlessness of the soul

For you have no reason, just no clue

Nor understanding, for out the window flew,

Reason, logic and common sense

Leaving clouds thick, heavy and dense

When despair the mind clouds

And sadness the heart crowds

Lord then will I, my soul counsel

That amid all the tussle

To You, I need to afresh commit

All of myself, with absolutely no limit

I will remind myself to remember
How you faithfully kept the ember
Of my soul glowing in the past
Even when troubles came full and fast
When faced with problems anew
How afresh Your faithfulness I knew

So, will I rejoice for this I know
You, as in the past did keep aglow
With no condition but love unending,
Will take and lead ever so gently, mending
My heart, and you my heavenly Friend
Will take me through this too, to the end

Extended Reading — Psalm 121, 123-125, 128-130

LIFE
Life is Sacred

*David asked him, "Why weren't you afraid to lift your hand to
destroy the LORD's anointed?"*   *2 Samuel 1:14*

King Saul is dead.

Saul and his three sons had been killed in battle against the Philistines
(1 Samuel 31:1-8). An Amalekite brings the news of Saul's death to
David. There were contrary views on whether his report was correct or
whether he found Saul already dead and brought his crown and band
on his arm to David in hope of a reward.

When this Amalekite said he was the one who killed Saul, David is
genuinely angry and sad and asks his men to put the Amalekite to death.
He didn't simply put on a false display of grief and then secretly honor
the man who killed him.

Now David though he had many opportunities to legitimately defend
himself against Saul, he refused to be the one to destroy Saul. He knew
that since it was God who put Saul on the throne it was also God's job
to end his reign, not his.

Saul who had come to the throne of Israel as its first ever king, humble
and anointed by the Lord, left the throne and his life, bitter and hardened
against both God and man. What a tragic end of a life that could have
gone to such great heights. Now Saul may have been rebellious and had
a hardened heart. But that is no reason to kill.

Except in war, no other reason is good enough to take life. We are called
to honor and respect life and not take it, in any circumstance. Life is
the Lord's to give and take.

How will you lead those around you to honor and respect life?

*Lord help me be ever conscious that life is yours alone to give and
take, I pray.*

Extended Reading — 2 Samuel 1-4

GOD'S PRESENCE
Journey of Life

You make known to me the path of life; you will fill me with joy in your presence, with eternal pleasures at your right hand.

Psalm 16:11

God's presence with us is the greatest blessing.

When the people of Israel rebelled against the Lord by forming for themselves a golden calf to worship, the Lord was angry. He refused to go with the people anymore. He said he would keep his promise. He would give them the lands, he would drive out all the people of the lands before them. The only change was that the Lord would not go with them. Shouldn't be much of a problem, right?

But Moses knew better. He refused to go without the Lord's presence. Moses knew that the presence of the Lord was way more precious than all the lands and victories. Without the presence of the Lord, the lands or even the greatest wealth was simply not worth it. And so, he insisted that if the Lord would not go with them, then he would not send them from that place (Exodus 33:15).

God is the one who created us and has a wonderful plan for each one. He alone knows the way we need to take and can direct us. God is sovereign. He is the only one who can protect and keep us and bring us safely to heaven at last. Having the Lord go with us and before us, is by far the greatest blessing.

To experience and practice God's presence we need to have a relationship with him and spend time with him. We need to talk to him in prayer and listen to him from his word.

Are you living life by yourself or is God your constant companion on your journey?

Help me journey with you Lord each day, I pray.

Extended Reading — Psalm 6, 8-10, 14, 16, 19, 21

BIBLE
Authentication, and Proof

Adam, Seth, Enosh, 2 Kenan, Mahalalel, Jared, 3 Enoch,
Methuselah, Lamech, Noah.   *1 Chronicles 1:1-3*

Genealogies have their own place of significance.

The book of Chronicles opens with a genealogical record. This to most of us seems irrelevant and boring. We tend to skip over these pages, right? But if it is in the Bible it must be there for a purpose for all scripture is God-breathed says the Bible in 2 Timothy 3:16. So what are genealogies and why are they in the Bible?

Genealogy is the study of families tracing their lineage and history. They have a powerful part in the Bible.

Genealogies help prove the Bible's accuracy historically. Often, we come across people who insist that the Bible is a mere story or parable by which we are to live our lives. But genealogies help prove that the Bible is a historically proven account of people with names, who did really exist in specific times.

Genealogies also confirm prophesy. Jesus' birth was prophesied through the line of David (Isaiah 11:1). The scripture confirms that Jesus was indeed born of David's line (Matthew 1:1-17, Luke 3:23-28).

Genealogies reflect the character of God. God is interested in each of his people by name. The detailed lists of names tell us that God did not see Israel as just a group of people. Each one of them mattered to God, by name.

Genealogies reveal that Gentiles like Ruth, Rahab were in the Messianic line. God valued these people though they were not part of his covenant people. The Bible is the inspired word of God, who is lovingly interested in each of his people by name. How does knowing these truths change your relationship with God and his word?

Lord may this refreshing reminder help me love you and your word more, I pray.

Extended Reading — 1 Chronicles 1-2

PRAYER
From Depression to Delight

Why, my soul, are you downcast? Why so disturbed wit in me?
Put your hope in God, for I will yet praise him, my Savior and
my God.   *Psalm 43:5*

The psalmist is miserable.

The psalmist is unjustly accused and surrounded by ungodly wicked people with deceitful tongues. He took his sense of injustice to the Lord. He cried to the Lord for vindication and deliverance. The reason he turned to the Lord is because he had a relationship with him. He says for you are *my* God. Not just for you are God, but my God.

The psalmist is basically saying, Lord I am in a mess, I am miserable, and what I need is you. I need your light and truth to lead me. Not just to look at or admire. But to lead me.

The psalmist who began with feeling miserable and depressed moved on to praise God. And why? He allowed God's word, God's light and truth to lead him. And so, he could close the psalm with this strong counsel to his own soul, telling his soul not to be downcast, but to put its hope in God. And that hope leads to praise.

All of us go through times of feeling miserable, especially when people are not fair to us. Often our natural response is to justify ourselves. But the psalmist sets us a worthy example. He turned to his God with whom he had a personal relationship. He asked for his guidance to face the situation. And finally finishes with praising God because he completely hoped in the Lord.

What do you need to move from your depression to delighting yourself in God?

Lord help me grow in my love and trust in you, I pray.

Extended Reading — Psalm 43-45, 49, 84-85, 87

PRAYER
Power of Trust

Jabez cried out to the God of Israel, "Oh, that you would bless me and enlarge my territory! Let your hand be with me and keep me from harm so that I will be free from pain." And God granted his request. 1 Chronicles 4:10

A simple yet powerful prayer.

Jabez is a man in scripture about whom very little is said. The Bible tells us in 1 Chronicles 4:9 that Jabez was more honorable than his brothers. It also tells us that his mother named him Jabez saying, "I gave birth to him in pain." And that just about summarizes all that is said about Jabez. And yet the prayer this man prayed has become a watchword.

This one verse prayer begins with Jabez crying out to the God of Israel in desperation. He knew whom to cry to. Do we? Or do we cry to a friend, our spouse, by ourselves sometimes, wallowing in self-pity?

Jabez asked God to bless him and enlarge his territory. Jabez recognized the source of all his blessing was the Lord. Jabez asked that the Lord's hand be upon him and keep him from pain. The Lord is the only one who can protect and keep us.

Interestingly, nowhere in his prayer does Jabez give God any guidelines or suggestions on how his requests are to be answered. And the Bible says God granted his request.

This prayer though very famous and well accepted is by no means to be a rote prayer nor does it have some magical charm. Rather it gives us guidelines on how we need to pray. When you pray, do you trust he will answer, or do you end up trying to 'help' him?

Father, I choose to trust you with my needs today, just as Jabez did.

Extended Reading — 1 Chronicles 3-5

QUESTIONS
Go into the Sanctuary

Surely in vain I have kept my heart pure and have washed my hands in innocence.   *Psalm 73:13*

Asaph is frustrated and perplexed.

Asaph was one of the greatest singers and musicians during the time of David and Solomon. Asaph begins the psalm with a strong declaration of a truth that he was confident about, 'Surely God is good to Israel.' And yet there is another truth that he knew that troubled him and almost caused him to stumble. He says for I envied the arrogant when I saw the prosperity of the wicked (v3). And with this, he has a serious problem.

As he looks around Asaph sees that the wicked seemed to have no struggles in life. And as if that was not enough, they are arrogant and wear pride like a necklace (v6). Though they are violent and malicious people they seem to get away with all the evil they do.

And on the other hand, Asaph was ridden with troubles. He had trouble all day long and new punishments every morning (v14). So, he was frustrated and felt he had been faithful and pure for nothing. He could not understand how a good God was allowing the wicked to prosper while the godly seemed to only have suffering and punishments.

But that was until he went into the sanctuary of God. When he went into God's presence, he understood a perspective of eternity. He gained understanding and the larger picture.

Getting the right perspective of God and gaining understanding makes all the difference in our lives and to the questions that plague us too. Do you go into God's presence regularly, to gain understanding?

Lord help me regularly come into your sanctuary that I may live with the right perspective, I pray.

Extended Reading — Psalm 73, 77-78

WORSHIP
Power of Music

These are the men David put in charge of the music in the house of the LORD after the ark came to rest there.   1 Chronicles 6:31

Music was an important part of worship for God's people.

The book of Chronicles begins with the genealogies of all the tribes of Israel. Each one was recorded by name, including the Levites. David appointed the temple musicians, people specifically for the task of music in the house of the Lord. The Bible says these men ministered to the Lord. Worship through music is a ministry and an integral part of worship. It was to be structured and organized.

The worship of God was a very important part of Israel's life as a nation. And music had an important role. The Bible records the songs of Miriam, Moses, Hannah, and many others.

Music is a positive and powerful tool that can bless and help in worshipping God. The book of Psalms is the songbook of the Bible and a wonderful example of the right way to use music in worshipping God. Music can be a way to praise God and express our gratitude to him for all that he does for us. The right kind of songs can be a powerful tool for spiritual teaching (Colossians 3:16).

Music can be a very powerful tool in relaxation. David was very skillful in playing the harp. His music "refreshed" King Saul, the Bible says in 1 Samuel 16. Music in the Bible is widely used for consecrating hearts unto the Lord. Music is also a very powerful tool to pass on faith from one generation to another (psalm145:4-5).

Does the music you listen to cause you to worship God more meaningfully?

Lord help me use music well, I pray.

Extended Reading — 1 Chronicles 6

GRATITUDE
Need to Give Thanks

*It is good to praise the Lord and make music to your name,
O Most High, 2 proclaiming your love in the morning and your
faithfulness at night.*   *Psalm 92:1-2*

This is the only psalm titled, the Song for the Sabbath.

Praise is the business of the Sabbath. God's work and rest is the cause for the Sabbath. Praising him is the focus of Sabbath. The Sabbath must be a day, for not only holy rest, but also of holy work.

This psalm begins with a simple yet profound statement. It is good to give thanks or praise the Lord. It is our duty, our tribute due to our great God. We are unjust if we withhold praise rising from our hearts and lips.

The psalmist then moves on to suggest how we can express our worship. We are to make music in the name of God. Music is an integral part of God's plan for worship. There is great power and impact in music. It is a wonderful way to express our love and adoration to God.

Finally, the psalmist says we are to worship him when we rise and when we go to sleep and all the times in between. We are to praise God through the good times of sunshine and through dark and difficult times. Praise is to be continually on our mouths.

An attitude of gratitude keeps our perspective straight and keeps us from a critical, whining spirit. Giving thanks to God sets an example to those watching us.

What is keeping you from praising and giving thanks to God every day and night?

Lord give a heart of worship that gives thanks to you every day, I pray.

Extended Reading — Psalm 81, 88, 92-93

DISCIPLINE
From a Place of Love

All Israel was listed in the genealogies recorded in the book
of the kings of Israel and Judah. They were taken captive to
Babylon because of their unfaithfulness.   1 Chronicles 9:1

God disciplines those he loves.

The first eight chapters of Chronicles gives a detailed account of Israel by name. This is a small but powerful statement. Judah was taken captive to Babylon because of their unfaithfulness. Not because of the clash of kingdoms that doomed the kingdom of Judah. It was simply because of their own unfaithfulness. If they had remained faithful, God would have protected them through the rise and fall of many empires and kingdoms.

We have all experienced the discipline of our parents. At times they may not be pleasant memories and yet we accept that discipline has taught us important values and life lessons which we use even today. Parents are called to train their children and teach them life values. Often discipline may be unpleasant,but that does not keep responsible parents from disciplining children from a place of love until they learn and change their ways.

We often have questions about God who punishes his people. About how he sometimes used even pagan kings to discipline his children. But God is a compassionate and gracious God, slow to anger and abounding in love and faithfulness (Psalm 86:15). And yet, God disciplines his children from a place of love. The Bible says, do not make light of God's discipline and do not lose heart when he rebukes you (Hebrews 12:5).

What is God trying to teach you through the difficult experience you are going through?

Lord help me learn quickly, to turn to you, I pray.

Extended Reading — 1 Chronicles 7-10

LOVE
Beyond Ourselves

For her stones are dear to your servants; her very dust moves
them to pity.   *Psalm 102: 13*

The psalmist is referring to the ruined and broken Jerusalem.

The psalmist begins with his plea to God for mercy. He was in distress and was going through great affliction and challenges. He was going through so much heartache that he forgot to eat. He had become so thin that he was almost skin and bones (v5). He was taunted by his enemies (v8). The psalmist was in tears.

Though he is overwhelmed by his own ruin and need (v1-11), yet, in his sorrow, the psalmist turns his attention to the city of God. He looked outward rather than staying focused on himself. That is an important learning for all of us, especially in times that we are going through exceptional difficulty, it would be very powerful to turn the focus outside of ourselves.

The psalmist says, the stones of Jerusalem are precious to the Lord's servants and the dust moves them to pity. By nature, we tend to reject that which is broken or torn down. But if every broken-down stone of God's city was precious to his servants, then how much more the broken and hurting people around should be precious to us. 1 Peter 2:5 says every stone represents the people of God in his great building. The poorest, the most difficult person, the most ignorant convert, every single one is precious to the Lord and so is to be precious to the church of God.

How are you caring for the people in pain and need around you?

Lord give me your love to go beyond my own pain to love those who are needy, I pray.

Extended Reading — Psalm 102-104

DEPENDENCE ON GOD
How much Longer Lord?

David was thirty years old when he became king, and he
reigned forty years.   *2 Samuel 5: 4*

Run David, run.

This seems to have been the motto for many years of young David's
life. The youngest in his family, David, was a mere lad when Samuel
anointed him king over Israel. Though not given specifically, Bible scholars
agree that David was but a teenager, when he was anointed. And yet,
it was years later, at the age of thirty, that David finally ascends the
throne of Israel. That was no short wait indeed. Nor was the wait easy.

David was on the run for many years from King Saul, who over time
became jealous of him. For no fault of his, David was constantly on the
run, for killing him became Saul's mission in life. David was forced to
live among the caves. The life of a fugitive was his lot, for a long time
before he reached the throne of Israel. The Lord took David through
many difficult situations and circumstances before he could be transitioned
from shepherd to king.

And this is a pattern we see all through the Bible. Abraham waited
twenty-five years for Isaac. Joseph thirteen years as a slave, before he
became the second in command to the King of Egypt. Moses had
forty years in the palace and forty in the wilderness before leading the
Israelites out of Egypt. Paul had three years in Arabia before he started
his ministry. There is a time of preparation between promise and actual
fulfillment. Are you asking, how much longer Lord about the promises
he has given you?

The Lord never fails or goes back on his promises. Trust him and wait patiently
for his perfect time.

Lord thank you that you always keep your word.

Extended Reading — 2 Samuel 5:1-10; 1 Chronicles 11-12

CHURCH
Love, So Live

Behold, how good and how pleasant it is for brothers to dwell together in unity!   *Psalm 133:1*

The Psalmist is calling us to behold!

Psalm 133 is attributed to King David. He probably wrote it when he was finally received as king over all the tribes of Israel, ending a terrible season of national division and discord.

After a long time of violence, war, and fighting, finally, there is unity and peace. And David says behold, it is worthy of notice. David points out how good and pleasant unity amongst God's people is.

Good is what we ought to do, what God requires of us, it is our duty. And it is good to live in unity. But if it is only good, then it could become a chore. But when it not just good but pleasant, it makes a big difference. Pleasant is when we rejoice, it is our delight. So, to dwell together in unity is right and our duty, but it is also our delight and joy.

To dwell in unity is to have oneness of heart, of mind, of spirits. David was referring to relationships among God's people. This unity will be tested because this dwell together. Often it is easier to dwell in unity with those who are distant and far away.

This was a song that was especially relevant for pilgrims who came from many different walks of life, regions, and tribes, gathering together for the one purpose of worshipping God in Jerusalem. Our love for God should bind us to joyfully live in unity among believers. How can you be a channel of peace and reconciliation in your church?

Lord may my love for you drive me to be a channel of your peace and unity, I pray.

Extended Reading — Psalm 133

REBELLION
Precious Memories

Our fathers in Egypt did not understand nor appreciate Your miracles; They did not remember the abundance of Your mercies nor imprint Your loving kindnesses on their hearts, but they were rebellious at the sea, at the Red Sea.   Psalm 106:7

Memories often define our attitudes.

The psalmist is burdened by the forgetfulness of the people. In the above verse, he confessed the sin of the entire Israelite nation. They were rebellious. They did not understand or appreciate the miracles that the Lord had done on their behalf. Miracles to rescue, to take care and provide for them. Neither did they remember the abundant mercies of the Lord. They did not imprint the loving-kindness of the Lord on their hearts. And the fact that they did not remember, was rebellion!

Rebellion was one of the dark sins of the Israelites. They rebelled by being disobedient, worshipping idols and being proud. Their rebellion was also evident by the fact that they did not remember. They did not remember God's goodness and faithfulness to them. And when they did not remember they were not grateful. And ungratefulness comes from a heart of pride and self-sufficiency. Human minds are rather peculiar. We often tend to remember the bad things that have happened in our lives rather than the good. We are quick to complain when things don't go the way we would like. Rarely do we remember the many wonderful things that we have enjoyed.

Take a moment to pause and look back over your life and observe what you remember. Are you being rebellious?

Gracious Lord as I look back, I realize I have been quick to complain, but slow to remember your goodness to me. Give me an increasingly grateful heart, I pray.

Extended Reading — Psalm 106-107

DEPENDANCE ON GOD
On him Alone

*So David inquired of the Lord, "Shall I go and attack
the Philistines? Will you deliver them into my hands?"
The Lord answered him, "Go, for I will surely deliver the
Philistines into your hands."*   2 Samuel 5:19

David was a veteran soldier.

David had been anointed as king over Israel. And David had a
much-needed perspective. He recognized that it was the Lord who
had established him as king over Israel and had exalted his kingdom
for the sake of his people Israel (5:12). And that kept him humble and
dependent on God.

As David was settling down as king, he heard the news that the Philistines
had arrived in the Valley of Rephaim. He could easily have gone right
out and attacked and routed them. After all, he was a great warrior
and he knew the Philistines and their army well. He had even been on
their side to fight on their behalf. He sure knew how to attack them.
So, what was the delay?

But David did not go out against them immediately. He went to the
Lord to seeks counsel. And the Lord assured him that he will deliver
them into David's hands.

God allows us wealth and positions of power not just for us but for the
sake of his people, for us to be a blessing to others. David knew that
all he had and all he was from the Lord and for the Lord. He chose
to call on him. He depended on God and not on his own knowledge
or abilities. On whom or what do we depend each day for wisdom
and counsel?

Lord help me humbly depend on you every day, I pray.

*Extended Reading — 2 Samuel 5:11-25; 2 Samuel 6:1-23; 1 Chronicles
13-16*

ABORTION
Blessed Forgiveness

Blessed is the one whose transgressions are forgiven, whose sins are covered. Blessed is the one whose sin the Lord does not count against them and in whose spirit is no deceit.   *Psalm 32:1-2*

How could I?

There are times in life when we do things that seem so very bad that we feel we can't or don't deserve to be forgiven. And one such time is abortion. Abortion is an irreversible action but can continue to haunt for the rest of life!

An unwanted pregnancy can be a frightening experience, especially for someone who is not financially, emotionally, mentally or physically prepared for such a responsibility. In their search for answers, perhaps they were fooled into believing that the unborn child was an expendable "lump of tissue," not really a pre-born human being. And now every day and night are haunted by remorse and guilt.

And one wonders, will the guilt and regret ever end?

Yes, it can end. There is blessed forgiveness and healing in Jesus. The Bible in Romans 3:22 says we are made right in God's sight when we trust in Jesus Christ to take away our sins. All of us, no matter who we are, no matter what we have done, can be saved. It is never too late. No sin is too great that the Lord cannot forgive. Only Christ can and will forgive you. In him, there is peace that passes all understanding. But we need to choose to go to him.

Is there some sin that has been haunting you that need to seek Jesus' forgiveness and healing?

Dear Lord, I come to you, broken and bleeding. Have mercy on me, I pray.

Extended Reading — Psalm 1-2, 15, 22-24, 47, 68

WORSHIP
Heart of Worship

Enter his gates with thanksgiving and his courts with praise;
give thanks to him and praise his name. For the Lord is good and
his love endures forever; his faithfulness continues through all
generations.   *Psalm 100: 4-5*

When we sing together with joy and gusto,
The many hymns and choruses too.
What exactly are we doing?
Just the music and harmony enjoying?

Or do the words so powerful and so sweet,
Penned so beautifully from the heart.
To your soul joy and comfort bring,
And help you worship him as you sing.

To encourage you as through life you plod,
And times that hurt and make you sad,
To raise your voice in worship sweet,
And your God and Creator humbly greet.

So next time you raise your voice to sing,
And as the powerful melodies ring,
Would you pause to ponder and to think?
And into your heart, allow, the words truly sink.

To be ever faithful, as you sing each day,
And mean the words that you say,
And so, to your Maker, who reigns up above,
You sing with a heart full of gratitude and love.

Extended Reading — Psalm 89, 96, 100, 101, 105, 132

GRATITUDE
What Can I Do in Return?

He said to Nathan the prophet, "Here I am, living in a house of cedar, while the ark of God remains in a tent." 2 Samuel 7:2

God had finally given King David rest.

From the days of being anointed as the next king of Israel, till now, David faced so many challenges and wars. It took years of running from jealous King Saul before David even became king. And after that, he faced so many wars, assassination attempts, and even mutiny. And now finally, he had rest. He had truly earned it. He could comfortably rest and enjoy himself wouldn't you think?

Well, not King David. His heart was so full of gratitude to the Lord. His heart burned with the desire to do something for the Lord. He was uncomfortable. How could he live in the opulence of his cedar palace while the ark of the Lord remained in a tent? So, he thinks of building a temple for the Lord.

David never forgot his humble beginnings. He never forgot from where to where the Lord had brought him. David says, who am I, Sovereign *Lord*, and what is my family, that you have brought me this far? (1 Sam 7:18). And as he remembers, he is overwhelmed with gratitude. His response, what shall I return to the *Lord* for all his goodness to me? (Psalm 116:12). This humble man tried to find ways to glorify God and honor him.

A humble heart never forgets the past goodness of God. A humble heart is a grateful heart. A humble heart is constantly trying to return something for God's goodness.

How are you reflecting a humble heart today?

Lord may I ever live my life in gratitude, I pray.

Extended Reading — 2 Samuel 7; 1 Chronicles 17

DIRECTION
Which Way Now?

*In you, LORD MY GOD, I put my trust.² I trust in you; do not let
me be put to shame, nor let my enemies' triumph over me. ³ No
one who hopes in you will ever be put to shame, but shame will
come on those who are treacherous without cause. Psalm 25:1-3*

David's strategy.

Every so often in life, we come to crossroads. We may be confused,
wondering which way to go, wanting to make the right decision
and yet not sure how. When David was confused and weary, wondering
which way to turn, he had a plan.

David in this psalm shows how he handles the challenges that came
his way. He turns to God when in trouble. Matthew Henry the great
theologian and commentator said, prayer is the ascent of the soul to God.

David displays a close and intimate relationship with his Lord. He
knew the Lord as his personal God, not just some God seated on his
throne far, far away.

For David, the choice was clear. The fact was, he was surrounded by
enemies and troubles galore. But his strategy was simple and clear. He
puts his trust in his God, whom he knew enough to call **his** God!

David puts his trust in God because of his relationship with and knowledge
of this personal God. He knew that whenever he went to his God, he
could be sure that he will not be put to shame or embarrassed. He also
knew that it is true for anyone who would trust God!

David turned to God in prayer when he needed direction. Is that your
strategy too?

Lord may I know you and confidently turn to you first, I pray.
Extended Reading — Psalm 25, 29, 33, 36, 39

GRACE
From Fear to Honor

So Mephibosheth ate at David's table like one of the king's sons.

2 Samuel 9:11

Mephibosheth was scared.

There was a loud knock on the door of Makir. There stood the king's soldiers with the summons for Mephibosheth, son of Jonathan, King Saul's grandson. Mephibosheth who had been living in hiding was petrified. It was a common practice for the leader of the new dynasty to execute every potential heir from the previous dynasty. At the news of the death of Saul and Jonathan, his nurse had gathered Mephibosheth and fled, leading to an accident that left him lame in both his legs. And Mephibosheth had been living in hiding ever since.

On arriving at the palace, Mephibosheth fell face down in David's presence. But David was quick to allay his fears. He assured him that he wanted to honor his covenant to his father Jonathan to show kindness to his descendants, (1 Samuel 20). David promised to restore all the lands of Saul to him. Further, he gave him the honor of a close relationship with himself saying that he shall eat at David's table for the rest of his life.

David is a picture of God's grace and we are Mephibosheth. We were weak, hiding and poor, separated from our King because of our ancestors and our own deliberate actions. But our King sought us in his love. Our King's kindness to us is based on a covenant. We have the invitation to be part of the heavenly banquet of our King.

But we need to accept his offer of grace in humility. We are also called to be like David and minister and serve others.

Thank You Lord for your grace and may it flow through me too, I pray.

Extended Reading — 2 Samuel 8-9; 1 Chronicles 18

THANKSGIVING
A Sacrifice that Honors

He who offers a sacrifice of praise and thanksgiving honors Me.
Psalm 50:23

Anything that you really value in life will have the smell of your blood, sweat, and tears.

Sacrifice is to give up something that you want to keep in order to get or do something else. In the above verse, the Lord clarifies that it is the one who offers him a sacrifice of praise and thanksgiving that honors him.

When life is tough, and tears seem ever ready to fall, you praise God not necessarily for *what* you are going through rather you praise God for *who* he is. You praise God because you recognize that God is more than able to see you through your situation, however tough and depressing it may seem.

A sacrifice of praise requires unflinching confidence in the one you praise. It requires that you move your eyes and thoughts from the storms that surround you. To move your eyes from the storms of health, finance, relationships, to the only one who can see you through these storms.

Offering praise and thanks when life is full of good things barely involves sacrifice. Sacrifice is when you praise through the fears and pain. Sacrifice is when you praise God when all you want to do really is to give in to the emotions that seem to engulf. To trust that your God is bigger than all your problems, and so to praise him sure requires sacrifice.

In what situation of life do you require to turn your focus from the what to the who and praise him?

Teach me, Lord, today to honor you with my praise and thanksgiving when I face tough situations, I pray.

Extended Reading — Psalm 50, 53, 60, 75

FAITH
Trust Leads to Victory

Now this I know: The Lord gives victory to his anointed. He
answers him from his heavenly sanctuary with the victorious
power of his right hand. ⁷ Some trust in chariots and some in
horses, but we trust in the name of the Lord our God.

Psalm 20:6-7

This is another of David's psalms.

Yet this psalm is different as it is in the voice of a multitude that
prays for King of Israel, as he stands ready to go into battle. It could
be that David took the spontaneous prayer of the people and made it
into a song to recall the spiritual strength of the moment.

This was stirring cry from the hearts of the people for their king, who
are tensely aware of the life and death issues of battle. They pray for
his safety and they pray for God's blessing and protection over him.

And in the above verses, David draws a strong contrast and affirms his
own stand. He points out that some trust in chariots and horses, but
his trust was in God alone. David was counting on God, not human.
David put his trust in the person, the character of God. He didn't carry
the name of the Lord as a magical charm.

The name of God speaks of the comprehensive character of God. The
name of God is an expression of his faithfulness to his covenant with
Israel. David recognized that God had anointed and appointed him.
And so, he was confident that God would give him victory too.

We are all engaged in spiritual battle. And God gives us victory too when
we depend on him and refuse to trust people or the world.

Are you living in victory each day?

Lord increase my trust in you I pray.

Extended Reading — 2 Sam 10; 1 Chronicles 19; Psalm 20

WITNESS
Looking Back

Come and hear, all you who fear God; let me tell you what he
has done for me.   *Psalm 66:16*

Looking back over the years gone by,

Through the many happenings along the way,

What has been the growth, what the gain?

What has been the learning through the pain?

How have the numerous blessings left you?

A bigger blessing, or just the same, nothing new?

Life is rich with experiences unlimited,

These can us, grow or keep restricted.

Yet if on our own we choose to face life,

Life can be overwhelming and full of strife.

And yet the Lord is our strength and hope,

He promises to equip and help us cope.

Would you rest in the knowledge of his love?

Unconditional, and seek his grace from above.

To deal with your every day, and let,

Him be your Shield and Defender yet.

May he ever be your anchor and stay,

In experiences and years coming your way.

So that when all is said and done,

Those who, your life has known,

Would say, surely here lies one,

Who depended on him alone.

For he ever the strength and fortress,

Of this his child, even through distress.

Extended Reading — Psalm 65-67, 69-70

SIN

Sin is Always Against God

Then David said to Nathan, "I have sinned against the Lord."

2 Samuel 12:13

David stayed back in Jerusalem.

It was the time of war. David sent Joab his commander with the army to fight against the Ammonites. But David did not go. Instead, David who could not sleep was pacing on the roof of the palace. And that is when David saw Bathsheba bathing.

David was tempted. And it didn't stop there. He enquired about her and sent for her. Bathsheba too was bathing in an inappropriate place where she could be easily seen. And soon enough she was pregnant. And that led to the next sin. To cover up the adultery David murdered Uriah her husband.

God sent Nathan the prophet to David. Nathan explained his sin to him through a story. David recognized his sin and was deeply repentant. He did not try to explain or give excuses. He did not blame anyone. He took responsibility for what he had done. His response was something very powerful and relevant to every Christian today.

Sin is always against God. And trying to hide our sin is only a deception. We may be able to hide our sin with difficulty from our conscience. But our sin is never hidden before God. Sin hinders our relationship and fellowship with God and people.

As soon as we are conscious of having sinned, the only way is to confess and repent. Not to try to reason, justify or explain it away. We need to go to the Lord in prayer, acknowledge our sin to him, confess and seek his forgiveness. Unconfessed sin is a barrier to our spiritual life and power. What sin do you need to bring to the Lord today?

Lord give me a humble and contrite heart, I pray.

Extended Reading — 2 Samuel 11-12; 1 Chronicles 20

RESTORATION
A Symptom, Not Disease

Create in me a pure heart, O God, and renew a steadfast spirit within me. ¹¹ Do not cast me from your presence or take your Holy Spirit from me. ¹² Restore to me the joy of your salvation and grant me a willing spirit, to sustain me.   Psalm 51:1-2

Psalm 51 is perhaps the best known of the penitential psalms.

Written by David after he committed both adultery and murder (2 Samuel 11-12) this psalm portrays more vividly than anywhere in Scripture the heartfelt plea for mercy from the fallen sinner. David recognized that his sin separated him from God and he was heartbroken. He cried to the Lord.

David pleaded for cleansing and restoration. He prayed for a steadfast spirit, a spirit that was firm and established in the Lord. He wanted to be done with the kind of instability that he had just experienced. He prayed for a spirit that was joyfully willing to follow God's word rather than exploit people.

A heart that is rooted in the Lord is not easily wavered but is firm and steadfast. David knew that his sexual sin was only a symptom, not the disease. The root of the problem was his lack of joy and gladness in God. His prayer was that God would restore to him the joy of his salvation, for that was his actual need.

God in creation gave us the gift and privilege that allows us individuality and freedom. Willful misuse of these however leads to rebellion and subsequent fall. As a result, all through life, all of us have a the tendency to rebel against God. And you and I are no exception.

David came to the Lord for cleansing and restoration. Have you?

Lord restore the joy of your salvation in me, I pray.

Extended Reading — Psalm 32, 51, 86, 122

DISAPPOINTMENT
Rock that is Higher than I

Then David said to all his officials who were with him in Jerusalem, "Come! We must flee, or none of us will escape from Absalom. We must leave immediately, or he will move quickly to overtake us and bring ruin on us and put the city to the sword."   *2 Samuel 15:14*

Absalom committed treason under the guise of worship.

Absalom, David's son, worked carefully and intentionally. He was impatient for the throne which would anyway be his one day. He stole the hearts of the people with his cunningness and carefully cultivating an exciting and enticing image. And soon under the guise of fulfilling a vow, he left for Hebron, presumably. He instead went and conspired against his own father, Davidand declared himself as king. David was forced out of the kingdom and away from the Tabernacle. What a sad day.

In the pain of being forced to flee for his life, and the disappointment of being betrayed by his own son, King David penned Psalm 62. Huge waves of trouble washed over him, and he found himself submerged, his head and heart and all. His deep pain was too much for him to bear. He cried in anguish to the Lord, asking to be led to the Rock that is higher than him, his God, his salvation, his hope.

Loneliness, rejection, and hurt are real. We all go through times when those closest to us, turn against us. The pain is almost unbearable and disappointment and grief wash over our souls.

Would you like David, turn to the Rock that is higher, that can be your safe place too.

Heavenly Father lead me through my pain, to you my Rock that is higher than I, I pray.

Extended Reading — 2 Samuel 13-15

ABORTION
Life Over Fear

Cast your cares on the LORD AND HE WILL SUSTAIN YOU; He will never let the righteous be shaken.   Psalm 55:22

Life is precious, we all agree.

Then why is abortion so rampant today? Research shows that over 95 percent of the abortions performed today involve women who simply do not want to have a baby. Only less than 5 percent of abortions are for the reasons of rape, incest, or because of risk to the mother's life.

A closer look reveals that the 95 percent of women who don't want to have the baby are driven by fear. Fear that one is too young or immature to have a baby. Fear of not having the required resources to take care of the baby. Fear that the arrival of the baby will require too many adjustments. Fear that the father will not provide the needed support. And finally, the fear that one will not be able to handle another baby with the babies she already has. Fear causes women to take this irrevocable step of putting an end to the life that is growing within them.

Life is a gift from God and is not ours to take. The child forming in the womb is very much a life and not just a blob of flesh as some would have us believe. Irrespective of the difficult situations we find ourselves in, we are to turn to God. He will help us if we turn to him. We are to choose him and life over our fear.

How will you help someone you love, value life and choose life over their fear?

Help me Lord to always choose life over my fear, I pray.

Extended Reading — Psalm 3-4, 12-13, 28, 55

WORDS
Choose to Bless

*As King David approached Bahurim, a man from the same clan
as Saul's family came out from there. His name was Shimei son
of Gera, and he cursed as he came out. ⁶ He pelted David and
all the king's officials with stones, though all the troops and the
special guard were on David's right and left.   2 Samuel 16:5-6*

Shimei's words hurt!

Shimei falsely accused David that his situation and the loss of his
kingdom was because of his past sins against the house of Saul (what
sins?). Abishai, David's bodyguard, and nephew wanted to attack Shimei
and curse him back (v9). But David prevents him.

David did not defend himself or react in anger. He recognized the
sovereignty of God, responded humbly, and received Shimei's curse as
from the Lord (v10-12).

Curse words are words that are intended to inflict harm or damage,
to belittle or to wish one evil. Being a child of God does not make
you immune to others cursing. But how you respond makes a world
of difference. You can either respond in anger and 'curse' back or like
David choose to recognize the sovereignty of God even in those painful
situations.

Curses only have power over us if we believe them (Proverbs 26:2) and
we invest power in them. As a child of God, you are blessed, regardless
of what others say to you. Choose to reject words that do not line up
with God's word and forgive those who curse.

Forgiving the other frees us to live victoriously in God's blessing. Speak
blessing over others. Words of blessing cause growth, hope and healing.
Choose to become a blesser!

Lord help me believe what you say about me and be a blesser, I pray.

Extended Reading — 2 Samuel 16-18

WAITING
A New Song

I waited patiently for the Lord; he turned to me and heard my cry. ² He lifted me out of the slimy pit, out of the mud and mire; he set my feet on a rock and gave me a firm place to stand. ³ He put a new song in my mouth, a hymn of praise to our God. Many will see and fear the Lord and put their trust in him.

Psalm 40:1-3

David had been waiting for the Lord.

In the previous psalms we see that David had been waiting for the Lord, but without an immediate answer. David continued to wait. He waited patiently, diligently, perseveringly, until God helped him.

As David waited, God inclined or turned to him. Inclining pictures God bending down to David in his affliction, removing any perceived distance between the Lord and his servant. Almost like God's attention was arrested and riveted, now David was confident of a favorable answer.

David's patience for the Lord resulted in God lifting him up. He delivered him from his crisis. David's prayer for deliverance was answered. God set him in a much better and more secure place. He helped him stand.

And that deliverance caused David to sing a new song. God gave him a fresh understanding of himself and new experience of walking with him. The Lord gave him a new song, a new reason to praise him.

How good and right it is for the creature to praise the creator, the redeemed to praise the redeemer, the delivered to praise the deliverer. We are grateful that God gives us the ability to praise him.

Are you willing to wait patiently in prayer?

Lord give me a new song as I wait patiently for you, I pray.

Extended Reading — Psalm 26, 40, 58, 61-62, 64

BEREAVEMENT
When We Forget to Remember

The king covered his face and cried aloud, "O my son Absalom!
O Absalom, my son, my son!"   2 Samuel 19:4

Absalom is dead.

However, a day of victory was turned into a day of mourning for all the people because of David's excessive mourning. David's loyal and sacrificing supporters won that day for the glory of God and the good of Israel. But then they couldn't enjoy their victory because David was overcome with excessive weeping for Absalom. David was mastered by feelings and so he lost perspective.

God is not against feelings but at the same time, feelings were never meant to master us. Excessive mourning is when mourning is rooted in unbelief and self-indulgence. In 1 Thessalonians 4:13, Paul says, brothers and sisters, we do not want you to be uninformed about those who sleep in death so that you do not grieve like the rest of humankind, who have no hope.

David, in his excessive sorrow, forgot that God was still in control. He forgot that a great victory was won and that he had many loyal supporters. He forgot that God had shown great grace and mercy to David.

When someone is overcome by tragedy or sorrow, the problem is not in what they know, but in what they forget. Loss of a loved one is always painful, and tears and deep sorrow are only natural. But some Christians mourn at times in death as if they have no hope in God and that is wrong. It is important to retain perspective, forgetting the sovereignty of a loving God.

In your sorrow are you forgetting God's love and sovereignty?

Lord help my grief be rooted in what I know about you, I pray.

Extended Reading — 2 Samuel 19-21

QUIET TIME
Faith in Expectancy

In the morning Lord, you hear my voice; in the morning I lay
my requests before you and wait expectantly.   Psalm 5:3

The Lord testified that David was a man after his own heart

Was it because David was a perfect person? Of course not! The Bible records that David committed many sins, including adultery and murder. Then what set him apart for God himself to testify about him?

David had a powerful relationship with God. In verse 1 we find that David longs for an audience with God, basically saying Lord, please listen to me. Then in verse 2, we find David prayed to God. We often come to God so full of our own requests or feelings that we forget to focus on God and sense his presence. David's prayer was focused on God.

In today's text, we find a couple of pointers. The NKJV says, "in the morning you **shall** hear my voice, in the morning I **will** direct my voice to you." It is his commitment to God. He was essentially saying, "Lord, that's an appointment, I commit to meeting you every morning to bring my requests to you."

Then David says, "and then I wait expectantly. Not only will I place my requests before you every morning, Lord, but after that, I will wait, **expectantly**." That reflects faith. Having placed his requests before God, he knows and believes God will act. So, he looks forward to that, eagerly, expectantly to watch how God answers his prayers.

Is the Lord sure to hear your voice every morning? Do you look forward expectantly, to watch as he answers your prayers?

Lord help me make my time with you my priority every morning and in faith wait expectantly as you answer, I pray.

Extended Reading — Psalm 5, 38, 41-42

EXPERIENCE GOD
The Power of 'My'

He said: "The Lord is my rock, my fortress, and my deliverer;
³ my God is my rock, in whom I take refuge, my shield and the
horn of my salvation. He is my stronghold, my refuge, and my
savior— from violent people you save me. ⁴ "I called to the Lord,
who is worthy of praise, and have been saved from my enemies.
2 Samuel 22:2-4

David needed more than one title to describe his God.

David piled title upon title in praising God. And every single title is prefixed with the personal pronoun 'my.' The God David was talking about was not a distant God, He was not someone else's God, nor someone who David had seen in other people's lives. Each title came from his very own personal experience of how he had experienced God in the different times of his life. Each title was meaningful to David because God fulfilled the meaning of each title in David's experience.

David had experienced the Lord's deliverance. He had tasted and known that God could be counted on, that he was firm as a rock. David had experienced God's protection multiple times when he ran to him for refuge. And so David's praise rose from his very personal experience.

When we experience God personally, it brings great strength and beauty to our faith. The power of 'my' comes when we see God for who he is. When we know him as our rock,fortress,deliverer,shield,stronghold and savior, it is natural to trust him completely.

How have you experienced God? What titles would you use to praise God?

Lord I want to experience you in new and powerful ways, I pray.

Extended Reading — 2 Samuel 22-23; Psalm 57

WORSHIP
The How and Whom of Worship

Come, let us bow down in worship, let us kneel before the Lord our Maker; [7] for he is our God and we are the people of his pasture, the flock under his care.   *Psalm 95:6-7*

A Gentle plea to worship God.

The psalmist is calling the people to do what is right before God, get low before God. The psalmist calls us to bow down, to worship and to kneel before God.

The call is to bow down and worship. We are to worship God with humble hearts.. God deserves our complete submission as we bow down in his presence. We are to bow down in worship before our maker, not before a crucifix or an image that we have made.

The psalmist further calls the people to join him in kneeling before God our maker. In the previous verses, the psalmist talked about God's reign and rule over all of creation. And now he includes humankind under God's creation. He reminds us that God is our maker, who created us. And so we are to worship our creator. We are to bend our knees before our God in a posture of supplication and request.

The psalmist reminds us that we are the sheep of his pasture. There is a sense of belonging in this phrase. God personally takes care of each one of us. The redeemed have two great reasons to humbly worship God because we are twice his, once at creation and then at redemption.

Is your heart posture one of humility and submission when you come before God?

You alone are worthy of all my humble worship, my Creator and my Redeemer.

Extended Reading — Psalm 95, 97-99

SATAN
Know Your Enemy

Satan revolted against Israel and incited David to take a census of Israel.   *Chronicles 21:1*

The devil is a very real spiritual being.

David had been doing well. God had been giving him victory on every side. But then, the devil rose in him the form of pride. David wanted to gauge his military strength by taking a census. He wanted to know how many fighting men Israel had.

David's dependence moved from God to his own ability and the strength of his army. Joab, commander of David's army tried to dissuade him but David was insistent. So Joab took the census. This angered the Lord and he punished Israel.

The devil appears in the earliest accounts of the Bible (Genesis 3:1-7). He tricked Adam and Eve into disobeying God. He is always around and prompts people into the wrong action.

Satan rebelled against God (2 Peter 2:4, Luke 10:18) and fell from heaven. His sole purpose is to destroy or hinder the work of God (1 Peter 5:8-9). Satan's attacks are sometimes subtle, disguising his motives. Other times his opposition is clear and direct, taking control of people (Mark 5:1-13). However, Satan's time is limited. He will be finally destroyed at the end of time by God (Revelation 20:10).

Satan cannot possess those of us who are indwelt by the Holy Spirit. He sure can tempt us. But we are victors in Christ Jesus, for he that is in us is greater than he that is in the world (1 John 4:4). But we are to put on the full armor of God to stand against the evil schemes of the devil (Ephesians 6:11). Have you put on your armor today?

Lord help me know my enemy and daily put on my armor, I pray.

Extended Reading — 2 Samuel 24; 1 Chronicles 21-22; Psalm 30

PRAYER
With a Heart for God's Glory

Help me, Lord my God; save me according to your unfailing love. ²⁷ Let them know that it is your hand, that you, Lord, have done it.   Psalm 109:26-27

David is in trouble again.

David is surrounded by many enemies. The wicked have been speaking against him. And so he prays that God would not be silent. He did not want the mouth of the deceitful to have the last word.

David was humble and honest about his need. He was poor, needy and was hurt deeply (v22). He was tired and worn. And his cry was simple and straightforward. Help me, Lord my God! His plea was much like the Canaanite woman with the demon-possessed daughter (Matthew 15:21-25).

David's prayer was based on God's unfailing love. He had nothing to claim for himself. He pleads because of God's mercy, not his own merit. His calls on God's character and goodness to save him.

David wanted deliverance not just for himself but also for the glory of God. David wanted his enemies and all who look at him to know that his rescue was from God's hand, that it was the Lord who had done it.

"Ungodly men will not see God's hand in anything if they can help it, and when they see good men delivered into their power they become more confirmed than ever in their atheism; but all in good time God will arise and so effectually punish their malice and rescue the object of their spite that they will be compelled to say like the Egyptian magicians, 'this is the finger of God.'" (Spurgeon). What's your attitude when you come to God in your need?

Lord may 'Your finger' ever be evident in my life, I pray.

Extended Reading — Psalm 108-110

PRAYER
A Set Apart Privilege

The sons of Amram: Aaron and Moses. Aaron was set apart to consecrate him as most holy, he and his sons forever, to burn incense before the LORD, attend to His service, and to bless [worshipers] in His name forever.   *1 Chronicles 23:13*

Aaron and his descendants were set apart forever.

David now old and full of years makes his son Solomon, king over Israel (v1). And then, David proactively gathers all the leaders of Israel, to organize them to help Solomon with the work of building the temple and administering the affairs of the kingdom.

The Levities were numbered and organized. Although all the tribe of Levi was involved in different work in the temple, only Aaron and his descendants were to offer incense and minister before God. Incense is a picture of intercessory prayer. The priest had to represent the people before the Lord.

Intercessory prayer simply means praying on behalf of others. There were many in the Old Testament who were mediators, like Abraham, Moses, David, Samuel, Hezekiah, Elijah, Jeremiah, Ezekiel, and Daniel. Christ is pictured in the New Testament as the ultimate intercessor.

By dying on that cross Jesus closed the gap between God and us. And so we can now intercede in prayer on behalf of other Christians or for those who are lost. 1 Timothy 2:5 says, for there is one God and one mediator between God and humankind, the man Christ Jesus.

Every Christian is called to be an intercessor. Intercession is work and commitment. To pray for the needs of other believers and those who are lost is also a privilege. Who needs your prayers today?

Lord give me a burden to raise my brothers and sisters to your throne of grace, I pray.

Extended Reading — 1 Chronicles 23-25

ASSURANCE
Overwhelming Knowledge

*Such knowledge is too wonderful for me, too lofty for me to
attain.*   *Psalm 139:6*

David knew his God and what he knew overwhelmed him.

D avid is famously known as the man after God's own heart. King
David sets the premise for this psalm by stating some facts. God
had already taken the effort and had searched him. God knows him,
when he sits and when he rises. God also knows and understands his
thoughts

It is not a question nor speculation. God knows each of us, just as he
knew King David.

God's knowledge is not restricted to the past. He continues to know
each of us, every day, every minute of each day. He knows when we sit,
stand, and think, even where we go. He knows it all.

And this our God knows not just our past and our present but knows
our future too. He knows what we will think or say, what we will do
in the future. He knows more about us than we know about ourselves.

Our God knows and understands us and yet he loves us. He is our God
who protects us, from all sides. He lays his hand upon us.

And this knowledge overwhelms David. He found it difficult to
understand how and why God loves us so much. But the truth is God
knows, loves and protects each of us. And this truth should be our
assurance and comfort as we go through life.

Does what you know of God and his love to overwhelm you too?

May I increase in my knowledge and love for you Lord, I pray.

Extended Reading — Psalm 131, 138-139, 143-145

LEGACY
More than a Physical House

> *Unless the Lord builds the house, the builders labor in vain.*
> *Unless the Lord watches over the city, the guards stand watch in*
> *vain.*   Psalm 127:1

We are creating a legacy.

In this psalm, the Bible gives us three word pictures. We are to be workmen, watchmen, and warriors. The goal of all three is that we will leave a legacy of godliness to our children, our grandchildren, and generations to come.

The 'workman' is not simply building a physical house. He is building a home, a heritage – a godly family line. He is building a legacy that will take the heart, faith, and ways of God into the next generation. That kind of building is more demanding, exacting and even exasperating sometimes.

Leaving a godly legacy will not happen by chance. It needs to be done intentionally and prayerfully. Leaving a godly legacy takes effort and has so much at stake. We cannot afford to not do it well. We are to build lives, homes, and churches that reflect God's glory long after we are gone. We want to leave behind a godliness that people are encouraged by and want to embrace in the generations to come.

God is building his kingdom, one home at a time, and we are workmen with him. Our children are a sacred stewardship from the Lord for whom one day we will need to give account. That does not diminish their responsibility. But we, as adult believers, will one day stand before God and give an account for how we built, watched over the city, and fought the battle on behalf of the next generation. What are you doing today to leave a godly legacy?

Lord help me be a good and effective workman for you, I pray.

Extended Reading — 1 Chronicles 26-29; Psalm 127

FEAR
When Fear Grips

The Lord is with me; I will not be afraid. What can mere mortals do to me? ^{7} The Lord is with me; He is my helper. I look in triumph on my enemies.   *Psalm 118:6-7*

Fear is real.

All of us experience fear in one way or the other. And the Bible recognizes this reality. Throughout the Bible, we are continually encouraged not to be afraid.

One of the many reasons we are afraid is because our vision is limited. The truth is that God is on our side and is fighting powerfully on our behalf. And yet, we cannot see him. The truth is, we often, tend to live our lives by what we see rather than by faith. When challenges and troubles come our way, we focus on them, which we can see, rather than the Lord, whom we cannot see. And fear grips us.

The only way to fight fear is to know this God who is ever with us. We get to know him when we read the Bible and pray regularly. The more we read the Bible, the more we know God. And the more we know God, the more we will be able to trust him and so live a life directed by him.

The apostle Paul had his own times of fear. In Ephesians, he asks them to pray for him to fearlessly make known the gospel (Ephesians 6:19-20). David had his fears too. And he said, when I am afraid, I will put my trust in you (Psalm 56:3).

Everyone has fears. When fear tends to grip you, would you like be willing like Paul to ask for prayer and like David choose to trust him.

Lord, when I am afraid, help me put my trust in you, I pray.

Extended Reading — Psalm 111-118

SUFFERING
Your Plan for Me

Be still before the Lord and wait patiently for him; do not fret when people succeed in their ways when they carry out their wicked schemes.   *Psalm 37:7*

When my head is bowed,

And tears unstopped flow,

And all I can think and see,

Is the injustice done to me.

Open my eyes, Lord, help me see,

You have a marvelous plan for me,

And You will not stop until You see,

Your reflection in a sinner, such as me!!

When at me fly accusations daily,

Slander, gossip are constant company,

When life seems too hard to bear,

And I am in stooped in despair,

Open my eyes, Lord, help me see,

You have a marvelous plan for me.

And You will not stop until You see,

Your reflection in a sinner, such as me!!

When doubt, fear are my regular stalkers,

When I am done, can take it no longer,

When confusion refuses to leave my side,

And all I want to do is run and hide,

Open my eyes, Lord, help me see,

You have a marvelous plan for me.

And You will not stop until You see,

Your reflection in a sinner, such as me!!

Yes, Lord help me remember,

That nothing in my life does enter.

Outside of your loving perfect plan,

For You are my God truly sovereign.

So, open my eyes, Lord, help me see,

You have a marvelous plan for me,

And You will not stop until You see,

Your reflection in a sinner, such as me!!

Extended Reading — 1 Kings 1-2; Psalm 37, 71, 94

QUIET TIME
The Soul's Chewing

I have hidden Your word in my heart that I might not sin against
You.   *Psalm 119:11*

The Bible is the inspired Word of God.

The 66 books of the Bible are collected into two 'libraries' that were written over a period of around 1500 years. Though a very old book written to guide people in their lives centuries ago, this love letter from God remains alive and relevant, still able to answer the needs of people today.

Though this psalm has no title, its style suggests that it originated with David the shepherd boy who became the king of Israel. This is the longest of the psalms and focuses on the Word of God.

This psalm glorifies God and his word. It refers to the scripture in almost every verse. The psalmist says he has hidden God's word in his heart. He spends much time with the word and he meditates on God's word. How can you meditate on God's word?

To meditate is 'the soul's chewing' said the Yorkshire preacher, William Grimshaw, two hundred fifty years ago. To meditate is to focus, to fix our eyes on his ways (v15) so that we understand (v 27).

And as we meditate and remember all that God has done, we are inclined to worship him and delight in his Word. The outcome of our meditation is that we apply what we learn from his word leading to lives transformed for him. Lives that are transformed are aligned with God and his will, bringing him glory and honor.

How are you growing in your love for God's word?

Lord help me meditate on your word and may my life be transformed
for your glory I pray.

Extended Reading — Psalm 119:1-88

OBEDIENCE
Which Direction?

So give your servant a discerning heart to govern your people and to distinguish between right and wrong.   2 Kings 3:9

Solomon is now king of Israel.

The Bible says Solomon showed his love for the Lord by walking according to the instructions given him by his father David. And so God appeared to him and asked him to ask for whatever he wanted.

Solomon's now-famous request for wisdom pleased God. God responds to Solomon's request by promising him three different gifts, two unconditional and one conditional.
God gave Solomon the gift of wisdom that he asked for (v12). 1 Kings 4:29-34 records the details of Solomon's immense wisdom that God gave.

God also gave Solomon wealth and fame. God gave him something that he had not asked for, riches and honor (v13). Solomon would be known as the wealthiest king of his era.

The third gift God gave him was conditional, a long life based on Solomon's obedience. If Solomon would walk in obedience to God, then he would live long (v14). The Bible records that Solomon's obedience was mixed. Though Solomon began well, as his humble request for wisdom shows, he did not end well. He later disobeyed God.

It is not enough to begin well, we need to finish well too. Obedience to God proves our love for him (1 John 5:2-3), shows our faithfulness to him (1 John 2:3-6), glorifies him in the world (1 Peter 2:12) and opens paths of blessing for us (John 13:17). The extent of our obedience to God will determine the direction our lives will take. In which direction is your life going?

Lord, please help me be faithful to you to the very end of my life, I pray.

Extended Reading — 1 Kings 3-4; 2 Chronicles 1; Psalm 72

BIBLE
The Blessing of Hiding

Your word, Lord, is eternal; it stands firm in the heavens. [90] Your faithfulness continues through all generations; you established the earth, and it endures. [91] Your laws endure to this day, for all things serve you.   *Psalm 119:89-91*

God's word is perfect and all-sufficient.

This psalm written by a man who went through great trouble in his life has come through it with a deep and passionate understanding of God's unfailing love (v75-77). The author through his pain and suffering has learned to cling to the truths that he learned from the scriptures.

This psalm affirms the character of God. In almost every verse, the word of God is mentioned. This psalm magnifies the law of God and points to its excellence and relevance. And the psalmist speaks from his own experience of the benefits of the law. There are different terms that refer to the word of God throughout this psalm – law, testimonies, precepts, statutes, commandments, judgments, word and ordinances.

The word of God reflects God's nature and we learn that we can trust his character. God's word is enough to make us wise, to train us in righteousness and equip us for every good work (2 Timothy 3:15-17). The word of God is a wonderful reflection of the amazing character of God. We also learn about God's plans and purposes for humankind. And we are blessed if we delight ourselves in this law and meditate on it day and night (Psalm 1:2).

This psalm reminds us that if we hide God's word in our hearts, it will keep us from sinning (v11). What are you hiding in your heart?

Lord increase my love for your word, I pray.

Extended Reading — Psalm 119:89-176

MARRIAGE
The Priority of Love

Let him lead me to the banquet hall and let his banner over me
be love.   Song of Solomon 2:4

Song of Solomon also known as the Song of Songs, is a superlative, meaning this is the best of all of Solomon's works.

This lyric poem is written to extol the love between a husband and his wife. This poem clearly presents marriage as God's design. A man and woman are to live together within the context of marriage, loving each other spiritually, emotionally, and physically.

The poetry takes the form of a dialogue between a husband (the king) and his wife (the Shulamite). This book is a literal depiction of marriage, there are some elements that foreshadow the Church and her relationship with her king, the Lord Jesus. Today's verse describes the experience of every believer who is sought and bought by the Lord Jesus. We are in a place of great spiritual wealth and are covered by his love.

We live in a world that is confused about marriage. The increasing prevalence of divorce and modern attempts to redefine marriage are in sharp contrast to Solomon's song. This biblical poet says that marriage is to be celebrated, enjoyed, and revered. It also gives some practical tips on strengthening one's marriage.

This book reminds us to prioritize and know our spouse. Encouragement and not criticism is to be the watchword. We are to make it a priority to enjoy each other and delight in God's gift of married love. We are to renew our vows and work through problems. Divorce is not a solution.

God intends marriage to be a place of deep secure love.

Lord help me work at building my marriage and my spouse, I pray.

Extended Reading — Song of Solomon 1-8

FAITH
Let Go

Trust in the Lord with all your heart and lean not on your own understanding; [6] *in all your ways submit to him, and he will make your paths straight.* Proverbs 3:5-6

To let go is the need of the hour,
To let go is the strength of the heart.
Yet, to hold on is the will of the flesh,
But, to hold on, is the knell of death.

Let go of the past, and its pain,
Let of go of failures that bring no gain.
Let go of bitterness and of anger,
And every thought leads to slander.

To hold on is death, of faith,
Of trust and confidence, of the truth.
That the Lord alone is the One,
Who can be trusted, more than anyone.

If only in child-like trust,
You would to him entrust.
Your every care, strife and test,
For in Him is perfect peace and rest.

Storms of life though may assail,
Yet inexplicable peace that will never fail.
Would be your assured portion,
No matter what your life's commotion.

Extended Reading — Proverbs 1-3

DISCIPLINE
Away with the Snooze Button

Go to the ant, you sluggard; consider its ways and be wise! [7]
It has no commander, no overseer or ruler, yet it stores its
provisions in summer and gathers its food at harvest.

Proverbs 6:6-8

There is great value in hard work.

The Bible often points to nature to help us learn valuable lessons.
Christ sends us to the school of the birds of the air, the lilies of the
field, to learn to depend on God to provide for us (Matthew 6:25-29).
In Jeremiah 8:7, we are pointed to the stork, the dove, and the thrush,
to learn to take the seasons of grace and not to lose opportunities that
God puts in our hands.

The difference between success and failure is often hard work. The ant is
the proverbial insect of hard work. It is considered even more laborious
than even the bee and careful of its young. And King Solomon, speaking
to the sluggard or lazy person, says go take some lessons from that small
insect, the ant.

The ant is wise and worthy of being imitated because she works hard
without being told to work hard. She has no captain. No one who gives
instructions or imposes work. The ethics of diligence comes from within.

The ant does not work hard because someone is watching. The ant works
hard when the work is to be done, in summer and in the harvest. She
works with forethought. She plans ahead.

Parents often find that their children need to be watched, monitored
and even nagged sometimes to do the work they need to do. But as
adults, each one is to take responsibility to do their work. Where do
you need to work harder without having to be monitored?

Lord help me work hard and be diligent, I pray.

Extended Reading — Proverbs 4-6

WISDOM
Guarded by the Word

My son, keep my words and store up my commands within you.
² Keep my commands and you will live; guard my teachings as
the apple of your eye. ³ Bind them on your fingers; write them
on the tablet of your heart.   *Proverbs 7:1-3*

Solomon emphasizes the need to keep and understand God's word and a father's wisdom.

The implication is not that reading the Bible will provide any magical protection. And yet a person who begins to know the Bible, treasure it and meditate on it, will soon enough begin to keep God's commands. And keeping these commands will lead to life.

Solomon says, to his son, be intentional, work at storing up these commands. He is to guard these teachings as the apple of his eye. The apple of the eye refers to the pupil of the eye, which we go to great lengths to protect. So also, we are to honor and protect God's word by obeying it.

Solomon counsels his son to have a living breathing relationship with the word of God. The word was not just to be in his mind but to be engraved on his heart. It was to rule his heart and all his actions.

God's word is powerful and relevant for every aspect of life. All scripture is God-breathed and is useful for teaching, rebuking, correcting and training in righteousness (2 Timothy 3:16)

How will you increase your time with reading, studying and applying God's word?

Lord, increase in me love for your word, I pray.

Extended Reading — Proverbs 7-9

GOSSIP
Filter Your Words

A gossip betrays a confidence, but a trustworthy person keeps a
secret.   *Proverbs 11:13*

Anyone who gossips to you will also gossip about you.

Gossip is the casual or unconstrained conversation or reports about other people, typically involving details which are not confirmed as true.

The unfaithful talebearer or gossip is one who goes from person to person making it his or her business to scatter reports. Such a person loves the power and intrigue of revealing secrets. To be able to reveal secrets gives a sense of power that is used for their own advancement.

A person of a faithful spirit is one who conceals a matter. A trustworthy person is guided by love and wisdom and knows when it is appropriate to conceal a matter.

Socrates who was lauded for his wisdom advocated the 'Test of Three' as a filter to be applied on any rumor. The tests of truth, goodness, and usefulness. In this test, you are to filter the information you intend to pass on through three questions. First, ask yourself if the information you are about to pass on is true and not some hearsay. The second is to ask yourself if the information that is being passed on is something good about the person. And finally ask yourself if the information to be conveyed is useful, either to the hearer or the person about whom it is. And if the information you intend to share does not pass all these tests, do not pass it on.

This filter has been found to be very practical and effective in stemming unnecessary gossip. You will be surprised how little information passes through all three filters. Would you choose to apply the 'Test of Three' to your conversations?

Lord guard my mouth that I may not sin with my words, I pray.

Extended Reading — Proverbs 10-12

WORDS
Are You a Murderer?

The soothing tongue is a tree of life, but a perverse tongue crushes the spirit.   *Proverbs 15:4*

How many people have you murdered in the past week?

That would be a ridiculous question to ask decent law-abiding citizens, right? Yet if the question is when was the last time you were angry with someone or the last time you expressed yourself in sharp, cutting words would it seems as ridiculous?

We all get angry, and quite often too. And in our anger, we end up saying things that are sharp and painful. The Bible is very clear about anger and does not take it lightly. In Matthew 5:21-22, the Lord Jesus says, anyone who is angry with his brother or sister, will be subject to judgment. And anyone who says, 'you fool' will be in the danger of the fire of hell.

Our words matter. We are called to use our words with caution. Proverbs 18:21 says that the tongue has the power of life and death. Words have a lot of power. Words once spoken cannot be taken back. Children who have been told 'you will never amount to anything' or 'you are useless' or 'you are a failure' often have grown up and lived it out.

The Bible says the words we speak have immense power. The power to give life or crush the spirit. Words have the power to encourage, give life or break the spirit of a person. Good words are like a tree that continually brings life from its shade and fruit.

So, the next time you are furious and are about to lash out, would you pause and ask God for grace to bless instead.

Lord help be one who blesses with my words, I pray.

Extended Reading — Proverbs 13-15

PRIDE
Watch Where You Go

Pride goes before destruction, a haughty spirit before a fall.

Proverbs 16:18

Pride is overinflated self-confidence or the attitude of a haughty spirit.

The Bible is full of examples of proud people, from Goliath and King Nebuchadnezzar to the rich fool and King Herod. God judged all of them for their pride. Lucifer the beautiful and powerful archangel is the ultimate example of pride. He was not satisfied with his God-given glorious position. He wanted the honor and worship that belonged to God. He rebelled against God. He lost his position and fell from heaven and took a third of the angels with him (Revelation 12:4). And so, Lucifer became Satan and has been corrupting the world ever since, with his pride.

Pride wrongly exalts self. At the root of all pride is the sense that we know better than everyone else, including God. Pride keeps us from a close relationship with God. The Lord will not tolerate anyone with a haughty look or an arrogant heart (Psalm 101:5). Pride in the heart is reflected in the face and attitudes, through our lifted brows, turned up noses or critical looks and attitudes. Pride leads to idolatry.

Pride is a heart condition that we need to continually guard against by seeking humility (1 Peter 5:6). We are to continually examine ourselves in the light of the Scripture (2 Corinthians 13:5). Remembering God's grace to us and how undeserving we are (Ephesians 2:8-9) gives a much-needed perspective. We are also to practice the art of considering others better than ourselves (Philippians 2:3) and seek to serve rather than to be served (Mark 10:44-45). How would you say you are doing on pride?

Lord keep me ever humble in your sight I pray.

Extended Reading — Proverbs 16-18

BIBLE
Care for Some Knowledge?

Stop listening to instruction, my son, and you will stray from the words of knowledge.   *Proverbs 19:27*

Listening requires humility.

Solomon counsels his son to listen to his instruction. He also warns him that to stop listening is to go astray from the path of wisdom. To stay on the path of wisdom is a matter of choice. And yet to stop listening is to ask for trouble.

To listen means to give heed to or pay attention. Listening is other-focused activity. To listen one must, first, take the focus off, of yourself and shift it to the other who is speaking.

When you listen to another what you are saying is, you are important to me, what you are saying is important to me. When you listen, you are also showing a teachable spirit, acknowledging that you may not be the expert on the matter. When you listen, you display a humble attitude of one who is willing to listen and learn.

The Bible says, if you stop listening to instructions, you will stray from knowledge. When you buy a new product, the first thing you do is read the instruction manual. Only then can you figure out how to use the product in the right and most effective way.

Instruction for life often comes from parents, elders, mentors. But most importantly instruction for our lives come from the one who created us, in the owner's manual, the Bible. Who better than our creator to guide and instruct to live out our lives to the best potential. The Bible guides and instructs us helping us grow in knowledge. So, would you say you are growing in knowledge?

Lord help me humbly listen to your instruction and so grow in knowledge, I pray.

Extended Reading — Proverbs 19-21

PARENTING
What are You Passing On

Train up a child in the way he should go, even when he is old,
he will not depart from it.   Proverbs 22:6

Children need training.

The job of a parent is not to simply let them grow up anyway, but to train them, in the way he or she should go. The child needs to be guided and directed in the way he or she must go.

Parents are stewards of the children God entrusts in their care. And so, the way the child should go refers to training your child in God's ways. To help the child grow in the path of wisdom and life as against the way of folly and destruction (v5). Parents are to teach and discipline their children in the ways of the Lord and for the Lord.

The way he should go also refers to the child's individual way or inclination. Parenting involves discerning and working on the strengths and weaknesses of each child, recognizing that no two children are the same. According to the child's way is to respect each child's individuality and build them. And yet that does not mean to give in to their self-will.

And a child so trained, will not depart from it. This is a wonderful promise especially to parents troubled over their adult children. A child that is trained in the proper way, though they depart for a season, will return and not depart from it.

The pressures on children today are so high. And the pressures on parents even higher. And in a world like this to teach the children the ways of the Lord and to model them in one's own life, is often the greatest challenge parents face.

Lord help me rely on you for wisdom as I train up my children in the
way they should go, I pray.

Extended Reading — Proverbs 22-24

CALLING
Uniquely You

So Solomon built the temple and completed it.   1 Kings 6:14

Solomon builds the temple of God.

David, Solomon's father had wanted to build a great temple for God a generation earlier, but God had forbidden it because he was a man of war and had shed blood. The Lord had said that Solomon his son was the one who would build the temple of the Lord (1 Chronicles 28:3, 6). And God kept his word.

Solomon builds the house of the Lord, in Jerusalem on Mount Moriah. That was the place where the Lord had appeared to his father David, on the threshing floor of Araunah (2 Chronicles 3:1).

The new, stationary temple was to replace the portable tabernacle constructed during the wilderness wanderings. This temple was an extremely beautiful and ornate structure. The construction and dedication of Solomon's temple are described in 1 Kings 6-8.

The Bible says, no hammer or chisel or any iron tool was heard in the temple while it was being built (v7). This speaks of how God works in his people who are his Temple. Often the greatest work in the Kingdom of God happens quietly.

Though David was more than willing and wanted to build the temple of the Lord, the Lord assigned that task to his son, Solomon. God has different tasks and roles that he has for each of his children, and one cannot do what another is to do. Each of us is to do what God is uniquely calling us to do, not what someone else is doing. And as each of us do our respective parts, the Grand Weaver, weaves his beautiful design. What is God calling you to do today?

Lord help me to willingly obey you and do all that you call me to do, I pray.

Extended Reading — 1 Kings 5-6; 2 Chronicles 2-3

PRIORITY
Order of Priority

It took Solomon thirteen years, however, to complete the construction of his palace.   *1 Kings 7:1*

Simple but unexpected tests often reveal the deepest truths of the human heart.

Solomon spent seven years building the temple (1 Kings 6:38), but thirteen years building his own house. The temple was glorious, but it seems that Solomon wanted a house that was more glorious than the temple.

It seems like Solomon's priority for his own personal comfort and luxurious tastes was higher than God's house. Solomon's house was magnificent (v6-12). And at the end of a detailed description of Solomon's palace, the writer almost as an afterthought mentions that some of the great architectural features of the palace were also found in the temple. It seems like, as great as the temple was, Solomon's palace was better.

When Solomon made his palace more spectacular than the temple, it said something about his values. Old Europe has many magnificent churches and cathedrals and that reflected the values of the people of those times. Most magnificent buildings in today's world are used for business, shopping, or entertainment and that says something about our values. God reminds us to give careful thought to our ways in Haggai 1 and speaks powerfully to those who think more about their house than they do for the house of God.

Solomon finished the work of building the temple. But the work of spreading the gospel is never complete for a Christian. The Bible says the harvest is plenty and the laborers are few (Luke 10:2). There is much to be done yet to build the church of God today. What priority do God and his work have in your life?

Lord may I never put anything above my love for you, I pray.

Extended Reading — 1 Kings 7; 2 Chronicles 4

HOLINESS
Stricken and Awed

When the priests withdrew from the Holy Place, the cloud filled the temple of the Lord. [11] And the priests could not perform their service because of the cloud, for the glory of the Lord filled his temple.   *1 Kings 8:10-11*

The Temple was not ready until the Ark of the Covenant was brought.

Solomon assembled the elders of Israel and all the heads of the tribes. This was to be a spectacular opening ceremony for the temple. And the priests brought the ark, the most important item, as God had commanded.

And when the priests withdrew from the temple, the cloud filled the temple.

This was the cloud of glory, seen often in the Old and New Testaments, sometimes called the cloud of *Shekinah* glory. It is hard to define the glory of God. It could be called the radiance of his character and presence which was manifested here in a cloud.

This is the cloud that stood by the Israelites in the wilderness and the door of the temple. It also from which God met Moses and spoke to Israel. This is the cloud that was present at the transfiguration of Jesus (Luke 9:34-35) and the cloud of glory that received Jesus into heaven at his ascension (Acts 1:9). It is also the cloud that will display the glory of Christ when he returns triumphantly (Revelation 1:7).

God is good and loving but he is also holy. Isaiah, Peter, John, and others felt awed in the presence of God. They were stricken by the extent of the difference between their own sinfulness and the holiness of God.

What is your response to God's holiness and your own sinfulness?

Lord help me ever live aware of your holiness, I pray.

Extended Reading — 1 Kings 8; 2 Chronicles 5

PRIDE
My Pride Blocks

If my people, who are called by my name, will humble themselves and pray and seek my face and turn from their wicked ways, then I will hear from heaven, and I will forgive their sin and will heal their land.   *2 Chronicles 7:14*

Our nation needs our prayer.

King Solomon has just finished building this amazing temple of the Lord. The Lord now appears to him. The Lord tells him that he has heard his prayer and accepts the place for himself as a temple of sacrifices (v12).

The Lord talks about the future, possible problems, and its solution. He tells King Solomon, there would be times in the future when he shuts the heaven and there is no rain, or he sends some plague, or there is some national catastrophe. And when that happens, if his people would humble themselves and pray, then the he would hear and answer and deliver.

Every nation of the world has its own challenges. We, as God's people, are called to pray for our nations. God says his people, those who believe in him, are to seek and call unto him.

Prayer comes from a place of humility. Prayer says, Lord I can't but I believe you can. Prayer shows need and dependence. Prayer shows our inability and God's amazing ability.

Our prayers matter.

Even if you and I are not in positions of governing authority, we are still in powerful positions. We are called to humble ourselves and pray. We are to be prayer warriors for our nation.

Is there any form of pride in you that is keeping you from praying for your nation?

Lord give me the grace to be humble and to pray for my nation, I pray.

Extended Reading — 2 Chronicles 6-7; Psalm 136

PEACE
Ever Safe Remain

He heals the brokenhearted and binds up their wounds.

Psalm 147:3

When situations and people cause your peace to yearn,

And persons and personalities cause you pain,

When people and situations around you confuse,

And to make any logic or sense, they simply refuse,

When moods, tantrums that challenge reason,

Consume you, your days and last beyond a season,

Lean on him and not your own understanding,

For you will gain his peace and precious learning.

If you choose to walk with him, to him stay near,

Though life is tough and filled with unnumbered fear,

He will teach, and you will continue to learn,

That in his arms you safe and accepted remain.

His arms will envelop and comfort you,

As you run to him, he is waiting for you,

With arms outstretched, and love overflowing,

Choose to run to him, as each day is unfolding.

His love is unconditional and to him you are special,

Just as you are, with your wrinkles, warts and all.

And may that ever remain your confidence and song,

Not cause all the pain is suddenly just gone.

But because your Lord he does over you rejoice,

For you are his child, and that is his choice.

For you, he chose to die and rise again,

So that in his precious arms, ever safe you remain.

Extended Reading — Psalm 134, 146-150

PRAYER
Patiently Wait

The Lord said to him: "I have heard the prayer and plea you have made before me; I have consecrated this temple, which you have built, by putting my Name there forever. My eyes and my heart will always be there."   1 Kings 9:3

The Lord visits Solomon a second time.

God graciously appeared to Solomon at the beginning of his reign (1 Kings 3:5-9). And now he appeared to him a second time. What a blessing and a privilege.

And at the dedication of the temple, Solomon had prayed a great prayer of dedication (1 Kings 8:22-53). God gave Solomon an immediate answer of approval at the time of dedication, when the sacrifices were consumed with fire from heaven (2 Chronicles 7:1-7). And now the Lord said to him, after what seems like some years, that he has heard his prayer.

The Lord says, that he has consecrated the temple that Solomon built. Solomon in the power of the Holy Spirit did the physical, outward work of building the temple. But the consecration of the temple, however, was God's work.

We can do the physical outward work but only God can do the inward and spiritual part. When God calls us to a task, we are to be faithful to obediently do all that God asks us to do. And then we need to trust God to do the heart work.

When we pray for people, sometimes for years, it can be tiring. Fear, doubt and unbelief tend to creep in. But wait patiently on God. He will show up and answer. He will bring change in the hearts and minds of the ones you are praying for. Don't give up. Pray expectantly.

Lord help me wait on you patiently in prayer, I pray.

Extended Reading — 1 Kings 9; 2 Chronicles 8

RECONCILIATION
Exhaust All Possibilities

What you have seen with your eyes [8] do not bring hastily to court, for what will you do in the end if your neighbor puts you to shame? [9] If you take your neighbor to court, do not betray another's confidence, [10] or the one who hears it may shame you and the charge against you will stand.   *Proverbs 25:8-10*

Going to court should never be the first resort.

A court of law may sometimes be necessary. Solomon reminds us to always try to resolve the dispute outside of court anyway possible. Only if really needed to go to court. Paul reminds the church what a bad testimony it is when one believer takes another to court to have disputes between them settled by unbelievers (1 Corinthians 6:1-8).

Another strong reason to avoid going to court is the high probability of being put to shame. You might just lose. There is also the possibility that when you debate your case outside of court with your neighbor you discover some truth, they know that could put you to shame.

And if you finally do end up in court, Solomon says, be careful not to betray another's trust. What someone has said to you in confidence should not be used in public to win your case.

When you consider all these possibilities, the option of going to court to resolve an issue should slide to the bottom. Prayerfully consider other ways to settle. Be humble in your approach and willing to accept your role in the problem. Exhaust all other possibilities. Never do anything that will tarnish your Christian witness. Whom can you pray for and encourage to resolve their dispute in other ways?

Lord help me be a channel of your peace when reconciliation is needed, I pray.

Extended Reading — Proverbs 25-26

HUMILITY
One Day At a Time

> *Do not boast about tomorrow, for you do not know what a day may bring.*   *Proverbs 27:1*

Stay humble.

Solomon cautions against the human tendency to be overly confident in what the future holds. While the fact is that you and I don't know what the future holds. We are not even able to control what will happen in the next half hour.

There are some of us who are tempted to consult different medium of astrology, tarot cards or people who claim to be able to tell what our future holds. But the Bible is clear that we are not to try and figure out our future (Leviticus 19:31). We are to trust God with our futures.

Spurgeon said, "To know the good might lead us to presumption, to know the evil might tempt us to despair. Happy for us is it that our eyes cannot penetrate the thick veil which God hangs between us and tomorrow, that we cannot see beyond the spot where we now are, and that, in a certain sense, we are utterly ignorant as to the details of the future. We may, indeed, be thankful for our ignorance."

This is not, however, to say that we are not to plan wisely for the future. We are to use our God-given wisdom and resources to make wise choices about our future. At the same time, we are cautioned against over-confidence in one's ability to control the future. Only God holds our future. So we are called to live and plan our lives wisely in total God-confidence and not self or people confidence.

How will you reflect your God-confidence about your future, to those around you?

Lord may I trust you completely, even about my future, I pray.

Extended Reading — Proverbs 27-29

LIFE PURPOSE
Closer to You, Daily

Yet when I surveyed all that my hands had done and what I had toiled to achieve, everything was meaningless, a chasing after the wind; nothing was gained under the sun.   Ecclesiastes 2:11

What a state of utter hopelessness.

The book of Ecclesiastes paints a perfect picture of life when God is taken out of the frame. It is presented as the experiences of the Philosopher or 'Teacher' who deliberately places himself in the shoes of a godless person. And the resulting worldview is one of emptiness and meaninglessness (1:2). The writer shows that the human mind is unable to come up with convincing answers to the meaning of life, without the help of God.

Humans have great potential for creativity and technical advancement. And yet, when that potential is not governed by a God-centered worldview, it leads to indiscipline and slavery of different kinds. Identity and significance elude those who do not know God. Revelation 3:17 says that without God we are wretched, miserable, poor blind and naked and we do not even know it. And that is the sorry state that a life away from God looks like.

Jesus and the apostles taught that man's problems don't so much stem from the outward circumstances as from the inner state. Problems and relationship issues stem from jealousy, selfishness, pride, greed, covetousness, and all wrong motives. And that a choice to be friends with the world makes one naturally the enemy of God. A heart that is proud God opposes. But if we come near to God, he will come near to us (James 4:1-10). Is yours a life that is experiencing God near to you each day?

Lord draw me close to you, never let me go, I pray.

Extended Reading — Ecclesiastes 1-6

JUDGMENT
Day of Reckoning

That's the whole story. Here now is my conclusion: Fear God and obey his commands, for this is everyone's duty. Ecclesiastes 12:13

A spirit of hopeless despair the predominant theme of this book.
The book of Ecclesiastes is an unusual and difficult book in the Bible. The words of the preacher show us the futility and foolishness of a life lived with an eternal perspective.

Ecclesiastes does not question the existence of God. The author is no atheist. God is always there in the picture. The question, however, is whether God matters or not. The answer to that question is vitally connected to a responsibility to God that goes beyond this earthly life.

In search for this answer, the preacher thoroughly examined the emptiness and futility of a life lived without the perspective of eternity. And then finally concludes the necessity of eternity.

And so, after writing much of the book about the futility of life if not for a perspective of eternity, the preacher concludes the whole matter. We are to fear God and keep his commandments and that is our ultimate responsibility. Obedience to God pleases God. Obedience to God also fulfills our destiny.

There sure is a day of reckoning, a day when each of us will indeed need to give an account.

The preacher warns us that God will call into account every person and every work, including every secret thing, whether good or bad (v14). And so living with a perspective of eternity brings purpose to life.

How does knowing that you will be called to give an account impact what you do and think daily?

Lord help me live each day ever aware that I am accountable to you, I pray.

Extended Reading — Ecclesiastes 7-12

JUDGMENT
Deserved Judgment

Then he said to Jeroboam, "Take ten pieces for yourself, for this is what the Lord, the God of Israel, says: 'See, I am going to tear the kingdom out of Solomon's hand and give you ten tribes.   *1 Kings 11:31*

God ordained the division of Israel.

Solomon had a rich heritage of faith from his father David. He had his personal experiences too. And yet Solomon went after other gods. God was displeased with Solomon's embrace of idolatry. He ordained the division of Israel.

Solomon's kingdom was an outstanding example of wealth, military power, and prestige. God had promised the entire kingdom of Israel to the descendants of David forever. The only requirement was that they remained obedient to him They could not remain faithful for even one generation.

God announces the division of the kingdom. A part of the kingdom would be faithful to the descendants of David and part of it will be under a different dynasty. Even in this great judgment, God mingled undeserved mercy with deserved judgment. For the sake of David, he even delayed this judgment until after Solomon's generation.

Jeroboam and David were appointed by God to follow disobedient kings. David waited for the Lord to give him the throne, and God blessed his reign. Jeroboam did not wait for God but made his own way to the throne, and God did not bless his reign.

We sometimes think that great spiritual experiences will keep us from sin and will keep us faithful to God. That was not true for the wisest man who ever lived, and it will not be the case with us either.

Lord keep me from allowing anything to take priority over you, I pray.

Extended Reading — 1 Kings 10-11; 2 Chronicles 9

INTEGRITY
A Wise Prayer

*"Two things I ask of you, Lord; do not refuse me before I die:
keep falsehood and lies far from me; give me neither poverty nor
riches but give me only my daily bread. ⁹ Otherwise, I may have
too much and disown you and say, 'Who is the Lord?' Or I may
become poor and steal, and so dishonor the name of my God.*

Proverbs 30:7-9

Agur earnestly asked God for two things, on this side of eternity.

Proverbs 30 is a collection of wisdom from Agur son of Jaekh, a man
known only in this chapter of the Bible. The author recognizes his
tendency to forget God when life is too easy and to turn in desperation
away from God when life is hard.

Agur has two requests. The first is for personal integrity. He wanted to
be a man known by truth, not lies. He didn't want the deceptiveness of
wealth and poverty anywhere near him. While riches give the impression,
we don't need God, poverty makes us feel that God is of no help or
that his laws are impossible to keep.

Agur's second request was, give me neither poverty nor riches. He
wanted to be satisfied with God's provision in his life. Agur's concern
was that either extreme might lead him to profane the name of God.
He didn't want to arrogantly deny God because he felt he was so rich
he didn't need God. Nor did he want to be so poor that he would use
poverty as an excuse to sin.

Agur was a wise man and yet if he felt tempted to allow riches to profane
the name of God, how much more each of us.

God's glory motivated Agur's prayer. What motivates yours?

Lord that my prayers would be motivated by your glory, I pray.

Extended Reading — Proverbs 30-31

COUNSEL
Itching Ears

But Rehoboam rejected the advice the elders gave him and consulted the young men who had grown up with him and were serving him.   *2 Kings 12:8*

Rehoboam became king after his father, Solomon.

Rehoboam, the son of Solomon, was assumed to be the next king. This was a logical continuation of the Davidic dynasty. But interestingly, Rehoboam was the only son of Solomon that we know by name. Solomon had 1,000 wives and concubines, yet we read of one son he had to bear up his name, and he was a fool.

Solomon was a great king, but he took a lot from the people. The people of Israel wanted relief from the heavy taxation and forced service of Solomon's reign. They approached Rehoboam and offered their allegiance if he agreed to this.

Wisely, Rehoboam asked the counsel of these older, experienced men. They seemed to advise Solomon well. The elders knew that Rehoboam could not expect the same loyalty from the people that Solomon had. Rehoboam had to relate to the people based on who he was, not on who his father was.

If he showed kindness and a servant's heart to the people, they would love and serve him forever. This was good advice. But Rehoboam rejected the advice of the elders and chose to go by the wicked counsel of the younger men.

Advice shopping is a familiar, but unwise practice. Here you keep asking different people for advice until you find someone who will tell you what your itching ears want to hear. It is wise to have a few trusted counselors who tell you even what you don't want to hear. Do you have godly people in your life who give you wise counsel?

Lord give me a humble and wise heart to even accept counsel that is difficult, I pray.

Extended Reading — 1 Kings 12-14

WITNESS
Impact of Independence

The leaders of Israel and the king humbled themselves and said,
"The Lord is just."   *2 Chronicles 12:6*

Rehoboam became established as king.

And the Bible says, after Rehoboam's position as king was established and he had become strong, he and all Israel with him abandoned the law of the Lord (2 Chronicles 12:1). Rehoboam trusted God till the time that he felt he needed him and abandoned God when he grew. And he led the people away from God and led the entire kingdom into sin with him.

And so, the Lord gave them into the hands of Shishak, king of Egypt. Shishak took the fortified cities of Judah and came to Jerusalem. This a serious threat to the southern kingdom. Shemaiah the prophet met the leaders of Judah and reminded them that because they had abandoned God, he had now abandoned them to Shishak' (v5). This was a correction that matched the offense.

If Judah insisted on forsaking God, they would find themselves forsaken in the day of their need. The danger of telling God "leave me alone" is that someday he may answer that prayer.

But the leaders and the king, realize their mistake and humbly accept that the Lord is right. This national repentance was initiated by the leaders of the kingdom.

Great moving of the Spirit of God in history, have been seen when leaders have passionately turned to God in repentance and humility. As leaders in different areas of life, be it as parents, or leaders at work or church, or just leaders to those younger in the faith, each of us are accountable for our spiritual walk. How is your spiritual walk enabling others to turn to God?

Lord may my walk with you encourage those watching, I pray.

Extended Reading — 2 Chronicles 10-12

SEEKING GOD
Stay on Course

The Lord is with you when you are with Him If you seek Him,
He will be found by you, but if you forsake Him, He will forsake
you.   *2 Chronicles 15:2*

King Asa was someone who knew what the Lord wanted of him.

Interestingly, this promise and warning that the Lord sends Azariah with, came not at the beginning of his reign as king of Judab, but much after.

Now the Bible records that King Asa did what was right in the eyes of the Lord (2 Chronicles 14:2). He had already done much to remove all the idols and pagan gods from Judah. He had sought the Lord and the Lord had also given him victory against the Cushites. And then, Azaria is sent by the Lord with this warning and promise to the king

To seek is to go in search or quest of, to pursue, and to follow.

Seeking the Lord is not a one-time activity but an ongoing, lifelong habit of the believer. And we are to seek the Lord all through life and its choices and decisions, not just in the initial walk with the Lord. Nor is seeking the Lord to be restricted to some areas of life but is to pervade every decision and choice.

And yet, if after knowing the truth, we still choose to forsake him, then the Bible says it very simply, he will forsake us too. If after knowing the truth we still insist on delighting in wickedness, then the Lord himself will send a powerful delusion so that we believe the lie (2 Thessalonians 2:11-12).

Are you walking with him daily or have you abandoned him somewhere along the way?

Lord may I ever seek you, all the days of my life.

Extended Reading — 1 Kings 15:1-24; 2 Chronicles 13-16

SPIRITUAL WARFARE
Are You Armed for Battle?

*They taught throughout Judah, taking with them the Book of
the Law of the Lord; they went around to all the towns of Judah
and taught the people.*   *2 Chronicles 17:9*

Jehoshaphat strengthened his kingdom.

Jehoshaphat, the son of Asa came to the throne of Judah. He Jehoshaphat
recognized that the northern kingdom was a danger to Judah militarily,
politically, and especially spiritually. And so he strengthened his defenses
against this threat.

And the Bible says the Lord was with Jehoshaphat because he followed the
ways of his father David before him (v3). Now David was Jehoshaphat's
ancestor, not his father. Asa his father though a good king did not finish
well. And yet Jehoshaphat chose to do right in the sight of the Lord.

There are some who use the excuse of unbelieving parents for one's own
spiritual failure. But the fact is today, unlike the days of Jehoshaphat, we
have the Bible and many godly examples to follow. We have no excuse.

By the third year of his reign, Jehoshaphat had the Levites brought in.
They were assigned the task of teaching God's law throughout the towns
of Judah. This was the wisest and best policy the security-conscious
king of Judah could adopt. Teaching God's law not only equipped the
people spiritually but also sent out the message to the surrounding
nations that Jehoshaphat's power was much more than the physical
army. Though Jehoshaphat had strengthened his military defense, it
was when he established a preaching ministry in all the cities, that his
enemies were afraid and made no war. Are you arming yourself for
life's battles with God's word?

Lord help strengthen myself in you and our word, I pray.

Extended Reading — 1 Kings 15:25-34; 1 Kings 16:1-34; 2 Chronicles 17

DEPRESSION
Miserably Miserable

*while he himself went a day's journey into the wilderness. He
came to a broom bush, sat down under it and prayed that he
might die. "I have had enough, Lord," he said. "Take my life; I
am no better than my ancestors."*   1 Kings 19:4

Elijah was depressed.

God had used Elijah mightily. Elijah's prophecy, under God's direction,
had closed the skies. There had been a drought in the land for three
whole years. Rains would come again only at Elijah's word. During the
drought, God had so wonderfully provided for Elijah through a raven
and a brook. And when the brook dried up, God sent him to a widow
in Zarephath.

And then came the spectacular victory on Mount Carmel. Elijah
contested the prophets of Baal and Asherah and proved that Yahweh
the Lord God of Israel was God indeed. God had sent down fire from
heaven and consumed a soaking wet sacrifice and a waterlogged altar.
The victory was decisive.

When Jezebel, King Ahab's evil queen, threatened to kill him, Elijah ran.
He was ready to give up everything and simply die. Forgotten were the
recent amazing victories. Forgotten was God's faithfulness experienced
in abundance. All forgotten.

But God did not judge or blame him, instead provided him what he
needed for the moment. He gave him food and rest. God did not give
up on Elijah. He was not done with Elijah but prepared him for the
next phase of his ministry. God does not give up on us either, nor is
he done with us yet. Will you remind yourself to trust God when you
feel like just giving up?

*Lord remind me that you understand and have not given up on me,
I pray.*

Extended Reading — 1 Kings 17-19

CHOICES

Choice to Make, Daily

> *Ahab said to Naboth, "Let me have your vineyard to use for*
> *a vegetable garden since it is close to my palace. In exchange I*
> *will give you a better vineyard or, if you prefer, I will pay you*
> *whatever it is worth."* ³ *But Naboth replied, "The Lord forbid*
> *that I should give you the inheritance of my ancestors."*
>
> *1 Kings 21:2-3*

King Ahab coveted.

King Ahab asked Naboth for his vineyard and promised to pay for it. But Naboth refused the offer. Naboth's response was out of reverence and obedience to God's command not because he was selfish. He had a God-given right to keep his land and not sell it (Numbers 36:7).

King Ahab was evil and did not respect God's laws (1 Kings 16:30). He married Jezebel, who was not an Israelite, but an idol worshipper who practiced witchcraft (2 Kings 9:22). Jezebel killed the Lord's prophets (1 Kings 18:4).

And when Ahab did not get what he wanted, he pouted like a child rather than repent and turn away from it. When Jezebel finds out she takes matters into her own hands. She has Naboth an innocent man put to death so that her husband could now own the vineyard he wanted (v7-16).

But God sees everything and remains the righteous judge. Ahab had no excuse for living a wicked life. God had sent him prophets with his truth. And now he sends Elijah to Ahab to tell him what punishment his wickedness would bring on him (v17-19).

God reveals his truth to us each time we hear God's Word. To walk in his light or continue in a life darkened by sin, is a choice we make. What's your choice?

Help me Lord to respond in obedience each time, I pray.

Extended Reading — 1 Kings 20-21

COURAGE
In the Face of Danger

Then Micaiah answered, "I saw all Israel scattered on the hills like sheep without a shepherd, and the LORD said, 'These people have no master. Let each one go home in peace.'" 1 Kings 22:17

Micaiah was a fearless and true prophet of God.

King Ahab of Israel asks King Jehoshaphat of Judah to help him in this dispute against Syria. Jehoshaphat agrees but suggests that they enquire of the Lord. Now that was a bold request to someone like King Ahab who set against the prophets of the Lord.

Ahab had prophets who would tell him just what he wanted to hear. They were not faithful prophets of the Lord rather they were keener to please their kings. And so these prophets prophecy victory for Ahab.

But Jehoshaphat insisted on hearing from a prophet of the Lord (v7) Ahab knew there was Micaiah, a prophet he did not like because he never prophesied good concerning him. But he obliges Jehoshaphat and has Micaiah brought in. Micaiah, unlike the others, was clear that his loyalty was to the Lord more than the king and that he would only speak what the Lord tells him (v14).

When he was asked, Micaiah states "I saw all Israel scattered on the hills like sheep without a shepherd" (v17). Zedekiah, Ahab's leading prophet, struck Micaiah on the cheek and called him a liar. Ahab chose to believe Zedekiah's predictions of victory and had Micaiah imprisoned. However, in the battle that followed, Ahab was killed, just as Micaiah predicted.

It took Micaiah courage and resolve to stand for the Lord, in the face of danger and threat from the evil king, but he did. Would you?

Give me Lord the courage to stand for you even in the face of danger, I pray.

Extended Reading — 1 Kings 22; 2 Chronicles 18

TRUST
Depend on God

Amplified Bible - *¹² O our God, will You not judge them? For we are powerless against this great multitude which is coming against us. We do not know what to do, but our eyes are on You."*   *2 Chronicles 20:12*

When in crisis, we turn to those we trust.

King Jehoshaphat was cornered by this huge army that was advancing in a battle against him. He was petrified. Jehoshaphat recognized his need. He knew he was weak, he knew that the armies of Judah were no match for this huge approaching army. But the beauty is, when he was in need, Jehoshaphat also knew exactly what to do and whom to turn to.

Jehoshaphat turns to the Lord as his first resort. He did not go and count the strength of his army or call a council of his ministers. He knew the Lord well enough to turn to him in trust and that the Lord was more than able to handle his crisis.

Jehoshaphat was humble to acknowledge his need. He clearly expresses his own powerlessness and inadequacy in the situation. He is very candid about the fact that he does not know what to do

And then Jehoshaphat fixes his eyes on the One who knows. Once he places his need before the Lord, he then clearly trusts God with unwavering faith to provide a solution and take care of him.

Challenges and battles in life are real in every one of our lives. We need to have our battle strategy in place. Jehoshaphat's strategy was to acknowledge his own need and fix his eyes on the God who could help. His strategy gave him victory. What's your strategy?

Father help me keep my eyes fixed on you rather than my challenges, I pray.

Extended Reading — 2 Chronicles 19-23

PRIDE
Selfish Pride

You should not gloat over your brother in the day of his misfortune, nor rejoice over the people of Judah in the day of their destruction, nor boast so much in the day of their trouble.
Obadiah 1:12

Edom was proud and selfish.

The book of Obadiah is just a single chapter making it the smallest book in the Old Testament. Obadiah means "worshipper of Yahweh" or "servant of Yahweh." Obadiah's prophecy is different from the others. His focus was more on the sin of Edom rather than on Judah or Israel.

The Edomites were the descendants of Esau, Jacob's brother. Edom was known for their pride and how they did not help the Israelites in their time of need. And so Obadiah's focus is on the destructive power of selfishness and pride. He warns against being proud and gloating over another's fall. Obadiah also reminds us not to be so focused on our own feelings and desires that we don't consider the impact on those around.

Instead, Obadiah calls us to come under God's authority. To allow our appetites and desires to be controlled by him used for his divine purposes. Unlike Edom, we are to help people. If we stay true to him, God will overcome on our behalf. We have nothing to be proud of except Jesus Christ and his finished work on the cross for us.

If we think hard enough, all of us will surely be able to identify at least such a person in our lives, who by their selfish pursuits have caused us pain. But the bigger question is, do we also come under this section of people?

Lord help me trust you enough to be selfless and humble with those around me, I pray.

Extended Reading — Obadiah; Psalm 82-83

COMMITMENT
Tenacious Commitment

When they had crossed, Elijah said to Elisha, "Tell me, what can I do for you before I am taken from you?" "Let me inherit a double portion of your spirit," Elisha replied.   2 Kings 2:9

Elijah was soon to be carried into heaven in a whirlwind.

This chapter opens with the phrase, '**when** the Lord was about to take Elijah up to heaven' (v1). And so it was apparently common knowledge, at least among some of the prophets.

Elijah tests Elisha's devotion.

Elijah tells Elisha to return, while he goes on ahead. Elisha refuses. Elisha knew there was an anticipated unusual departure and wanted to stay as close to his mentor as possible, in these last moments of his life on earth. Elijah tests Elisha repeatedly but Elisha tenaciously refused to leave his mentor.

When they reach the banks of the Jordon, Elijah asks Elisha what he could do for him before he is taken away. Elisha asks for a double portion of the mighty spirit of Elijah.

The idea of a double portion was not to ask for twice as much as Elijah had, but to ask for the portion that went to the firstborn son (Deuteronomy 21:17). Elisha asked for the right to be regarded as the successor of Elijah, as his firstborn son regarding ministry.

Elijah tells Elisha that if he sees him being taken up, then his request would be fulfilled. Elisha saw (v10). And when Elijah was taken up, he picked up the mantle that had fallen and put it on.

If God were to test your devotion to him today, would he find you as tenacious as Elisha?

Lord help me ever be found faithful in my devotion to you, I pray.

Extended Reading — 2 Kings 1-4

FEAR
Who is With You?

"Don't be afraid," the prophet answered. "Those who are with us are more than those who are with them."   2 Kings 6:16

The King of Aram was a frustrated man.

Aram was at war with Israel. But what the King of Aram did not count on was the God of Israel who directed and protected his people through his servant, Elisha. Time and time again, as God revealed to him, Elisha warned the King of Israel, of places to watch out for, where the Arameans were waiting to attack them. This made the King of Aram furious. He even began doubting that his own people may be traitors and leaking their battle plans and secrets.

But soon enough the King of Aram figured out that Elisha was the root of all his troubles. He had Elisha located at Dothan and sent a mighty army to capture him. The army of horses and chariots surrounded the city by night. When Elisha's servant got up the next morning he was taken aback and petrified. But Elisha reassured him and prayed that God would open his eyes. Then the servant saw the chariots of fire that stood around them. The chariots of the army of angels who surrounded them.

Many a times, we are so overwhelmed by our circumstances that we can see that we forget the strength we have in our God. But the fact is that he that is in us is way greater than he that is in the world (1 John 4:4). We have no reason to be afraid.

Whom can you encourage with this truth today?

Open my eyes, Lord, to see that I have all that I need in you, I pray.

Extended Reading — 2 Kings 5-8

COURAGE
Dare to be a Jehosheba

Joash was seven years old when he began to reign. 2 Kings 11:21

Like the boy Samuel, Joash grew up in the temple.

Jehu had destroyed all of Ahab's descendants in Israel including Ahaziah the king. Athaliah, the queen mother, used the occasion to take power for herself. She reigned over the land for six years. She was the daughter of Ahab and Jezebel, and the wife of King Jehoram of Judah. She was a bad influence on both her husband and her son, Ahaziah. She tried to destroy all of David's household.

But Jehosheba, Joash's aunt and the wife of Jehoiada, the high priest, saved him and hid him in the temple for six years (2 Chronicles 22:11). This little-known woman had an important place in God's plan for the ages. Through her courage and ingenuity, she preserved the royal line of David through which the Messiah would come.

Jehoiada, a godly man, was concerned with restoring the throne to the line of David. He carefully prepared for the dramatic moment when Joash was revealed. He presented the young king Joash, to the people amidst great security. Joash was introduced and anointed and presented with a copy of the Law of God as was required for a king (Deuteronomy 17:18). The people joyfully accepted him.

One reason Athaliah was able to reign for six years was because no one knew of any other alternative. Many people live under the reign of Satan today because they don't really know there is a legitimate king ready to take reign in their lives.

Evil people like Athaliah will begin their work, but God can always raise up a courageous Jehosheba. Would you be a Jehosheba, for the Lord?

Lord give me courage and a willing heart to take risks for you, I pray.

Extended Reading — 2 Kings 9-11

FAITH
Receive Boldly

Then he said, "Take the arrows," and the king took them. Elisha told him, "Strike the ground." He struck it three times and stopped. ¹⁹ The man of God was angry with him and said, "You should have struck the ground five or six times; then you would have defeated Aram and completely destroyed it. But now you will defeat it only three times."   *2 Kings 13:18-19*

Jehoash, king of Israel, pays the dying Elisha a visit.

And during the visit, Elisha asks Jehoash to shoot arrows through the window. Jehoash understood that these arrows represented the Lord's deliverance of Israel against Syria.

Then Elisha tells Jehoash to shoot his arrows to the ground and he shoots three times and stops. Elisha was angry with him. So Elisha tells him, Israel would enjoy only three victories over the Syrian army, instead of the many more they could have enjoyed.

King Jehoash should have continued until the prophet said enough. When God calls us to take something by faith, we need to receive it boldly. There are times when we need to persist and not stop with just a small effort. We are to keep shooting, be it in the battle against sin, or growing in our Christian knowledge, or to grow in our faith. We are not to give up.

Jehoash's excuses could have been that he was not a good archer or that he thought three times was enough. It could also be that Jehoash didn't think it will do much good or that he was just not in the mood.

Do these excuses sound familiar? Let us walk by faith and ask big of God, rather than give excuses.

Lord help come to you boldly to receive all that you have for me, I pray.

Extended Reading — 2 Kings 12-13; 2 Chronicles 24

OBEDIENCE
How Much Will You Pay?

Amaziah asked the man of God, "But what about the hundred talents I paid for these Israelite troops?" The man of God replied, "The Lord can give you much more than that."

2 Chronicles 25:9

King Amaziah of Judah prepared for the battle.

Amaziah assembled his army and numbered the troops. He also hired men from the northern tribes of Israel. This was a common practice in the ancient world.

But the Lord sent an anonymous prophet to warn the king. The king was not to use the Israelite troops for battle. If he did, the prophet warned him that God would make him fall before his enemy. Now, though it made perfect military sense for Amaziah to hire and use these troops, according to the word of God, it made no spiritual sense.

Amaziah heard and understood the message that the Lord sent him, but he had a relevant question. What about the money he had to pay them? The prophet wisely answered the Lord can give you much more.

So Amaziah discharged the Israelite troops that had come. He paid them as promised and he trusted God to provide and to protect. Then Amaziah went and fought and defeated the Edomites, who apparently rebelled against Judah's authority. He saw the victory that God promised.

Amaziah's question was what will it cost me to be obedient to God? Obedience to God often comes with a price. Jesus said, whoever wants to be my disciple, must deny themselves and take up their cross and follow me (Matthew 16:24). Whatever the cost of obedience, it is always ultimately cheaper than disobedience. Are you willing to pay the price of being obedient to God?

Help me choose to obey you Lord, whatever the price, I pray.

Extended Reading — 2 Kings 14; 2 Chronicles 25

SELF-RIGHTEOUS
A Jonah Spirit

But the Lord replied, "Is it right for you to be angry?" Jonah 4:4

Jonah runs away.

God told Jonah to prophesy to Nineveh. He instead ran away from God, in a ship bound for Tarshish. God sent a violent storm that threatened the ship. On casting lots the terrified sailors discover that Jonah was the reason for the storm. Jonah accepted his fault and told them to throw him into the sea for it to calm down.

But thankfully, God was not done with Jonah. He sent a big fish to swallow Jonah and he remained in the stomach of the fish three days and three nights. (Imagine the poor fish's state, it had food in its belly but is not allowed to eat it).

A repentant Jonah prayed to the Lord from the belly of the big fish. The fish threw out Jonah on to the shore. The Lord commanded Jonah again to go to Nineveh and proclaim that Nineveh would be overthrown in forty days. This time Jonah obeyed the Lord.

The king of Nineveh and his people repented and turned to God. God relented and did not send destruction that he had threatened. This strangely, made Jonah angry.

Jonah was angry at God's compassion. Jonah himself enjoyed the mercy of God. And yet, Jonah had a problem when God extended mercy to Nineveh, whom he preached to? What if God treated him the way Jonah wanted God to treat Nineveh?

Jonathan Swift so rightly captured Jonah's heart:

We are God's chosen few, All others will be damned;

There is no place in heaven for you,

We can't have heaven crammed.

Is there a selfish, self-righteous Jonah spirit in you?

Lord forgive me when I resent your grace upon another needy soul just like me, I pray.

Extended Reading — Jonah 1-4

PRIDE
Finish Well

But after Uzziah became powerful, his pride led to his downfall. He was unfaithful to the LORD his God and entered the temple of the LORD to burn incense on the altar of incense.

2 Chronicles 26:16

Uzziah's reign was generally good.

Uzziah, also called Azariah (2 Kings 15), largely did good in the sight of the Lord. And he reigned 52 long years. He did not remove the high places, traditional places of sacrifice to the Lord and sometimes doorways to idolatry. He was active in opposing the enemies of Israel. Neighboring countries brought him tribute. His fame spread among the nations because of his many achievements.

The main reason for Uzziah's success was God's help. But he is a great example of one who handled adversity better than success though his success got to his head.

The law of God was clear that no king should also be a priest. And only a priest is to offer sacrifices in the temple. But Uzziah overstepped this law. He entered the temple of God to burn incense. He was not content with the authority God had given him. He wanted to add more priestly functions to his royal power.

Azariah the priest confronts him. Rather than repent, Uzziah became furious. 'While he was raging at the priests in their presence before the incense altar in the Lord's temple, leprosy broke out on his forehead' (v19). He had to rush out of the temple never to return. He remained and died a leper.

Interestingly, God's righteous anger and punishment against Uzziah only broke out when he raged at the priests in his rebellious anger (v19). With prosperity, there is always the danger of pride. What will you do to guard yourself?

Keep me humble Lord and help me finish well, I pray.

Extended Reading — 2 Kings 15; 2 Chronicles 26

REPENTANCE
Call to Reason

"Come now, let us settle the matter," says the Lord. "Though your sins are like scarlet, they shall be as white as snow; though they are red as crimson, they shall be like wool.   *Isaiah 1:18*

The book of Isaiah begins with this stunning invitation from God to his people to a legal debate.

God had faithfully led and provided for his chosen people, Israel, for years. The people should have lived in eternal gratitude to him for his goodness to them. Instead, they are accused of being corrupt, having betrayed and neglected this awesome God. And the Lord is saying, come let us reason together. The Lord says come let's talk about it. He is calling them to come and discuss their options or argue their case. To weigh the facts and evidence.

In verses 16 and 17, God states what he requires of his people. To be clean, to stop doing wrong, learn to do right, seek justice, encourage the oppressed, to defend the cause of the orphan and widow. The people have not been doing these things. They have rebelled. They have sinned. But the Lord says, yet if they are willing to repent and return, then he would still forgive and cleanse them.

The word "scarlet" also means 'double-dyed.' The Lord is saying to his people the stain of sin is deep, and yet if you repent, I will cleanse and make white as snow. Christ paid the price for our sin and we are made righteous through him. What a gracious God!

The Lord's requirement of his people remains the same today, to do right and seek justice. If the Lord were to call you to reason with him how would you measure up?

I need your forgiveness, Lord. Would you cleanse, as you have promised?

Extended Reading — Isaiah 1-4

CALLING
Cleansed to Serve

Then I heard the voice of the Lord saying, "Whom shall I send? And who will go for us?" And I said, "Here am I. Send me!"   Isaiah 6:8

King Uzziah had died. Judah was in great national crisis.

Judah was facing God's displeasure because of their neglect of God and his word. In the first five chapters, Isaiah had proclaimed woe after woe on the people for their numerous sins. But then he has this awesome vision of God. God gave Isaiah this vision during a time of great loss and sorrow. What a reminder that he can and does bring beauty out of ashes and works all things for good, even the painful, sorrowful ones.

Isaiah saw the Lord high and exalted and seated on the throne, the train of his robe filled the temple. To view the holiness of God and his crystal-clear purity brings to a sharp perspective on how short we as humans fall of this perfect and holy God. God is so holy, so set apart, so totally other than we are. This vision changes Isaiah's entire response. From woes on the people the searchlight turns on to himself and he declared 'woe to *me*!' '*I* am a man of unclean lips!'

We do not know what wastroubling Isaiah but whatever it was, it prevented his lips from being God's messenger to others. Unconfessed sin prevents us from worshipping him with all our heart. God took the initiative to see his servant cleansed. Then the Lord calls Isaiah. And Isaiah's most natural response was 'here am I, send me.'

God continues to call his people to serve him with clean hearts. What is your response to him today?

Here am I, Lord, cleanse me and send me, I pray.

Extended Reading — Isaiah 5-8

CALLING
Just a Nobody

The words of Amos, one of the shepherds of Tekoa—the vision he saw concerning Israel two years before the earthquake when Uzziah was king of Judah and Jeroboam son of Jehoash was king of Israel.   *Amos 1:1*

Amos was just one of the shepherds of Tekoa.

The book of prophet Amos is the only place that this man of God is mentioned in the Old Testament. He is not to be confused with Amoz, father of Isaiah (Isaiah 1:1). The name Amos means 'burden' or 'burden bearer.' Amos was a man with a burden about the judgments against Israel and the neighboring nations.

Amos does not seem to have had any theological or prophetic training. He describes himself as neither a prophet nor the son of a prophet, but a shepherd who also took care of sycamore-fig trees (Amos 7:14-15). He was just a simple man uniquely called to ministry.

Amos' mission was mainly directed to the neighboring nation of Israel. His messages of impending doom and captivity because of her great sins, were largely unpopular and unheeded. The country was having good times, so his messages were not taken seriously.

Amos was not a prophet or a priest, he was 'just-a' shepherd, a small businessman in Judah. Why would anyone listen to him? But Amos obeyed God's call instead of making excuses. He ended up becoming one of God's powerful voice for change.

God has and continues to use many 'just-a' such as salesmen, shepherds, carpenters, housewives, fishermen. God can use you, whatever you are or not. The question is, are you willing to be used for the Lord?

Lord make my heart ever willing and available to you, I pray.

Extended Reading — Amos 1-5

SIN
Complacent Woe

Woe to you who are complacent in Zion, and to you who feel secure on Mount Samaria, you notable men of the foremost nation, to whom the people of Israel come!   Amos 6:1

Israel's sin was complacency.

To be complacent is to have a feeling of contentment or self-satisfaction, often combined with a lack of awareness of pending trouble or controversy.

The prophet Amos saw in the people of Israel a complacency or a sinful rest. A rest of indifference, laziness, and self-indulgence. A confidence of one who is based on sandy foundations of self and man. Not a confidence on the rock-solid foundation of God. A confidence of the man who thought he could hide his sin from God.

Israel's complacency was seen in the fact that they counted on and felt secure in Samaria. They were not quick to act, they procrastinated. They put off the day of disaster (v3) they didn't take it seriously. They were self-indulgent. They were so caught up in enjoying themselves they didn't pause to grieve over the ruin around them. They were willfully ignorant in their revelry, they didn't seem to care less (v4-6).

The idea of rest is not bad. Jesus calls to rest (Matthew 11:28-29). There is a promised rest for the people of God (Hebrews 4:9-11). But complacency is wrong.

"Self-indulgence! Oh, this is the god of many! They live not for Christ – What do they do for him? They live not for his Church – What care they for that? They live for self, and for self only. And mark there are such among the poor as well as among the rich, for all classes have this evil leaven." (Spurgeon) How is complacency seen in your life?

Lord help me act and repent about the sin in my life, I pray.

Extended Reading — Amos 6-9

KNOW YOUR GOD
Where is Your Trust?

> *For to us a child is born, to us a son is given; and the government shall be upon his shoulder, and his name shall be called Wonderful Counselor, Mighty God, Everlasting Father, Prince of Peace.*   Isaiah 9:6

God does not take sin lightly.

In the days of King Ahaz of Judah, the people turned away from God. They even turned to occults to interpret their circumstances and future rather than to God. The law was very clear that the people of God were not to turn to mediums or spirits (Leviticus 19:31). And so, the Lord hid his face from Judah (8:17) but only for a season. God himself gave his people the way they could come back to him.

God used Isaiah to give his people hope. Isaiah prophesied the coming of the Lord Jesus seven hundred years before Christ was born. God so beautifully describes his Son. He is called wonderful because of the miracles he would do. He was called mighty God speaking of his power and might. He is called everlasting father reflecting that he was and is and remains our eternal father who cares and protects his people. And finally, the prince of peace, who brings peace to the world.

Young and old even today seek the world of the dead to find answers rather than turning to the living God. Ouija boards, tarot cards, astrology are just some such ways. When we turn to other sources for our solutions it is sin. All sin has its roots in refusing to acknowledge God as the supreme authority in one's life. Beware.

What or whom are you trusting with your life?

Forgive me Lord for the times I have trusted others rather than you, I pray.

Extended Reading — 2 Chronicles 27; Isaiah 9-12

DISCIPLESHIP
Called to Walk

He has shown you, O mortal, what is good. And what does the Lord require of you? To act justly and to love mercy and to walk humbly with your God.   Micah 6:8

Micah was called.

The prophet Micah was very confident in his call and knew that God had filled him with his Spirit to declare their sin to Israel (3:8).

In chapter six of this book, Micah pictures a courtroom with Israel on trial before God. The Lord had a complaint against Israel. As Israel stepped into the witness box, God asked Israel to testify against him. He asked, what have I done to you? God had not only done them no evil but rather he had done Israel immense good.

Israel's response is one of bitterness and resentment. Almost like Israel is asking 'what exactly is it you want from me?' (v6-7). And the Lord said three things.

God calls his people to be just and fair in how we deal with people. Then the Lord said, love mercy. Treat people with the measure of mercy that you want the Lord to treat you with.

And finally, the Lord said, walk humbly with your God. Spurgeon says, "True humility is thinking rightly of thyself, not meanly. When you have found out what you really are, you will be humble, for you are nothing to boast of. To be humble will make you safe. To be humble will make you happy. To be humble will make music in your heart when you go to bed. To be humble here will make you wake up in the likeness of your Master by-and-by."

How is your walk with the Lord today?

Lord help me grow in my walk with you each day, I pray.

Extended Reading — Micah 1-7

CHOICES
Your Mark on History

> *Ahaz was twenty years old when he became king, and he reigned in Jerusalem sixteen years. Unlike David his father, he did not do what was right in the eyes of the Lord.* [2] *He followed the ways of the kings of Israel and made idols for worshiping the Baals.*
> *2 Chronicles 28:1-2*

Ahaz did not do what was right in the eyes of the Lord.

This is a crisp description of the reign of perhaps the worst king of Judah. While many of the previous kings did fall short in some area or the other, king Ahaz, the Bible simply says, did not do what was right in the eyes of the Lord. What a way to be remembered.

Though Ahaz had many good examples to follow of his father king Jotham or even examples in history like David, he chose to walk in his own ways. Ahaz not only rejected the godly heritage of the kings of Judah, but he also chose to walk in the ungodly ways of the kings of Israel. The extent of Ahaz's depravity is seen in the fact that he even sacrificed his children in the fire (v3).

Today we are not short of godly examples. We have the Bible, which is full of great men and women of God. We also have the examples of saints who have lived and many who even today live wonderful lives among us, of love and service to the Lord.

And yet many continue to choose the ways of the world, as against God's ways. It finally comes down to each one's choice. Choices small and big will define the mark we will leave on history.

How will you be remembered?

Lord may I chose you every day of my life I pray.

Extended Reading — 2 Chronicles 28; 2 Kings 16-17

PRIDE
What is Your Position?

*I will punish the world for its evil, the wicked for their sins.
I will put an end to the arrogance of the haughty and will
humble the pride of the ruthless.*   *Isaiah 13:11*

Pride goes before a fall.

Chapter thirteen begins with an oracle Isaiah delivers against Babylon
and Assyria. An 'oracle' could be translated a 'weighty message'
or 'burden.' Isaiah delivers this oracle against Babylon and addresses
questions like what will happen to an individual or nation that elevates
himself against the Lord Almighty.

Babylon was a powerful nation. It was the center of world trade where
people of different nationalities came together. In their brutal power,
they had put Judah and the other nations through immense suffering.
And now Isaiah delivered this oracle against Babylon and how it will
be brought low by the Medes. Verses 14-16 talk about the judgment
on Babylon. Babylonians would be cruelly massacred while the people
that came to do trade with them fled in fear in all directions.

In today's world, promoting oneself is almost the norm and expectation.
News channels and media today are full news of killings, revenge and
all kinds of evil. About how people vie with one another to outdo and
exalt themselves to positions of power and wealth in every field including
politics, economics, and entertainment. We almost never hear stories of
how God delivered his people.

Self-exaltation is elevating oneself above God. It is shaking a fist in
his 'face' and his ways. And that is pride. Beware. For God opposes
the proud but shows favor to the humble (1 Peter 5:5) Where are you
positioned today, above or below God?

Lord give me a humble and a contrite heart I pray.

Extended Reading — Isaiah 13-17

FAITH
Where is Your Security?

This is what the Lord says to me: "I will remain quiet and will look on from my dwelling place, like shimmering heat in the sunshine, like a cloud of dew in the heat of harvest."

Isaiah 18:4

Wherever Judah looked there was doom.

The threat of Assyria loomed large. Damascus to the north, Philistia to the west, Moab to the east, Cush to the south, all the nations are faced with doom. Envoys from 'the land of whirring wings' come. These good-looking messengers from Cush, have come in papyrus boats to Judah to presumably to offer to support them against Assyria.

The situation was gloomy, and Judah felt helpless. Sadly, they were looking to alliances for help rather than to God. But Isaiah sends the messengers from Cush back. He explains that the Lord quietly observes from his dwelling place on high. And when the time is right, he will do away with Assyria like a farmer prunes spreading branches (v5). And at that time the people of Cush would join with all the peoples of the world in bringing gifts of praise to the Lord to Mount Zion (v7).

There is a lot to be concerned about in today's world. We often look at the instability in the world with concern and look for solutions around us.

But God is sovereign. He sure is watching and is in absolute control. Rather than look around, we are to look up to the Lord for his grace and love. He is our strength and our tower of refuge. God sometimes removes our false security so that we would trust him.

Is your trust and security in peoples and powers or in the Lord?

Lord help me trust you rather than looking at people for my security, I pray.

Extended Reading — Isaiah 18-22

FAITH
Compassion in Warning

*Therefore a curse consumes the earth; its people must bear their
guilt. Therefore, earth's inhabitants are burned up, and very few
are left.*   Isaiah 24:6

To warn is to tell someone that something bad or dangerous may happen
so that they can avoid it or prevent it

Isaiah's prophecy warned that the whole earth would be laid to waste,
made desolate. And that the reason for the coming judgment is the sin.

Isaiah lived in a time when greater military powers annihilated their
weaker enemies, who must have felt like their world was laid waste. His
prophecy could be seen as the overthrowing of Judah and its neighbors.
People in all positions and walks of life would come under judgment
(v2). Very few would be left.

Isaiah also says the earth is defiled by its inhabitants in three specific
ways namely, disobedience to God's law, violation or altering God's
statutes and breaking the everlasting covenant. And yet there are a few
left. The few that honor God (v5).

Isaiah's warnings may not have been very comfortable on the ear. And yet,
life without the Lord is always ridden with fear, joys are only superficial,
and relationships hang under the fragile thread of individual will. Living
away from the purity of God's will spreads like a virus. Immorality
becomes the basis for entertainment, families are shattered, and people
are bloated with self-interest and competition.

To be told of danger is to be shown compassion.

Many people seem to live successfully without honoring God. But living
apart from him and disregarding his commands and promises leads to
spiritual deadness. Are you among the few that honor God or the crowd
that is stooped in self and superficiality?

Lord help me to honor you and live for you all my life, I pray.

Extended Reading — Isaiah 23-27

CHOICES
What are You Holding On To?

Hezekiah trusted in the Lord, the God of Israel. There was no one like him among all the kings of Judah, either before him or after him. ⁶ He held fast to the Lord and did not stop following him; he kept the commands the Lord had given Moses.

2 Kings 18:5-6

Hezekiah was the son of the wicked King Ahaz.

And yet, he was one of the few kings of Judah who had a close relationship with God and did what was good and right and faithful before the Lord his God (2 Chronicles 31:20).

Hezekiah boldly cleaned house.

After Ahaz's wicked reign, there was much work to do. Hezekiah brought down pagan altars, idols, and temples. The temple in Jerusalem, whose doors had been nailed shut by Hezekiah's own father, was cleaned out and reopened. The Levites were reinstated as priests. Under Hezekiah's reforms, revival came to Judah.

Though Hezekiah did not have a good role model in his father, Ahaz, he still chose to obey God. And because King Hezekiah put God first in everything he did, God prospered him. Hezekiah held fast to the Lord and kept the commands of the Lord, and the Lord was with him (2 Kings 18:6–7).

Hezekiah's life is, for the most part, a model of faithfulness and trust in the Lord. His faith was more than superficial, as his bold reforms show. Hezekiah's trust in the Lord was rewarded with answered prayer, successful endeavors, and miraculous victory over his enemies. When faced with an impossible situation, surrounded by the dreadful and determined Assyrian army, Hezekiah did exactly the right thing—he prayed. And God answered. Do you use your corrupt family background or difficult upbringing for not choosing to serve God?

Lord help me like Hezekiah choose to do right, I pray.

Extended Reading — 2 Kings 18:1-8; 2 Chronicles 29-31; Psalm 48

PRAYER
An Inward Relationship

They do not cry out to me from their hearts but wail on their beds. They slash themselves appealing to their gods for grain and new wine, but they turn away from me.   *Hosea 7:14*

The people of Israel are unrepentant and insincere.

The Lord had faithfully led his people for years, provided for their every need. And yet, time and time again, these people went away from God. They went after other gods, gods of the people around. God describes them as an adulterous woman who keeps going after her lovers and is not faithful to her husband.

And so God used this Old Testament prophet Hosea, to call the Israelites to repentance. God commanded Hosea to marry a prostitute, Gomer to send a powerful message to his people. The names of three children they have also God used to send specific messages to them.

The Lord also says that the people are insincere in their prayer. They make a show of praying to the Lord, but their hearts are turned away from the Lord. Their trust is not in the Lord, but rather in the people and the gods around them.

Prayer in its simplest form is talking to God. Prayer directly addresses God. Prayer can be audible or silent, corporate or personal, but all prayer is based on faith (James 1:6). Paul exhorts us in Philippians 4:6-7 to worry about nothing but pray about everything. We are to pray without ceasing (1 Thessalonians 5:17). We are to keep a running conversation going with the Lord through the day. Our prayer reflects our inward relationship with God.

What do people see through your prayer life?

Lord may my prayer reflect my abiding trust in only you, I pray.

Extended Reading — Hosea 1-7

LOVE
Love Remembers

"When Israel was a child, I loved him, and out of Egypt I called my son.² But the more they were called, the more they went away from me.   *Hosea 11:1-2*

God remembered Israel.

God loved Israel. He remembered that he had promised Abraham that his seed would be as numerous as the stars in the sky. And so Israel was born. God remembered Israel when they were in bondage in Egypt and he brought them out with his mighty Hand. God remembered and so he brought them safe into Canaan, the land that he had promised. But the people forgot.

Israel forgot God. Soon after the Lord brought them out of Egypt, they forgot how he had led them with such mighty wonders, they grumbled about food in the desert. When God provided them manna and quail they grumbled about water. When God provided for all their needs, they still went after other gods and idols. The more the Lord provided and cared for his people, they went further away from him.

Love remembers. Love remembers to be kind, even when the person doesn't deserve it. Love remembers to forgive when the other hurts you.

God tenderly cares for his children, he loved us enough to buy us back from the wages of our sins, eternal death. He sent his only son to die that cruel death on the cross and bought us back with his blood. He continues to provide for our every need. But we often forget. We forget his goodness in our lives and focus on what we don't have. We are ungrateful and grumble like the Israelites. How does your life reflect that you love God and remember his goodness to you?

Lord help me have a grateful heart that remembers you every day, I pray.

Extended Reading — Hosea 8-14

KNOW YOUR GOD
Quiet Strength

This is what the Sovereign Lord, the Holy One of Israel, says: "In repentance and rest is your salvation, in quietness and trust is your strength, but you would have none of it.   Isaiah 30:15

Woe to an obstinate nation.

This chapter begins with the Lord's declaration of woe on Israel. Woe to them because they are obstinate. They seek man's help instead of God's. They carry out plans that are not the Lord's and so they heap sin upon sin on themselves. (v1).

To be obstinate is to stubbornly refuse to change one's opinion or chosen course of action, despite attempts to persuade one to do so. Israel had opportunity after opportunity to see the mighty hand of God, to experience his protection and provision. And yet time and again, they seem to choose to seek man's help, make their own plans, refusing to turn to the Lord. Now does that attitude ring a bell somewhere? Are we very different from Israelites?

The Lord continues by saying repentance, quietness, and trust are the solutions to all of Israel's problems.

Repentance is to regret for past wrongs and commit to change for the better. Repentance takes humility. And yet, unrepentance is like cholesterol in the arteries which block the flow of blood, clogging our relationship with the Lord.

Have you noticed that when we have been wronged or when fear and worry grip, we often feel compelled to act? We feel we need to do or say something. It is very tough to be quiet. We want to justify, fight back or just do something. And yet, the Lord says to be quiet and to trust him is where our strength lies. How can you display your repentant and trusting heart today?

Lord help to quietly trust you through my day, I pray.

Extended Reading — Isaiah 28-30

OBEDIENCE
Distinct Will

he will dwell on the heights; his place of defense will be the
fortresses of rocks; his bread will be given him; his water will be
sure.   *Isaiah 33:16*

The distinction is clear.

In the earlier part of this chapter, the Lord had pronounced woes on those who destroy, who betray, those who sin. He says these sinners in Zion are terrified and gripped with fear. And yet, those who are righteous, their lives are distinctly different. And he describes a righteous person.

A righteous person intentionally keeps away from sin. His senses and his actions are controlled. He walks right, he talks right. He shakes his hand to keep clear of bribes. He is careful about what he hears and sees. The future of such a person is secure, his needs are provided for and his position is high and secure.

God's word is distinctly clear about his will for us. The Bible is full of clear instruction about how we are to live, what we are to do and not.

We are often anxious to know and do God's will especially when we are at crossroads of life and have important decisions to make. Decisions maybe regarding education, career, and even marriage. Everyone longs to know that their future is safe. But the important and pertinent question to ask is if we are doing all that we know to be his will as revealed in his Word, in the everyday life.

When you are living out God's will in the everyday life, you will end up knowing and doing God's will in the big decisions of life too.

How are you living out God's revealed will for you today?

Lord help me live my life every day by what I already know in your word, I pray.

Extended Reading — Isaiah 31-34

FAITH
Who is Taunting You Today?

You say you have counsel and might for war—but you speak only empty words. On whom are you depending, that you rebel against me?   Isaiah 36:5

The Assyrian king captured Judah.

Sennacherib, a tenacious warrior defeated Babylon on his east and then turned to Judah and other kingdoms on his west. He captured Hezekiah's fortified cities. Though Hezekiah had joined Moab, Philistia, and others in rebelling against Sennacherib, he soon tried to back down. He even stripped the gold from the temple to buy peace, but it was not enough.

Hezekiah's worst fears had come true. He had seen the fall of the northern kingdom of Israel because of its disobedience to God (2 Kings 18:9-12). He had faithfully removed all the idols from his nation. And yet, here were the invaders at his gates.

Backed by a strong army and their recent successes, Rabshakeh, commander of the Assyrian army taunted the people of Israel. He stopped outside the walls of Jerusalem and spoke insolently to the people even inciting them to rebel. But the people remained silent, for Hezekiah had commanded his people not to answer him (36:21).

Isaiah had consistently warned Judah that God had brought Assyria to punish them for their sins but would also cause Israel to turn to God (chap 1-35). Now the time had come. The temptation to doubt God's presence must have been very strong. But Judah was not to resist Assyria nor think that they could stand on their own. They were not to seek outside help either. They were to trust the Lord, completely. In what situation is God asking you to trust him completely, though you are tempted to look for outside help?

Lord the wave of fear is strong but give me the courage to trust you completely, I pray.

Extended Reading — Isaiah 35-36

FAITH
Him Dependent

*Hezekiah received the letter from the hand of the messengers,
and read it, and Hezekiah went up to the house of the Lord and
spread it before the Lord. ¹⁵ And Hezekiah prayed to the Lord.*

Isaiah 37: 14-15

King Hezekiah is upset.

The taunting content of the letter from the Assyrians had King
Hezekiah tear his clothes and put on sackcloth (official signs of
expressing sorrow in those days). But he did not stop there. He went
into the temple of God.

In this chapter, we see Hezekiah going into the temple three times (v4,
15, 21). That was his natural response to a crisis. He did not allow the
content of the letter to dominate his thoughts and defeat his faith. He
took the letter and went into the house of the Lord. Hezekiah spread
it before the Lord the God of Israel, who he knew to be holy and real.
He knew that the best place to bring his problems was before the Lord.
So he went and prayed.

Hezekiah's prayer is a great model for all of us who find ourselves
overwhelmed by our circumstances. Hezekiah's prayer begins with him
recognizing that God is completely sovereign (15-16). He brought his
requests before the Lord in humility, recognizing that God is sovereign
and knew his troubles fully well (v17-19). He also recognized that the
ultimate purpose, even through this crisis, is that God is lifted for all
to see and know, that he alone is God (v20). What an excellent model
of prayer.

The Lord answered Hezekiah's prayer. Sennacherib's army was routed.
Sennacherib fled and was soon killed by his own sons (v36-38). Like
Hezekiah, what troubles do you need to humbly bring before the Lord
today?

Lord increase my dependence on you I pray.

Extended Reading — Isaiah 37-39; Psalm 76

FAITH
A Call to Prepare

A voice of one calling: In the wilderness prepare the way for the Lord; make straight in the desert a highway for our God.

Isaiah 40:3

To prepare is to make ready for use.

The exiled nation of Israel wondered how they would return from Babylon to Jerusalem. It was not going to be easy. In this verse, Isaiah says that the Lord is going to return to Jerusalem and the voice is ordering for preparation. The people reading Isaiah's prophecy would have been comforted that God would indeed make a way and lead them back to their land. And yes, he sure did. They did travel back home from Babylon to begin rebuilding the temple (Ezra 1-2).

But this call was for more than just the return from exile. This call also predicted the coming of the Messiah and a forerunner to announce his arrival. Isaiah was foretelling that the King of Glory, the Lord was coming to his people.

A forerunner is one who precedes an arriving king, announcing the royal arrival. His announcement was meant to enable the great amount of preparation needed for a royal visit.

John the Baptist was the forerunner who announced the coming of the Messiah (Luke 1:17). And this Messiah who came lived died and rose again, will come again (Acts 1:11).

If near eastern towns made so much physical preparation for a king's arrival, then how much more do we need to prepare for the return of the King of kings and Lord of lords. We are to prepare our hearts for him morally, spiritually. We need to confess our sins and seek him in his word. How are you preparing to meet the Lord when he returns?

Lord give me a humble and repentant heart that is fit for your coming, I pray.

Extended Reading — Isaiah 40-43

SUBMISSION
Beyond the Questions

"Woe to those who quarrel with their Maker, those who are nothing but potsherds among the potsherds on the ground. Does the clay say to the potter, 'What are you making?' Does your work say, 'The potter has no hands'?   *Isaiah 45:9*

Israel's deliverance is coming but from unexpected sources.

This chapter begins with the Lord addressing Cyrus as his anointed. The Lord says that he will take Cyrus by the hand to subdue nations and strip kings of their armor. And this form of deliverance was most unexpected and even unacceptable to at least some of the exiles.

It is to those exiles who resented deliverance through a foreign conqueror, that these verses (v9-13) are addressed. They are likened to a clay pot scolding the potter for his design. A woe is pronounced on such a person, who would "quarrel with his Maker."

There are many events around us that cause us to wonder at God's ways. Natural disasters, the rise of oppressive governments, deprivation among those who are hardworking, suffering from sickness, the difficult people or situations in our lives, the list seems long.

And we don't understand. We have questions. And that is okay. But when we come to him with our questions, we are to come to him with a humble spirit, not as one who quarrels with his maker.

God's word says when we don't understand, we humbly submit to the One we trust. We trust our just God who will ensure righteousness and salvation will prevail on earth and in his people's lives. We trust in the sovereignty of our loving father who holds our future. Who needs to be encouraged by your humble trust in the Lord, today?

Lord help me trust you more especially when I don't understand, I pray.

Extended Reading — Isaiah 44-48

PURPOSE
Why Do You Pray?

Now, LORD our God, deliver us from his hand, so that all the kingdoms of the earth may know that you alone, LORD, are God."   *2 Kings 19:19*

Hezekiah is in deep trouble.

Sennacherib, King of Assyria threatens Judah. His commander comes to the people of Jerusalem and taunts them. The commander ridicules Hezekiah's trust in the Lord. He incites the people to fear them and rebel against Hezekiah. He tried to turn their hearts away from Hezekiah and the Lord. And the palace officials carry this message back to the king.

Hezekiah was distraught and he tore his clothes in sorrow and he put on sackcloth. He sent his officials to the prophet Isaiah to enquire of the Lord. Isaiah sent them back with a reassuring message from the Lord. The Lord had indeed heard the blasphemy of the commander of the Assyrian army and promised to destroy the enemy.

Hezekiah also went to the Lord in his time of need. He went to the temple and prayed one of the most powerful prayers in the Bible, which has a lot to teach us even today.

Hezekiah tells God about his problem. He begins his prayer by acknowledging the Lord as sovereign and supreme over all. Hezekiah recognized the Lord as the one who created the heavens and the earth and so affirming that he trusts the Lord can help him. And then Hezekiah simply presents the problem without giving the Lord any instructions. Finally, he states the purpose of his prayer, which is that all the kingdoms of the earth may know that the Lord alone is God. What is the purpose of the prayers you pray?

Lord help me turn to you with pure motives in my prayers, I pray.

Extended Reading — 2 Kings 18:9-37; 2 Kings 19:1-37; Psalm 46, 80, 135

GOD'S LOVE
Love Unparalleled

Can a woman forget her nursing child, that she should have no compassion on the son of her womb? Even these may forget, yet I will not forget you. [16] Behold, I have engraved you on the palms of my hands; your walls are continually before me.

Isaiah 49:15-16

God's love for us is beyond our understanding.

Chapter 49 begins an altogether new section in the book of Isaiah. A section that has reference to a message that would be for the ends of the earth (49:6) and God's promises that transcend time. The perfect faithfulness God displayed in history would be seen in future too.

God is aware of his people and their situations. God's love for Jerusalem and his people goes beyond the love of a mother for her nursing baby. God will never abandon his children. He will never forget them or their needs.

As though he is holding up his hand for them to see he says, see I have engraved you on the palms of my hands. The word "engraved" and "ever" give the sense of permanence. Jesus' nail-pierced hands so beautifully remind us how he has indeed inscribed us on the palm of his hand. And the Bible says, nothing can separate us from this love of God (Romans 8:35-39).

Life has its share of challenges over which one has no control. It is so easy to focus on "bereavement and barrenness." We are instead to focus on God, whose love surpasses that of a nursing mother for her child, whose protection is everlasting, and whose triumph is certain. Those who hope in him will not be disappointed.

Is your hope and trust in the unfailing love of this savior?

Lord may I ever remember your amazing love for me, I pray.

Extended Reading — Isaiah 49-53

PRIDE
Humble Dwelling

For this is what the high and exalted One says – He who lives forever, whose name is holy. I live in a high and holy place, but also with the one who is contrite and lowly in spirit, to revive the spirit of the lowly and to revive the heart of the contrite

Isaiah 57:15

Our God is an amazing, all powerful, all knowing God.

He is the Creator of the entire universe. He is the one who has placed each star in the sky and calls them by name (Psalm 147:4) He is the one who owns the cattle on a thousand hills (Psalm 50:10), Who has measured the waters in the hollow of his hand, or with the breadth of his hand marked off the heavens (Isaiah 40:12). He is the high and lofty one whose throne is the heavens and footstool, the earth (Isaiah 66:1).

Yet this awesome God who lives in the holiest of holies, in the high and lofty places, also lives in one other place. In the heart of one who is humble and contrite. Two absolute ends of the spectrum. The amazing awesome God who dwells in the highest heavens is also willing to come down to live in the hearts of mere humans.

But, God only dwells in the heart of those whose hearts are humble before him.

Pride is a foolish and corrupted sense of one's personal value, status or accomplishments. It leaves room for only self. While a humble person lovingly and honestly obeys God, because he recognizes that God is the Creator of the universe. It makes room for God's will and ways.

Is yours a heart that God dwells?

Lord give me a humble heart and dwell in my heart, I pray.

Extended Reading — Isaiah 54-58

DISCOURAGEMENT
Arise and Shine

> *Arise, shine, for your light has come, and the glory of the Lord rises upon you. ² See, darkness covers the earth and thick darkness is over the peoples, but the Lord rises upon you and his glory appears over you.*   Isaiah 60:1-2

God is light.

Chapter 59 closes with a grand description of the glory and brilliant splendor of our Lord. And this chapter is the climax of Isaiah's vision of the completion of the promises of God to Israel. It begins with a call to Israel to arise and shine.

The command to arise assumes the nation is lying down, perhaps prostrate in their shame and sinful misery. But now the moment has come for her to stand. To arise from her discouragement and distress. Israel is called to shine because her salvation has come. This light or salvation refers to the "glory of the Lord," which comes from knowing the Lord's presence and his deity (60:19-20). The Lord has come. His beautiful presence has come over Zion like a sunrise that banishes the night. And so Israel is called to arise and shine with the radiance of God's light which would be with them and in them, always.

God is consistently associated with light in Scripture. The Bible opens with the creation of light (Genesis 1:3-5). The Lord led Israel through the wilderness with a pillar of fire at night (Exodus 13:21-22). The psalms are filled with descriptions of the Lord in figures of light. In the New Testament Jesus, himself said "I am the light of the world. Whoever follows me will never walk in darkness but will have the light of life (John 8:12). How is knowing this light helping you arise from your discouragement today?

Lord help me shine your light to the world around me, I pray.

Extended Reading — Isaiah 59-63

SURRENDER
White Flag, Finally!

Yet you, Lord, are our Father. We are the clay, you are the potter;
we are all the work of your hand.   Isaiah 64:8

Isaiah here is reflecting a worshipful recognition of God.

He is recognizing the amazing greatness of the sovereign creator, who can do as he will with his creation but who chooses to relate to them as a Father. We are just mere clay in his hands.

And yet how often we as his creation, protest and fight against his ways with us? How often we rebel by insisting on taking things into our hands, doing things our way, refusing to accept his will and sovereignty in our lives.

Lord all these years I have tried,

I have fought, and I have cried.

To make things go my way,

Make people listen to what I say.

And what I got in the bargain,

Are sorrow and stress over again?

Lord, now I see, and this I know,

I have nothing but a mess to show.

This is it, my Lord, I am done,

Of managing life on my own,

This is it, my Lord, I am done,

Of letting others my mind to run.

When fears, doubts lift their ugly head,

May I that dangerous path not tread,

I will choose to call on you that very instant,

Keeping my gaze on you constant.

Here Lord I commit, here I finally wave,

My white flag of surrender and I give.

To You alone my heart, to sway,

To your will forever, from today.

Extended Reading — Isaiah 64-66

OBEDIENCE
Expect Consequences

But the people did not listen. Manasseh led them astray so that they did more evil than the nations the Lord had destroyed before the Israelites.   *2 Kings 21:9*

Manasseh was twelve when he became king of Judah.

Though Manasseh, was the son of the godly king Hezekiah, he did evil in the sight of the Lord. He reversed all the reforms of his father Hezekiah. He rebuilt the high places and erected altars to Baal. He even sacrificed his own son in the fire.

Not only did Manasseh sin personally, but as a king, he led Judah in forsaking the Lord and worshiping idols. The extent of their sin was so great that God declared he would wipe out Jerusalem. According to Jewish tradition, it was King Manasseh who murdered the prophet, Isaiah.

Second Chronicles 33 says that God sent the Assyrians who captured Manasseh and took him away to exile. And while in exile, Manasseh sought the Lord and greatly humbled himself before the Lord. And the Lord was moved and listened to his plea. So he brought him back to Jerusalem and his kingdom. The repentant Manasseh was restored to his kingdom and started to rebuild Judah militarily (2 Chronicles 33:14), and began to institute religious reforms.

Even though Manasseh had a personal conversion, he was never able to lead Judah out of the sin that he had previously led them into. They did not follow him in his reforms, they continued in their idolatry (2 Chronicles 33:17). His son Amon followed his evil ways.

Manasseh demonstrates that while any sin may be forgiven when we repent, repentance does not remove the natural consequences that come from our disobedience. Would you choose to grow in your obedience to the Lord?

Lord help me obey you and worship you alone, I pray.

Extended Reading — 2 Kings 20-21

PRAYER
The Attitude of Yet

In those days Hezekiah became ill and was at the point of death.
He prayed to the Lord, who answered him and gave him a
miraculous sign.   *2 Chronicles 32:24*

King Hezekiah fell ill.

Immediately after independence from King Sennacherib of Assyria, Hezekiah fell ill to the point of death. The Lord sent Isaiah to tell him to put his house in order because he would not recover from this illness. Hezekiah was unhappy and begged the Lord. The Lord granted him another fifteen years.

Hezekiah soon recovered. But sadly, this healing made Hezekiah proud and selfish. When a delegation from Babylon, carrying well wishes for his healing, their intention was also to figure out how Hezekiah's God had defeated the Assyrians. Hezekiah had an excellent opportunity to testify to God's faithfulness and answered prayer. Instead, Hezekiah in his pride chose to show off his wealth and military strength. What a sad choice.

This choice, Isaiah prophesied would lead to the invasion of Judah by Babylon some years later (2 Kings 20:16-18). It was also during the years of his recovery that Hezekiah fathered Manasseh, one of the most-wicked kings that Judah ever had. Answered prayer led Hezekiah to pride and selfishness.

We don't always know what is best for us. When we believe we know better than God, it leads to pride. It takes humility to submit to God. Our supreme example is found in Christ himself, who submitted to the Father, even unto death on the cross. He prayed all his desires and fears to the Father. But he finished his prayer with a small yet powerful word, YET. He prayed yet not my will but yours be done. Are yours, 'yet' prayers that submit to God?

Help me trust and submit to you Lord, I pray.

Extended Reading — 2 Chronicles 32-33

KNOW YOUR GOD
Jealous Love

The Lord is a jealous and avenging God; the Lord takes vengeance and is filled with wrath.   Nahum 1:2

Nahum is a short yet powerful message for the people of Nineveh.

Nahum is one of the small books of the Old Testament that we may not have turned to recently. And yet the message of Nahum is one of great relevance to the people of Nineveh and remains relevant to us today.

Nineveh was the ancient Assyrian capital city. And this city had heard the preaching of Jonah just a hundred years back and had repented. But here was Nahum now called to preach to this city again. The people of Nineveh had fallen back into sin and were ripe for God's judgment again. This is often true in each of our lives too. We hear God's word, we recognize our sin, we repent and yet soon enough we go back to our old ways.

Today's text reminds us that the Lord is a jealous God. Have you ever wondered how can that be? How can it be said that God is jealous? God is not jealous *of* us, he is jealous *for* us. God's jealousy is love in action. He refuses to share the human heart with any rival. Not because he is selfish and wants us all to himself, but because upon that loyalty to him depends our very moral life.

The truth is also that we cannot fight against God and hope to prevail. Everyone who sets themselves against God will end up receiving his vengeance. And that is sure not a nice place to be. Knowing God's power should make us trust and fear his judgment. Are you trying to fight God today?

Lord help me accept and enjoy your jealous, protective love for me, I pray.

Extended Reading — Nahum 1-3

OBEDIENCE
Not Too Young

Because your heart was responsive, and you humbled yourself before God when you heard what he spoke against this place and its people, and because you humbled yourself before me and tore your robes and wept in my presence, I have heard you, declares the Lord.   *2 Chronicles 34:27*

Josiah was just eight years old when he came to the throne of Judah.

Josiah was a godly king, though he was the son of King Amon and grandson of King Manasseh, two of the wickedest kings of Judah. The Bible says, 'he did what was right in the eyes of the LORD and followed completely the ways of his father David, not turning aside to the right or to the left (2 Kings 22:2).

Josiah raised money to repair the temple, and during the repairs the high priest, Hilkiah found the Book of the Law. When Hilkiah read it to Josiah, the king tore his clothes, a sign of mourning and repentance (v11). King Josiah called for a time of national repentance. He led the people in making a covenant with the Lord to keep all his commands and testimonies with all his heart and soul. The people followed him. (2 Kings 23:3).

The temple was cleansed and the high places demolished. Josiah restored the observance of the Passover (2 Kings 23:2–23) and removed mediums and witches from the land. The judgment on Judah because of the evil King Manasseh had done was delayed because of Josiah's godly life and leadership (2 Kings 22:20).

Josiah was a strong positive influence though he came to the throne as a child. You are not too young to live a life committed, obedient life to the Lord.

Lord help me love and obey and be a blessing to those around me, I pray.

Extended Reading — 2 Kings 22-23; 2 Chronicles 34-35

KNOW YOUR GOD
Love that Breaks into Song

The Lord your God is with you, the Mighty Warrior who saves.
He will take great delight in you; in his love, he will no longer
rebuke you, but will rejoice over you with singing."

Zephaniah 3:17

Zephaniah the ninth of the twelve Minor Prophets, was from the royal lineage of Hezekiah. He prophesied against Nineveh during the time of King Josiah.

Zephaniah's message was against the people of Nineveh who had done great evil in the sight of the Lord. And yet, his message ends with this comforting assurance from the Lord to restore the remnant of Israel. God promises to restore his people.

And in the light of this great restoration that God promises his people, God calls his people to rejoice with singing. Rejoice because God who is Mighty and able is with you. Rejoice because God takes joy in you. Rejoice because you can rest in his love for you. And most interestingly, rejoice because God rejoices over you with singing.

God has great joy in his people. We often are so focused on the image of God who is waiting to correct or punish us that we forget that God loves us deeply and rejoices over us. We don't often think of God singing, but he does. Think of the great Jehovah singing. God sings over us, his children. What an amazing thought.

God did not sing when he made the universe. He simply said it was good. But when it comes to his redemption, He is so filled with joy that he breaks into song. If God sings, shall we also not sing? Are you one of God's redeemed that he is singing over today?

Lord help me rejoice in you my loving God, I pray.

Extended Reading — Zephaniah 1-3

ABORTION
It's My Life

"Before I formed you in the womb, I knew you, before you were born, I set you apart; I appointed you as a prophet to the nations."   *Jeremiah 1:5*

Life is precious, even in its very nascent form.

Though the Bible does not specifically address the issue of abortion, the scripture is abundantly clear about God's view of life and its value.

In Jeremiah, the Bible tells us that God knows us even before he formed us in the womb. Each of us is made with a purpose. Not even one of us is an accident. The Lord says he has a plan and a purpose for each one of us (Jeremiah 29:11).

The psalmist in Psalm 139:13-16 talks about how intently God is involved in the creation of every human being in the womb. And in Exodus 21:22-25 we see that the exact same penalty is prescribed for someone who causes the death of a baby in the womb as for someone who commits murder. Thus, God considers a baby in the womb as precious and valuable as a full-grown adult.

And so for a Christian, abortion is not a matter of a woman's right to choose as it is a matter of life and death of a human being made in God's image (Genesis 1:26-27, 9:6).

The Bible makes it clear that God values life very highly. Every life is precious. And the Lord himself is involved in the formation of every life in the womb. If that be true, then whose decision is it to be really? Do you and I have the right to take life that God has created?

Lord for times I have not regarded life as precious, forgive me I pray.

Extended Reading — Jeremiah 1-3

REPENTANCE
Plow and Prepare

This is what the Lord says to the people of Judah and to Jerusalem: "Break up your unplowed ground and do not sow among thorns. ⁴ Circumcise yourselves to the Lord, circumcise your hearts.   *Jeremiah 4:3-4a*

God is calling his people to repent.

Fallow ground is uncultivated farmland. Land that was plowed before but now has been dormant for an extended period. Land that was fruitful at one time has become hardened over time. And unless it is plowed and broken up no useful crop can be grown on it.

Fallow ground implies resistance. To break up fallow ground is hard work. The Lord says do not sow among the thorns. It is not that fallow ground does not yield anything, it only yields weeds and thorns. Nothing useful comes out of it. Fallow ground needs work and preparation to be made useful.

Jeremiah is using circumcision as a metaphor. Spiritually speaking Judah was to work on having repentant, prepared hearts. They were to return to the Lord with hearts softened by repentance. God is interested in the inward change of heart rather than the physical conformity to rules. Ultimately it is not the physical circumstance but a changed and purified heart that the Lord desires.

A circumcised heart is a pure heart separated unto God (Romans 2:29), a heart that is aware of its own sin and the need for God's forgiveness. True circumcision is a matter of the heart, performed by the Spirit of God. Only the Holy Spirit can purify a heart and set us apart unto God. And only when our hearts are plowed and prepared by the Spirit can we be used by the Lord. Is yours a circumcised heart?

Spirit God would you purify my heart, I pray.

Extended Reading — Jeremiah 4-6

GOD'S JUDGMENT
Not Enough Tears

Oh, that my head were a spring of water and my eyes a fountain of tears! I would weep day and night for the slain of my people.

Jeremiah 9:1

Jeremiah was known as the weeping prophet.

In the previous chapter, Jeremiah lamented over Judah, as he prophetically saw them conquered, exiled and many killed. And here he is saying that he does not have enough tears to lament over the coming destruction of Judah.

Jeremiah looked ahead and saw that payday was coming. Just as there is a bill at the end of a meal or stay at a hotel, so also there is a time of accounting. There is a day of reckoning when God will call his people to account. Jeremiah saw the connection between the way the people were living and the ultimate judgment of God. He also saw what the people did not. He made connections that the people didn't make. And he was grieved. He wept.

God's coming judgment is a repeated theme in the book of Jeremiah. Jeremiah was a clear minority with his message. The people were not interested. God's judgment is never a popular message. It is not a message that people want or like to hear. Not then, not now. And yet, you and I are called to tell.

We are a minority today too. But we are called to proclaim God's love and impending judgment to people. People need to hear the truth about Christ, His death and life-giving resurrection. They also need to know that there will be a day of reckoning.

Does your heart break over people who don't know about Christ?

Lord help me be bold and willing to share about you, I pray.

Extended Reading — Jeremiah 7-9

FAITH WALK
In Preparation

If you have raced with men on foot and they have worn you out, how can you compete with horses? If you stumble in safe country, how will you manage in the thickets by the Jordan?

Jeremiah 12:5

Why do the wicked prosper?

Jeremiah asks the question that plagues the minds of many, within and without the church. He couldn't understand why the wicked prosper, while he often suffered. Jeremiah also thought that the wicked could not enjoy any prosperity or pleasure unless God allowed it. Jeremiah had questions, but he asks with humility (v1).

Jeremiah was going through spiritual, mental and emotional struggle through the persecution from his fellow villagers from Anathoth. They had evidently mocked him and laughed at him. Later on, Jeremiah would have to spend a night in the stocks (Jeremiah 20:1-3), confinement in a cistern (Jeremiah 38:6), and imprisonment in the court of the guard (Jeremiah 28:13). But the troubles he was having in Anathoth were nothing compared to the troubles he would have later.

God's answer to Jeremiah was both powerful and profound.

God does not answer Jeremiah directly but encourages him to regard his present challenge as a preparation for greater challenges to come. God tells him to make his face like flint and not care for them. If he found it difficult in Anathoth, how would he fare in Jerusalem? Jeremiah needed to learn to trust God in his present challenge, in order to prepare him for the horsemen or greater challenges in the future.

God never calls us to contend with horsemen until he has trained us with run with men. Have you considered that the Lord might be preparing you for greater things through your struggles today?

Lord help me trust you as I go through today's challenges, I pray.

Extended Reading — Jeremiah 10-13

REPENTANCE
To Turn Away

Although our sins testify against us, do something, Lord, for the sake of your name. For we have often rebelled; we have sinned against you.   Jeremiah 14:7

Judah was going through a drought.

Sustained or multiple droughts could mean life and death situations in ancient societies where most people made their living by farming. A drought was also a special issue for ancient Israel and Judah because they often worshipped Canaanite idol Baal who was thought to be the god of weather and rain. And so many ancient Israelites were drawn to Baal worship because they wanted rain.

A drought was part of the covenant curses and was a possible punishment for disobedience (Deuteronomy 28:23-24). The Lord intended that the drought would bring the nation to repentance.

Jeremiah, using his prophetic imagination, thought of what true repentance would look like from Judah in response to the droughts. It began with an utter confession of guilt and an appeal to pure mercy, not what they deserved.

In the Bible, the word *repent* means "to change one's mind." The Bible also tells us that true repentance will result in a change of actions (Luke 3:8–14; Acts 3:19). Repentance includes conviction of sin, which is God's work in us (John 16:8-11), sorrow for sin and turning from it (2 Corinthians 7:10).

Repentance and faith are often considered two sides of the same coin. You cannot place your faith in Jesus Christ as the Savior without first changing your mind about your sin and about who Jesus is and what he has done. Have you chosen Christ as your Savior? Is there a sin in your life that you need to change your mind about and turn away from?

Lord help me turn to you with a genuine heart of repentance I pray.

Extended Reading — Jeremiah 14-17

GOD'S WILL
Re-shaped for His Use

He said, "Can I not do with you, Israel, as this potter does?"
declares the LORD. "Like clay in the hand of the potter, so are
you in my hand, Israel.   *Jeremiah 18:6*

God had a message for Israel.

In the Bible, God has often used daily life examples to teach deep truths. And this time God has one such lesson through Jeremiah.

God asked Jeremiah to go down to the house of the potter. Jeremiah went. As he observed the potter making his pots, the pot that the potter was making got marred in the potter's hand. And so the potter formed it into another pot, shaping as seemed best to him (v4).

The Lord used this analogy, to remind Jeremiah of his sovereign right to do what he pleased with a marred or uncooperative vessel. Israel marred themselves morally and spiritually before God.

Interestingly, the potter does not throw away the clay that got marred. He re-uses and re-shapes. And thankfully that is what God does with Israel and each of us too. The Lord does not give up on us when we mess up. He re-shapes and re-orders our lives that we would still be useful in his hand.

God has created each of us, fearfully and wonderfully (Psalm 139:13-16). We are to take what he has given us and use it for his glory and pleasure. Rather than live with disappointment and dissatisfaction with what God has or has not given us, we can choose to thank him in everything.

Just as the clay finds its highest purpose when it remains pliable in the hands of the potter, so our lives fulfill their highest purpose when we let our Potter have his way in us.

Lord mold me and make me, for your glorious purposes I pray.

Extended Reading — Jeremiah 18-22

RESTORATION
Opportunity to Return

I will give them a heart to know me, that I am the Lord. They will be my people, and I will be their God, for they will return to me with all their heart.   *Jeremiah 24:7*

Judgment came and was still to come on Judah.

The entire nation of Judah was to be exiled to Babylon. And when judgment came on a nation or community, it means that all suffer, even those who may be innocent of the sins that brought God's judgment. And yet that did not mean that everyone in Judah was the same in God's eyes.

What God said to Jeremiah through the two baskets of figs means that even when all suffer, God still knows the difference between those caught up in the judgment and those who brought down the judgment.

Some like the good figs were sent out of Judah to Babylon for their own good. And Jeremiah's message was that those first taken in exile to Babylon were the good figs, not the bad. They would be blessed even in captivity. God also promised to bring them back to this land. And when they returned to the land, God would establish them securely again (v5-6).

And then the Lord promised that he would give them a new heart to know him to know that he is the Lord. The great change after the exile was that Israel no longer went after the idols of the nations. They were separated and devoted to Yahweh in a way they had not been before.

How does this promise that God gave Israel encourage and strengthen you today?

Thank You, Lord, that you are a God of restoration and healing, even today.

Extended Reading — Jeremiah 23-25

HOPE
Hope and a Future

For I know the plans I have for you," declares the Lord, "plans to prosper you and not to harm you, plans to give you hope and a future. ¹² Then you will call on me and come and pray to me, and I will listen to you. ¹³ You will seek me and find me when you seek me with all your heart.   Jeremiah 29:11-13

Jeremiah 29 contains a letter from Jeremiah, writing as the Lord's prophet, to the exiles in Babylon.

The Israelites were in Babylon by the will of God, because of their rebellion. But exile didn't mean that God forgot about them or wanted to destroy them. They would be in Babylon for a long time but defined time, seventy years. And in that time God wanted them to settle in and make the best of their lives. God wanted the Jewish people to multiply. They were to do good, pray for and be a blessing to their Babylonian neighbors.

God reminds them of his own thoughts toward these exiled Jews in Babylon. For these exiled Jews, it was easy to think that God was against them; that he intended evil for them. But the Lord assured them that his thoughts toward them were of peace. In his heart and mind, God had a future and a hope for them, even in their exile.

The Lord promises to listen to them when they pray and seek him. Their seeking and God is found, and the fact that God would bring them back from captivity was part of their future and hope.

The devil works hard to rob us of our hope in God's future for us. What will you do to trust and seek God today?

Thank you, Lord, that you remember me, help me seek you daily I pray.

Extended Reading — Jeremiah 26-29

RESTORATION
A Reason to Sing

This is what the Lord says: Sing with joy for Jacob; shout for the foremost of the nations. Make your praises heard, and say, 'Lord, save your people, the remnant of Israel.'

Jeremiah 31:7

God's restoration is always worth singing about.

God assures his people that he will again take them into a covenant relationship with himself. He will save and restore his people. God promises to gather his people from all over the earth. The people will not just return to God but also to their land. And this is no small matter, but one that warrants great rejoicing and praise.

In this great restoration (v24) Israel will return to God with tears and supplications. The Bible says in Zechariah 12:10, I will pour out on the house of David and the inhabitants of Jerusalem a spirit of grace and supplication.

When we go through times of difficulties, one of the first things the enemy tries to steal is our joy. But the Bible says the joy of the Lord is our strength (Nehemiah 8:10). We don't have to stay in that valley of despair and depression. Don't have to allow what people say to control you. Maybe everyone isn't happy about us. But God is. We are who God created us to be. He is happy about you!

When times of suffering come, it is also reassuring to remember that the church has already been there. Nothing new has come over us. And that God in his goodness calls each of us back to him. He will draw his children to himself, by the influence of the Holy Spirit, he will restore to us the joy of our salvation (Psalm 51:12). Would you draw near to him? He promises to draw near to you (James 4:8).

Lord restore to me the joy of your salvation, I pray.

Extended Reading — Jeremiah 30-31

OBEDIENCE
'Foolish' Obedience

'This is what the Lord Almighty, the God of Israel, says: Take these documents, both the sealed and unsealed copies of the deed of purchase, and put them in a clay jar so they will last a long time. ¹⁵ For this is what the Lord Almighty, the God of Israel, says: Houses, fields, and vineyards will again be bought in this land.'   Jeremiah 32:14-15

A property deal from prison.

God gave Jeremiah a tough message for King Zedekiah and that landed him in the palace prison. King Zedekiah was angry that Jeremiah told the people that the Babylonians would succeed in conquering the city that Zedekiah was trying so hard to defend.

And now in prison, God tells Jeremiah to buy a field in his hometown Anathoth, from his cousin Hanamel. Anathoth was about three miles outside Jerusalem. With Babylonian armies surrounding Jerusalem, the enemy had already occupied Anathoth. Jeremiah was offered the purchase of land that was already under Babylonian control. The land itself was worthless and Jerusalem's days were numbered. To buy such a land in a time like that seemed like foolishness.

But Jeremiah obeyed the Lord. He bought the field following all the legal requirements for the purchase. Then he instructed Baruch, a scribe and his assistant, in everyone's hearing. Baruch was to preserve and hide the title deed and details of the transaction in a clay jar, to be read later.

The property purchase from prison was an expression of confident trust in God's promise that the land would be possessed again. Jeremiah obeyed what God asked him to do, however foolish it seemed. Do we obey to what God wants us to obey, even though it may seem foolish?

Lord help me to be more concerned about obeying you than looking smart to the world, I pray.

Extended Reading — Jeremiah 32-34

GOD'S JUDGMENT
Hear and Turn

Take a scroll and write on it all the words I have spoken to
you concerning Israel, Judah and all the other nations from
the time I began speaking to you in the reign of Josiah till
now. ³ Perhaps when the people of Judah hear about every
disaster, I plan to inflict on them, they will each turn from their
wicked ways; then I will forgive their wickedness and their sin.

Jeremiah 36:2-3

God called Jeremiah to write.

Jeremiah has been speaking God's messages to the people. And now God calls him to write these messages on a scroll. He was to write all the prophetic sayings he had been given up to that point, which meant all the earlier messages too.

Jeremiah was to write so that the message might be more effectively delivered. The written word would be more easily remembered, consulted, and meditated upon. The purpose was that the people of Judah will hear, turn from their wicked ways so that the Lord would forgive them.

There were another twenty years before the final conquest of Jerusalem. There was still time. It was still possible that God would rescue Judah, to avert the coming judgment. But for this every man needed to hear what God has spoken, turn from his evil ways and then God would forgive their sins.

The day of the Lord's return is imminent, there is no two ways about it. The time and date we do not know. And yet, when there is still time, God continues to give us opportunity after opportunity for us to hear his word and turn from our sins, so that we may experience his forgiveness and redemption. Have you taken up this offer?

Lord help me not delay in accepting you as my Savior, I pray.

Extended Reading — Jeremiah 35-37

COMPROMISE
Falsely Accused

So they took Jeremiah and put him into the cistern of Malkijah, the king's son, which was in the courtyard of the guard. They lowered Jeremiah by ropes into the cistern; it had no water in it, only mud, and Jeremiah sank down into the mud.

Jeremiah 38:6

The officials did not like Jeremiah's message.

Jeremiah did not enjoy preaching his message of catastrophe and doom either. But God called Jeremiah to give God's message to the people, which was their only chance of surviving the Babylonian threat. Jeremiah obeyed.

The officials asked King Zedekiah to execute Jeremiah. They said his message was bad for the morale of those defending Jerusalem and that Jeremiah did not seek the good of the people, rather their ruin. This was the exact opposite of the truth.

Zedekiah being the puppet king he was, did not have the courage to stand up to these officials. So he allowed them to do to Jeremiah as they pleased. They lowered him into a cistern of mud. Like many other servants of God, Jeremiah was wrongly accused. Moses the humble man was accused of pride. Job the righteous man was accused of great sin. Jesus the spotless son of God was accused of being demon-possessed.

Jeremiah had a very difficult message to deliver. He loved Judah, but he loved God much more. As painful as it was for Jeremiah to deliver a consistent message of judgment to his own people, Jeremiah was obedient to what God told him to do and say. He prayed for God's mercy on Judah but also trusted that God was good, just, and righteous. Are you being obedient to the Lord, especially in the difficult things he has called you to do?

Lord help me never compromise on doing your will, even when it is tough, I pray.

Extended Reading — Jeremiah 38-40; Psalm 74, 79

JUDGMENT
Multiple Chances

He set fire to the temple of the Lord, the royal palace and all the houses of Jerusalem. Every important building, he burned down.   2 Kings 25:9

Solomon's great temple was now a ruin.

T he beautiful temple that was built almost four hundred years back, was destroyed by the Babylonians, in the eleventh year of Zedekiah. And it would stay a ruin for many years until it was humbly rebuilt by the returning exiles in the days of Ezra.

History records that when the Babylonians entered the temple, they held a two-day feast there to desecrate it; then, on the third day, they set fire to the building. Nebuzaradan the commander, also carried away the valuable things from the temple.

Nebuzaradan methodically demolished the beautiful city, the palace and important buildings. He broke down the walls of Jerusalem, destroying the physical safety and security of the city. The walls would remain a ruin until they were rebuilt by the returning exiles in the days of Nehemiah.

Nebuzaradan also carried the people who remained in exile. He left behind some of the poorest people of the land to work the vineyards and fields.

Jerusalem was left desolate, completely plundered under the judgment of the Lord. The Lord had given his people this land and they possessed it for more than eight hundred years. A land that was taken by faith and obedience was lost through idolatry and sin.

God is loving and gracious. He is a God of not just second chances, but multiple chances. But his judgment is real too and will surely come. Would you choose to turn to him now, before it is too late?

Lord may I use every opportunity to draw closer to you, I pray.

Extended Reading — 2 Kings 24-25; 2 Chronicles 36

FAITH
From Why to Who

Lord, are you not from everlasting? My God, my Holy
One, you will never die.   Habakkuk 1:12

Habakkuk is overwhelmed.

Habakkuk the prophet, had a burden. He had a message from God
and it was heavy and saddened him. It was a message of coming
judgment on Judah. It was also a heavy message. Habakkuk deals with
some tough questions that he brings to God and God's answers.

The book of Habakkuk begins with his complaint. Habakkuk looks
around and he sees the violence and injustice of the world around him.
He is upset. He wails, and he complains. He can't understand why God
was allowing him to see all this. But in his complaining, he does not
lose focus of who he was addressing.

Habakkuk says, Lord are you not from everlasting, you will never die?
He moves from why to who. He remembers that God is infinite, unlike
us finite human beings. He also affirms and reiterates his relationship,
my God, my holy one.

Two things stand out here. One, the fact that Habakkuk has a personal
intimate relationship with God. He is not praying to some far away,
distant God, but as he says, my God, my Holy One. There is a very
personal relationship there. And yet, though he has a personal relationship
with this God, Habakkuk also knows that God is holy. He recognizes
and acknowledges that God is holy and way above in purity.

When faced with challenges, Habakkuk turned from his many 'whys' to
the 'who' of the one he was trusting, because he knew him as his personal
and holy God. Life is never easy. Challenges and discouragements are
part of life. What's your strategy?

Help me Lord to increasingly focus on who you are rather than my
problems, I pray.

Extended Reading — Habakkuk 1-3

AMBITION
Who is the Focus?

Should you then seek great things for yourself? Do not seek them. For I will bring disaster on all people, declares the Lord, but wherever you go I will let you escape with your life.

Jeremiah 45:5

Baruch certainly suffered much for his faithfulness to God and Jeremiah.

Baruch was an educated man, qualified as a secretary, whose brother was an officer of high rank under Zedekiah (Jeremiah 51:59). As Jeremiah's faithful partner and scribe, Baruch had to endure a great deal of opposition and abuse. And now he was exhausted and discouraged. Part of his disappointment though seemed to come from seeking great things for himself. He probably wanted to be in a different place than where he found himself. And God had a word for him.

God wanted Baruch to turn away from his self-focused state and not obsess too much about his own perceived growth and success. God tells Baruch, not to seek great things for himself. He reminds Baruch, worldly power, fame and reputation will not last long. He was going to bring disaster on all the people. But God promises to take care of Baruch wherever he went.

Paul in Philippians reminds us not to seek anything out of self-ambition (Philippians 2:3). And yet Paul, Peter and even Jesus were ambitious men. The difference, however, is that they were ambitious for God's glory and his name to be lifted.

God's word to Baruch reminds us that we are to focus on and exalt God and not ourselves. The Bible says, for all those who exalt themselves will be humbled, and those who humble themselves will be exalted (Luke 14:11). What are you ambitious for?

Lord, I desire to be ambitious for you, but I often fail. Please help me I pray.

Extended Reading — Jeremiah 41-45

FAITH WALK
Keep at It

*The swift cannot flee nor the strong escape. In the north, by the
River Euphrates, they stumble and fall.   Jeremiah 46:6*

God is God of all nations.

The book of Jeremiah mostly deals with the judgment God would
bring on Judah. And yet, in these few chapters, Jeremiah brings
word about the judgment on the Gentile nations. God's sovereignty is
over all the earth and not restricted to just Judah. God did not ignore or
neglect the Gentile nations. He would righteously judge each of them too.

Jeremiah begins his prophetic vision about the nations, with Egypt.
God called the proud Egyptian army to this battle, bringing them for
the purpose of judging them.

This battle between Egypt and Babylon was to take place on the banks
of the Euphrates. Though Egypt came to battle with Babylon expecting
to crush them, the Babylonians route them completely. Jeremiah could
see the captains of the Babylonian army calling out orders, commanding
all their soldiers to pursue and utterly defeat the retreating Egyptians.

God is fair and the true Judge. Jesus says his judgment is just for he seeks
not to please himself but his Father who sent him (John 5:30). God is
impartial in his judgment (1 Peter 1:17). The scriptures are also very
clear that God will punish all who do not obey him (2 Thessalonians
1:8). But God gives eternal life to those who by persistence in doing
good seek glory, honor, and immortality (Romans 2:7).
God will judge everyone. And he is fair and righteous in his judgment.
Are you persisting in being faithful in serving your Lord and Master
that you may have eternal life with him?

Lord may I be found faithful in serving you I pray.

Extended Reading — Jeremiah 46-48

FAITH WALK
Live Out Your Inheritance

Concerning the Ammonites: This is what the Lord says: "Has Israel no sons? Has Israel no heir? Why then has Molek taken possession of Gad? Why do his people live in its towns?

Jeremiah 49:1

The Ammonites were often in conflict with Israel.

The Ammonites lived in the area on the east side of the Jordan River, north of the Moabites. They opposed Judah during Jehoiakim's reign and joined in the invasion of Judah (2 Kings 24:2).

Ammonites occupied land that was given to the tribes of Gad, Reuben, and Manasseh. They lived in that land as if Israel's inheritance didn't matter. But to God, it was clearly Israel's inheritance and did not belong to Ammon.

This was not just a political matter but also a spiritual matter. The Bible says Molek has taken possession of Gad. Molek is mentioned as the invader who took possession and occupied the lands. Molek or Molech was also worshipped with rites of child-sacrifice for many years.

God's word is packed with promises for his children to claim as our inheritance. Yet we live as spiritually poor people, struggling to stay afloat. The Bible has promises to encourage us and direct us. Whatever your situation, there is a promise that you can claim.

Peace, love, and power in Jesus is ours as our inheritance as children of God. And yet, we often forfeit our inheritance and live in constant worry, fear, and doubt. The Bible says, be doers of the word, not hearers only (James 1:22). Are you daily enjoying the rich inheritance that is yours in Christ Jesus?

Lord help me live the rich life of love hope and joy that is my inheritance in you, I pray.

Extended Reading — Jeremiah 49-50

SUBMISSION
In Humble Adoration

He made the earth by his power; he founded the world by his wisdom and stretched out the heavens by his understanding. When he thunders, the waters in the heavens roar; he makes clouds rise from the ends of the earth. He sends lightning with the rain and brings out the wind from his storehouses.   *Jeremiah 51:15-16*

God is the Creator of all that is.

A creator is one who makes something new. The fact that God is the Creator of all that is seen and unseen, is one of the foundational truths of the Bible. Isaiah 40:28 (ESV) says, have you not known? Have you not heard? The LORD is the everlasting God, the creator of the ends of the earth. He does not faint or grow weary; his understanding is unsearchable.

Yahweh is not only a God of judgment; his power, his wisdom and his understanding are also evident in creation. God's power in creation is not just a thing of the past. He is presently working in and through creation. God is the maker of all things.

God is the designer and craftsman of everything in the universe. When God created the heavens and the earth, he did so by speaking it into existence. But when he created human beings, he took some clay that he had already made and formed a man. Then he breathed his own life into that man, and "man became a living soul" (Genesis 2:7). This means that human beings are more like God than any other created thing.

The wise person bows before the Creator and willingly submits himself or herself to the only one who truly knows how we are made (Romans 9:20). What's your response to this Creator God?

Lord may I ever bow in humble adoration to you my Creator, I pray.

Extended Reading — Jeremiah 51-52

WAITING ON GOD
Remind Me

I say to myself, "The Lord is my portion; therefore, I will wait for him. ²⁵ The Lord is good to those whose hope is in him, to the one who seeks him; ²⁶ it is good to wait quietly for the salvation of the Lord.   *Lamentations 3:24-26*

Lord when I fret and fume over unfairness and terror,
And I am inclined to major on the minor,
When I am envious of those who get away with evil,
And choose to focus on people, more than your will,
Remind me, Lord, Remind me.

Remind me, Lord, to commit my ways to you,
Remind me, to trust you in all I do.
That in Your presence I would be still,
And know that justice bring, ou surely will!!

Lord when evil men work against yyour people,
And that too, at the cost of the poor and feeble.
When these people seem to get their own way,
And they seem to prosper, every day,
Remind me Lord remind me.

Remind me, Lord, to wait for you,
Remind me, to keep your ways in all I do,
That I would consider the blameless and upright,
And see and know that, you do uphold alright!

Extended Reading — Lamentations 1; Lamentations 2; Lamentations 3:1-36

BACKSLIDING

Return

Restore us to yourself, Lord, that we may return; renew our days as of old [22] *unless you have utterly rejected us and are angry with us beyond measure.*   Lamentations 5:21-22

Jerusalem has fallen.

The Book of Lamentations is a   collection of five poems where Jeremiah is lamenting the catastrophic defeat and conquest of Jerusalem and the Kingdom of Judah.

Jeremiah recounts and contrasts between happy, prosperous Jerusalem and the lonely, empty conquered city after Babylon's conquest. Jerusalem that once was full of people is now empty and desolate. Once she was great among the nations, now she is like a slave. Jeremiah weeps with and for Jerusalem and Judah.

God seems to have forgotten his people. The only hope they have is to cry out to God, to repent. But these people didn't even seem to have the power to repent properly on their own. Jeremiah recognized that they needed God to turn back to them. And if God would turn back to his people, they would surely be restored.

Our hearts are so often hardened or too low or helpless that we are not even repentant. God alone can give us hearts of true repentance and restore us completely. While 'I repent' is a good and right prayer, 'turn me back to you Lord, and give me the gift of true repentance' may be a better prayer.

And then Jeremiah asks that the Lord renew and revive his people. When God turns us back to him, we can and should expect a revival. If we have backslidden or declined, we can pray that God would grant us hearts that are repentant so that we may be renewed. Do you need to come back to the Lord in repentance?

Lord give me a heart of repentance and turn me back to you, I pray.

Extended Reading — Lamentations 3:37-66; Lamentations 4; Lamentations 5:1-22

CALLING
A Captive Called

He said to me, "Son of man stand up on your feet and I will speak to you." ² As he spoke, the Spirit came into me and raised me to my feet, and I heard him speaking to me.   *Ezekiel 2:1-2*

Ezekiel was in captivity.

God called Ezekiel to his prophetic ministry during tough times. Though Judah still stood as an independent nation they were under Babylon's powerful domination. And though the temple still stood and functioned in Jerusalem, the people had been carried away as captives. Ezekiel, the priest, was one among the captives. It is in this setting, that God calls Ezekiel to his prophetic work.

Ezekiel's call began with a glorious vision of God. Ezekiel sees the heavens, God's throne, and the cherubim. Ezekiel has an amazing vision of the likeness of the glory of God (1:28). The vision was so overwhelming that it caused Ezekiel to fall face down.

After the vision, God now calls him for the work he has for him. He asks him to stand up on his feet and receive his call. The Spirit entered Ezekiel and worked in him to do what God commanded. This same Spirit continues to help believers do what God commands.

The Holy Spirit still works and enters his people through the word of God. And when God calls us to do a certain thing, then he gives us the power to do it. The best position we can have is to recognize our own needs and his all-sufficient grace and strength.

God continues to call and equip his people, even though our tough situations. What is God calling us to do today?

Lord help me be obedient to all you call me to do, I pray.

Extended Reading — Ezekiel 1-4

JUDGMENT
Take Heed and Act

Now, son of man, take a sharp sword and use it as a barber's
razor to shave your head and your beard. Then take a set of
scales and divide up the hair.   *Ezekiel 5:1*

Ezekiel means "strengthened by God."

Ezekiel grew up in Jerusalem and served as a priest in the temple. He
was among the second group of captives taken to Babylon along
with King Jehoiachin. While in Babylon Ezekiel became a prophet of
God. God often asked Ezekiel to do things that served as prophetic
demonstrations to the people, of coming judgment.

And this shaving of his head and dividing up the hair is another such
object lesson. God asks Ezekiel to shave his head, using a sword. A
sword is not usually used to cut hair, rather is used in battle. As this
was, however, an acted-out prophecy regarding the judgment that the
Babylonian army would bring on Jerusalem, a sword was appropriate.
The burning, chopping, and scattering of his hair represented the fall
of Jerusalem and the bringing back of God's remnant.

Ezekiel delivered God's messages with straightforward language that
everyone could understand, whether they listened or not (Ezekiel 2:7).
Ezekiel did not hesitate to obey God's instructions faithfully, though he
faced considerable opposition. Ezekiel had a passionate view of judgment
and hope, and he reflected God's own sorrow over the people's sins.

Ezekiel was told to groan with a broken heart and bitter grief for the
coming judgment. And that message remains relevant for us today.
Judgment day is coming. It will surely take place. With whom will you
prayerfully share the good news of the Gospel this week?

Lord give me a burden to share your love to those around me, I pray.

Extended Reading — Ezekiel 5-8

FAITH
Are You Seeing?

*Son of man, you are living among a rebellious people. They have
eyes to see but do not see and ears to hear but do not hear, for
they are a rebellious people.*   Ezekiel 12:2

Ezekiel lived among a rebellious people.

The Lord has been speaking through his prophet Ezekiel to the people
of Israel. In the earlier chapters, the Lord pronounces judgment
on idolaters. The glory of the Lord departs from the Temple. The Lord
pronounces sure judgment on Israel and yet promises that they will
return too if they repent.

And now the Lord went further to describe the people of Israel as
rebellious because they had eyes but did not see and ears but did not
hear. And what were these people not seeing or hearing?

The Lord had been using Ezekiel as an object lesson to the people to
warn them. The Lord gave his people ample opportunity take heed,
to be warned. They had been seeing the many things that the Lord
had asked Ezekiel to do as a message. And yet they behaved like they
could not see or hear.

In the following verses, we see God asked Ezekiel to pack his belongings
and leave as if on exile. Ezekiel was to dig through the wall and take his
belongings through the hole in the wall. And when the people asked,
he was to explain his actions as a sign of the exile that was to come.

The Lord continues to graciously warn us today from his word and
through the lives of people around us. Are we taking warning and
repenting or are we rebellious too?

**Lord help me heed what I hear and see and return to you in
repentance, I pray.**

Extended Reading — Ezekiel 9-12

Faith
Be Aware and Alert

My hand will be against the prophets who see false visions and
utter lying divinations. They will not belong to the council of
my people or be listed in the records of Israel, nor will they
enter the land of Israel. Then you will know that I am the
Sovereign Lord.   *Ezekiel 13:9*

False prophets often have seemingly optimistic, positive messages.

Among the Jewish people of Ezekiel's time, there were many false
prophets, both in Israel and in the Babylonian exile. These false
prophets of Israel prophesied that God will deliver Jerusalem and Judah
from the Babylonians, and those already in exile will come home soon.
Though this was soothing to the ears of the suffering people, these
prophecies were not true or from God.

The prophecies of these false prophets came from their own hearts and
desires. These self-proclaimed prophets made their prophecy sound
spiritual and mysterious. But God called them foolish prophets who
had seen nothing (v3) and who spoke lies (v6).

And God said, his hand will be against these self-proclaimed prophets.
God's judgment upon these false prophets meant that they had no share
in Israel's assembly, in Israel's house, or in Israel's land. This exclusion
would declare that Yahweh is God. These three punishments strike the
core of what it meant to be an Israelite.

False prophets are very much part of today's church. 2 Peter 2:1 says,
false teachers are not a possibility, but a reality and right within the
church. False teachers do not get their message from God.

The message of a true teacher leads one to be effective and productive
in the knowledge of Christ (2 Peter 1:8). Would you ask God to keep
you alert to false teachers and prophets?

Lord help me know and accept only your Truth, I pray.

Extended Reading — Ezekiel 13-15

COMMITMENT
Watch Your Word

Surely as I live, declares the Sovereign Lord, he shall die in Babylon, in the land of the king who put him on the throne, whose oath he despised and whose treaty he broke.

Ezekiel 17:16

An oath made had to be honored.

Zedekiah rebelled against Nebuchadnezzar, king of Babylon, much against strong warnings from Jeremiah. He ignored the promises of submission that he made to Nebuchadnezzar, king of Babylon (2 Kings 24:20).

If he had remained faithful to his oath of loyalty, Judah could have continued to prosper as a tributary kingdom. He had favorable conditions for his reign. Nebuchadnezzar's benevolent attitude helped Zedekiah prosper. Instead, Zedekiah rebelled.

An oath was sacred in Israel. Violating an oath was an offense against God. Even an oath made fraudulently was to be honored. God expected Zedekiah to be loyal to the covenant he made. He had bound himself by oath, in the presence of God to be faithful to the covenant he made with Nebuchadnezzar, but at the first given opportunity, he broke it.

Jeremiah 52:11 says that Zedekiah remained in Babylon until his death. God promised severe judgment on Zedekiah for not keeping his word. Through Ezekiel, God said Zedekiah would die during Babylon. And as it was told, he died in the most terrible of circumstances (2 Kings 25:7).

When Zedekiah gave his oath to Nebuchadnezzar, God regarded it as an oath to him also. The implications of this attitude are far-reaching. Agreements entered by worshippers of God are binding as if they had been made with God. God's people are called to be people of their word. Are we ?

Lord help me be careful to honor you with my word, I pray.

Extended Reading — Ezekiel 16-17

SALVATION
Take the Offer

For everyone belongs to me, the parent, as well as the child—
both alike, belong to me. The one who sins is the one who will
die.   *Ezekiel 18:4*

Everyone belongs to the Lord.

This chapter begins with God's answer to a false proverb which says,
the parents eat sour grapes, and the children's teeth are set on edge
(v2). The proverb was a protest, a complaint. The idea was that the present
generation was being unjustly punished for what their fathers did. The
one who eats the sour grapes should have the sour taste in their teeth.

But the fact is, God has authority over all, the parent and the child. And
he promised to pronounce judgment over anyone who sinned because
everyone belongs to God, the fathers as well as the children. None who
should be punished for their sins would escape that judgment. God will
deal with each one in justice and mercy.

God judges the heart of each individual and deals with each one according
to their own faith. Salvation is offered to all. John 3:16 says **whoever**,
believes in Jesus shall not perish but have everlasting life. Each of us
has the option to accept Jesus' offer of salvation and be adopted into
God's family and inherit a new nature.

And yet, sin is never private, it has consequences. Adam and Eve's sin has
marred all of us, we are all born with a sinful nature (Romans 3:23). The
sins of the parents will affect the children. Those who grow up watching
sinful behavior are often likely to do the same in their own lives.

Do we take Jesus' offer or do we blame others for our condition?

Lord, I accept you as my Savior today, in Jesus' name.

Extended Reading — Ezekiel 18-19

COMMITMENT
Single-Minded Devotion

As for you, people of Israel, this is what the Sovereign Lord says:
Go and serve your idols, every one of you! But afterward, you
will surely listen to me and no longer profane my holy name
with your gifts and idols.   *Ezekiel 20:39*

God is now getting to the bottom line.

Having walked through Israel's history of sin and God's history of mercy to Israel, in the previous verses, the Lord now brings the matter to a head. God gives them a challenge.

God is asking his people to decide. They needed to choose. If they wanted to serve their idols, then they might as well make up their minds and do it. They could become Babylonians in every regard now if that is what they really wanted. But if they chose God then they were to worship him with all their hearts. God was telling them they needed to pick a side and stay there.

God clearly longed for Israel's restoration to the land. It would be a pleasing sacrifice unto him and it would glorify him before the Gentiles (v41). But God did not want a divided heart.

When the Israelites brought Yahweh worship from hearts that were also given to idols, it profaned God and his name. In New Testament phrasing, God called Israel to be either hot or cold, but not lukewarm (Revelation 3:15-16). If anyone loves the world, the love for the Father is not in them (1 John 2:15).

Today the idols we worship may or may not be graven images. However, anything that takes priority over God is an idol. And this could range from our achievements, careers, physical looks to relationships and addictions. Do you have an undivided heart?

Lord may my heart ever be committed to you alone, I pray.

Extended Reading — Ezekiel 20-21

PRAYER
Stand and Build

I looked for someone among them who would build up the wall and stand before me in the gap on behalf of the land, so I would not have to destroy it, but I found no one. Ezekiel 22:30

Stand in the gap and build the wall!

The image of the wall connects back with the false and weak wall of the false prophets just a few verses before this (v28). The false prophets build by smearing whitewash. God looked for a man to bring strength, stability, and security to Israel but found no one.

God was looking for a man of prayer, like Abraham, Moses, and David, God looked for one who would, through prayer, stand in the gap between a holy God and his disobedient, rebellious, profane people. God found no one in Ezekiel's time, but fortunately, he did find the man to stand in the gap, Jesus Christ. He is the one who ever lives to pray for his people (Hebrews 7:25).

The Bible says the end of all things is near. And every follower of Christ is called to stand in the gap and build the wall. We are to pray earnestly for the lost in our nations. The enemy is on a warpath, like a roaring lion, looking for those he can devour. Therefore, we are called to be alert and of sober mind and pray (1 Peter 5:8).

Sometimes when things look so hopeless and wasted in the world around us, we get discouraged and give up. But despite what it looks like, however hopeless it seems, we need to keep praying. Nothing is too hard for God. He will answer our prayer and every nation will be changed! Will you stand in the gap?

Lord help me be diligent in praying for my nation, I pray.

Extended Reading — Ezekiel 22-23

OBEDIENCE
Obedience Even Through Pain

Son of man, with one blow I am about to take away from you the delight of your eyes. Yet do not lament or weep or shed any tears.   *Ezekiel 24:16*

Ezekiel was going to lose his wife.

This was a shocking message God had for Ezekiel. God said, his wife would suddenly and unexpectedly die, 'with one blow.' But Ezekiel was not to mourn. He was forbidden to be sorrowful. He was to groan silently. He was not to weep nor show any outward, traditional signs of mourning or loud wailing. Furthermore, he was to announce to the people that this was to happen.

Wonder what that must have been like for Ezekiel. What would he have told his wife? The loss of his wife would naturally be painful. The phrase 'delight of your eyes' indicates a dear and loving relationship between Ezekiel and his wife. All through the book of Ezekiel, we see him as a man of deep emotion. He often wept over the fate of Jerusalem and Judah. He would be deeply affected by this sudden loss.

And yet, the Bible says Ezekiel obeyed God. Ezekiel was determined to honor God by obeying him despite his own feelings and pain. So Ezekiel the prophet, reported to the people the next morning that his own wife would die. And she died that evening.

Mourning the loss of a loved one is natural. This is a one-off incident in the Bible and not a pattern. Jesus wept at the tomb of Lazarus (John 11:35). Ezekiel needed a specific command from God not to do it.

Ezekiel's obedience even in this painful situation is a powerful example.

Lord may I honor you in all circumstances of life, I pray.

Extended Reading — Ezekiel 24-27

HOPE
Something Beautiful, Something Good

This is what the Sovereign Lord says: When I gather the people of Israel from the nations where they have been scattered, I will be proved holy through them in the sight of the nations. Then they will live in their own land, which I gave to my servant Jacob. *Ezekiel 28:25*

God was not through with Israel as a nation.

This promise shows that God's plan for Israel in their land did not end with the Babylonian conquest of Jerusalem; nor has it ended today. Ezekiel looked forward to an aspect of the new covenant. A time of restoration when the Lord would bring his people back together again (Deuteronomy 30:3). There was still hope.

In God's design, the Babylonian exile would not last forever. After 70 years of forced captivity, the Jewish people could go back to the Promised Land. During the days of Ezra and Nehemiah, there was a partial return.

God promised that they will live in their own land again. And that all danger and opposition would end. And as part of the new covenant promise, there was a greater fulfillment to come. And this would be just another way that God would reveal himself to Israel and to the world. As a God who is truly sovereign and faithful to his word and his people. This message was a source of encouragement to the people in exile.

God is not through with each of us either. However bleak and hopeless our situations may seem, God's not done yet. Suffering is not the end, he will restore and make us strong and firm (1 Peter 5:10). He is working something beautiful, something good even through all your pain. Hope in him.

Lord help me never keep my hope in you I pray.

Extended Reading — Ezekiel 28-31

WITNESS
Watchman for God

Son of man, I have made you a watchman for the people of Israel; so, hear the word I speak and give them warning from me.   *Ezekiel 33:7*

You wicked person, you will surely die.

This was the general message Ezekiel was to give the people of Israel. God appointed Ezekiel as a watchman for the people of Israel to warn them of the coming danger. Ezekiel heard from God that judgment was coming soon, and he was to announce it.

Now if Ezekiel faithfully delivered the message to the people, then the response of the one he warned was the responsibility of one who heard it. But if Ezekiel did not tell the people, giving them the opportunity to repent and turn from their evil ways, then Ezekiel would be held responsible for their blood (v2-6)

The Lord reiterates a basic principle about his nature and dealings with humanity. God takes no special pleasure in the death of the wicked (v11). God's heart is for people to repent, to turn from their way and live. God is not sadistic and cruel, making repentance impossible because he loves to see humanity suffer. But he will not spare the requirements of justice and holiness for those who refuse to turn to him.

The Great Commission in Matthew 28:19-20 reminds us that every disciple of the Lord Jesus is to share the gospel to the ends of the earth. We are watchmen who are responsible to tell people the gospel and warn them of the coming judgment of God. We are to tell and live a life that points to Christ. Changing hearts is the Holy Spirit's work.

Are you being a watchman for the Lord?
Lord may my life and words always point to the truth of your word, I pray.

Extended Reading — Ezekiel 32-34

SALVATION
Transformed for Life

I will give you a new heart and put a new spirit in you; I will remove from you your heart of stone and give you a heart of flesh. [27] And I will put my Spirit in you and move you to follow my decrees and be careful to keep my laws.   Ezekiel 36:26-27

The Lord promises spiritual transformation.

There is to be a radical change. From the law working from outside in, God promised a new heart to work from inside out. God says he would take the heart of stone out and replace it with a new heart, of flesh.

A heart of stone implies a heart that is hardened by sin. An inflexible and stubborn heart that is not receptive to God's word or Spirit's leading. While a heart of flesh is a picture of submission and compliance. A heart that can feel, can enjoy and can be a welcome dwelling place for the Spirit of God.

God promises a new heart and a new spirit. 2 Corinthians 5:17 says a believer is a new creation in Christ Jesus. God promised a new nature, which would be taught in accordance with the truth in Jesus. In the new nature, you put off your old self, which is corrupted by deceitful desires and put on the new self, created to be like God in true righteousness and holiness (Ephesians 4:21-24).

God also promises the indwelling holy spirit. The Spirit dwells in every believer (Romans 8:9) and is promised to fill the believer with special presence and power (Acts 1:5, 8) and help the believer obey God's law.

Is this transformed life yours?

Change my heart O God, make it ever new, I pray.

Extended Reading — Ezekiel 35-37

SALVATION
Not By Our Merit

I will no longer hide my face from them, for I will pour out my Spirit on the people of Israel, declares the Sovereign Lord.

Ezekiel 39:29

It was their sin that caused God to hide his face.

The Israelites in exile in Babylon, after the fall of Jerusalem and Judah, were in a tough situation. Return and restoration seemed almost impossible. And it is to these people, that Ezekiel first spoke his message of hope and restoration. To them these promises were precious. There was a minor fulfillment in the return from captivity under Ezra and Zerubbabel. The greater and complete restoration still awaits, as the New Testament recognizes (Romans 11:26).

Israel's restoration would come from a spirit of repentance. They would see all that God did for them and it would humble them considering his generous love. They would see and admit that it was their own sins that sent them into captivity and suffering.

God says he will pour out his Spirit. The restoration was to be complete and permanent. He promises never to hide his face again. With God's Spirit poured out upon Israel, they would have a relationship with God based on God's work and grace, not on their own merits.

God can never tolerate sin. But God always loves the sinner. And the extent of God's love for us sinners is seen in the cross. For God so loved the world that he gave his one and only Son, that whoever believes in him shall not perish but have eternal love (John 3:16). God's love is not limited, but available to *anyone* who believes. What an amazing God and what amazing love!

Who needs to hear of this amazing love from you, today?

Lord help me be generous in sharing your wonderful love, I pray.

Extended Reading — Ezekiel 38-39

BIBLE
Yardstick For Our Lives

He took me there, and I saw a man whose appearance was like bronze; he was standing in the gateway with a linen cord and a measuring rod in his hand. ⁴ The man said to me, "Son of man, look carefully and listen closely and pay attention to everything I am going to show you, for that is why you have been brought here. Tell the people of Israel everything you see."

Ezekiel 40:3-4

This is the longest vision that Ezekiel receives.

This vision is about a new temple and city. In chapters 41 and 42, Ezekiel saw a glorious vision of the temple. In chapter 43 God took possession of the temple. Chapter 44 is about the priests who are to minister in this temple. Chapter 45 and 46 talk about the division of the land. And chapters 47 and 48 talk about the holy waters that border the holy land, portions assigned to the tribes and dimensions of the gates of the holy city.

The vision begins with Ezekiel seeing the temple. He is taken to Israel, where he sees a mountain and a city. A man of angelic beauty meets him with a linen cord and rod in his hand. He asks him to pay close attention so that he can go back and tell the people of Israel.

The temple of God is built by line and rule. The church is formed according to the scripture, which is the cord and measuring rod in the hands of Christ. The Bible is the standard by which we called to live our lives. How do you measure up?

Who needs to hear from you today, about the Bible being our yardstick and standard for life?

Lord help me daily live by the standard of your word, I pray.

Extended Reading — Ezekiel 40-41

REPENTANCE
Turn and Return

> *Now let them put away from me their prostitution and the*
> *funeral offerings for their kings, and I will live among them*
> *forever.*   *Ezekiel 43:9*

God takes possession of his temple.

Ezekiel having given us a view of the glorious temple, now moves to describe God taking possession of the temple. God promises his continued presence with his people on the condition that they repent. Their repentance meant that they turn from their idols, abandon their idolatrous practices and worship God in the way he commands.

The repentance of the people of Israel was to come from their shame of looking back and recognizing their pattern of sin (v10). And as God describes the pattern for this temple, it reflects the mercy God has in store for them despite their utter unworthiness. This understanding should cause them to be ashamed of their conduct.

God's unending goodness is all ours. All he asks is, repent.

We are to turn away from our sins and return to him. Charles Spurgeon says 'repentance is a discovery of the evil of sin, a mourning that we have committed it, a resolution to forsake it. It is, in fact, a change of mind of a very deep and practical character, which makes the man love what once he hated, and hate what once he loved.'

The whole church under the new covenant today has the privilege of access to God (Hebrews 10:19). And for the same reason, not just the priests, but every believer now is obliged and called to press toward the perfection of holiness. We are to be holy for he who called us is holy (1 Peter 1:15-16). Does looking back over your life and pattern of sin cause you to repent?

Lord give me a humble and repentant heart, I pray.

Extended Reading — Ezekiel 42-43

KNOW GOD
I Am Unworthy

*Then the man brought me by way of the north gate to the front
of the temple. I looked and saw the glory of the Lord filling the
temple of the Lord, and I fell facedown.*   *Ezekiel 44:4*

All through the Bible, the response to God's holiness has always been
worship.

God is holy. In Isaiah 6, Isaiah's response to God's holiness was to
recognize the sinfulness and the filthy state of his own heart and
mouth. One way to describe God's holiness is perfection. God is unlike
any other (Hosea 11:9) and his holiness is the essence of that 'otherness.'
There is absolutely no trace of sin in him (James 1:13). God is way
above any other. No one can compare to him (Psalm 40:5). His holiness
fills his entire being and is reflected in every one of his characteristics.

Only when we glimpse the holiness of God will we recognize our own
sinfulness. And only when we see our own sin for what it is before God,
can there be true repentance. Realizing the dreadful consequence of sin
and the fact that the sinless Son of God suffered our punishment, should
bring us to our knees and join Job in saying 'I am unworthy' (Job 40:4).

Understanding God's holiness should cause us to be awed by his
compassion, mercy, grace, and forgiveness towards us. And then say
with the Psalmist, 'if you, Lord, kept a record of sins, Lord, who could
stand? But with you there is forgiveness, so that we can, with reverence,
serve you (Psalm 130:3-4).

Our reasonable response to this holy God is to offer our bodies as
living sacrifices and live lives that are transformed by the renewing of
our minds (Romans 12:1-2).

*Lord may I never lose the awe of your holiness and my own sinfulness,
I pray.*

Extended Reading — Ezekiel 44-45

KNOW GOD
The River of Life

> *The man brought me back to the entrance to the temple, and I saw water coming out from under the threshold of the temple toward the east (for the temple faced east). The water was coming down from under the south side of the temple, south of the altar.*
>
> *Ezekiel 47:1*

Waters in the sanctuary.

The first twelve verses of this chapter talk of Ezekiel's vision of the holy water, their rise, extent, depth. It also tells about the healing property of these waters and gives an account of the trees growing on its banks.

The waters of the sanctuary are running waters, like a river, not standing waters as in a pond. The waters were increasing and spreading. As Ezekiel watched, the waters grew from just a trickle to a mighty river (v3-5).

This parable gives a picture of the River of Life. Throughout the Scriptures, water is associated with the Holy Spirit. And here we see the outpouring of the Holy Spirit and is associated with the outpouring of the Holy Spirit on the church on the day of Pentecost.

And since Pentecost, the gospel has been spreading and it continues to spread even today. Through the witness of his people, the gospel continues to spread to the ends of the earth. We see the work of the Holy Spirit moving in our own hearts and churches bringing with it blessings, healing and growth. It is the river of life that flows from the temple and the Spirit of God. And the ultimate fulfillment of this passage will come when Christ returns to reign on the earth.

What difference has this River of Life made in your life?

Spirit of the Living God, fall afresh on me, break me, fill me and use me, I pray.

Extended Reading — Ezekiel 46-48

RESTORATION
Turn to God

will repay you for the years the locusts have eaten – the great locust and the young locust, the other locusts and the locust swarm – my great army that I sent among you.   Joel 2:25 I

True repentance leads to restoration.

Joel means 'Jehovah is God.' Joel prophesied during a time of great turmoil and transition, to the southern kingdom of Judah without reference to the northern kingdom of Israel.

In chapter one, Joel speaks of the judgment that had arrived in Judah through a plague of locusts and drought. In chapter two, he begins describing the judgment that will come. A large and mighty army is set against Judah. But Joel continues with the hope of the restoration of the Lord if Judah is willing to repent.

The people who hear the warning of the Lord are called to repent. True repentance is to turn *to* God and turn away *from* sin. They are to repent with all their hearts. They are to repent with fasting, with weeping, and with mourning. Repentance is to be genuine not a show. They are to rend their hearts, not their garments.

And if there is true repentance, God promised to restore what was taken away in chastisement. God promises to restore what the locusts had eaten away. Locusts ate the fruit of the years of labor, not the years themselves. Time lost cannot be restored, but God promises to restore the fruit of the years lost.

God is still in the business of restoring lives and hearts of those who truly repent. Have you truly repented, turned to God and away from sin?

Lord that I may truly turn to you with all my heart, I pray.

Extended Reading — Joel 1-3

OBEDIENCE
Would You Dare?

> *But Daniel resolved not to defile himself with the royal food and wine, and he asked the chief official for permission not to defile himself this way.*   *Daniel 1:8*

Nebuchadnezzar confiscated more than the holy things from the temple. He brought to Babylon the young and brightest minds of Judah. Teenagers, Daniel, and his three friends were among these slaves who were brought back to Babylon. They were put under the care of Ashpenaz, to be groomed for civil service.

Indoctrination was the simple purpose of grooming. The young Jewish men were to leave behind their Hebrew God and culture and look to Nebuchadnezzar for all their needs. But Daniel and his friends refused, insisting that they would look to God alone.

Daniel did not object to the change of name. He knew who he was in the Lord, so it didn't matter what others called him. Daniel also knew what he believed in and hence he did not object to the foreign education. But the food and wine were a different matter.

Daniel and his friends objected to the food and wine, on at least three counts. The food served did not follow the requirements of the Jewish law. The food was probably sacrificed to idols. And eating the king's food implied fellowship with the Babylonian culture.

Daniel and his friends were committed to obedience at all costs. Refusing the king's order could mean punishment, even death. The food itself was a much better alternative to a vegetarian diet and water for three years. Being separated from family and home would have made it only more difficult not to compromise. It took courage for Daniel to choose to honor God. Would you dare to be a Daniel?

Lord give me the desire and courage to obey you against all odds, I pray.

Extended Reading — Daniel 1-3

INTEGRITY
Obedient Disobedience

Now when Daniel learned that the decree had been published, he went home to his upstairs room where the windows opened toward Jerusalem. Three times a day he got down on his knees and prayed, giving thanks to his God, just as he had done before.   *Daniel 6:10*

There were no skeletons in Daniel's closet.

Daniel distinguished himself from the other officials. And so King Darius intended to set him above the entire kingdom. Daniel shined above the other officials because he had an excellent spirit. This was more than what those leaders could bear. Daniel had a good attitude in his work and life, and this made him the object of attack.

Try as they might, the officials could find no fault with Daniel. And they finally concluded that there was no way to get at Daniel, except through the law of God (v5). And so they come up with a devious plan to trap him where they suggested the king should issue a decree that anyone who worships or bows down to any god other than him, should be put into the lion's den.

The decree didn't change anything for Daniel. He continued to get on his knees and pray to God, three times a day. And that was just what the officials needed and informed the king. The king was forced to implement the decree. He reluctantly put Daniel in the lion's den. But as we know, God came through for Daniel and shut the mouths of the lions.

Daniel did break the king's law, but he did not go *against* the king or against the king's *best interests*. Daniel is an example of obedient disobedience. He was preserved through faith. What is preserving you?

Lord give me an excellent spirit like Daniel, I pray.

Extended Reading — Daniel 4-6

PRAYER
Not Just for 'Super Believers'

*In the first year of his reign, I, Daniel, understood from the
Scriptures, according to the word of the Lord given to Jeremiah
the prophet, that the desolation of Jerusalem would last
seventy years. ³ So I turned to the Lord God and pleaded with
him in prayer and petition, in fasting, and in sackcloth and
ashes.*   Daniel 9:2-3

Daniel intercedes.

A wonderful model of intercessory prayer is found in this chapter.
Daniel prays in response to God's Word. The fact that he understood
from the scriptures indicates that he spent much time with the scriptures,
to understand it. He didn't just understand or stop with academic
knowledge, he acts on it. He prayed. He pleaded with God in earnestness.

There is a fervency and urgency to Daniel's prayer. His prayer is based on
the character of God (v4). He personally knows the God he is praying
to. A God who keeps his covenant of love to his people. And what
he knows gives him the confidence to approach him.

Daniel's prayer is undergirded with confession, not just of his own sins
but that of the people he identifies unselfishly with God's people (v5).
His prayer is dependent on God's character and its goal is God's glory
(v16-19).

True intercessory prayer seeks to know God's will and glory and see
it fulfilled, regardless of what it costs us. All Christians have the Holy
Spirit in their hearts and, just as he intercedes for us in accordance
with God's will (Romans 8:26-27), we are to intercede for one another.
Intercession is not a privilege restricted to some 'super believers', rather,
not to intercede for others is sin (1 Samuel 12:23). Are you interceding
for others?

Lord that I may be diligent in praying for others, I pray.

Extended Reading — Daniel 7-9

PRAYER
The Twenty-First Day

Then he continued, Do not be afraid, Daniel. Since the first day that you set your mind to gain understanding and to humble yourself before your God, your words were heard, and I have come in response to them.[13] But the prince of the Persian kingdom resisted me twenty-one days.   Daniel 10:12-13a

Prayer matters.

Daniel had been in serious prayer for three full weeks (Daniel 10:2). God responded to Daniel's prayer the very moment he made his request known and an angel was dispatched with the answer. This is just another reminder that prayer is powerful.

But the Bible says the prince of the Persian kingdom resisted him. Since this prince was able to oppose the angelic messenger to Daniel, we know this was more than a man. This prince was angelic being, but evil, because he opposed the word of God. Apparently, this was a demon of high rank that opposed the answer to prayer. Jesus referred to Satan as the prince of this world (John 12:31).

Since Daniel's period of prayer and self-denial and the period that the prince opposed the angel was also 21 days, we see there is a link between Daniel's prayer and the angelic victory. We can surmise that if Daniel would have stopped praying on the 20th day, the answer may not have come.

Prayer isn't merely a therapeutic exercise. We are to persist in prayer even when answers are delayed. God forbid that we forfeit the answer because we gave up on the twentieth day rather than persisting to the twenty-first day.

Is there something you have been praying for long enough that you feel like giving up on? Would you persist, like Daniel.

Lord help me to persist in prayer, I pray.

Extended Reading — Daniel 10-12

FAITH
New Beginnings

*But many of the older priests and Levites and family heads,
who had seen the former temple, wept aloud when they saw the
foundation of this temple being laid, while many others shouted
for joy.*   Ezra 3:12

Israel was on the brink of new beginnings.

The Israelites had hit an all-time low in their relationship with
God which had resulted in their exile. The Lord used king Cyrus
of Persia, a pagan king to bring his people back. The Israelites return
joyously. The second chapter of Ezra gives the detailed account of all
those who returned from the exile, by name.

As soon as the people settle into their towns, they rebuild the altar to
the Lord and offer sacrifices. Immediately after, they begin the process
of rebuilding the temple and gave generously to the work of the Lord.
The temple was soon completed and ready. There were many new
beginnings for the people of Israel.

However, to many of the old-timers, this new temple didn't seem like
much. They were comparing it to the former temple built by Solomon.
And so they wept. But the younger ones who had not seen the earlier
temple rejoiced. But God used this new beginning to reestablish his
people in their worship to him.

We all need at some point in life, need new beginnings. We may have
gone so far away from the Lord that we often wonder if it is even possible
to return. Returning can sometimes be scary because you don't want to
risk another failure. And yet our God is a God of new beginnings. He
waits with open arms to welcome his children back.

Would you return to the Lord today?

*Lord, you know my heart like no one else. Forgive me Lord and help
me return to you I pray.*

Extended Reading — Ezra 1-3

RELATIONSHIPS
Unholy Partnerships

But Zerubbabel, Joshua and the rest of the heads of the families of Israel answered, "You have no part with us in building a temple to our God. We alone will build it for the LORD, the God of Israel, as King Cyrus, the king of Persia, commanded us."   *Ezra 4:3*

An offer of a dangerous alliance.

Judea had not been completely emptied of the local people. There was a remnant that remained. And when they saw the Israelites begin to rebuild the temple, they were not happy. They were enemies of Judah and Benjamin. But they suddenly pretend to be very friendly and want to help. They wanted to partner in the work either to ruin it or to influence it to their benefit.

But Zerubbabel, Joshua and the rest of the leaders, were unified in their response. They firmly and sternly decline any help from these people. They did this knowing that they had the permission of Cyrus, king of Persia to rebuild the temple. But they also knew they lacked human and financial resources. And yet, they knew that allowing these enemies would be dangerous for them and their work.

It takes courage and great faith to refuse partnerships that may seem helpful but are from the wrong kind of people. Especially in times of crisis, men of faith have fallen into the blunder of associating themselves with those who do not share their faith. And that has often led to experiences of great opposition to their work.

Would you seek God's wisdom and counsel to make the right decisions regarding your partnerships and associations?

Lord fill me with your wisdom I pray, in the decisions and choices I make.

Extended Reading — Ezra 4-6; Psalm 137

PRIORITIES
Give Thought

Now this is what the Lord Almighty says: "Give careful thought to your ways. ⁶ You have planted much but harvested little. You eat but never have enough. You drink but never have your fill. You put on clothes but are not warm. You earn wages, only to put them in a purse with holes in it."   *Haggai 1:5-6*

There is a problem.

The people of Judah had been in Jerusalem eighteen years after returning from exile in Babylon. They were all settled into their homes and hadd cultivated their lands. But the temple of the Lord still lay in ruins.

They found that though they worked hard, their harvest was little. They did not seem to have enough. Haggai called them to think. What could be the reason?

Wrongly ordered priorities.

While the people lived in paneled houses, the temple of God lay in ruins. They showed little or no reverence for God or his temple. They should have taken no rest until the work of God was as prosperous as their own personal lives. They should have been as willing to sacrifice for the work of God. Instead, they focused on rebuilding their own lives.

The people had their own share of excuses. The land was still desolate. The work was hard. They didn't have a lot of money or manpower (1:6). They suffered crop failures and drought (1:10-11). Hostile enemies resisted the work (Ezra 4:1-5). They feared opposition. And on and on.

God saw through their excuses just as he sees through our excuses today. Haggai's call to think and re-order life's priorities is like an alarm clock, unwelcome but necessary. What is the priority for God and his work in our life?

Lord may you ever be the topmost priority in my life I pray.

Extended Reading — Haggai 1-2

KNOW GOD
But By My Spirit

So he said to me, "This is the word of the Lord to
Zerubbabel: 'Not by might nor by power, but by my Spirit,' says
the LORD Almighty.   *Zechariah 4:6*

The name Zechariah means 'The Lord Remembers'.

Zechariah is a fitting name for a prophet of restoration. Zechariah
lived in a time along with others like Haggai, Zerubbabel, and
Ezra. Zechariah's mission was to encourage and mobilize the people
to complete the task they had begun and yet lost momentum for,
completion, rebuilding the temple.

Zechariah warned them of the consequences of neglecting God's work.
He emphasized that God wants to do a work through his people.
Zechariah adds to Haggai's prophecy, that God is interested in his
people, not just buildings.

Zechariah's prophecies were rich with visions. Today's passage is about
the vision he had regarding Zerubbabel, who was the civic leader of
Jerusalem. Zerubbabel had the responsibility to finish the work of
rebuilding the temple. The work had stalled, and Zerubbabel needed
encouragement to complete the work.

The Lord's message to Zerubbabel was, not by might nor by power, but
by my Spirit, you will accomplish this work. Might focuses on collective
strength, the resource of a group or army. While power focuses on
individual strength. God is saying, "Zerubbabel, you will accomplish
the task of rebuilding the temple. But not by the strength of those with
you nor by your own individual abilities. You will surely accomplish,
because of my spirit." As the church of God today, we are to rely on
the holy spirit for all our needs and not on our own might or power.
Where is your confidence today?

Lord help me rely on your spirit for my every need, I pray.

Extended Reading — Zechariah 1-7

KNOW GOD
Driven By Compassion

I will strengthen Judah and save the tribes of Joseph. I will restore them because I have compassion on them. They will be as though I had not rejected them, for I am the Lord their God and I will answer them.   Zechariah 10:6

God promises to strengthen.

Like the other books of prophecies, though Zechariah begins with warnings to the people, it closes with promises. The Israelites had listened to and followed false and deceptive leaders. Lack of godly leaders was partly the reason for this.

But the Lord has compassion on his people. He tells them to ask for the latter rains and He would give it to them (v1). In his mercy God assures that he would transform his people from a flock of sheep to a herd of war horses, ready for battle. He promises that his people would be like mighty men who would defeat their enemies (v3).

Lord promises to strengthen his people. He would bless and restore them. And the reason was that he had compassion on them. This blessing is for all the tribes of Israel.

God has the strength for each of us too. Ephesians 6:10 says, finally, be strong in the Lord and his mighty power. The availability of God's strength for us means there will be opportunities to use it. We are not promised lives free of trouble and challenges. But we are promised God's strength and his might to go through times of difficulty with his grace and come out victorious. Are you going through difficult times? There is a compassionate God who is waiting to strengthen and restore you. Would you trust him?

Lord help me to rely on your love and compassion and seek your strength for each day, I pray.

Extended Reading — Zechariah 8-14

CALLING
Positioned for What?

*And who knows but that you have come to your royal position
for such a time as this?"*   Esther 4:14

From orphan to a queen.

Esther, an orphan, young Jewish girl won the heart of Xerxes, King of Persia. She became queen in place of Vashti. This victory and position came with responsibility. Her people, the Jews, were under the threat of annihilation, thanks to the pride and arrogance of Haman, the Agagite. Mordecai her uncle calls her to act on behalf of her people reminding her maybe she came to her position for this very purpose.

The lives of the Jews in the kingdom rested on Esther's action. She needed to present the needs of the Jewish people to the King and get him to repeal the decree that threatened their very lives.

Esther displays great wisdom, discernment, and courage in dealing with the situation. She first calls for three days of fasting and prayer by all the Jews, including herself to seek the Lord's wisdom for the matter. Then she invites the king and Haman to a banquet. The king is pleased with her and is willing to give her up to half of his kingdom. But Esther invites them to a second banquet the next day.

On the second day, Esther presents her request to the king, saying that she and her people have been sold to be killed and annihilated by Haman. She requests that this order is repealed. The king is furious and is quick to act. He takes immediate action to stop this cruel order.

Esther rose to the task for which she was positioned. What is the task that God has for us, where he has placed us today?

Lord help me live out the calling you have for me, I pray.

Extended Reading — Esther 1-5

WITNESS
To Be Remembered Well

Mordecai the Jew was second in rank to King Xerxes, preeminent among the Jews, and held in high esteem by his many fellow Jews because he worked for the good of his people and spoke up for the welfare of all the Jews.   Esther 10:3

Mordecai was a kind and a good man.

Esther's uncle, Mordecai, chose to take her in when her parents died and took care of her like his own daughter. When he heard of the king's decree calling for young women to be brought to the palace for the king to choose from, as a replacement for Queen Vashti, he was quick to enroll Esther. The king chose Esther as his queen.

Mordecai stayed close to the palace and kept an eye on Esther. One such day, he overheard two guards Bigthana and Teresh conspire to assassinate the king. Mordecai's quick action to inform Esther who in turn informed the king, saved the king's life when the report was investigated and found to be true (2:19-23).

Mordecai was keenly involved in ensuring the safety of his people the Jews. When Haman drew up the evil plan of destroying all the Jews, he enlisted Queen Esther's help to repeal the decree. He guided and encouraged her to use her good offices for the good of her people. The Jews were saved when Esther was able to help the king see through the cruel plot that Haman had hatched. Mordecai was a powerful mentor and guide to Esther. He was a blessing not just to his niece but his people too. He is remembered as one who worked for the good of his people. How will you be remembered?

Lord may all I do and say honor you and bless those around me, I pray.

Extended Reading — Esther 6-10

BIBLE
To What Are You Devoted?

For Ezra had devoted himself to the study and observance of the Law of the Lord, and to teaching its decrees and laws in Israel.

Ezra 7:10

Ezra was a teacher of the Law.

Ezra the prophet, had an effective ministry which included teaching the word of God, initiating reforms and restoring the worship of God. He believed in the need and use of God's word as the only authoritative rule for living. Ezra was also instrumental in leading spiritual revival in Jerusalem.

When Ezra returned from captivity in Babylon, he expected to find the people serving the Lord, joyfully. Instead, he found the opposite. He was frustrated and sad. But he did not lose trust in God. He wanted the people to know how important and essential the word of God was. He taught the people the Law.

As a teacher of the Law, Ezra devoted himself to three things – to the study of the Law of God, to the observance of this Law that he studied and then, only then to the teaching of this Law in Israel. Ezra did not just flip through the Book of Law whenever he found the time. He did not just read through the Law but studied it. He studied it and then observed, acted on it.

The Bible records that Ezra devoted himself to the study of the law. To devote is to give all or most of one's time or resources to a person or activity. So for Ezra studying the Law of the Lord was not a casual, once a week activity. He gave most of his time and resources to the study of the Law. What are you devoted to?

Heavenly Father increase in me the desire to study and obey your word, I pray.

Extended Reading — Ezra 7-10

WITNESS
Spurred to Action

The king said to me, "What is it you want?"   *Nehemiah 2:4*

Nehemiah was the cupbearer to the Persian king.

Nehemiah seems to have remained after the exiles had been allowed to go home. The prestigious position of being cupbearer to the king reveals something of Nehemiah's upright character. But though he was still in Persia, he was keenly interested in the state of affairs in Judah. And he had just received sad updates from his brother Hanani about the condition of Jerusalem and his people.

Nehemiah was heartbroken. His response was to mourn fast and pray. He confessed the sins of his people and interceded on their behalf. But he did not stop there. He asked the Lord to grant him favor with the king. Nehemiah wanted to go and do something about the problem. He couldn't just be a spectator.

When Nehemiah went into the king's presence, the king noticed that he was not his usual self and asked him what happened. The king recognized that it was not a physical illness but sickness of heart. He obviously knew Nehemiah well enough and cared that he was not well. The king valued Nehemiah.

Nehemiah responded prayerfully to the king's question and sought permission to go back and rebuild his city and the temple of God. The king not only granted permission but provided Nehemiah all the material he needed to rebuild the walls of Jerusalem. Nehemiah found favor with the king.

Nehemiah was not indifferent to the needs of his people. He cared enough to do something about it. Are you indifferent to the needs of those around you or are you spurred to action?

Lord help me prayerfully act where you need me to, I pray.

Extended Reading — Nehemiah 1-5

SERVICE
Serve With An Attitude

So the wall was completed on the twenty-fifth of Elul, in fifty-two days.   *Nehemiah 6:15*

Nehemiah arrived in Jerusalem, armed with support and supplies from the Persian king.

Nehemiah began by assessing and planning the work involved to rebuild the walls of Jerusalem. He then called together the people and explained the plan. The people supported Nehemiah and were willing to do all that he said. Nehemiah wisely delegated work to the people, along the wall. They began the work of rebuilding the walls though they faced much opposition.

Sanballat, Tobiah, and Geshem were three enemies of the Jews. They were very unhappy to see that Nehemiah had come to lead the work of rebuilding the wall. They made several attempts to block the work of the Jews. They mocked and ridiculed them. They suggested they were rebelling against the king. But Nehemiah encouraged and led the people to go ahead. Though Sanballat and his friends used several ploys to disrupt the work, they failed. Nehemiah and his team continued their work, with their swords by their sides. Though under pressure, they worked together unfazed, encouraged and strengthened in the Lord. And they completed the work a record time of fifty-two days.

Nehemiah wisely led the people to complete this stupendous task in the least time possible. Nehemiah was selfless and willing to work hard. Oppositions were real, but he did not rely on his own strength. His focus was the Lord and all he did was saturated in prayer. And God used him mightily for his glorious purposes. What is your attitude to the work that the Lord has called you to do?

Lord help me serve you with all my heart only to glorify you, I pray.

Extended Reading — Nehemiah 6-7

CHURCH
How Much is it worth?

> *He read it aloud from daybreak till noon as he faced the square before the Water Gate in the presence of the men, women and others who could understand. And all the people listened attentively to the Book of the Law.*   Nehemiah 8:3

The walls of Jerusalem had been rebuilt.

Nehemiah had led the people in the humongous effort of rebuilding the walls of Jerusalem in a staggering 52 days. The people had settled into their towns. And the first recorded event that took place in Jerusalem was the reading of the Law, as we see in this text.

The first activity that the people chose to do, was to call Ezra, the teacher of the Law and have him read from the book of the Law (v1). That was the *priority* given to the word of God.

And that is what Ezra did. He read and read from the book of the Law to an audience who stood (v5) before him for hours. From daybreak to noon is easily five to six hours. The people stood listening to the word. The word of God was not to be taken lightly but to be read in *reverence*.

The people longed to hear the word of God. They recognized that the Law that was being read to them was straight from God and they wanted to hear. Many of those listening would not be educated to read themselves. Nor was the word available as easily as it is today. They *valued* the word of God.

In a world which is increasingly about fast and instant, too much, too easily, is God's word and worship a priority or an option for you?

Help me prioritize worship and your word, I pray.

Extended Reading — Nehemiah 8-10

RESTORATION
Time to Celebrate

At the dedication of the wall of Jerusalem, the Levites were sought out from where they lived and were brought to Jerusalem to celebrate joyfully the dedication with songs of thanksgiving and with the music of cymbals, harps, and lyres. Nehemiah 12:27

It was time to celebrate.

The walls were rebuilt. A difficult task was completed in record time, against many odds and much opposition. The city of Jerusalem now needed to be re-populated. So the leaders of the people settled in Jerusalem. The rest of the people cast lots to bring one out of every ten of them to live in Jerusalem, the holy city, while the remaining nine were to stay in their own towns. Those who volunteered to live in Jerusalem were commended by the people (11:1-2).

Now that every detail had been taken care of and there was more than enough reason to celebrate. It was time to say thank you. Thank You to the Lord for helping them complete this task. Celebration to the Lord because they knew well that without the Lord it would have been impossible to complete.

The celebration was to the Lord and with God's people. The Levites were sought and brought to lead the celebration. The celebration was with musical instruments and songs of thanksgiving.

We have many reasons to celebrate. Birthdays, weddings, are just a few. The times that we experience God's goodness and mercies are numerous each day. How often do we stop to say thank you to the Lord, acknowledging his goodness and faithfulness? How do your celebrations point to the Lord and his goodness?

Lord increase in me the attitude of gratitude and may all my celebrations point to you I pray.

Extended Reading — Nehemiah 11-13; Psalm 126

FAITH WALK
Refiner's Fire

He will sit as a refiner and purifier of silver   *Malachi 3:3*

Malachi, the final book in the Old Testament, is an oracle.

God is warning his people through Malachi to turn back to God. God pronounces his justice and the promise of his restoration through the coming Messiah. Four hundred years of silence ensues, ending with a similar message from God's next prophet, John the Baptist, proclaiming, "Repent, for the kingdom of heaven is near" (Matthew 3:2).

And Malachi says, He will sit as a refiner and a purifier of silver. What a comfort to know that the Lord himself will sit as the refiner. He does not give this task to even the angels. He may give the angels charge over us, but our purification is only done by him. And the Bible says he *sits* as the refiner.

The sitting posture reflects patience. The refiner is in no hurry. He is close to the silver that he is refining. He personally takes time to carefully work with the silver to burn away the dross. He refines until all the dross is burnt away and he can see his image clearly in the molten silver.

"If any of you, my hearers, are seeking the Lord at this time, I want you to understand what it means: you are seeking a fire which will test you and consume much which has been dear to you. We are not to expect Christ to come and save us in our sins, he will come and save us from our sins; therefore, if you are enabled by faith to take Christ as a Savior, remember that you take him as the purger and the purifier, for it is from sin that he saves us." (Spurgeon)

Purify my heart Lord and may I reflect you, I pray.

Extended Reading — Malachi 1-4

SUBMISSION
Against All Odds

"I am the Lord's servant," Mary answered. "May your word to me be fulfilled." Then the angel left her.   Luke 1:38

Mary received extraordinary news.

Mary a young girl from Nazareth was betrothed to be married to Joseph. She looked forward to her wedding with great joy and anticipation, as any young girl would. Mary was extra thrilled because she had recently heard that her older cousin, Elizabeth who had been barren all these years, had conceived.

Even as Mary busily went about her chores, humming away, thinking of all these things, she had an unexpected visitor. Standing before her in all his heavenly form was Gabriel, the angel of the Lord. He came bearing startling news.

Gabriel told Mary that she would be with child, by the Holy Spirit! That she, a virgin, would become pregnant and deliver God's own son. She was to call him Jesus.

All kinds of thoughts raced through her mind in that short time. How could that even be? She had never heard of something like this ever before. What would she tell Joseph? What would people say when they found her pregnant out of wedlock? And yet, Mary's response found in today's text was priceless. What courage,what humility. Though the questions and doubts were all real, she responded with a heart of submission and complete trust in God.

Mary's willingness to submit to God against all odds and challenges gave the world Jesus Christ the Savior. Now could God have done it if Mary had refused? Of course. But thank God that he chose to use mere mortals like us to fulfill his divine purposes.

What is your response to what God is asking you to do?

Lord give a humble and submissive heart, I pray.

Extended Reading – Luke 1; John 14-1:1

CHRISTMAS
The Person of Christmas

While they were there, the time came for the baby to be born, [7]
and she gave birth to her firstborn, a son. She wrapped him in
cloths and placed him in a manger because there was no guest
room available for them. Luke 2:6-7

As the world moves with elation,
Into a time filled with celebration.
My friend, my wish for you,
Is that you would truly know.
The Person, who is the reason,
Bringing meaning to the season.
To all the fun and laughter,
The love and joyful chatter.

He is the King of kings,
He alone the Lord of everything.
Who with his word did bring,
To life, everything.
He is the one who owns the cattle,
On a thousand hills.
The heaven is his throne,
And the earth his footstool.

Yet this amazing, Almighty one,
His heavenly glory did disown,
That he might our pardon buy,
As on the cross, he did die.
So, my friend this Christmas,
Amidst all the hustle and fuss,
Let your love for him be the meter,
And of all the fun he, the center.

Extended Reading – Matthew 1; Luke 2:1-38

OBEDIENCE
In spite of Questions

So he got up, took the child and his mother and went to the land
of Israel.   Matthew 2:21

Joseph found himself in a very difficult position.

Joseph was a good man. But he simply did not understand what Mary, the girl he was soon to marry just told him. What was she talking about anyway? How could it even be true? Was she lying? No, she couldn't be, he knew she was an honest girl. But then how could she be pregnant other than through another man? Could what she said be really true.

All kinds of questions, doubts, and fears filled Joseph's mind. And yet soon enough the angel of the Lord visited him in a dream. The angel comforted and assured him that all that Mary had said was true. And that Mary was indeed with child only by the holy spirit.

Joseph accepted Mary.

Joseph and Mary went together to their hometown, Bethlehem, to be numbered under the census. And Jesus was born there. However, after Jesus was born, when King Herod tried to have him killed Joseph fled with Mary and the child, as instructed by the angel. He later returned as the angel had instructed.

It is interesting that after that initial vision to Mary, the rest of the communication by the angel is to Joseph. Often, Joseph and his faithful obedience get missed out in the story of Christmas. Even before he fully knew or understood, Joseph a good man, wanted to protect Mary from public disgrace. And once he knew, Joseph played a key role. His willing obedience had a big impact.

Are you hesitant to obey God?

Lord help me obey you completely, even when I don't understand fully, I pray.

Extended Reading – Matthew 2; Luke 2:39-52

CHOSEN
Affirmed and Launched

And a voice from heaven said, "This is my Son, whom I love;
with him I am well pleased."   Matthew 3:17

Jesus grew up in Nazareth.

As the son of a carpenter, Jesus grew up in wisdom and stature and in favor with God and man (Luke 2:52). He lived thirty years of his life, in submission to his earthly parents. As he grew, his cousin John the Baptist, went ahead of him, preparing the way for him. John preached repentance from sin and baptized the people in the river Jordon.

At age thirty, Jesus also went to be baptized. John tried to resist saying that he needed to be baptized by Jesus and not the other way around. But Jesus insisted so that all righteousness would be fulfilled. John agreed and baptized Jesus.

As soon as Jesus came out of the water, something spectacular happened. The heavens opened and the spirit like a dove came and rested on him. And a voice from heaven affirmed Jesus saying this is my son, whom I love and with him, I am well pleased. Imagine the watching crowd. All kinds of people including the Pharisees and the Sadducees saw and heard this amazing event.

God had sent his son into the world for a purpose. He was to redeem humankind from their sins by paying the ransom with his life. And as Jesus was to begin his ministry, God the father affirms him.

Those who love and have accepted Jesus Christ as their personal savior are God's children and have God-given purposes for life.

How does knowing that you are loved and have a God-given purpose comfort and strengthen you today?

Lord help me live each day knowing that you love me and have a purpose for my life, I pray.

Extended Reading – Matthew 3; Mark 1; Luke 3

FAITH
But Because You

Simon answered, "Master, we've worked hard all night and haven't caught anything. But because you say so, I will let down the nets.   *Luke 5:5*

Jesus the new teacher on the block, is visiting.

Simon and his companions finished an exhausting night of fishing. They had worked themselves to the point of exhaustion says the Amplified Bible and yet had caught nothing. Disappointed and dejected they were washing their nets. Jesus, the teacher came by, choosing to use their very boat to teach from, that day.

Jesus settled down and taught the crowd from the boat and that sure took some time. When he had finished, then, only then, does the Lord address Simon's need. He told him to cast the nets out in the deep again.

Now, Simon was no rookie. He knew that if he had tried all night and caught nothing, then he was not going to catch any now either. But Simon Peter's reply to the Lord is precious. He said that they had worked long and hard, **but because he said so they would** let down the nets. And they did. Simon Peter got a haul so large that he needed help to bring it in (v6-7).

Today when all our knowledge, wisdom and own will, tell us to do it this way, would we like Simon Peter say, "because you say so Lord, I will. Because you say so I will trust you, I will not worry, I will keep myself pure, I will choose to love, even those who hate me, trouble me and will go the extra mile with joy."

Lord help me go beyond my own knowledge and understanding and do as you ask me to, I pray.

Extended Reading – Matthew 4; Luke 4-5; John 1:15-51

KNOW GOD
Inclusive Love

For God so loved the world that he gave his one and only Son, that whoever believes in him shall not perish but have eternal life.   *John 3:16*

This verse is a crisp but by far the most celebrated declaration of God's love and the gospel. This is a verse that most Christians can quote from memory.

God loved the world first. He did not wait for the world to turn to him first. The God of the entire universe, the all mighty, all powerful all knowing, all wise God, loved, so loved this world. He loved enough to give his one and only son who lowered himself to the level of a mere man. The Creator became the created. He came down so that ***whoever*** believes on him would not perish.

The word of God emphatically says whoever believes. The extent of his love includes every single person, whoever they might be and whatever they may have done. The worst terrorist, heartless murderer, the most notorious criminal. That includes that one person who hurt you so bad or that absolutely impossible person with whom you are struggling to have a civil conversation. Just anybody at all, who believes.

And the reward of believing and accepting this amazing love leads to nothing short of eternal life. Life for all eternity in the presence of this awesome God, where there is no more sorrow, no more pain. Instead, unending peace and joy that never ends.

In a world where everything is about self and questions like what I stand to gain, are the norm, God displays a love that is completely selfless and inclusive. What dear friend, is your response to this wonderful love? How inclusive is your love?

Help me Lord to accept your amazing love and share it with others too, I pray.

Extended Reading – John 4-2

FAITH
Where there is a Will

Since they could not get him to Jesus because of the crowd, they made an opening in the roof above Jesus by digging through it and then lowered the mat the man was lying on.   Mark 2:4

There simply had to be a way!

This great teacher, Jesus was the talk of the town. Everyone was talking about how he healed so many people of their different diseases. And now he was actually in town. If only they could get their friend to Jesus, thought his friends, he would be healed too. They just had to get him to meet Jesus. But it almost seemed like all of Capernaum had gathered at this house where Jesus was. How would they get him through the crowds?

Finally came the 'aha' moment. They would lower him down from the roof! It sure was a crazy thought, but this was an opportunity of a lifetime. It was going to be tough and yet if he did get healed, it sure would be worth every minute of it.

And so, with great effort and difficulty, the four friends managed to carry their friend on a mat, to the roof of the house. They opened the roof enough to let him down to where Jesus was. And the rest, as they say, is history. Jesus saw their faith and healed the man.

What effort, what commitment, what love. Have you ever wondered, what if these friends did not go to the great effort? What if they tried, but gave up? These four friends went to great lengths to get their friend to Jesus. Would we ?

Who do we need to bring to Jesus today?

Lord help me persevere in love to bring my friend to you, I pray.

Extended Reading – Mark 2

HOLINESS
More than Physical Healing

Later Jesus found him at the temple and said to him, "See, you are well again. Stop sinning or something worse may happen to you."   *John 5:14*

Do you want to be healed?

Jesus was back in Jerusalem. He went to the pool called Bethesda and saw this man lying on his mat. The pool of Bethesda was where many sick gathered for healing. Maybe the healing was real or maybe it was just a hopeful legend, that the first one in the pool when the waters were stirred, would be healed. There was hope that there was healing in this pool.

Jesus knew that the man had been paralyzed for thirty-eight years. And yet, he asked him if he wanted to be healed. Jesus knew that not every sick person wanted to be made well. Sometimes they were so discouraged that they had put away all hope of being healed. Also as Barclay comments, "An eastern beggar often loses a good living by being cured of his disease."

The man's answer interestingly was not the expected simple yes. Instead he gave a long explanation of why he could not get to the waters on time. Jesus tells him to "Get up! Pick up your mat and walk." (v8) And he did.

Jesus later sought him out in the temple because he was more concerned about the man's spiritual condition. Jesus told him to stop sinning. Jesus' greater purpose of healing him physically was to heal him spiritually.

Jesus continues to be concerned with the condition of our hearts and wants to heal our sin-sick souls. Jesus is asking us today, if we want to be healed?

Heal all of me Lord, my body mind and soul, I pray.

Extended Reading – John 5

OBEDIENCE
When You Say Lord, Lord

"Why do you call me, Lord, Lord," and do not do what I say?
Luke 6:46

Jesus told the story of the wise and foolish builder to explain this question.

In this story, Jesus talked about two kinds of builders, wise and foolish. The wise one built on a strong, firm foundation, while the foolish one built on moving, passing unsure foundations.

This story is so well known that we even have songs about it. But the question is do we really live by this powerful truth? Jesus is asking this very pertinent question – why do you call me Lord, Lord if you are not willing or doing what I say.

Lord means the one who has authority, control or power over others. So when we call someone Lord it means that we acknowledge and accept the person's authority, control or power over us. And if that is true then all that we do and say is to be in line with the will and wish of the one we call Lord.

In essence, Lordship goes hand in hand with obedience. Research says obedience is closely related to the proximity to the authority figure. So also, the closer we are in our relationship to the Lord Jesus, the greater our obedience to him.

Jesus is our sure foundation our hope and source of all wisdom. We are to build our lives on him by obeying his word. However, often our own fear, pride or even unbelief keeps us from submitting to his authority and lordship in our lives.

What is keeping you from being able to truly call him Lord today?

Father help me willingly bring every area of my life under your lordship, I pray.

Extended Reading – Matthew 12:1-21; Mark 3; Luke 6

PRAYER
Daddy my Daddy

Our Father in heaven.   *Matthew 6:9*

The prayer that our Lord Jesus taught his disciples in these verses of Matthew 6:5-13 is famously known as the Lord's Prayer.

This is one prayer that is so well known that not just Christians, but even people of other faiths know it by heart, but many a times it is repeated meaninglessly, more as a rote or even as a magic charm.

This prayer begins very simply, yet emphatically, with a phrase so simple yet so pregnant with meaning. Our father in heaven! The whole pivot of this prayer is contained in this phrase.

Our father, which reminds us that we are praying to someone with whom we have a close relationship. Without the relationship, this prayer is invalid. Only those who can truly address God as father, with a personal relationship that allows him to even be addressed as Daddy *my* Daddy, can pray this prayer meaningfully.

Interestingly though the relationship is *my* Daddy, the prayer is *our* Father or *our* Daddy. This prayer reminds us of our responsibility to pray for others and with others.

Now prayer is always addressed to someone who is believed to be able to answer. When we pray, we acknowledge that we are relying on God and his ability and willingness to answer.

The phrase 'in heaven' reminds us to direct our prayers to God who is in heaven. 'In heaven', points to the fact that he is in control of not just the earth but that he is sovereign over all of the universe.

How is our relationship with this God?

Help me grow in my relationship with you my Father, I pray.

Extended Reading – Matthew 5-7

FAITH
Amazing Faith

"Lord, don't trouble yourself, for I do not deserve to have you come under my roof. ^{7} *That is why I did not even consider myself worthy to come to you. But say the word, and my servant will be healed.*   Luke 7:6-7

Jesus had just delivered the most famous sermon the world has known.

As he entered Capernaum, Jesus was met by a delegation of Jewish elders who came to him with a strange and yet urgent request for their friend, a Roman centurion. That was not a very common friendship. Jewish elders did not take kindly to the Roman officers. And yet here they were.

The Roman centurion's servant was very ill and close to death. And these Jewish elders had been sent to see Jesus would be willing to heal this servant. The elders defended their rather strange request by quickly adding that this centurion loved the nation and had even built their synagogue. Jesus agreed to go.

But as they neared the place, there was another message from the centurion. The centurion sent word to tell the Master, that he was not worthy to have him under his roof. And yet if the Lord would but just say the word, his servant would be healed.

The centurion was a gentile with a pagan upbringing. A man of war, stationed in Palestine to ensure that the Jews submit to the Roman emperor. And yet he had great faith. Jesus was amazed and he turned to the crowd and said that he had not seen such faith in all of Israel.

The men who had been sent with the message returned to the house to find the servant well. What area of our life needs this kind of faith today?

Lord increase in me humble faith, I pray.

Extended Reading – Matthew 8:1-13; Luke 7

SUBMISSION
Whose Reign?

Take my yoke upon you and learn from me, for I am gentle and humble in heart, and you will find rest for your souls.

Matthew 11:29

Reign he does, in the hearts of those,
Who do with him daily walk close.
And theirs is peace and pure joy untold.
As with him, life's journey does unfold.

Theirs it is, to trust him, to see and to know,
How as through ups and downs of life they go.
The Master Weaver in them does draw and design,
Patterns breathtaking, as they submit to his reign.

To watch him their little, use and multiply,
To make the lame to walk and the blind to see.
How he does calm, storms in many a breast,
As those who trust him, leave it to him and rest.

Does he, dear friend in your heart too reign?
Or to surrender to him you still feel constrained.
He is worthy of your complete trust, he alone,
For without him you remain in-want, all on your own!!

Extended Reading – Matthew 11

CHOICE
Either Or

*"Whoever is not with me is against me, and whoever does not
gather with me scatters.*   *Matthew 12:30*

There is no room for neutrality.

Jesus had just healed a boy who was demon possessed and faced
much opposition over it. The people were amazed and wondered
if this indeed was the boy who grew up next door? Was this the same
person, the Son of David? The Pharisees claimed it was by the power
of Beelzebub, the prince of demons, that Jesus drove out the demons.

And Jesus in this one piercing statement made it amply clear that there
was absolutely no room for sitting on the fence. Barclay state three
possible reasons why a person tries to stay neutral. Sheer inertia is one
reason. People tend to stay away from anything that disturbs them. They
just want to be left alone. Even making a choice is seen as a disturbance.

Fear and cowardice is another reason. Taking a stand for Jesus means
courage. The fear of what others will say and think cripples them. The
voice of the neighbor is louder than the voice of God.

Preference for security rather than adventure is the other reason. Following
Christ involves adventure and action while selfish inaction is much easier.

This statement of Christ is a test that we need to apply to ourselves.
In the spiritual war against Satan's strongholds, there are only two
positions that one can take. We are either for Christ or against him.
There is nothing in between. Either we are gathering with Christ or
scattering with Satan.

Who are we, those who gather or scatter?

*Lord fill me with your courage to confidently take a clear stand to
gather with you always, I pray.*

Extended Reading – Matthew 50-12:22; Luke 11

JUDGMENT
A Time of Sorting

*Let both grow together until the harvest. At that time I will tell
the harvesters: First, collect the weeds and tie them in bundles to
be burned; then gather the wheat and bring it into my barn."*

Matthew 13:30

Weeds growing among good seed is a real threat to any farmer.

Tares were a kind of weed that was familiar to the people of Galilee. In
their early stages, tares so resembled the wheat that it was impossible
to distinguish one from the other. As they grow, they are distinctly
different from each other, but by then the roots are fully intertwined.

And so the farmer leaves them until the time of harvest when the tares are
sorted and burned first. And then the good grain is gathered into barns.

Jesus told this parable to teach about the Kingdom of God. The world
is the field and the enemy is the devil. The evil one is constantly trying
to influence each soul with wrong teaching. We are to be on our guard.
The day of judgment is for real and is sure to come. A day when there
will be a sorting of the good seed from the bad.

This parable also reminds us not to judge others. Those that seem like
the good seed to us may turn out to be the ones that are cast away to
be burnt. While those that seem as bad seed may be in heaven before
us. It is not our place to judge. Our focus is to keep our hearts free
from the evil that could ruin us. The Lord alone is the judge of all.

How will you protect your heart from the tares of the evil one?

**Lord help me guard my heart against the influences of the evil one,
I pray.**
Extended Reading – Matthew 13; Luke 8

WITNESS
This Little Light of Mine

He said to them, "Do you bring in a lamp to put it under a bowl or a bed? Instead, don't you put it on its stand?

Mark 4:21

Light is meant to be revealed.

Jesus is saying a lamp gives light and the light is meant to shine. Interestingly, he is not mentioning any specifications for the lamp. He just says a lamp. If the lamp is big or small, if it is fancy looking or not, whatever might be the shape or size, the fact is, a lamp is a lamp. It is to be put on its stand so that it gives light in a dark place.

The Bible says God is light; in him, there is no darkness at all. If we claim to have fellowship with him and yet walk in the darkness, we lie and do not live out the truth (1 John 1:5-6). If we have this light, the truth of God, we are not to hide this light. It is our solemn responsibility to spread that truth in whatever way God gives us the opportunity. God did not light our lamp so that it would remain hidden.

The Bible also says you are the light of the world (Matt 5:14). And you need to keep shining your light. Just keep doing what you know is right by the word. Read the Word, live by it. Keep praying. The rest is for the Lord to handle. We need to keep shining our light, faithfully, consistently. Sometimes our little light may just be the light that those around us need to see.

Are we faithfully shining our little light in our corner?

Lord may my light shine so all around me may see you in me, I pray.

Extended Reading – Matthew 8:14-34; Mark 4-5

GOD'S LOVE
Sin Sick Souls

On hearing this, Jesus said, "It is not the healthy who need a doctor, but the sick.... For I have not come to call the righteous, but sinners."   Matthew 9:12-13

Jesus was born and lived as a human.

As a child, Jesus lived and grew as the son of a Jewish carpenter. He lived through all of life's normal experiences. He knew hunger, thirst, need, pain, loneliness, and rejection. He was even tempted by Satan for forty days. And yet he did not sin.

Jesus walked and lived with ordinary people. At the beginning of his ministry, Jesus called twelve ordinary men to be his disciples, some fisherfolk some even tax collectors. Levi was one of the twelve that Jesus called and he was a tax collector.

As Levi sat at his tax booth that day, Jesus called him to follow him. Levi's response was decisive and immediate. He left everything and followed Jesus. In his joyful response to Jesus, Levi arranged a banquet for Jesus at his home. The Pharisees and Sadducees who saw this were quick to criticize and judge. They questioned why Jesus would eat and drink with sinners. And it was in response to their criticism that Jesus replied saying that he came to the sick, the sick at heart and not for those who are righteous.

The Bible is very clear that all have sinned and have fallen short of the glory of God (Romans 2:23). That there is no one who is righteous no not one (Romans 3:10). And so Jesus came to save each and every one of us.

Has Jesus healed us from the sin-sickness in our heart? What are we waiting for?

I need the healing that you alone can bring. Lord heal me I pray.

Extended Reading – Matthew 10-9

COMFORT
Come Away My Child

Then, because so many people were coming and going that they did not even have a chance to eat, he said to them, "Come with me by yourselves to a quiet place and get some rest." Mark 6:31

Life with all its challenges and tasks,
Many a times seems heavy and overwhelming.
How does one balance, one tends to ask,
This act of juggling, all that life is demanding.
Demanding our love, our attention, our time,
Our presence and availability, that's an uphill climb,
Phew now is that one tall order methinks, do you?

Is there anyone who does know or understand?
This pain which sometimes is so hard to stand.
Stress and strain, caused by the constant need,
Of loved ones, which though I would love to meet,
But yet deep down my heart does cry,
I am drained and this task is too heavy,
Not anymore, I can't, is your helpless plea?

If that my friend is your heart's deep cry,
Do know and remember, you are not alone!
Yes dear one, there is one and only One,
Who alone knows, who fully understands,
Like no else ever could, for he with his own hands,
Did you create in his image, his precious child,
And to you he says, come away my child spend time with me

You, he waits to gather, in his everlasting arms,
To comfort, to strengthen, through life's storms.
To give you his peace that passes all understanding,
As your load, he lightens, and your way he brightens.
For his yoke easy and his burden light,

Giving for every challenge, his grace, and his might!!
And he says, come away my child spend time with me.

So would you heed him, as he tenderly calls,
Come away dear child even as evening falls.
Before the day breaks and to your many tasks you rush,
Pause a while, spend time with me, ere you they crush.
Let me comfort and strengthen you for your day,
And remind you from my word, that all along your way,
I am ever with you, so would you come away my child?

Extended Reading – Matthew 14; Mark 6; Luke 9:1-17

I AM
I Am the Bread

Then Jesus declared, "I am the bread of life. Whoever comes to me will never go hungry, and whoever believes in me will never be thirsty.   John 6:35

I AM says the Lord,
I AM the bread of life,
I AM the only one who can feed you,
The only one who can satisfy your hunger.

As the world rushes on,
Along its many busy ways,
Do you long, do you hunger,
For someone to listen, to understand?

As people each day,
Are quick to blame and criticize,
Do you long, do you hunger,
For someone who accepts, without fault?

As the world and its many pressures,
Constantly remind, you are not good enough,
Do you long, do you hunger,
For someone who believes in you, your worth?

I AM says the Lord,
I AM the Bread of life,
I AM the only one who unconditionally,
Loves and accepts you, now and forever.

So come away, dear one, says he,
Spend time with me, feed on me,
Through my word each day, that I may,
With my love and my truth, you ever satisfy.

Extended Reading – John 6

FAITH WALK
Traditions or Faith

'these people honor me with their lips, but their hearts are far from me. ⁹ They worship me in vain; their teachings are merely human rules.'"   *Matthew 15:8-9*

These scribes and Pharisees were on a mission.

They went to Galilee all the way from Jerusalem to investigate and assess the works and words of the man called Jesus. They had heard all kinds of reports about him and had come to understand the situation for themselves.

They began by questioning why the disciples broke the tradition of the elders. Interestingly, by their own admission, the disciples were breaking tradition, not scripture. Jesus did not answer their question directly. Instead, he went to the root of the problem and asked, what made a person pure?

The Bible gives no command about washing hands before meals. The religious leaders' problem was they substituted their own rules and rituals for real love and worship of the living God. Jesus used the words of the prophet Isaiah to reveal their hypocrisy. Their lofty words and impressive prayers were of no use when their hearts did not belong to God.

For all their outward attention to rituals and apparent devotion, their worship of God was man made custom and ceremony. Their traditions might ease their conscience but God knew their hearts. They were empty of real love for the living God and neither did they have love for their parents through whom they received physical life (v4-6).

People today often know their church's rituals and programs better than their church's actual faith and belief. Could it be that we use the rules and traditions of the church to cover our lack of true personal commitment to Jesus Christ?

Lord give me a heart that is pure, that lead to pure actions, I pray.
Extended Reading – Matthew 15; Mark 7

DISCIPLESHIP
Life with a Difference

Then he called the crowd to him along with his disciples and said: "Whoever wants to be my disciple must deny themselves and take up their cross and follow me.   *Mark 8:34*

Discipleship comes with a cost.

Peter has just confessed that Jesus was the Messiah. But then he also rebuked Jesus. Though his intent was love for Jesus, he was unwittingly used by Satan. This could happen to any of us too. We don't have to be demon possessed for Satan to use us. And so it is important that you and I are constantly on our guard against his evil ways. Jesus rebukes Peter.

And then Jesus laid down the terms and conditions for those who wanted to be his disciples. If we are to follow him we have to be willing to be different. Our standards and yardsticks may not always make sense to those around. We live in a world that says, 'take all you can get' while Jesus teaches us to 'give all that we have.'

Throughout the Bible, our mind is seen as the key to our spiritual growth. If our thoughts are wrong our actions can never be right.

To follow Jesus is to live and do as he wishes. If our lives are to change then it has to begin with our minds. Our minds need to be renewed. The Bible never says 'don't' without also saying do. And so, God remolds our hearts from the inside (Romans 12:2) putting in his love and laws. He tells us to concentrate on that which is good, holy and of God (Philippians 4:8). Our new way of thinking will be characterized by humility and concern.

Are we willing to pay the cost?

Lord help me follow you whatever the cost, I pray.
Extended Reading – Matthew 16; Mark 8; Luke 9:18-27

PRAYER
Recipe for Growth

After Jesus had gone indoors, his disciples asked Him privately,
"Why couldn't we drive it out?" He replied, "This kind can come
out only by prayer."   Mark 9:28-29

Prayer is powerful.

Jesus often looked for a quiet place away from all distractions so he could pray to his heavenly Father. There are times that he prayed all night. And here he is telling his disciples that some works of God could be achieved by concentrated periods of prayer.

Remarkable things happened when Jesus' early disciples prayed. Prison doors were miraculously opened. Many people became believers because of their preaching. Many were healed because of their prayer.

Prayer helps us grow in our relationship with God. Prayer is the way to keep in touch with God and his purposes. When we neglect prayer, it is easy to stray away from his plan. Every decision we take, every situation we are in, gives us reason to pray. We are also called to pray for others, that they might know God's power too.

There is much truth in the statement 'a prayerless Christian is a powerless Christian.' God often chooses to channel his power to us and others when we pray. But it is human nature and often the devil's tempting that we find all kinds of excuses for avoiding prayer.

It is a good practice to set aside a fixed time to pray every day, just as we set aside time to eat or sleep. Have a list of things to pray for. Mark the date you start praying for each request. And when God does answer that request, put that date down again. To look back and see the numerous prayers God has answered, strengthens our faith.

How can we strengthen our prayer time?

Lord help me spend much in secret with you, I pray.

Extended Reading – Matthew 17; Mark 9; Luke 9:28-62

HUMILITY
How Great are You?

And he said: "Truly I tell you, unless you change and become like little children, you will never enter the kingdom of heaven. ⁴ Therefore, whoever takes the lowly position of this child is the greatest in the kingdom of heaven.   Matthew 18:3-4

Jesus noticed the disciples bickering and whispering.

As Jesus and his disciples walked from Caesarea Philippi to Capernaum, the disciples' conversation became a dispute among them. Later in the day, Jesus knowing their hearts, addressed the question that was on their mind, who would be the greatest in the kingdom?

The disciples were asking the wrong question.

Before they could be great, they needed to enter the kingdom and for that they needed to be humble. For the Bible says, the kingdom of God belongs to the humble and poor in spirit (Matthew 5:3)

Jesus, however, did not rebuke the disciples for desiring greatness in God's sight. Rather he showed them how God's idea of greatness was different using the illustration of a child.

In a world where pride and self-promotion are the norm, Jesus calls his disciples to be pure at heart as a child and completely without self-sufficiency. They must trust him completely in humble dependence.

To follow Christ is to understand that not only greatness but true happiness comes from knowing that in ourselves we have and are nothing. Our Father in heaven possesses everything. He has given us all that we need for life and godliness.

Anyone who wants to be first must be last and servant of all. The world despises the weak and helpless and calls someone superior to others as great. But God calls the one who serves others as great, like his Son Jesus Christ. How are we serving the Lord today?

Lord help me increasingly trust and depend on you, I pray.

Extended Reading – Matthew 18

CHRISTIAN LIVING
The Fence of Truth

To the Jews who had believed him, Jesus said, "If you hold to my teaching, you are really my disciples. ³² Then you will know the truth, and the truth will set you free."   John 8:31-32

The truth of God sets us free from Satan's clutches.

Christian life is based on the truth that God has shown us in his word. We are to put that truth into practice. We are to live by the truth of God's laws and obey it. God's truthful laws are like a fence at the top of a steep cliff. They prevent us from harming ourselves and others.

When we accept God's truth about ourselves, our needs and Jesus' death and resurrection, we are set free from the prison of sin. God's truth also sets us free from ourselves. Jesus helps us overcome our faults and failings that hurt others, which we are unable to overcome.

God promised when we know him personally, we will also know and understand the truth about him, his world and his purposes. Jesus said you will know the truth and the truth will set you free (John 8:32).

God never does wrong, nor does he lead his people to do wrong. We are to think, speak and act honestly, even if those around us do not. It is easier to be truthful in practice if we are truthful in our thinking.

Truth is not just about knowledge but also about living truthfully. The truth of God's word teaches us to love God, care for others, and look after the things he has given us.

In which area of our life are we struggling to live by the truth of God's word?

Lord help me accept your truth and live by it, each day, I pray.

Extended Reading – John 7-8

FAITH WALK
Journey Heavenward

I am the gate; whoever enters through me will be saved. They will come in and go out, and find pasture.									*John 10:9*

Life is not a set of accidents.

The previous chapter concludes a great conflict with the religious leaders of the time, regarding Jesus healing a man born blind. The leaders had shown themselves so unhelpful and cruel to the man, his parents, and the common people. Jesus felt it necessary to talk about the contrast between his heart and work as a leader to God's people and the heart and work of many of the religious leaders of the day.

Jesus used the picture of a shepherd and describes himself as the good shepherd. And in this verse, he further described himself as the door or gate. Out in the pasturelands for sheep, pens were made with only one entrance. The door for those sheep pens was the shepherd himself. He laid his body across the entrance, to keep the sheep in and to keep the wolves out. The shepherd was, in fact, the door.

Religious leaders gained their place among God's people through ambition, manipulation, and corruption. While Jesus the true shepherd comes in the legitimate and designed way: through love, calling, care, and sacrificial service.

Jesus the Good Shepherd calls us to journey with him. He walks ahead of us and leads the way, calling us by name. Jesus promises that we will never walk alone. He is like an expert guide who knows the way and the difficulties that lie ahead. He has many new things he wants to teach us as we follow him, eventually to heaven.

Have we begun our journey to heaven, with this Good Shepherd?

Lord help me trust you completely as I journey with you, I pray.

Extended Reading – John 9:1-41; John 10:1-21

PRIORITY
If Today Were

"Martha, Martha," the Lord answered, "you are worried and upset about many things, ⁴² but few things are needed—or indeed only one. Mary has chosen what is better, and it will not be taken away from her."   *Luke 10:41-42*

If today were to be my last,
Would my day change? Would it be different?
Oh yes, it would Oh yes it would!!

If today were to be my last,
Things would change and real fast.
Much less my concern with unwashed dishes,
And much more with unsaid wishes.
Much less with untidy beds and bathrooms,
And much more loved ones' eternal rooms.

If today were to be my last,
Things would change and real fast.
Much less my concern with airs and graces,
Much more that from me overflows his graces.
Much less with petty, insignificant points to prove,
Much more that loved ones know his love is true.

Yes, if today were to be my last,
My greatest desire would surely be.
To plead with those around, one last time,
That they eternally his would be!!!
So to live each as if it were my last,
Would be the wisest choice, wouldn't you agree?

Extended Reading – Luke 10-11; John 10:22-42

HYPOCRISY
True Through and Through

Jesus began to speak first to his disciples, saying: "Be on your guard against the yeast of the Pharisees, which is hypocrisy. ² There is nothing concealed that will not be disclosed, or hidden that will not be made known.   Luke 12:1b-2

A hypocrite is not genuine but is play-acting.

Jesus has been teaching the crowds many things. As he continued in the general direction towards Jerusalem, vast multitudes came to hear him. The crowds were so large that some were injured because they trampled on one another. And Jesus began speaking to his disciples to warn them against the great danger of hypocrisy.

The basis of hypocrisy is insincerity. God would much rather have a blunt and honest sinner than someone who puts on an act of goodness. Repentance in a state of hypocrisy is impossible. If one does not even realize that he is sinning, then how can there be repentance? God does not shut him out, but by his repeated refusal the sinner shut himself out.

Jesus likened hypocrisy to leaven. It takes only a little bit to affect a great mass, it spreads, swells and sours the whole meal. If we are insincere in one area it soon spreads to the rest of life.

The temptation to hypocrisy is often strongest to those who enjoy some measure of outward success. In light of their growing popularity, it was especially important for the disciples to remember this. The solution to avoid hypocrisy, however, is not that we never aspire to a higher standard. But that we aspire, yet be honest about our difficulty in fulfilling that standard.

How honest and transparent is our life?

Lord help me be a true person on the inside, I pray.
Extended Reading – Luke 12-13

SALVATION
Handing Over the Keys

So he got up and went to his father. "But while he was still a long way off, his father saw him and was filled with compassion for him; he ran to his son, threw his arms around him and kissed him.   Luke 15:20

A rebellious child comes home.

In Jesus' parable of a lost son, a repentant, rebellious son who wasted his life and brought shame on the family, decides to return home. His father who saw him from a distance went out and welcomed him home. His sin was forgiven and the family celebrates his return.

Our God and creator of all that exists, also knows just how each of us thinks and feels. He is holy and can do nothing wrong.

But we do wrong. Our self-will, self-indulgence, and self-confidence separates us from God. The Bible calls this barrier, sin. Sin keeps us from knowing God personally.

We cannot get to know God unless we are willing to say sorry to him and when needed to others. We must put sin behind us and promise him that we will not to willfully go on our own again. And that is called 'repentance'

Becoming a Christian is like starting life all over again, by handing over control of our lives to Jesus. We come to Jesus just as we are. We don't need to try to reform ourselves. Once we say yes to Jesus, he will do the transforming.

The lost son's return caused the family to celebrate. Heaven rejoices over every child that returns to God.

Who or what is keeping us from handing over the keys of our life to God?

Lord forgive me for having left you out of my life. Take charge of my life I pray.

Extended Reading – Luke 14-15

COMMITMENT
Only One Master

"No one can serve two masters. Either you will hate the one and love the other, or you will be devoted to the one and despise the other. You cannot serve both God and money."   *Luke 16:13*

No two ways about it.

Jesus was referring to the slave and master relationship. A slave cannot not belong to two masters. A master possessed a slave   exclusively. A slave is different from a servant or workman. A workman can have more than one job but a slave has only one master.

Jesus was talking about the heart condition. Many say they love God, but their lives and priorities show otherwise. Serving God can never be a part-time job. Once you choose Christ as your savior, every moment of our time and all that we are and own belong to him alone. God is the most exclusive of masters. We either belong to him totally or not at all.

If we think we are successfully serving two masters, we are deceiving ourselves. One can have both money and God, but one cannot serve both money and God.

We cannot call ourselves a child of God and steal stationery or work time from our job. We cannot sing and praise God on Sundays at worship, and then use our mouth for bad language, angry words, lies, gossip and slander during the week. If Christ is truly Lord of our lives, we cannot allow our hearts and minds to be filled with dirty thoughts and images. As a child of God, we cannot abuse our body, which is the temple of God, with substances that are harmful.

Who is truly the master of our life?

Forgive me and help me be ever faithful to you alone my Master, I pray.
Extended Reading – Luke 16; Luke 17:1-10

I AM
I Am the Resurrection and the Life

Jesus said to her, "I am the resurrection and the life. The one who believes in me will live, even though they die; John 11:25

I AM says the Lord,
I AM the Resurrection and life,
I AM the One who alone gives,
Eternal life beyond earthly lives.

As you look around and see,
The rush to amass wealth, power,
Do you question, do you wonder,
Is this all life is meant to be?

As crowds look for heroes,
And follow the gurus and weirdos,
Do you question, do you wonder,
Is this what life is meant to be?

As you rush headlong each day,
A task to next, no time for another,
Do you question, do you wonder,
Is this all life is meant to be?

I AM says the Lord,
I AM the Resurrection and life,
I AM the only One, who in the strife,
Gives purpose, who lead to everlasting life.

So, choose to walk with me, says he,
I long to direct and guide thee,
Where peace and joy yours will be,
And life abundant, found only in me.

And when life's journey is done,
And over the Jordan, you come,
I will be there, waiting to embrace thee,
In my everlasting arms, eternally.

Extended Reading – John 11

PRAYER
A Sinner's Prayer

> *"But the tax collector stood at a distance. He would not even look up to heaven, but beat his breast and said, 'God, have mercy on me, a sinner.'*   *Luke 18:13*

Two approaches to prayer.

In this parable, there are two men praying. But their prayers and attitudes are distinctly different. The Pharisee prayed, not to God, but to himself. His short prayer had more 'I' than any other word. He praised himself and compared himself to others and gave a list of his many deeds. The Pharisee was full of himself and had no room in his prayer for anyone else, even God.

The tax collector, however, approached God in prayer, not on his own merit but based on who God is. He didn't say, "God, be merciful to me, I'm not a Pharisee or because I am a repentant sinner. He did not justify himself saying he was only human or that he will try to better. He simply prayed, praying body, soul, and spirit, "God, be merciful to me a sinner!"

The Pharisee relied on his own power and deeds before God and tried to impress God with his many words. But the tax collector relied on the mercy and compassion of God barely having words to express himself. The Pharisee thought he was not like other men; that he was *better* than them. The tax collector also thought that he was not like other men; that he was *worse* than them.

The Pharisee saw prayer and his spiritual life as a way to be exalted, but the tax collector approached God in humility. But the Bible says, God resists the proud but gives grace to the humble (James 4:6).

What is our attitude in prayer?

Lord have mercy on me, a sinner!
Extended Reading – Luke 17:11-37; Luke 18:1-14

IDENTITY
No Bar ... Just You

Then they came to Jericho. As Jesus and his disciples, together with a large crowd, were leaving the city, a blind man, Bartimaeus (which means "son of Timaeus"), was sitting by the roadside begging.   Mark 10:46

Insignificance personified.

If being blind was not bad enough, Bartimaeus was forced to beg too. But the story doesn't even end there. He was just known as Bar-Timaeus, which means the son of Timaeus, Bartimaeus was not significant enough to even to be given a name of his own. And begging by the side of the dusty road to Jericho seems to be about all that he was good at.

But little did Bartimaeus know that his life was about to change radically.

Bartimaeus heard the rumble of an approaching crowd. And as the noise kept growing louder and people's voices clearer, he figured that this crowd was following Jesus of Nazareth, the healer. Bartimaeus was excited and hopeful too. Maybe Jesus would heal him too?

He raised his voice and called out in his most appealing cry. Wonder if he would be heard above the din of the crowd. But that didn't stop him. Bartimaeus cried out loud. And Jesus stopped!

And the moving crowd came to a grinding halt. Jesus asked for Bartimaeus to be brought! Among the crowd of people of varying importance, the cry of Bar-Timaeus the blind beggar mattered to Jesus. He may have had many important things waiting for Him, but Bar-Timaeus mattered enough to Jesus for Him to stop, give him time and hear his cry.

You matter to Jesus.

However insignificant we may feel, to Jesus we are of worth, and worth stopping for. Would we call out to him today?

Thank you for reminding me that I matter to you Lord.
Extended Reading – Matthew 19; Mark 10

KNOW YOUR GOD
Saving Knowledge

They crowd rebuked them and told them to be quiet, but they shouted all the louder, "Lord, Son of David, have mercy on us!"
Matthew 20:31

This is a parallel account of Jesus healing blind Bartimaeus found in Mark 10:46-52.

Blind Bartimaeus sat along the road to Jericho, along with his friend. His was a small world. He probably had been sitting in this same spot for years. The place for him to sit and beg. Beg for alms, for alms that he needed to sustain himself. He didn't know much else. He knew how to plead and cry for alms.

But that day   something very different happened. The crowds were much more than usual. He could sense a lot of excitement in the air. He could hear the noisy chatter of young and old alike, men and women. The bits of conversation he heard hinted that someone special was passing by. It was Jesus!

Oh yes, he had heard so much about this man. Jesus was this carpenter from Nazareth, he was from the family of King David. And what was more, he had healed all kinds of illnesses, he had calmed the sea and the list goes on. What if Jesus could heal him too?

Bartimaeus was not very educated, but he knew. He **knew** this had to be the one that the prophets foretold. He knew Jesus was no ordinary man. He knew that Jesus could heal him and make a world of a difference in his life.

Bartimaeus was not going to let this opportunity go by. He raised his voice and called out to Jesus. And guess what? Yes, Jesus stopped and healed him. Bartimaeus knew Jesus and his power. Do you?

Father that I would know you more and more, I pray.

Extended Reading – Matthew 20-21

DISCIPLESHIP
Above All Else

"Truly I tell you," Jesus said to them, "no one who has left home
or wife or brothers or sisters or parents or children for the sake of
the kingdom of God [30] will fail to receive many times as much
in this age, and in the age to come eternal life." Luke 18:29-30

The rich young ruler had just asked Jesus what he needed to inherit
eternal life.

Jesus reminded him about keeping the law. The man's response shows that
he believed he had kept the law. Jesus perceived that he was misguided
and empty. He responded to this man in love says Mark 10:21. Jesus
challenged the man to love God more than money and material things.
The man failed this challenge.

Essentially, this man was an idolater: he loved money and material things
more than God. It seemed like he had climbed to the top of the ladder
of success, only to find his ladder leaned against the wrong building.

The word 'disciple' means a follower, one who learns from their teacher.

Jesus calls us to be active disciples who will go on to discover the richness
of Christian life. Christian discipleship means giving top priority to
Jesus in our life. Nobody or nothing should come between Christ and
the disciple. Christ is to be above family, relationships and all that we
possess. We and all that we have are to be at his disposal.

Disciples are willing to do whatever Jesus wants, being sure that his way
is always the best. And when we do, Jesus promises us immeasurable
rewards in this life and the next.

Would you say that **you** and **all** that you have is at the Lord's disposal?

Lord help me worship you alone I pray.

Extended Reading – Luke 18:15-43; Luke 19:1-48

FORGIVENESS
Answered Prayers, Anybody?

*Therefore I tell you, whatever you ask for in prayer, believe that
you have received it, and it will be yours.*   Mark 11:24

Every one of us wants answers to our prayers.

Prayer is often the only hope for some who remember to pray when they seem to hit roadblocks or challenges that overwhelm, financial or emotional breakdown, a health crisis etc. Answered prayer is the end purpose even for those for whom prayer is a way of life and consistent relationship and dependence on the Lord. Answered prayer helps us grow in our faith and encourages us to pray more.

Prayer undergirds faith. There is no faith without prayer and there is no point in praying without faith. The Bible lays down a very key pre-requisite to be fulfilled if we want our prayers to be answered. A pre-requisite that is not easy to fulfill always and also could make us uncomfortable many a times. A pre-requisite that we would rather ignore or side step, not even talk about. And yet, without fulfilling which we should not even expect answers to our prayers, either.

The Lord assures us that our prayers will be answered, as long as we forgive. (Mark 11:24-25). In the Lord's Prayer, the petition is clear, forgive us our sins as we forgive those who sin against us. (Matthew 6:12).

Prayers that rise from an unforgiving heart, will not and cannot be answered. Forgiveness is the basis of our salvation. God forgave our sins, in Jesus name. And that is why we are to forgive those who have wronged us.

Have you been wondering about some prayers not being answered? Could it be that there is un-forgiveness lurking in the dark corners of your heart?

Give me the grace to forgive the Lord as you have forgiven me, I pray.

Extended Reading – Mark 11; John 12

SALVATION
Dressed for the Occasion

"But when the king came in to see the guests, he noticed a man there who was not wearing wedding clothes. [12] He asked, 'How did you get in here without wedding clothes, friend?' The man was speechless.   Matthew 22:11-12*

Jesus told the story about a wedding banquet of a king's son.

He was picturing the kingdom of heaven and entry into it. God the father is the king, the Lord Jesus is the son. The banquet points forward to the 'marriage supper of the Lamb.'

In the parable none of those initially invited came. And so, the king sent his servants into the streets to invite everyone – of all classes and situations. Whoever will come, good and bad, Jew and Gentile, are invited and brought into God's kingdom.

The king invited everyone and accepted his guests in any condition. However, he did not expect them to remain unchanged. Guests were not to wear their own clothes. They were provided with wedding clothes.

Apparently, one man thought his own clothing was good enough. And when the king in the story questioned the man, he was speechless.

We can enter God's presence only through his Son, Jesus. People often want the relationship with God and to experience his promises, but believe they are good enough and don't need to accept Jesus.

God requires holiness from those who come to his feast. And we are clothed in his garments of salvation and righteousness (Isaiah 61:10). Those who rely on their own good behavior or religious practice are like one who is unclean and all our righteous acts are like filthy rags (Isaiah 64:6).

Are you appropriately dressed for the greatest banquet ever?

Renew my thinking and my living, prepare me for the your banquet Lord, I pray.

Extended Reading – Matthew 22; Mark 12

WITNESS
Walk the Talk

So you must be careful to do everything they tell you. But do not do what they do, for they do not practice what they preach.
Matthew 23:3

Jesus exposed the corruption, hypocrisy, and rebellion of the Pharisees.

Jesus recognized and acknowledged the leadership of the teachers of the law and the Pharisees. And when their teaching followed the Law of Moses, the people were to obey.

But Jesus warned the people not to imitate the example of the Pharisees because they did not live by God's intention for his people. Their motives were all wrong. They did what they did for the love of praise. They enjoyed the best seats in the synagogue and the prestige of being called 'Rabbi.' They were hypocrites. And unless they saw themselves as they truly were before God they could never be saved.

The Lord Jesus warned against loving even the small privileges of leadership, which distract from serving and loving God and his people. To be great is to serve where you are needed the most, according to God's will. God exalts those who humble themselves and become servants. He opposes all who exalt themselves (James 4:6).

We are also to be cautious when following leaders, when the leaders are blinded and are not walking their talk. Paul though humble and fully aware of his own faults and limitations, was able to say in absolute confidence, follow my example as I follow the example of Christ (1 Corinthians 11:1).

Paul was extremely confident of his own way of life of self-denial, humility, and service that he was unafraid to present himself as a model for others to follow.

Can those you lead afford to follow you?

Lord may I ever humbly reflect you in my walk, I pray.

Extended Reading – Matthew 23; Luke 20-21

SECOND COMING
Alert and on Guard

But about that day or hour no one knows, not even the angels in heaven, nor the Son, but only the Father. ³³ Be on guard! Be alert! You do not know when that time will come.

Mark 13:32-33

The return of the Lord Jesus is for certain.

B ut Jesus says even he does not know the day or the hour. How could that be right? Wasn't he God, and so didn't he know everything? Jesus did not know this, not because he gave up his omniscience, rather because he voluntarily, in submission to his Father, restricted his knowledge of this event.

There were things which even Jesus left without questioning in the hands of God. What greater warning can there be to those who try to work out times and timetables as to his return.

There are some who say, we don't know when he will come, so it really doesn't matter. While others say, we don't know when he will come, so we must find out and set a date. Neither of the response is right. The right response is I don't know when he is coming, so I need to be on guard and alert.

People are not ready because they fail to watch. Anyone who is alert is not caught by surprise. There is no reason for fearful and hysterical expectation. Rather we are to simply do our work day by day and work to make every day fit for him. We are to watch and pray. To be alert and live in such a manner that it does not matter when he comes. All of life is to be a preparation to meet our King.

Are you ready to meet him if he was to come today?

Lord help me live each day fit for you, I pray.

Extended Reading – Mark 13

SECOND COMING
The Offer of Hope

As Jesus was sitting on the Mount of Olives, the disciples came to
him privately. "Tell us," they said, "when will this happen, and
what will be the sign of your coming and of the end of the age?"
Matthew 24:3

Jesus is predicting the End.

The Bible's repeated use of the phrase "the last times" refers to the entire period between Christ's first and second comings. In this passage, Christ starts by telling his disciples about the "end" of something they would be familiar with, the temple (v1-2). In the gospels, Jesus' prediction of the destruction of the Jerusalem temple merges with His description of the last times.

Jesus speaks of a chain of events that would begin to happen to indicate his imminent return. Stress and social disorder will be the characteristic of the period before Christ's second coming. People will be arrogant, materialistic and immoral. There would be those who make a mockery of religion and of any talk of Christ's return (2 Timothy 3:1-5). Politically, wars and revolutions will be the norm.

Family relationships would be filled with hatred and division, loyalties strained to the point of betrayal (Mark 13:12). Fear and insecurity would rule the day. Aimlessness would be rampant, with people running from activity to activity yet with no real purpose.

These signs don't mean the end but would be the labor pains heralding the birth of the new order. Rather than waste time trying to know the precise details of his return, we are to use it as an opportunity to evangelize and offer hope.

Who needs to hear the hope of salvation from you today?

Give me Lord the burden and courage to share you with the needy world around me, I pray.

Extended Reading – Matthew 24

SECOND COMING
Are You Ready?

The bridegroom was a long time in coming, and they all became
drowsy and fell asleep.   Matthew 25:5

Jesus tells the parable of the ten virgins to illustrate the second coming
of Christ.

A wedding in first century Judea was one of the greatest celebrations in
village life. Ten young women, who apparently knew the bridegroom,
alike in so many ways, were invited to the wedding feast.

Each of the ten young women took her lamp to go out and meet the
bridegroom. But there was a delay and one by one each of them fell
asleep. Only at the midnight cry, 'here's the bridegroom' did the difference
between the two sets of virgins become evident.

Five of them were prepared for the bridegroom, while the other five were
not. The wise virgins were ready with their lamps filled with oil, trimmed
and burning bright. The foolish virgins soon realized that they lacked
what they needed to enter into the celebration. They didn't have oil.

In this parable, the ten virgins were those who claimed to follow Jesus.
The oil represents the holy spirit. The wise virgins with their oil are
the ones who have accepted Christ as savior and are ready to meet the
savior. The foolish virgins represent those yet to decide, probably in
their overconfidence, thinking they still have time to choose Christ.

But the truth is, the time of the Lord's return is near, though we do
not know when. Jesus wants every person to believe in him. To trust
him means a relationship with him today and readiness to meet him
with joy when he returns.

Are you ready to meet the savior?

Lord help me choose you as Savior and be ready to meet you, I pray.

Extended Reading – Matthew 25

GOD'S LOVE
Extravagant Love

Then he took a cup, and when he had given thanks, he gave it to them, saying, "Drink from it, all of you. [28] This is my blood of the covenant, which is poured out for many for the forgiveness of sins.   *Matthew 26:27-28*

Jesus gave everything for you.

Today's passage is the gateway to the 'most holy place' in Jesus' life. As you read these verses you get a glimpse into the very core of the Lord's heart. His deep love for his Father and his people.

Jesus is surrounded by people of varying attitudes. Despite three years with the Lord, Judas loved money, not the Lord. He resented Jesus for embracing the cross. This was not the kind of leader Judas wanted to follow. As the group's treasurer, Judas was known to embezzle money regularly. One coin here another coin there, led to him becoming increasingly hard of heart. Sin has a way of creeping in on us, slowly but steadily, if not dealt with immediately. Where are we in the danger of sin hardening our heart?

Peter boasted of how great his devotion to Jesus was. He refused to take Jesus' warning. He sincerely believed he would die for Jesus and yet Peter could not even stay awake to pray with Jesus. How often do we fail because we trust ourself more than we trust God?

But Mary loved Jesus enough to listen to him. She believed his words about the cross, though she did not fully understand. She wanted to give him what cost her everything. Mary anointed Jesus with the expensive perfume. Mary's extravagant gesture reflected her extravagant love for Jesus.

What would you give Jesus?

I want to give you my all, but I often fail, Lord like Peter, help me, I pray.

Extended Reading – Matthew 26; Mark 14

KNOW GOD
An Act of Remembrance

And he took bread, gave thanks and broke it, and gave it to them, saying, "This is my body given for you; do this in remembrance of me." [20] In the same way, after the supper he took the cup, saying, "This cup is the new covenant in my blood, which is poured out for you.   *Luke 22:19-20*

Christ left us a fellowship 'meal' to remember him by.

Jerusalem was the epicenter of Judaism. People from all over had come together to remember the event that had birthed their nation. This year was extra special with the Galilean teacher who had captured the hearts and minds of many. Could this be the year of political deliverance through him, they wondered.

And it is in this setting that Jesus instituted the Lord's Supper during the Passover meal that he had with his disciples. He broke bread with them and drank wine from the cup with them, commanding them to do it in remembrance of him until his coming again.

The bread and wine of the Holy Communion signify receiving of Christ's body and blood, given for us. When we participate in the Holy Communion, we worship a triumphant victorious Savior, we give thanks and renew our fellowship with him. When we take the bread and wine, we are no spectators, we are deeply involved. We are all family of believers that come together to remember and anticipate his imminent return. We come to the Lord's Table to receive grace and strength for living our Christian life until then.

What is your attitude as you participate in the Lord's Supper?

Lord help me ever be grateful and strengthened each time I come to your table I pray.

Extended Reading – Luke 22; John 13

I AM
I Am the True Vine

> *I am the true vine, and my Father is the gardener. [2] He cuts off every branch in me that bears no fruit, while every branch that does bear fruit he prunes so that it will be even more fruitful.*
> *John 15:1-2*

I AM says the Lord,
I AM the True Vine.
I AM he in whom you must abide,
For a life that bears much fruit.

Do lives around seem to surprise,
Lives that claim to be lived for Me?
Yet do you tend to wonder as you see
Why these lives so very dry, empty be?

Much this world needs my love unconditional,
To know the peace that only I am able.
Joy found in me is rare,
In a world ridden with so much care.

Patience in things small and big,
Come only when faithfulness to me is real.
Kindness and goodness will be grossly lacking,
Until self-control, gentleness is part of every deal.

I AM says the Lord,
I AM the true vine.
I AM he in whom you must abide,
To live a life that bears much fruit.

So abide in me, says he,
And let me abide in thee.

Let me grow and prune you each day,
That in you be seen, fruit in a great array.

Go bless this world, would you?
Thru all that you say and do
By living your life intertwined with me,
For I am the true vine, abide in me.

Extended Reading – John 14-17

GOD
What a Savior!

*And when Jesus had cried out again in a loud voice, he gave up
his spirit.*   *Matthew 27:50*

The cross was not a tragic accident.

A good part of the four gospels is taken up with the events surrounding
Christ's crucifixion. The cross was the entire focus and direction
of Christ's life on earth. Christ's death on the cross was the atonement
for the sin of humankind. The word 'atone' comes from two words 'at
one.' By dying on the cross for the sins of the world, Jesus Christ made
it possible for all humanity to be made 'at one' with God.

The crucifixion of Christ (Matthew 27:32-56) is an eyewitness account.
It was a very public death, watched by the soldiers (v36) visible to the
passersby (v39), to the religious hierarchy (v41) and witnessed by the
centurion and many women (v54-55). Now on Christ's death, the
curtain in the temple was torn from top to bottom (v51), putting an
end once and for all the separation between God and humans. Nature
shuddered, at his death (v52-53).

The cross is the guarantee that God has set his eternal love upon his
people. Human sin created a barrier of guilt between humans and the
creator. However, by willingly accepting responsibility for this sin and
dying on the cross, Jesus Christ took on the penalty for this sin. The
power of Satan's kingdom was broken and we are set free.

This earth-shattering, life-giving and atoning death of Christ should
cause us to be filled with awe at this amazing savior and to worship
him. It should give us the confidence to draw near to this God with a
sincere heart (Hebrews 19:22).

What is your response?

Lord I worship you for your amazing love and sacrifice for me.

Extended Reading – Matthew 27; Mark 15

KNOW GOD
Relentless Amazing Love

When he had received the drink, Jesus said, "It is finished." With that, he bowed his head and gave up his spirit.   John 19:30

Relentless amazing love,
Brought my Lord and king.
The maker of all the universe,
To earth, as a mere man, to traverse,
Only on Calvary's tree,
To be crucified, for you and me.

He left his heavenly glory,
To be born in a manger lowly.
To reach out to all of humankind,
Sin-sick in heart and mind.
But the Lord be praised, thankfully,
He didn't remain a helpless baby.

On mortal earth did he dwell,
To do away death's painful knell.
As son to Joseph and Mary,
He lived and worked, humbly.
And on Calvary's tree, did he die,
Man's pardon from sin, to buy.

When from the grave he rose again,
For us, eternal life he did gain.
On Calvary's tree, was from above,
Shown such relentless amazing love.
He did first, us love and forgive,
As every drop of blood, he did give.

Thus he is the cause, you see,
To forgive and let it be.
To love and share the joy,
The birth of this divine baby boy.
His love is truly the reason,
For all your celebration this season.

So as thru this season you go,
May the world thru you, truly know,
This wonderful loving Savior.

Extended Reading – Luke 23; John 18-19

WITNESS
Go, Tell

The angel said to the women, "Do not be afraid, for I know that you are looking for Jesus, who was crucified. ⁶ He is not here; he has risen, just as he said. Come and see the place where he lay. ⁷ Then go quickly and tell his disciples: 'He has risen from the dead and is going ahead of you into Galilee. There you will see him.' Now I have told you."   *Matthew 28:6-7*

The tomb was empty!

Mary Magdalene and the other Mary came to finish the preparation of Jesus' body, which had been cut short by the Sabbath (Luke 24:1-3). They came fully expecting to find the dead body of Jesus. They found the empty tomb instead.

These were two women had been there at the cross, when he was crucified. They were there when they had laid him in the tomb. And now it only seemed fitting that these women received their love's reward. They were the first two people in the world to be confronted with the empty tomb and knew the joy of resurrection. What an awesome privilege!

With that awesome privilege, came responsibility. The angel reminded them of the promise of Jesus that he would rise from the dead. Though this was so staggering that it seemed beyond belief, they needed to believe what they have seen to be true.

And now having seen for themselves, the angel urged them to 'go, tell.' That was their first duty. They were to proclaim the good news to others. 'Go, tell' remains the first command to the person who has discovered Christ for oneself.

Have you believed to 'go, tell?'

Lord help me be faithful in telling about you, I pray.

Extended Reading – Matthew 28; Mark 16

SURRENDER
My Lord and My God!

Thomas said to him, "My Lord and my God!"   John 20:28

Wow, what a heartfelt cry of surrender from a disciple full of doubts.

Thomas, one of the twelve disciples, had his own share of moods, doubts, and fears. Yet, he was also one of the most loyal of the disciples. Interestingly, he was the only disciple who was not there when the Lord appeared to his disciples for the first time (20:24), besides Judas, of course. And he being true to his nature refused to believe 'hearsay' and was very clear that if he needed to believe, he needed to see, touch for himself (20:25). And the Lord did come back, just for him.

The Lord knew Thomas for exactly who he was and yet he loved him dearly and accepted him.. The Lord didn't love him any less, criticize him in any way or judge him. He went back for just one doubting Thomas like the shepherd who goes after the one lost sheep (Matthew 18:10-14). Thomas mattered.

And that love and acceptance led to a disciple brought to his knees in humble and complete surrender with the all famous cry, My Lord and my God!!

Thomas had his own share of wrinkles and warts, but that did not hinder the Lord from loving him and using him. God can and does work with imperfect people. This same God loves and comes after each of us, weak and sinful as we are, and accepts each of us just as we are.

Is your heart's cry too one of true surrender, My Lord and my God?

Give me Lord a heart that is truly and completely surrendered to you, I pray.

Extended Reading – Luke 24; John 20-21

HOLY SPIRIT
The Divine Helper

All of them were filled with the Holy Spirit and began to speak
in other tongues as the Spirit enabled them.   Acts 2:3

The risen Christ has ascended into heaven.

The disciples returned to Jerusalem and regularly met for prayer. When the day of Pentecost came, they were all gathered in one place. And the Bible says, suddenly a sound like the blowing of a violent wind came from heaven and filled the whole house where they were sitting. They saw what seemed to be tongues of fire that separated and came to rest on each of them (v2-3).

In the Old Testament, 'Pentecost' referred to the Jewish 'Harvest Festival', which took place fifty days after the start of Passover. But for New Testament believers, 'Pentecost' is the day associated with the giving of the holy spirit in full to everyone who repents and turns in faith to Christ Jesus.

The Holy Spirit, the third person in the Trinity, is the Advocate or Counselor that the Lord Jesus promised his disciples that he would ask the Father to send (John 14:16). The Holy Spirit is also known as the spirit of truth. Malachi refers to the coming messenger of God as the refining fire (Malachi 3:2-3). The holy spirit came down in the form of a dove, on Jesus at his baptism, which pictures the gentleness of the holy spirit.

The character and activities of the holy spirit are emphasized through the various names and descriptions by which the spirit is known. We must be careful, however not to make these images anything more than helpful pictures.

Which of the names of the holy spirit warms you most? Why?

Thank you, Lord, for the gift of the holy spirit that guides and counsels me.

Extended Reading – Acts 1-3

FAITH WALK
Empowered for Life

After they prayed, the place where they were meeting was shaken.
And they were all filled with the Holy Spirit and spoke the word
of God boldly.   Acts 4:31

God empowers us to proclaim him.

Peter and John had just been released from prison. They were imprisoned for proclaiming Jesus. The believers pray for power and enabling to proclaim Christ more boldly. What a courageous lot.

Prayer, his word, his church and worship are wonderful ways that God equips us to proclaim his name with boldness.

Prayer is often the best way to ask God all the questions we have, tell him how we feel, share problems and opportunities we face. He often waits for us to ask before giving us what we need, because only when we come to him humbly can we receive.

We listen to God through the Bible. All what God wants us to know about him and how to live for him is contained in its pages. The Holy Spirit will make it come alive to us if we ask for his help. Also as part of God's family, our brothers and sisters in Christ have special gifts which God uses to help us. It often helps to talk to other Christians before making important decisions.

Worship is to express love and gratitude to God for all he is and has done. Praising God helps us remember how great he is. It also makes us more able to hear and obey him and to receive his power.

How well are you using the different forms of help God has given you to grow and proclaim Jesus more boldly?

Lord give me a heart that believes and worships you and proclaims
you with boldness, I pray.

Extended Reading – Acts 4-6

FAITH WALK
Spirit Filled Courage

But Stephen, full of the Holy Spirit, looked up to heaven and saw the glory of God, and Jesus standing at the right hand of God. [56] "Look," he said, "I see heaven open and the Son of Man standing at the right hand of God."   Acts 7:55-56

As the early church grew, its needs grew too.

Stephen was one of the seven chosen to serve in the daily distribution of food. The Bible describes him as a man full of God's grace and power (6:8). He performed great wonders and signs among the people.

But Stephen was accused of speaking blasphemous words against Moses and God, the temple and the law (6:11-14). Some Jews stirred up an opposition and brought him before the Sanhedrin. The high priest invited Stephen to explain himself in light of the accusations.

In his response, Stephen gave a beautiful panorama of Old Testament history. Stephen didn't try to defend himself. He simply proclaimed the truth about Jesus in a way people could understand and emphasized things in Jewish history they may not have considered.

And at the end of his response, Stephen saw heaven open and Jesus standing at the right hand of God. It is significant to note Jesus is standing here, as opposed to the more common description of him sitting in heaven at the right hand of the Father, almost as if giving him a standing ovation.

Stephen made history and was unique among believers. He was the first ever martyr of the church. Jesus stood in solidarity with Stephen at his moment of crisis. What a gracious savior who is not impassionate to the troubles of his children.

Is this savior yours too?

Lord give me the courage to accept you and proclaim you without fear, I pray.

Extended Reading – Acts 7-8

FAITH WALK
Decisive and Complete

*He fell to the ground and heard a voice say to him, "Saul, Saul,
why do you persecute me?"* 5 *"Who are you, Lord?" Saul asked.
"I am Jesus, whom you are persecuting," he replied. Acts 9:4-5*

In this passage, we have the most famous conversion story in history.

The day that Stephen died great persecution broke out against the
church. And Saul a zealous Jew, who approved of Stephen's murder
(7:58) led in persecuting the church. Saul had heard that certain Christians
had escaped to Damascus. So he went to Damascus armed with letters
from the Sanhedrin, to go and extradite them.

Saul wasn't seeking Jesus, rather he decided *against* Jesus. But Jesus
sought and decided *for* Saul.

Damascus from Jerusalem was around 140 miles and a week's journey by
foot. And as Saul walked this road to Damascus, a bright light flashed
from heaven and a voice called out to Saul.

Saul responded with the humble question, who are you, Lord? And the
Lord replied that he was Jesus. Paul spent the rest of his life wanting to
know more completely the answer to this question, to know the Lord
Jesus, more and more (Philippians 3:10). Saul's conversion was decisive
and complete. So into Damascus, he went a changed man.

Paul who had set out for Damascus like an avenging fury was finally
led in by the hand, blind and helpless. Up to this moment, Paul had
been doing what he liked and thought best. From this time forward he
would be told what to do.

The Christian is one who no more does what he wants but begins to
do what Christ wants. How about you?

Lord may I increasingly do what you want, I pray.

Extended Reading – Acts 9-10

FAITH WALK
Measured by Change

*So Peter was kept in prison, but the church was earnestly praying
to God for him.*   *Acts 12:5*

King Herod had just put James to death.

And when he found that it met the approval of the people he now
had Peter arrested and put in prison. But the church was praying.
And Peter is miraculously rescued from the prison. God works in and
through those who trust him.

Christian life is a growing experience and can be measured by the steady
changes in a person's life. As we trust him we continue to grow in our
dependence on him and become more and more like him.

God works things out even in the toughest of situations, showing that
he is in control, as you begin to trust God more and rely less on your
own abilities. And as you begin to turn to him for your needs, He begins
to help you overcome your fears and temptations.

As we begin to see God at work in our lives, our confidence in God
and his promises and power increase and our fears decrease. There is
no place in the Christian life for over-confidence rather we are to be
humbly dependent on God at all times. A growing Christian is used of
the Lord. God has something for each Christian to do.

Often a time of great blessing is followed by tough spiritual warfare
and testing. It has been said that the devil only concerns himself with
those who threaten his temporary hold on the world. So expect battles,
for the battle gets hotter as faith grows stronger.

What is the evidence in your life to show that you are growing as a
Christian?

*Lord change me that I may be more and more like you each day, I
pray.*

Extended Reading – Acts 11-12

FAITH WALK
Burdened and Set Apart

As they ministered to the Lord and fasted, the Holy Spirit said, "Now separate to Me Barnabas and Saul for the work to which I have called them."   Acts 13:2

They ministered to the Lord.

The leaders of the church were gathered at Antioch. The Bible says, they ministered to the Lord and fasted. Barnabas and the others ministered to each other but they also ministered to the Lord. To minister to the Lord is the primary role of every a servant of God.

The word 'minister' is used for the service of priests and Levites in the temple. And under the new covenant, ministering to the Lord means doing what pleases him and honors him. It is to worship, praise, prayer and listen to him, to honor him. To offer oneself as a living sacrifice (Romans 12:1).

They also fasted as part of their service to God. They sensed a need to seek God in a special way, about the need to spread the gospel. And God answered their prayer. He answered by using them. Often God uses those who have a burden to pray for a need, by using them as part of the solution, to do the work.

And as they waited on the Lord, the Holy Spirit directed them. Barnabas and Saul were to be set apart now, unto the Lord and sent into a specific work that the Lord had for them. The time was now. And they were to be set apart.

To be set apart to God means you must separate from some other things. We can't really say "yes" to God's call on our life until we can say "no" to things that will keep us from that call.

Lord help me be set apart to you to do what you call me to, I pray.

Extended Reading – Acts 13-14

FAITH
Faith Means Action

You see that his faith and his actions were working together, and his faith was made complete by what he did.   James 2:22

Abraham acted on his faith.

Abraham had been through an intense time of exercising faith, of hoping against all hope, to believe God for the almost ridiculous promise of a child when he was hundred and Sarah ninety. But he trusted God and God gave him the son that he had promised. But then soon, God asked Abraham to sacrifice Isaac, his promised son, the one he loved so, on Mount Moriah (Genesis 22:3).

Abraham simply could not understand. The Lord had promised to establish his covenant with Isaac (Genesis 17:19). Now he himself was asking Abraham to sacrifice the very same Isaac? But then his faith came into action.

Abraham was confident in God's love for him and that he could trust God completely. And so, he set out the very next morning (v3) and told his servants that they will worship and they **both** will return (v5). Abraham believed that God would provide (v8). Abraham went up the mountain and did everything needed for the sacrifice. Interestingly God did not stop him until he actually raised the knife.

Tough situations test our faith. Loss of a loved one, a broken marriage, struggling finances and many more, are all real challenges we face. But as believers, we are called to walk by faith, not by sight (2 Corinthians 5:7) like Abraham did. Faith also means obeying even when it hurts, even when it is hard…real hard.

God tests us to grow and mature us in our faith and trust in him. To build us not to break.

Heavenly Father, help me put my faith into action, obeying you even when things are tough, I pray.

Extended Reading – James 1-5

GRACE
Saved by Grace

Then some of the believers who belonged to the party of the Pharisees stood up and said, "The Gentiles must be circumcised and required to keep the law of Moses."   Acts 15:5

If the Pharisees believed anything, they believed one could be justified before God by keeping the law.

There rose an opposition to Paul and Barnabas over the issue of circumcision. And many who opposed were Christians who had been Pharisees, who were well known for their desire to obey the law in the smallest details. And circumcision was a big part of the law.

These Pharisees insisted that Gentile converts must also be circumcised and must live under the Law of Moses if they were to be embraced into the Christian community.

But the leaders soon come to the truth and crux of the matter. We are saved by the grace of the Lord Jesus (v11). Paul himself was a former Pharisee (Philippians 3:5) who became a Christian. But he knew that Jesus was his salvation, not the way to his salvation.

Galatians 2:16 says, know that a person is not justified by the works of the law, but by faith in Jesus Christ. So we, too, have put our faith in Christ Jesus that we may be justified by faith in Christ and not by the works of the law, because by the works of the law no one will be justified.

Grace gives a blessing we don't deserve. Grace is God choosing to bless us rather than curse us as our sin deserves. It is his generosity to the undeserving. Grace is God giving the greatest treasure to the least deserving—which is every one of us.

How is this truth seen in your life each day?

Lord may I never forget that I am saved by your grace alone, I pray.

Extended Reading – Acts 15-16

BIBLE
Faithful and True

Paul, an apostle—sent not from men nor by a man, but by Jesus Christ and God the Father, who raised him from the dead.

Galatians 1:1

An Apostle is one who is 'sent' or 'commissioned.'

Apostles described a unique group, invested with Christ's authority in the early church. The greatest qualification of an apostle was a first-hand knowledge of Jesus' earthly ministry. The apostle Paul had not been with Jesus from the beginning but the revelation he received was direct and his encounter with Christ unique to him alone.

When goods have been tampered with, they have to be taken off the shelves. Even if only a small part of the product is affected, the remedy has to be swift and radical for the welfare of the people. So with the gospel.

In this instance, the gospel has been tampered with by false teachers and so Paul writes this letter to the Galatians in AD 48 to defend two things, God's pure gospel and Paul's true apostleship.

Paul defends his apostleship. Though he was not with Jesus during his life on earth, his encounter with Christ was unique. Paul preached the gospel that he received directly from God. When God called him he simply obeyed. During the early days of his apostleship, Paul had minimal contact with the other apostles. He was alone in Arabia for three years listening and learning from the Lord.

Paul was an apostle of God, who was faithful and true to what he was called to do. And he wrote under the authority of God and was inspired by the Holy Spirit.

How does Paul's obedience to God inspire us to be faithful and true to what God is asking us to do?

Lord give me a heart of obedience to you, I pray.

Extended Reading – Galatians 1-3

FAITH
Walking with Jesus

So I say, walk by the Spirit, and you will not gratify the desires
of the flesh.   *Galatians 5:16*

Enoch walked with God.

To walk with God is to always have him in mind, to be aware of his purposes and to reflect his character. To walk with God is to be willing to wait for his perfect timing. To walk with God is to walk in faith.

Abraham sets us a wonderful example of faith. The Bible says, Abraham believed God and it was credited to him as righteousness (Genesis 15:6). Abraham showed that he believed God by obeying him and moving out to follow God to the land that was to become his inheritance.

When God told him that Sarah would bear him a son in their old age, he did not doubt it or look at his circumstances. Abraham believed God by not doubting or allowing unbelief any foot in ((Hebrews 11:8-12). Abraham's ultimate test of faith was when God asked him to sacrifice Isaac.

To walk with Jesus is to walk by faith and truth. We walk in the light as he is in the light (1 John 1:7). 'Light' is God's truth and holiness. The more we walk in God's light, he exposes our sinful nature and shows us how to live and enjoy fellowship with him and others.

The Holy Spirit enables us to walk in God's ways. Our natural tendency is to gratify our sinful desires and live self-centered lives. But Paul says, we are to walk daily depending on the Holy Spirit, who dwells in us.

To walk with Jesus is to live by depending on him each step of the way. Are we walking with Jesus, every day?

Lord help me walk in faith and obedience to you each day, I pray.

Extended Reading – Galatians 4-6

FAITH
Be a Berean

Now the Berean Jews were of more noble character than those in
Thessalonica, for they received the message with great eagerness
and examined the Scriptures every day to see if what Paul said
was true.   Acts 17:11

Paul and Silas arrived at Berea.

Paul, whenever he arrived at a place, had a practice of preaching the
gospel in the synagogue three Sabbath days. He did the same at
Thessalonica. While some of the Thessalonians received the gospel, some
stirred up trouble, forcing Paul and Silas to leave by night to Berea.

At Berea too, Paul went to the synagogue and preached. The Bereans
were a much more welcoming and accepting people. Two noteworthy
characteristics are mentioned about the Bereans. They received the word
with great eagerness. But they also searched the Scriptures daily to see
if what Paul said was true.

The Bereans were eager for the word. They had open hearts. But they
also had clear minds. Often people have clear heads but closed hearts,
and never receive the word with all readiness. It was *both* of these things
that made the Bereans more fair-minded and of more noble character
than those in Thessalonica.

Paul was the most famous apostle and theologian of the early church.
He was also the human author of thirteen books of the New Testament.
And yet the Bereans did not simply accept Paul's teaching without
checking for themselves.

They searched the Scriptures to see if Paul's teaching was truly biblical. It
was hard work, and they did it every day. It was not a one time, passing
look. They made it a point of diligent, extended study.

What is your attitude to what you hear preached?

Lord give me a heart that is eager and a mind that is alert to your
word, I pray.

Extended Reading – Acts 17; Acts 18:1-18

WORK ETHICS
Faith in the Market

Surely you remember, brothers and sisters, our toil and hardship; we worked night and day in order not to be a burden to anyone while we preached the gospel of God to you.

1 Thessalonians 2:9

An idle mind is a devil's workshop!

Paul is the spiritual father and the founder of the church in Thessalonica. It is he who brought the gospel to them during his second missionary journey. And yet Paul is reminding the Thessalonians, about how he physically worked hard, to pay for his own bed and stay. Interestingly, Paul mentions this topic of working hard in both his letters to the Thessalonians (also in 2 Thessalonians 3:8).

Paul being who he was to the Thessalonians could have easily said he had this huge God-given task of preaching the gospel and planting churches, and therefore need not work. He could easily expect to be taken care of. But no! He worked hard, worked day and night. Plied their trade, night and day.

Paul lived out his faith in the marketplace. And through his daily work in the marketplace reached out to the ordinary man on the street. His message and the aroma of the gospel came through ordinary, everyday activities. His life showed how to live out the gospel in the workplace.

Paul did not burden those whom he was staying with. He worked for his board and stay. He was not a burden on others. If we are called to serve in the mission field, it does not mean that we are to live off and be a burden on others.

Heavenly Father, forgive me for times I used your name as an excuse to be lazy, I pray.

Extended Reading – 1 Thessalonians 1-5; 2 Thessalonians 1-3

SERVICE
Faithful Service

Meanwhile a Jew named Apollos, a native of Alexandria, came to Ephesus. He was a learned man, with a thorough knowledge of the Scriptures. ²⁵ He had been instructed in the way of the Lord, and he spoke with great fervor and taught about Jesus accurately, though he knew only the baptism of John.

Acts 18:24-25

Apollos was an evangelist, apologist, church leader, and friend of the apostle Paul.

A Jew from Alexandria, Egypt, Apollos was a remarkable man. He didn't know much about Jesus, but what he did know genuinely excited him. Apollos was eloquent, strong in the scriptures. And what he knew he taught accurately and with bold passion.

Aquila and Priscilla helped Apollos fully understand about Jesus Christ and his resurrection. And that clearer understanding equipped Apollos to become truly effective in his ministry. He also received letters of reference from the church in Ephesus. With these Apollos served effectively in Achaia, especially refuting the Jews publicly.

However, among the Corinthians there arose a divisive spirit. Against Apollos' wishes, there was a group that claimed him as their mentor to the exclusion of Paul and Peter. Paul considered Apollos a trusted co-worker and colleague (1 Corinthians 3:9) where one sowed and the other watered. Paul deals with this partisanship in 1 Corinthians 1:12-13 by reminding the church that Christ is not divided, and neither should we be.

In summary, Apollos was a man with a zeal for the Lord and a talent for preaching. He labored in the Lord's work, aiding the ministry of the apostles and faithfully building up the church. He used his God-given gifts to promote God's work.

For what are we using our God-given gifts?

Lord help me use all that I am to serve you, I pray.

Extended Reading – Acts 28-18:19; Acts 41-19:1

HOLY SPIRIT
Cleansed and Transformed

These are the things God has revealed to us by his Spirit. The Spirit searches all things, even the deep things of God.

1 Corinthians 2:10

The Holy Spirit is the source and inspiration of all Christian growth.

A Christian is like a house with many 'rooms' or many interests, relationships and talents. The Holy Spirit comes to live inside our 'house' when we accept Jesus as our Savior. Slowly he moves from room to room cleaning away the dirt and dust of sin. But he will not force locks. He will only go in where we invite him to do his work and help us grow.

As Christians, we are to be 'holy.' The Holy Spirit does the work of sanctifying or making us holy by pointing out things that are wrong in our lives through our conscience, a Bible passage or a person. He gives us the strength to overcome our sinful habits and replaces them with the fruit of the Spirit expressed in service to God and other people.

The Spirit unites the Church which is made up of different people and opinions. We are to show our faith by working together despite our differences. He has given each of us varying 'gifts' so that we can both give and receive from each other.

The work of the Holy Spirit is powerful and fundamental to every Christian's spiritual growth and to the growth of the Church as a whole. To grow means submission to the Holy Spirit and willingness to learn from one another.

Is there any room in your 'house' the holy spirit is not allowed access?

Lord cleanse and transform me for your glory, I pray.

Extended Reading – 1 Corinthians 1-4

HUMILITY
His Alone

Do you not know that your bodies are temples of the Holy Spirit,
who is in you, whom you have received from God? You are not
your own;   *1 Corinthians 6:19*

Is it truly the desire of our heart,
That to him alone be *all* the praise.
Or somewhere deep inside is there a part,
Of us, that desires that others do raise?
A toast to say, how wonderful *we* are.

Now if for us it is our need and glory,
To rest on our own laurels gory.
Then why pray dear friend do we?
Only when in times of trouble,
Him seek, our needs to meet?

In times of trouble, and storms do brew,
It is almost always accepted and natural.
That one does try every single avenue,
And so among other things, we do call,
Him to come to our help and us rescue.

But he does in his word say and require,
We live *daily* under his provision, his leading.
For us to know him, yes that's his desire,
And it is in knowing him and in so living,
We grounded and humble remain.

For yes without him, we are truly nothing,
For we and all we own, belong to him alone.
Every single cell in our body is his, everything,
So, from our hearts may, we ourselves dethrone,
And allow him to reign, for we are his, his alone.

Extended Reading – 1 Corinthians 5-8

TEMPTATION
No Means No

No temptation has overtaken you that is not common to man. God is faithful, and he will not let you be tempted beyond your ability, but with the temptation he will also provide the way of escape, that you may be able to endure it.

1 Corinthians 10:13

Life is not fair!

That could well have been Joseph's line. Everything that could go wrong, did. Young Joseph was a slave in Egypt, sold by his brothers. He was far away from home and from his father who loved him to bits. He was away from the many comforts of home, good food, and familiar surroundings.

Joseph was bought by Potiphar, an Egyptian official of Pharaoh. And God was with Joseph. Even though a slave, Joseph found favor with Potiphar, he succeeded in all that he did. Joseph was Potiphar's personal servant who put him in charge of his entire household.

But then came trouble in the form of Potiphar's wife. She found Joseph very attractive, so much so that she called him to bed, not once not twice, but every day. (Genesis 39:7, 10) What an attractive offer for a young man. Joseph knew that if he gave in to this temptation, real and strong though it was, he would sin against God (Genesis 39:9). Sin, any sin is always first against God, and only then against another person.

Desperate situations call for desperate measures. Joseph literally ran for his life. When Potiphar's wife tried to get hold of him, he ran, even leaving his coat.

Temptations and sin are real in every one of our lives. But God gives the grace we need to overcome. How will you flee from the temptation you are battling today?

Father may I like Joseph flee and say NO to sin each time, I pray.

Extended Reading – 1 Corinthians 9-11

GIFTS
Blessed to be a Blessing

There are different kinds of gifts, but the same Spirit distributes them.⁵ There are different kinds of service, but the same Lord. ⁶ There are different kinds of working, but in all of them and in everyone it is the same God at work.

1 Corinthians 12:4-6

No believer is without a gift.

While the 'fruit' of the Spirit relates to character, the gifts of the Spirit are to do with abilities distributed among believers. All fruits of the Spirit are to be displayed by all believers but gifts vary from person to person.

Everyone has 'natural' God-given gifts from birth. Gifts are distributed among all and not restricted to some 'outstanding' individuals or leaders. Every believer has at least one gift. All gifts come from only one source, the spirit of God. God displays and pours out his miraculous power in different ways, but it is always the same God doing the work. Gifts when given back to him, he blesses and uses for his glorious purposes.

Gifts are to be used to glorify God and to edify and unite the body of Christ. Gifts are not to be a point of comparison or jealousy. Disciples are called to individually and collectively to use their gifts to share the gospel with the unreached. However challenging the circumstances, the ultimate aim for gifts that each disciple has, is to make Christ known.

Take time to prayerfully identify your gifts. Give thanks for the gifts that God has given you. Dedicate it back to God the giver. Find ways to use them as a blessing to those around you.

Lord may I ever use my gifts for your glory, I pray.

Extended Reading – 1 Corinthians 12-14

RESURRECTION
Approved and Sealed

For what I received I passed on to you as of first importance: that Christ died for our sins according to the Scriptures, ⁴ that he was buried, that he was raised on the third day according to the Scriptures.   *1 Corinthians 15:3-4*

The resurrection of Christ is the pivot of Christian faith.

Proof that the resurrection did actually happen, is both physical and psychological. The empty tomb with only the abandoned grave clothes provided the physical proof, backed by the persistent failure of all explanations to the contrary. The numerous reported appearances of the risen Christ, at different times and before different people point to the same truth.

Psychologically, the transformed lives of the disciples, the conviction of the early church in the face of severe persecution are ample proof that Christ did indeed rise from the dead.

In the resurrection, God set his seal of approval upon Christ as the Son of God. Christ's victory over death has taken out the finality of death.

Jesus would never have risen from the dead so triumphantly if he had not been first willing to give up his life. We receive new life in Christ, only when we are willing to give up control of our own lives.

It was the resurrection that transformed the followers of Jesus and sent them into the world to preach the Good News. And the same transformation even today causes his disciples to many a time face much persecution to reach the unreached for the Lord.

How has the death and resurrection of Jesus Christ transformed your views and lifestyle?

Lord may I never lose the wonder of your amazing love that took you to the cross for me, I pray.

Extended Reading – 1 Corinthians 15-16

GRATITUDE
To God be the Glory

All this is for your benefit, so that the grace that is reaching more and more people may cause thanksgiving to overflow to the glory of God.   *2 Corinthians 4:15*

Gratitude is the quality of being thankful. It is the readiness to show appreciation for someone.

Paul tells the Corinthian church that he is grateful for the ministry that God has entrusted the apostles with. Though they are hard pressed on every side, they are not crushed. Though they are persecuted and struck, they don't give up but press on. They carry around in them the marks of Christ, so that he may be revealed. And that comes from a heart of gratitude for Christ has done for them and through them (v7-12).

The message of the gospel requires from each of us the response of gratitude to God. Gratitude for the undeserved favor and merit that is ours because of Christ's death and resurrection. Gratitude that Christ took our place on that cross and rose in victory. Gratitude for the life eternal we have through faith in Christ. And when we show our gratitude and give thanks to God, it brings him glory.

An attitude of gratitude to God brings perspective. The fact is that I am deeply indebted to God for his grace and that all that he does for me is free and undeserved. An attitude of gratitude is the common factor in a life that gives glory to God and a life of joy.

Is our life glorifying God? How have we expressed our gratitude to God today?

Dear father help me never to be tired of thanking you for the undeserved grace I have in you, I pray.

Extended Reading – 2 Corinthians 1-4

FAITH WALK
Know your Privileges

We are therefore Christ's ambassadors, as though God were making his appeal through us. We implore you on Christ's behalf: Be reconciled to God.   *2 Corinthians 5:20*

We are privileged.

God has given us many privileges to inspire and encourage us in our Christian lives. God's children are part of his family. The 'family' of God are all those all around the world, who believe in him and love and serve him.

An ambassador is a chosen person who represents their country's interests in a foreign land. They tell people what their country believes in. Every Christian is an ambassador for Christ, representing God's Kingdom to this fallen world. Our first loyalty is always to Christ. We live by his standards rather than the world's standards. Our duties never stop, we are never 'off duty.' People judge our Lord by what we do and say.

We also have the privilege of being God's messengers. We have a message to pass on (Luke 8:38-39). Not all Christians have a special gift of teaching or preaching, but every one of us can tell others the simple facts about God and his saving grace. In a world full of people who feel lost and anxious, this is a message they badly need to hear.

Every believer is also a saint. We are highly regarded by God. We are called to live as saints, to continually grow in our faith and understanding so that we become more and more like him. We are to reflect Christ's love through our daily lives. What a privilege. An attitude of gratitude for who we are in Christ keeps us from taking it for granted.

How can we tell someone about Jesus this week?

Lord help me live like the privileged one I am, I pray.

Extended Reading – 2 Corinthians 5-9

THOUGHTS
Battle of the Mind

We demolish arguments and every pretension that sets itself up against the knowledge of God, and we take captive every thought to make it obedient to Christ.   2 Corinthians 10:5

As over life I turn back and look
This my learning from the Book
How powerful a weapon can be?
My thoughts in the hand of the enemy

He is waiting for me to weaken,
With his deceit and his accusation.
Lies pour forth like a torrent from him,
With not a single stop or pause even.

How easy it is for me,
To give in and miserable be.
One defeated and worn out me,
Is just what he would love to see.

And but for the grace of God,
That is exactly what I would be.
But, O am I ever so grateful,
For the master's love so faithful.

In him I am, a victor you see,
For he that is in me.
Is greater than he,
That in the world be.

So dear Lord, when next time to me,
He brings a thought, help me see.
With absolute confidence and clarity,
When it not a thought from Thee.

And then, with your grace alone,
May I quickly on that thought shone.
The light of your true and powerful word,
And thus, nip that crafty lie, right in the bud!

Extended Reading – 2 Corinthians 10-13

REBELLION
Completely Yours

As it is written: There is no one righteous, not even one; ¹¹ there is no one who understands; there is no one who seeks God.

Romans 3:10-11

Locks, keys, tickets have become a part of our daily lives.

The universality of sin reminds us daily that we live in a fallen world that cannot be trusted. In this passage, Paul is coming to the tail end of a careful argument. Sin and death are linked to each other. Paul declares that death is the payment we receive for sinning. And the fact is that no one is exempt. Not one who has not sinned, not even one.

Scripture teaches that the whole human race is involved in the original sin. But no one is condemned for the sin of another. We are guilty before God because we have rejected goodness and follow our own ways rather than God's.

Guilt is both a feeling and a fact. It is a feeling because our conscience tells us when we have done something wrong. We feel ashamed and guilty for the wrong we have done. It is a fact because God knows that we have rebelled against him.

It is evident that the world around us, though still a good place to live, is no more perfect. God is not the priority nor is he sought after. The world is increasingly self-focused. As a result, violence, hate, self-centeredness has become the norm of any regular day. And yet the Bible says, the eyes of the Lord move to and fro throughout the earth that he may strongly support those whose heart is completely his (2 Chronicles 16:9).

Is our heart completely his?

Lord I long to be completely yours, cleanse me and use me I pray.

Extended Reading – Acts 20:1-3; Romans 1-3

SUFFERING
Suffering is Good for me, Seriously?

³ Not only so, but we also glory in our sufferings, because we know that suffering produces perseverance; ⁴ perseverance, character; and character, hope. ⁵ And hope does not put us to shame, because God's love has been poured out into our hearts through the Holy Spirit, who has been given to us.

Romans 5:3-5

'*To glory in*', means to take great pleasure in, revel in or celebrate.

Things that make us happy, what we take pleasure in, things that we want to relive, are more often than not, situations of success and happy endings. Not suffering.

Paul, however, is setting a totally different trend. In this passage Paul talks about glorying, exulting, even rejoicing in our sufferings, as the Amplified Bible puts it. That would sound almost ridiculous except for the explanation he gives in the following verses.

Suffering is not an end in itself. Suffering, Paul says, produces perseverance, perseverance, character, and character, hope.

Perseverance simply means you just keep going and on *and on*, even when all you want, is to just throw your hands in the air and give up. Paul says suffering develops in us the ability to just hold on, to be tenacious, and simply hang in there.

Hold on to God, confident in his love and promises, which are true. And then Paul says, when we persevere and hold on to our faith in God, knowing for sure, that nothing comes to us, except through the filter of his immense love for us, that then produces in us, the character of God.

In our place of suffering can we hold on to God and his word, as he refines us to reflect him?

Lord, help me today in my pain and suffering to hold on to you and your word, I pray.

Extended Reading – Romans 4-7

DEPRESSION
When Tears Overtake Words

²⁶ In the same way, the Spirit helps us in our weakness, We do not know what we ought to pray for, but the Spirit Himself intercedes for us through wordless groans. ²⁷ And he who searches our hearts knows the mind of the Spirit because the Spirit intercedes for God's people in accordance with the will of God.

Romans 8:26-27

A true friend they say is one who sees the pain in our eyes, while everyone believes the smile on our face.

Jesus when talking to his disciples about his impending death on the cross, comforted them with the fact that he would not leave them as orphans, but send them a counsellor, a friend, the holy spirit, the comforter (John 14:16-18). The Holy Spirit is the seal of every believer, the One who walks with us through this life's journey.

The Holy Spirit is the gift available to believers only. The Spirit of God, understands us, like nobody else ever can, is also the one who knows and understands the heart and will of God. In this passage, Paul says the Spirit understands us, intercedes for us through wordless groans. The Spirit alone knows our deepest pain and our darkest fears. He knows our doubts and our confusions. The Holy Spirit knows and understands us better than our best friend ever can. He also knows the heart of God and is able to intercede for us according to God's will for us.

So, when we are so numb with pain and not even able to pray and tears overtake your words, take comfort. The Holy Spirit, our Comforter understands us and groans and intercedes on our behalf, according to the will of God.

Thank you, Lord, for the marvelous gift of the comforter, the Holy Spirit.

Extended Reading – Romans 8-10

PARENTING
Compare Not

*For just as each of us has one body with many members, and
these members do not all have the same function, ⁵ so in Christ,
we, though many, form one body, and each member belongs to
all the others.*   *Romans 12:4-6*

Why can't you be like your brother? See how well your sister sings, why
can't you be like her?

All of us have either been told similar lines or at least heard someone
say it. Some of us may even be saying things like this to our children.

The Psalmist in Psalm 139:14 says, that each one of us is fearfully and
wonderfully made. There are no two persons who are completely similar.
Today scientists are able to confirm with ample proof, what God in his
word stated thousands of years ago.

Paul in this passage of Romans reminds us that just as the body is made
up of many different parts, each distinctly different from the other, so
also each of us is different and in no way can be compared. Neither is
even one of us an accident. Not in the way we look or the family we
are born into nor the circumstances that we find ourselves in.

The plans and purposes he has for each one are varied and unique.
Each of us is different and has a different purpose to accomplish on this
earth. We have our roles to play, our very own little spots to complete
the wonderful tapestry that the Grand Weaver is weaving. I cannot do
what you are called to do just as you cannot do what I am called to do.

So compare not.

*Thank you Lord for fearful and wonderfully making me, unique as
I am.*

Extended Reading – Romans 11-13

COMMITMENT
Don't Major on the Minors

Therefore let us stop passing judgment on one another. Instead, make up your mind not to put any stumbling block or obstacle in the way of a brother or sister. ¹⁴ I am convinced, being fully persuaded in the Lord Jesus, that nothing is unclean in itself. But if anyone regards something as unclean, then for that person it is unclean.   Romans 14:13-14

Don't use your liberty to make another stumble.

Paul begins this chapter with a call to accept the one whose faith is weak, without quarreling over disputable matters (v1). We are not to judge others about what they eat or don't or minor things like that. In essence, Paul is saying, don't major on the minors.

Instead, we are to be mindful not to put a stumbling block in the way of another, who may be weak. This does not take away the need and responsibility to admonish (Romans 15:14). But that admonishing or rebuking is to be over scriptural principles. In matters of preference, we can offer advice but not judge them.

We can be stumbling blocks by discouraging the other with our legalism and rules. On the other hand, we can also be a stumbling block by causing them to sin through an unwise use of liberty.

The matter of uncleanness in matters of food, sacred days and the like are to be left to an individual's preferences. These mundane matters were not to come in the way of walking in brotherly love toward one another. Essentially, if Christ was willing to give up his life for the sake of that brother, you and I should be willing to give up our preferences.

Who needs to hear this freeing truth from you today?

Lord help me never be a stumbling block to my brother, I pray.

Extended Reading – Romans 14-16

FAITH WALK
Focus in Uncertainty

And now, compelled by the Spirit, I am going to Jerusalem, not knowing what will happen to me there. [23] I only know that in every city the Holy Spirit warns me that prison and hardships are facing me.[24] However, I consider my life worth nothing to me; my only aim is to finish the race and complete the task the Lord Jesus has given me—the task of testifying to the good news of God's grace.   *Acts 20:22-24*

Paul is saying farewell to the elders of Ephesus.

Paul didn't know what was ahead of him and he had every reason to believe it was not good. But that didn't trouble him nor was he moved by the uncertainty of things. Paul stayed faithful to his cause, spreading the gospel of Christ, for which he was willing to lay down his life.

Paul had apparently received many warnings of the holy spirit. He knew that prison and hardships lay ahead of him. And yet, that did not deter or set him off the track. Paul thought of himself as nothing compared to his God and how he could serve him. He wanted to finish his race, finish well and with joy. Paul considered the gospel he preached worth dying for.

Paul was not moved by uncertainty. He was able to trust God even when he didn't know what would happen. He could sing with the psalmist, I have set the Lord always before me; because he is at my right hand I shall not be moved. (Psalm 16:8).

Life is uncertain. And we often worry about possible difficulties and dangers. Can we like Paul, keep our focus instead, on the task of living for Christ and finishing well?

Lord give me the grace I need to serve you and finish well, I pray.

Extended Reading – Acts 20:4-38; Acts 21; Acts 22; Acts 23:1-35

FAITH WALK
Almost isn't Enough

King Agrippa, do you believe the prophets? I know you do.[28]
Then Agrippa said to Paul, "Do you think that in such a short
time you can persuade me to be a Christian?[29] Paul replied,
"Short time or long—I pray to God that not only you but all
who are listening to me today may become what I am, except for
these chains.   Acts 26:27-29

Paul asked for an audience with King Agrippa and got it.

Paul presents his defense to the top officials of the Roman Empire. He gives a full account of his life, heavenly vision, and subsequent conversion. And as he made his defense with joy in spite of his chains, Festus bursts out and calls him insane.

Paul used Festus' outburst to appeal to what King Agrippa knew. He brought the challenge directly to Agrippa, asking him 'do you believe?' Paul asked him if he believed the prophets because he knew that if Agrippa did believe the prophets, truth, and reason would lead him to believe upon Jesus. He wanted to connect what Agrippa already believed to what he should believe. This is a good and often necessary part of the presentation of the message of who Jesus is and what he did for us before calling the listener to a decision.

Agrippa almost believed but refused to say he believed. Paul almost persuaded him. But however close Agrippa was to becoming a believer, it wasn't close enough. Agrippa's reply is especially sad. It means that he almost had eternal life and was almost delivered from the judgment of hell. But almost isn't enough. Agrippa condemned himself further by admitting how close to the gospel he came, how clearly he understood it and yet he rejected it.

Is our belief almost or complete?

Lord help me completely trust you, I pray.

Extended Reading – Acts 24-26

FAITH WALK
A Blessing in Storms

Last night an angel of the God to whom I belong and whom I serve stood beside me [24] and said, 'Do not be afraid, Paul. You must stand trial before Caesar; and God has graciously given you the lives of all who sail with you.' [25] So keep up your courage, men, for I have faith in God that it will happen just as he told me.   *Acts 27:23-25*

Paul's unshakable confidence in God made him a leader among men, even though he was a prisoner of Rome.

Having set sail despite Paul's abundant caution against it, the ship with Paul and the other prisoners ran into stormy weather. The sailors were without food for days. The dark storm seemed to have hidden the sun, moon, and stars. And on an open sea, there was no way to navigate without the guidance of these celestial lights.

In this situation, Paul brought them hope. He told them the angelic vision he had. His message for them was a mixed one. He assured them that there would be no loss of life, though the ship and the cargo would be lost.

Paul had God's promise for his own safety. But for Paul that was not enough. He labored in prayer for the safety and blessing of those with him until God granted their safety.

God never forgets his own. That doesn't mean everything goes easy for those who serve him. Paul's present calamity proved that. It does also mean that God's watchful eye and active care is present even in every calamity.

Paul prayed for and encouraged those in the storm with him. How about us?

Lord help me bring your hope to those going through trouble, I pray.

Extended Reading – Acts 27-28

GRATITUDE
Your Thankful Best

And whatever you do, whether in word or deed, do it all in the
name of the Lord Jesus, giving thanks to God the Father through
him.   *Colossians 3:17*

Our lives are to be the natural overflow of a grateful heart.

Paul begins this chapter exhorting the Colossians to put off the old man by setting their minds on things above. To put to death things that are against God and part of this world. They were to remove all traces of worldliness from them. And then they were to put on the new man and live the life of a new man in Christ.

Every believer is a new person. And the new are the chosen people, holy and set apart unto God. And that knowledge is to cause us to live lives of gratitude to God. And so whatever we do, word or deed, we are to do it unto God. Every word and deed, with no exception, is to be done unto him, in complete dependence on him. And this dependence is to be coupled with grateful hearts.

A new person lives all of his/her life for Jesus. He/she will persevere to do what honors him, however difficult because he/she is doing it for Christ. A significant measure of our Christian life is found simply in how we treat people. We are to show compassion, kindness, humility, gentleness, and patience. We are to bear with one another and be quick to forgive (v12-13).

And so in our work life, our families, our communities, in every situation and relationship, we are to reflect the fact that we are his children, by our utter dependence on him and our hearts that display thankfulness.

Lord may my thankfulness to you be seen in all I say and do, I pray.

Extended Reading – Colossians 1-4; Philemon

GRACE
But for the Grace of God

For it is by grace you have been saved, through faith—and this is not from yourselves, it is the gift of God — *9 not by works so that no one can boast.*   *Ephesians 2:8-9*

You are dead.

Paul begins this chapter with this powerful doctrine of the Christian faith. He tells the Ephesian church that they are dead in their transgressions.

Transgression is an offense against the law. While sin is an immoral act, a transgression is against divine law. So basically Paul is telling the Ephesian church, either way, you are dead, be it under the law or be it under God's law. And yet he says, there is hope. You are saved. Saved from death and hell. Saved from punishment under the law.

Saved because of God's gift to humankind. God sent his son to pay the price for our sins. We are saved not because we deserve it or have in any way earned it. Saved only because God in his amazing incomprehensible love, chose to save us (John 3:16). If salvation was our accomplishment in any way, it would give cause to boast. But salvation is what God alone gave, and so he alone receives the glory.

Paul says we are saved only by the grace of God.

Grace is God's unmerited favor to us. Paul says, we are saved because of God's favor. Favor that we do not deserve by any reason or logic.

We can do nothing to earn our salvation. We can only accept this gift of salvation that God extends to us through his son Jesus Christ. Have we accepted this gift yet?

Lord help me never forget that but for your grace, I would dead, eternally, I pray.

Extended Reading – Ephesians 1-6

HUMILITY
Humility Personified

And being found in appearance as a man, he humbled himself by becoming obedient to death—even death on a cross!

Philippians 2:8

Relationships can be challenging.

Paul is exhorting the Philippian church and addressing issues they seem to be facing. He calls them to be like-minded doing nothing out of vain conceit or selfish ambition. They were to look out for the interests of others rather than their own. He also tells them that in their relationships with one another, have the same mindset of Christ (v2-5).

Paul specifies selfish ambition. Much of what we do is not done out of love for others but out of our own desires. And yet there is good ambition when it is to glorify God and serve him with everything we have.

'Conceit' is to think too highly of oneself, having excessive self-interest and being too occupied with self. Paul exhorts us to instead, put the interest of others ahead of our own. And the ultimate example of all what Paul was trying to say is found in Christ and his humility. And so he says, look at Christ, be like Christ.

Christ Jesus, who is God incarnate, chose to give up his divine glory to come down to the earth he created, as one who is created. He chose to become like one of us. He chose to obey the father, even unto the point of death on the cross. He chose humility.

Humility values the other and put the other's interest above your own. Christ valued us. He put our needs above himself. He came down to our level. Whom do you need to value and put above yourself?

Lord help reflect your humility and value others above myself I pray.

Extended Reading – Philippians 1-4

SALVATION
Eternal Consequences

Here is a trustworthy saying that deserves full acceptance: Christ Jesus came into the world to save sinners—of whom I am the worst.   *1 Timothy 1:15*

To fully appreciate what Jesus has done for us, we need to see ourselves as he sees us.

God has made every human being unique. And yet we all have certain things that are common too, like physical features, abilities of speech, thought and emotion. God has also given us a natural desire to seek him so that we live in harmony with him.

But every one of us is sinful. Nobody except Jesus has ever lived a fully perfect life. And our sinful nature separates us from God forever. God is a holy God. He cannot tolerate sin. But he loves the sinner. He sent his only son to die on our behalf (John 3:16).

To be saved is to accept Jesus' offer of salvation. When we do, we are saved from a fate of living without God eternally. We all need saving because all of us have sinned and fallen short of the glory of God (Romans 3:23). And because, the wages of sin is death, but the gift of God is eternal life through Jesus Christ our Lord (Romans 6:23).

Becoming like Christ is an ongoing experience. When we chose Christ as our Savior, he called us to set aside our sinful ways. It means abandoning the attitudes and thoughts that conflict with Jesus' love and purposes, not living in seclusion. This could sometimes mean saying 'no' to things that would hinder our relationship with Jesus and saying 'yes' to what he wants. Are we saved?

Lord help me live each day conscious of your sacrifice on the cross on my behalf, I pray.

Extended Reading – 1 Timothy 1-6

SALVATION
The Invitation is Open

At one time we too were foolish, disobedient, deceived and enslaved by all kinds of passions and pleasures. We lived in malice and envy, being hated and hating one another. But when the kindness and love of God our Savior appeared, he saved us, not because of righteous things we had done, but because of his mercy. He saved us through the washing of rebirth and renewal by the Holy Spirit. *Titus 3:3-5*

Somebody once said, "I didn't know I was lost until I was found."

Crete was the destination for this small but powerful letter from Paul to Titus, his trusted lieutenant. Crete a sizeable island had become a part of the Roman Empire. And Paul here is trying to reiterate the unchanging fundamentals of salvation.

Paul asks Titus to recall and remember. Before salvation, we were all foolish, disobedient and enslaved (v3). But by the mercy of God alone we are saved. We are saved not by our righteous works. We are saved only by the mercy of God through the washing and renewal by the Holy Spirit.

To become a Christian there are two distinct parts. We need to repent and turn to God, abandoning our old ways. And it is God who forgives us and empowers us through the Holy Spirit.

The basis for our salvation is the death and resurrection of Christ. There is the call of God to believe followed by the promise of God to all who respond. God has already made the way of salvation clear for everyone. And his invitation is open. But we can take the invitation, only if we choose to turn to him in faith and repentance.

Have we accepted his invitation?

Lord I come to you, change my heart and renew me I pray.

Extended Reading – Titus 1-3

PEACE
Harvest of Righteousness

They must turn from evil and do good; they must seek peace and
pursue it.   *1 Peter 3:11*

Peace is something everyone wants, yet few seem to find.

Peter says we are to do good and turn from evil. We are also to seek
and pursue peace.

Peace is tranquility, harmony or security. It could also mean prosperity
and well-being. Peace is directly related to the actions and attitudes of
individuals. Peace takes flight for many reasons. Sinful habits rob us of
our peace of mind. We cannot be at peace if we harbor discontentment,
envy or bitterness.

Bitterness they say is like an acid, which only damages the container
that holds it. If there is someone who has wronged, been unfair to you,
you need to make the choice to forgive that person. It is only when you
let go that God can take up your cause, and he will.

Believers are called to allow the peace of God rule in their hearts
(Colossians 3:15). We have peace when we trust and live by the promises
of God. When we rely on ourselves we reject the peace that God offers.
Peace is a fruit of the Spirit. If we allow the Spirit to rule in our lives
we will experience the peace of God.

James 3:18 says, those who sow in peace, reap a harvest of righteousness.
To live in peace we need to accept and live by the reconciliation that
Christ's death offers. Be quick to seek forgiveness of both God and man,
when you sin (1 John 1:9). Learn to be content (Philippians 4:11).
Develop a grateful heart (Ephesians 5:20).

Lord help me be one who lives in your peace, I pray.

Extended Reading – 1 Peter 1-5

FAITH WALK
A Growing Life

Anyone who lives on milk, being still an infant, is not acquainted with the teaching about righteousness. But solid food is for the mature, who by constant use have trained themselves to distinguish good from evil.   *Hebrews 5:13-14*

Christian life never stops.

The journey only begins, when we accept Christ as our Savior. There is always more to learn and heaven to look forward to. Jesus promised his followers' inner peace and joy. These don't come from an easy life but from the confidence that our heavenly father is in control, whatever happens.

Growing in faith can be an exciting yet exacting adventure. We grow in our faith and become perfect, by obeying God's will (1 Peter 1:14-16). The more we obey the more skilled we are at understanding and knowing what God wants us to do.

Sometimes we grow more like Jesus by applying our faith to the challenges we face. Christ promises to renew us and grow us in our faith. To grow in faith we also need to give. Christian faith is not meant to be kept to ourselves. We have the gospel to give others, which transforms people. Only when we give in faith will we grow in faith.

And yet, we are not meant to be "too heavenly minded to be of earthly use." Though our ultimate home is in heaven, we are to live this earthly life with our feet firmly planted on the ground, as long as we live.

Jesus said that Christian life is a narrow path, compared to the broad path of self-indulgence. But his way leads to abundant life here and in eternity.

How have we matured in our faith in the past year?

Lord help me increasingly obey and grow in you, I pray.

Extended Reading – Hebrews 1-6

FAITH WALK
Priestly Duties

But when this priest had offered for all time one sacrifice for sins, he sat down at the right hand of God.   Hebrews 10:12

The principle of mediation was basic for Israel.

The priests of the Old Testament nation of Israel were the agents of mediation through whom God was to be approached. God could not be approached lightly nor be approached directly. And without the shedding of blood, there was no forgiveness of sins. The priests were the foreshadowing of Christ, God's final and perfect mediator for all time.

Access to God is impossible unless sin is dealt with. But Christ through his atoning sacrifice for the sins of the world, became the passover lamb. He provided open access to God the Father, interceding on behalf of all believers. Never again would a sacrifice for sin be required. Christ by sacrificing himself made us perfect (v14). He removed everything that hindered our approach to God.

With Christ, a new priesthood came into being, that of all believers everywhere. 1 Peter 2:5 says believers like living stones, are being built into a spiritual house to be a holy priesthood, offering spiritual sacrifices acceptable to God. New Testament priesthood do not offer sacrifice for sins but offer the sacrifice of praise and thankful service to God, interceding on behalf of others.

Christians are to set a Christ-like example to the church in fulfilling their priestly duties. We are to be faithful in our worship of our savior our high priest. We are to serve him by strengthening our vision of God in each other and also among those who do not know him. We are to be intercessors for our fellow beings.

Who needs our intercession today?

Lord help me offer you a continual sacrifice of praise, I pray.

Extended Reading – Hebrews 7-10

FAITH WALK
Run Light

Therefore, since we are surrounded by such a great cloud of witnesses, let us throw off everything that hinders and the sin that so easily entangles. And let us run with perseverance the race marked out for us,   Hebrews 12:1

An athlete runs to win.

An athlete who prepares for a race ensures he runs by the rules and that he dresses light. Paul is calling every believer to run the race of life with diligence and perseverance, throwing off everything that hinders and the sin that entangles.

Past failures weigh us down. The devil is so crafty and is ever there to remind us that we have made the same mistake …again. He whispers, once a failure, always a failure. But the truth is, God is not limited by our failures but works all things for the good of them that love him (Romans 8:28), even our failures.

The devil tries to make sure you never forget. Sharp mean and painful statements that people have made about you can keep you in bondage and from doing what the Lord wants of you.

Guilt is another powerful tool of the devil. He whispers lies telling us that God could never forgive *that* one. And so, God could never love you or use you. But the word of God says, if we confess our sins, he is faithful and just and will forgive us our sins and purify us from all unrighteousness. (1 John 1:9) and that God has loved us with an everlasting love (Jeremiah 31:3).

Are we living by the truth of God's word or the lies of the devil? We should let go of these weights that pull us down and run light.

Father help me know the truth from lie and live by it, I pray.

Extended Reading – Hebrews 11-13

FEAR
No to Crippling

For the Spirit God gave us does not make us timid but gives us power, love, and self-discipline.   2 Timothy 1:7

Paul is writing his second letter to his son in the faith, Timothy.

He begins his letter with thanksgiving for Timothy, for his sincere faith and rich legacy. And then one of the first things Paul wants to remind Timothy is the gift that he has. Paul reminds Timothy that he does have a gift. And that gift is to be used, he is to fan the flame of that gift.

And then Paul says, for God has not given us a spirit of timidity or fear. Now he says that obviously because he senses fear in Timothy.

Fear cripples.

Fear is an unpleasant emotion caused by the threat of danger, pain or harm. Misplaced fear is not from God but the devil. Fear torments and damages us. Fear robs us of our peace and joy. Fear keeps us from being the best we can be, from rising to our full potential.

But when God calls us he also equips us. Each of us is gifted in one or the other. And the word of God says we are to use those gifts, by the power, love, and self-discipline that God gives us. Power to overcome our fears. Power to do all that he has called us to do and do it well. He gives us the power to do it with his confidence, for the word says I can do all things through Christ who strengthens me (Phil 4:13). God also gives us the love to drives our actions and the discipline to accomplish it.

What is fear crippling and keeping you from doing what God has called you to do?

Lord help me serve you, by your power, I pray.

Extended Reading – 2 Timothy 1-4

SERVING
Heart of Service

Therefore, my brothers and sisters, make every effort to confirm
your calling and election. For if you do these things, you will
never stumble.   *2 Peter 1:10*

Peter says we are to confirm our calling and election.

Which means that we are already called and elected. And we
confirm our calling by adding to our faith goodness, knowledge,
self-control, perseverance, godliness, mutual affection and love (v5-7).
And the more of these things are seen in our lives, we become more
like the nature of Jesus and we are being conformed to the image of
his son (Romans 8:29).

We are to confirm our calling by being more like Jesus. Jesus came to love
and to serve the ones he created. He commanded us to love God and
love our neighbors. This is our responsibility and calling, our ministry.

Ministry means to serve. It is to serve God and other people in his
name. And every believer is in ministry. Ministry, someone has said, is
giving when you feel like keeping, **praying** for others when you need
to be prayed for, **feeding** others when your own soul is hungry, **living**
the truth before people even when you can't see the results, **hurting**
with other people even when your own hurt can't be spoken, **keeping**
your word even when it's not convenient and **being** faithful when your
flesh wants to run away.

Ministry is to go beyond our comfort level and love and serve, God
and people. And when we love and serve, we grow to be like Jesus and
then we will never stumble.

How are we serving today?

Lord help to serve you each day in all I do, I pray.
Extended Reading – 2 Peter 1-3; Jude

WORSHIP
Consuming Passions

Dear children, keep yourselves from idols. 1 John 5:21

Parting words matter.

The Apostle John has come to the tail end of his first epistle. He had much warning to give his audience about false teachings, and at the end of it all, he gave his parting words in one simple short phrase - keep yourselves from idols. It is almost like he is saying, if you forget all that I have said until now, remember this one thing, stay away, keep away from idols.

Idols are more than graven images.

The word idol most often conjures up the picture of wooden or metal images and statues. But an idol is not restricted to a physical thing. An idol can be anything that is placed over and above God in our lives. Anything that takes more than what we give to God with respect to our devotion, our priority, and our time or mind space is an idol in our life.

Idols in our lives could be possessions, position, career, sports, hobbies, entertainment goals to even addictions. Sometimes our friends or even spouse could become an idol. Idols could also be an insatiable drive for money, prestige, 'success' as the world perceives it, or the desire to seek approval of others.

The things of this world will never fully satisfy the human heart. They were never meant to. They ultimately lead only to death (Romans 6:23). And when the created replaces the creator in our lives, we have fallen into idolatry. And no idol can infuse our lives with meaning or worth or give us eternal hope.

What consumes us?

Father give me the courage to remove the idols that consume me and to give you your rightful place in my life, I pray.

Extended Reading – 1 John 1-5

ROLE MODEL
A Choice to Make

Dear friend, do not imitate what is evil but what is good.
Anyone who does what is good is from God. Anyone who does
what is evil is not from God.   *3 John v11*

John is writing to his friend Gaius.

In his final epistle, John is writing to Gaius, whom tradition has it may be the one John appointed as bishop of Pergamum.

John commends Gaius for his hospitality to traveling preachers of the gospel (v5, 6,8); for his faithfulness (v5); for his love (v6); and for his walking in the truth (v3). And then in his final instruction tells Gaius not to imitate evil but to imitate good.

To imitate is to act like, follow or duplicate. Imitation comes from the Latin word 'imitatio' which means 'a copying, imitation.' It is where an individual observes and replicates another's behavior. It is also a form of social learning that leads to the development of traditions, and ultimately our culture. And John obviously knew the powerful impact of imitation.

John is essentially telling Gaius, be cautious who you choose as your role model. The apostle Paul in 1 Corinthians 11:1 says imitate me as I imitate Christ.

We all have role models who we admire and try to emulate. Role models can play a very powerful role in our lives. But just as we have role models, there are also those who are watching us and learning from us. As parents, older siblings, even among friends or those in our areas of influence, we are being observed and imitated.

What are people learning from us today? Peace, love, patience, forgiveness or strife, anger, bitterness, envy, jealousy?

Father help me be wise in choosing who I imitate and remain ever conscious of what others see in me I pray.

Extended Reading – 2 John; 3 John

MINISTRY
Hopelessness to Blessing

I, John, your brother and companion in the suffering and kingdom and patient endurance that are ours in Jesus, was on the island of Patmos because of the word of God and the testimony of Jesus.   Revelation 1:9

The book of Revelation is written by the Apostle John, the beloved disciple of the Lord Jesus Christ.

John had been exiled to the island of Patmos for incessantly preaching about Jesus Christ. History tells us that he was exiled because the Roman emperor Domitian was angry that John had not died when he had him dipped in boiling oil. John had suffered much. And now close to the end of his life, he found himself exiled for his faith.

Humanly that sure seems a hopeless situation. But not with God. With God, no situation is hopeless. The Lord had plans for John. He was not done with his beloved disciple. And what a grand plan. The Lord had preserved and kept John. And in that place of aloneness, he had a purpose for him. A wonderful absolutely amazing experience. A revelation from the Lord Jesus Christ himself. A revelation of things soon to happen (chap 1:1-2). A revelation that was to become part of God's inspired word, for generations to come. What a privilege indeed.

Often God turns a place of loneliness into a place of ministry and blessing. Even though we may find ourselves in a seemingly hopeless and lonely situation, the Bible reminds us he is not done with us.

We should not give up but trust and obey him. He can and will bring beauty out of the ashes of our life and use us to bless many.

Thank you, Lord, that you can and will bring beauty into my life too, help me trust you wholeheartedly, I pray.

Extended Reading – Revelation 1-5

ETERNITY
Victorious Celebration

After this, I looked, and there before me was a great multitude that no one could count, from every nation, tribe, people and language, standing before the throne and before the Lamb. They were wearing white robes and were holding palm branches in their hands. ¹⁰ And they cried out in a loud voice: "Salvation belongs to our God, who sits on the throne, and to the Lamb."

Revelation 7:9-10

There was great diversity in the multitude.

The multitude that John saw, was so great that it was not possible to count. John in this multitude saw people from different nations, tribes, peoples, and tongues. This multitude is evidence that the Great Commission (Matthew 24:14) will be fulfilled as Jesus promised. The promise of salvation is not restricted to just a few, but open to all

There were distinction and diversity in the multitude. It was not just a crowd of similar looking people. There will be differences among people in heaven, just as there is on earth. We are individuals and we will be individuals.

Everything that John saw was with reference to the throne of the Lamb. The central thought of heaven is the sovereignty of God. All the people were dressed in white. White robes signify the covering righteousness of Christ. It also reminds us of our priestly service.

The palm branches remind us of Jesus' triumphal entry into Jerusalem and are also emblems of victory. Dressed in the righteousness of Christ, they worship God for salvation. They recognize that God is the source of salvation, and no one else. Salvation isn't something we earn, it is something God gives.

The great multitude did not take their salvation for granted. Do we?

Lord may I live every day ever grateful for your gift of salvation, I pray.

Extended Reading – Revelation 6-11

GOSPEL
Everlasting Benefits

Then I saw another angel flying in midair, and he had the eternal gospel to proclaim to those who live on the earth—to every nation, tribe, language, and people. Revelation 14:6

John has seen the vision of the 144000 redeemed ones who 'follow the Lamb wherever He goes' (v4). He saw three angels flying in midair, the first of whom had the eternal gospel to proclaim. This is the only place in the Bible that the gospel is referred to as the eternal or everlasting gospel.

Gospel refers to the good news that Jesus Christ suffered and died on the cross to purchase humankind's pardon. And that he rose to life on the third day was exalted to the right hand of God. And the fact is this is eternal has significant.

The angel who proclaimed the everlasting gospel is flying "in midair" and with "a loud voice" (verse 7). The picture is of an angel in the highest possible place using the loudest possible voice to reach the maximum number of people with the good news of God's salvation. God is appealing to humankind one final time to reject the lies of Satan and respond to the eternal truth of God.

The gospel is "everlasting" because it is an unchanging message. False doctrines come and go, and new teachings are like wind and waves that toss the unsuspecting every which way (Ephesians 4:14). Countering the lies and false teaching of the beast is the everlasting gospel.

The message of salvation through faith in Christ is the eternal truth; it is as solid and unchanging as God himself, and those who believe the gospel will reap everlasting benefits.

Whom will you share this gospel with today?

Lord give me the courage and sense of urgency, to share this eternal gospel, I pray.

Extended Reading – Revelation 12-18

KNOW GOD
Knowing you Jesus

The armies of heaven were following him, riding on white horses and dressed in fine linen, white and clean.   Revelation 19:14

The very fullness of Christ defies human imagery and thought.

R evelation was written around the year AD 96 when the emperor Domitian tyrannized the Roman Empire. The believers then and the 'saints of God' down the ages, especially during times of stress and oppression, have been hugely encouraged by this book. Revelation portrays the victory of Christ, despite the terrifying ordeals that confront his people.

Apostle John described the end time collapse of the world of evil. He also identifies Christ through vivid imagery and a variety of titles. Christ is described as faithful and true (v11), the word of God (v13) and the King of kings and Lord of lords (v16).

In verse 11 Apostle John describes Christ as the Rider of the White horse. 'White' consistently stands for purity and heaven in the book of Revelation. And following this Rider were the armies of heaven dressed in fine linen, white and cleansed by Christ (v8). They are dressed in the righteousness of Christ and washed in the blood of the Lamb (Revelation 7:14)

The different names reveal the distinctive characteristics of the person and work of Jesus Christ. Knowing and understanding Christ keep us from being deceived by those who come in his name, claiming to be him (Mark 13:5-6). Which of Jesus Christ's titles mean the most to us?

As we step into another new year, let us try and make it a practice to mark the various titles of Christ in our Bible as we read? Use it to pray with confidence, especially through tough times.

Lord what an amazing God you are. Help me know and love you more in the coming years, I pray.

Extended Reading – Revelation 19-22

Special Readings

BIRTHDAY
Faithful and True

Take delight in the Lord, and he will give you the desires of your heart. ⁵ Commit your way to the Lord; trust in him and he will do this.   *Psalm 37:4-5*

As another year rolls by
With age increases the gray
Sometimes the challenges too
And yet as I look through
The pages of the years gone
One thing for sure, it is you alone
You Lord remain faithful and true.

You have kept me, Lord, and provided
You've been there though others deserted
You have comforted, strengthened me
To face the challenges that come at me
And the more I look, the more I see
You are growing me to be more like you.
Yes, Lord, you remain faithful and true.

And now as into the future, I look
No idea have I of even the next nook
Or what lies beyond the bend
But you will be faithful to the end
For you do not change, I know for certain
That you my Rock and Shepherd you remain
You, Lord, will still remain faithful and true.

WEDDING ANNIVERSARY
But as Form Me

But as for me and my household, we will serve the Lord.

Joshua 24:15

Joshua was making his stand clear.

After having led Israel in the conquest of the Promised Land, Joshua now is giving his final speech, at the close of his life. It is often said that the last words of a person are important and they are to be honored.

And in his final words, what Joshua has to talk about is God and his goodness and faithfulness to the nation of Israel. Joshua recounts the ways in which God had faithfully brought his people out of slavery with a mighty hand. God had blessed them and made them a mighty nation. He had given them a land flowing with milk and honey as their inheritance.

Joshua is also summing up the essence of his life and personal experience. And he affirms that the God he has served all through his life has been faithful to him. He has experienced and known this God. He has known this God to be loving, faithful, worthy of being worshipped. And now as he comes to the close of his life, Joshua reiterates that he his family will continue to live and serve this awesome God.

As you look back over your marriage, is it the faithfulness and goodness of God that you see? Or are you tempted to complain about your spouse and your situations? God who has led you thus far, will continue to lead you. Would you join Joshua in making your stand clear and committing together as a family that, you and your household, will serve this God who has been faithful and is worthy to be loved and served?

Lord may this prayer be true in our lives as a family, I pray.

CRISIS/TERMINAL ILLNESS
Remember

*Remember that you were slaves in Egypt and the L*ORD *your God redeemed you.*   *Deuteronomy 15:15*

When life is tough
And you are confused
When you feel you're done
And just cannot move on
When you simply cannot find
A single reason to smile
Remember.

When you feel all alone
And no one seems to understand
When your world seems
To be caving in on you
When your future to you
Seems all too bleak
Remember.

Remember who you are
Remember whose you are
Remember you are the child
Of the King and Lord
Of all the universe
And that you bear in you
His very image, fearfully made.

Remember the many ways
He has blessed you
Remember the times of need
When he has provided for you

Remember when time and time again
He has protected and kept you
Remember.

Remember that you are his
Who is the gentle Shepherd
Who in his arms will bear you
The heavenly Father's, who promises
Never to leave you nor forsake you
Your Redeemer's, who believes
That you were worth dying for.

So when life overwhelms you
Dear friend, would you turn to him
Let him hold you in his hands
And as you face life's challenges
Let him be to your Friend and Guide
Would you promise yourself today
That you will choose, to remember.

MEMORIAL
Pain that does not go

But our citizenship is in heaven. And we eagerly await a Savior from there, the Lord Jesus Christ, [21] who, by the power that enables him to bring everything under his control, will transform our lowly bodies so that they will be like his glorious body.

Philippians 3:20-21

Every face I see I wish it was you
Every place I go I wish I could go with you
After all these years I am still awestruck
At how unbearable still, the pain in my stomach.

Time doesn't seem to reduce
Nor memories their edge lose
Everything around points and draws
To you, your loss is as raw as it ever was.

Many a time I feel I can't
More like rather, I just don't
I don't want to live like this without you
I am so tired, of constantly missing you.

And yet, though I simply don't understand
Why Lord or what the plan that you had
Yet Lord I choose to trust you and obey
To find my strength in your word each day.

For you, Lord know and see my tears
You understand my doubts and my fears
And because you call me to keep my eyes
Fixed on you, I do, my Lord and my eternal Prize.

GRADUATION/ACHIEVEMENT
Perspective Please

But remember the Lord your God, for it is he who gives you the ability to produce wealth, and so confirms his covenant, which he swore to your ancestors, as it is today.   Deuteronomy 8:18

I am a self-made man/woman.

Does this phrase sound familiar? Have you heard someone say this or is this the thought in your own heart?

Having finally entered the Promised Land, after driving out many nations, Moses is now cautioning the Israelites. He reminds them not to forget God.

Moses says, remember that it is the Lord who has brought them out of Egypt and led them through the desert for forty long years. The Lord who sustained, fed them manna and quail from heaven, kept their clothes from tearing, their sandals from tearing. And now as they stand at the threshold of this land which flows with milk and honey, and the Lord blesses them with much grain and blessings.

It is the Lord who gives the ability to produce wealth and success. This may include the talent, the skill, the health, the stamina, the wisdom or anything else needed, to work and achieve. However, it is human tendency often to take pride in the success we attain. And so Moses sets the boundaries and perspective.

The Bible in Matthew 6:27 reminds us that none of us can add even a hair to our head. Then how do we even get the idea that it is *we* who have made it, on our own hard work and talent alone? As you stand at the peak of success, have you paused to acknowledge God's grace in your achievement?

Father help me never to lose perspective of your grace in my achievements and successes, I pray.

NEW JOB/PROMOTION
Are You a Star?

Do everything without grumbling or arguing... Then you will shine among them like stars in the sky.   Philippians 2:14-15

Who does not want to be a star right?

We consider movie actors, sports heroes and others, who excel in their respective field, like stars. Whatever the field, to rise to the position of star or leader in that field requires effort. For athletes, it means hours of training, strict hours of workout, even stricter diets and much more, every day. Whether they feel like or not, every morning could mean hours of exercise. There is a price to pay. No laurel is easily won.

Paul is calling the Philippians to develop a practice so they can be stars too. He says, develop the habit of not grumbling or arguing. Now that is easier said than done right? No grumbling no arguing is almost like saying no food and water to some of us. These are some things that we do almost naturally, about most everything. He doesn't say it's easy. But Paul says, don't do it.

And Paul explains why. He says so that, you will be like shining stars in a crooked and depraved generation. Stars are seen at night, in a dark sky. So also, the world around us is dark, depraved and needy. And we are called to be stars and shine for all we are worth, amidst the darkness. To be a star needs disciple and practice, many a time at the cost of things we really long for.

So as you stand at the brink of new opportunities, you are called to be a star wherever God is placing you.

Lord, it is tough, but I want to be the star for you, I pray.

EASTER
No, Not Some Fabricated Prose

In their fright, the women bowed down with their faces to the
ground, but the men said to them, "Why do you look for the
living among the dead? ⁶ **He is not here; he has risen!**

Luke 24:5-6

He arose! He arose!
That is the amazing truth
No, not some fabricated prose
He did die on that Roman cross
Two thousand years ago
But the third day, he arose.

He arose! he arose!
True, he was nailed to the cross
It is finished, Tetelestai cried he
Time froze and dark went the sky
No, that is not just a story
But an authentic fact of history.

He arose! he arose!
He didn't stay in the grave
But arose so he might save us,
To live with him eternally
And while on this earth
To live in absolute victory.

He arose! he arose!
So let us, when we still can
Come to the foot of his cross
And our burdens lay down
Accept his forgiveness
And live in victory, eternally.

CHRISTMAS
The Reason for the Season

While they were there, the time came for the baby to be born, [7]
and she gave birth to her firstborn, a son. She wrapped him in
cloths and placed him in a manger because there was no guest
room available for them. Luke 2:6-7 (NIV)

The birth of Christ remains the most pivotal moment in history.

Time literally parted. Periods of history are separated at his birth. His
birth is historically proven truth. His life, death and resurrection and
ascension remain as the most powerful events of history. His life, death,
and resurrection bring life, life in abundance here on earth and glorious
life eternal after. And that is the true reason for all the celebration at
Christmas. But is it your reason?

As the world moves with elation
Into a time filled with celebration
My friend, my wish for you
Is that you would truly know.
The Person, who is the reason
Bringing meaning to the season
To all the fun and laughter
The love and joyful chatter.

He is the King of kings
He alone the Lord of everything
Who with his Word did bring
To life, every single thing
He is the One owns the cattle
On a thousand hills
The heaven is his throne
And the earth his footstool.

Yet this amazing, Almighty One
His heavenly glory did disown

That he might our pardon buy
As on the cross, he did die
So my friend this Christmas
Amidst all the hustle and fuss
Let your love for him be the meter
And of all the fun he, the center.

How does your celebration reflect that Christ truly is the reason and the center of your celebration this season?

Lord may my celebration this season be the reflection of my heartfelt gratitude for what you have done for me, I pray.

A New Year Prayer

See, I am doing a new thing! Now it springs up; do you not perceive it? I am making a way in the wilderness and streams in the wasteland. Isaiah 43:19

At the close of the year, I trust you have experienced God and in his Word in powerful and personal ways. That God has been shaping you at the wheel of his word and making you more and more like him each day. Now as you move into the next year, would you make it your prayer that you would be a reflection of his love to the watching world, drawing many to him through your life?

Lord as into this New Year I step
This my prayer this my request
Give me joy Lord, Give me love
That to a watching world
I would live to show, the beauty
Of a life that in you is found!

Lord as into this New Year I step
No clue have I of what to expect
Of what the joys or what the tears
But this for sure I know and believe
The One who called me
Is with me and will never leave.

Lord as into this New Year I step
This my prayer this my request
With each day I would increasingly be
Aware and accepting of your love for me
So that to the hurting world that I see
Reflection of this love I would be!

www.ingramcontent.com/pod-product-compliance
Lightning Source LLC
Chambersburg PA
CBHW031958060726
47497CB00015B/309